THE TRUTH & LIES DUET

THE TRUTH & LIES DUET

C.W. FARNSWORTH

For all the hopeful romantics.

CONTENTS

FRIDAY NIGHT LIES

TUESDAY NIGHT TRUTHS

FRIDAY NIGHT LIES

CHAPTER ONE

CASSIA

He smells like cinnamon. Always.

Tonight—or today, technically, since it's past midnight—the spice is muddled by the strong scent of sweat and beer.

But still, beneath it, cinnamon.

"Cute PJ's, flower."

I tighten my fingers around the glass of water I'm holding as they twitch, resisting the urge to tug my plaid sleep shorts down so more of my legs are covered. My shoulders lift and tense as Holden approaches, even though I heard him walking toward the kitchen long before I caught a whiff of distinctive spice. I freeze like prey confronted with a predator, waiting to see what strategy will remove me from the situation emotionally unscathed.

Holden is always unpredictable.

My stiff posture doesn't scream casual or indifferent, the way I try to act around him. None of my senses can ignore him. And if I'm being honest with myself—which I rarely am on Friday nights—I have never been able to. Over time, I've just managed to make more successful attempts at it.

"Rough night?" I ask, ignoring his comment about my plaid pajamas and sipping some water hoping it'll douse the warmth pooling in my stomach.

He's just too much. Everything about him.

More than impossible to ignore; it's overwhelming.

I try to focus on the white cabinets and butcherblock counters instead. On the streak of moonlight beaming in from the window above the farm sink and casting an ethereal glow over the hardwood floor.

But my eyes always end up back on him.

A crooked grin appears, creasing the corner of his cheek. Hinting at the dimple I know is hiding there. "Refs got wasted and took the night off. I don't look that bad, do I?"

I swallow. "Worse."

Holden chuckles, a low, raspy sound that twists and snarls my insides. He laughs like he knows it's a lie. There's a streak of dried blood on one cheek and his left cheekbone is marred by a reddish streak. But beneath the battering and bruising, he's still ridiculously good looking. Perfect bone structure and messy brown hair.

I drink more water, just for something to do. Watching as he runs a dish cloth under the tap and rubs the wet cotton across his face. There's no cut, so the blood wasn't his, it seems.

I keep staring, long after I should look away. Track the dampened fabric as it trails lower, down the corded column of his neck and across the bunched muscles of his shoulder and farther south.

He's shirtless, wearing nothing but a pair of black mesh basketball shorts and a dirty pair of sneakers.

I swallow—twice. Try not to appreciate the view and fail at every attempt.

"Did you clean in here?" Holden asks, suddenly.

I down more water, trying to focus on the sensation of cold liquid sliding down my esophagus instead of how he's moved closer in order to toss the towel into the laundry room tucked off one corner of the kitchen. "A little."

A lot.

The Adamses' house is usually messier than mine and I'm the oldest of six, so that's saying something.

Holden pulls his phone out of his pocket and makes a face at the screen. Carelessly, he tosses the device on the counter and strolls toward the fridge, opening it and pulling a bottle of beer out.

I grip the glass that's now empty, feeling the leftover condensation slip against my fingers. "You already smell like a brewery."

He smirks. "Sober as a priest, flower."

"Priests are twice as likely as the average person to develop an alcohol addiction," I inform him.

Holden laughs before popping the top off and taking a long pull of beer. "Good thing I ruled out that career path, then."

"I know. Celibacy isn't your thing."

Holden raises an eyebrow; the only indication my response startled him. Usually, these late-night encounters begin and end with basic pleasantries.

I'm unsure what's loosening my lips tonight. Maybe I'm just sick of the predictability our interactions have become. That's mostly what my life seems to consist of.

Maybe I regret not pushing back at him years ago.

I step forward and take the brown bottle from him. Holden's eyes land and *burn* as he watches me take a drink from the bottle he was just sipping from.

I try not to think about the fact we're sharing spit. Not because I'm a germaphobe—although who knows where his mouth has been—but because it sends a secret thrill through me. The malty taste of hops coat my tongue and fizzes in my stomach.

Something shifts between us as I hold the bottle back out to him.

Something shifts on Holden's face as he takes it from me.

Our fingers brush, a warm contrast to the cold glass. He tilts his head, studying me more closely than he was before. "Asking for forgiveness instead of permission?"

"Neither." I say the word with more confidence than I feel.

His phone buzzes on the counter, and we both glance at it. Notifications cover the screen, most of them from Grace Harper.

I swallow the scoff that wants to release in response. Saying anything will give the impression I care. And even if I *do* care, that's not something I want Holden to know.

We haven't had that sort of friendship in years. The kind where you comment on each other's lives and have any right to do so. The sort where caring about each other's lives is expected, not something to hide.

I move away from him toward the sink. Refill my glass with water from the tap and drain it, trying to wash away the taste of beer since I'm too lazy to brush my teeth again before going back to bed.

I'm not even sure why I stole a sip. I wanted to do something different, I guess, not just say something unexpected.

Rather than spending Friday night in my pajamas, having a sleepover with my best friend, and then cleaning her kitchen, I wanted to be the girl who surprises the most popular guy in school.

I'm not sure it counts, though, considering that guy is Holden Adams. Once upon a time, it felt like he knew me better than I knew myself. I'm not sure if you *can* surprise someone you once knew like that.

Not sure of anything, honestly, when it comes to him. I used to be in love with him. Spent subsequent months hating him. Now remnants of those two extremes are stuck inside of me, swirling around with a mess of other complicated emotions.

Hurt and self-loathing.

Annoyance and appreciation.

Since I started the dishwasher earlier, I handwash the glass and stick it in the drain rack. After drying my hands on a clean dishtowel and looping it over the oven handle, I turn back around. "I'm going to bed."

Holden has blue eyes. Every time I look in them, especially when we're alone, I feel like I'm drowning in their depths. Fathomless and potentially devastating, just like the sea or the sky.

He picks at the orange label on his bottle of beer as he studies me. "You ever going to tell Sydney you don't sleep when you're over here?"

"You ever going to stop getting drunk and playing ball in the middle of the night?"

Holden's lips quirk. The small movement is not quite a smile or a scowl. Just a response—a reaction. An acknowledgement I spoke, and he listened. From most people, it would be meaningless. From him, it feels meaning*ful*. "Good night, flower."

I brush past him and hurry out of the kitchen as quickly as I can without appearing to run away. Even if that's exactly what I'm doing.

I hate how, despite never speaking to me most days, he knows my insomnia is worst when I'm sleeping somewhere different than my own bed. It doesn't seem to matter that it's a familiar place—Sydney and I have been having sleepovers since our parents decided we were old enough to in third grade. They've been a regular occurrence ever since, considering we live just across the street from one another.

The stairs creak as I creep up them, but I'm not worried about waking anyone up. Unlike me, Sydney sleeps soundly no matter what. Holden and Sydney's father, Joe, is gone for work, like usual. And Holden is downstairs and awake, doing...I have no idea what.

Maybe he's texting Grace.

Hopefully he's icing his face.

I've never gone to the old high school's basketball court where Holden and his friends allegedly spend most of their free time, so I have no idea how every pickup game seems to involve some sort of injury. I've seen Holden play on the school team in past seasons. He's fast. Agile.

Those games end unscathed. They also have actual referees, not drunk high schoolers shouting "Foul!" whenever they feel like it.

Sydney is sprawled out on her four-poster bed when I enter her room, snoring softly. Lily, the Adamses' dog, is curled up on the fluffy rug beneath the window. She raises her head when I enter the room and then lays it back down when she recognizes me. I close Sydney's bedroom door behind me and crawl onto the air mattress, settling on the inflated rectangle with a sigh as I slip under the sheets and pull the blankets up over me.

My ears strain, trying to catch any hint of sound downstairs. All I can hear is the steady thrum of my own heart, whooshing softly as the excitement from our encounter slowly fades.

I hate how much of an effect he has on me.

I hate how I was lingering in the kitchen, hoping he'd come home.

I hate how he only calls me *flower* when we're alone.

And if I'm honest with myself, I know Holden is the main reason I barely sleep in this room. Anticipation of a possible encounter acts as a powerful stimulant, followed by overanalyzing each word we exchange if he does come home. I know those sentences will be the highlight of my week.

But acknowledging that won't do me any good. It makes it harder to act normal around him, to act like it doesn't bother me that things changed between us.

That's why I lie to myself on Friday nights.

CHAPTER TWO

HOLDEN

Finn beelines for my truck as soon as I pull into my usual spot in the lot. He's outside my window before I've even turned the ignition off, knocking on the glass obnoxiously.

It's a beautiful fall day, crisp and clear. I climb out of the cab, listening to leaves as they crunch between my sneakers and the hard asphalt of the high school's parking lot.

"Where were you last night?" he asks as I sling my backpack on one shoulder.

"Sleeping," I tell him. "Did you forget what time Friday's match ended?"

"You slept all weekend?"

"I had some other shit to take care of too."

Finn scoffs, but he doesn't push me to elaborate. He's used to my vague answers, showing up an hour late at parties and forgetting when we made plans. I'm selfish, unmotivated, and I hate restriction.

I like doing what I want, when I feel like doing it. Honestly, it's a minor miracle I play a team sport. Commitment is a constriction that makes my skin itch, which is exactly what my mom used to say. At least I know my selfish tendencies won't result in abandoning two small children, the way hers did.

The only casualty of my choices this weekend is Finn pouting about me missing a fight. "You could've taken this guy down in minutes, Adams!" he exclaims as we walk across the parking lot.

I roll my eyes and tug the brim of my baseball hat down so it better shades my eyes from the sun. The bruise on my cheek twinges. "It wasn't supposed to be a regular thing, man. Just some easy cash now and then."

"Well, Declan needs you there next weekend. He said he'll sweeten the pot."

"How much?" I ask, fishing around my backpack for the granola bar I tucked inside before leaving the house this morning.

"Double."

"For real?"

"Uh-huh." Finn's eyes are alight with excitement. "He wants you up against some football player from Ridgemont."

I make a noncommittal sound as I unwrap the bar and take a large bite of my breakfast. Inside, I'm starting to spiral and second-guess. I knew that the start of the basketball season was going to add complications. Especially since I have no good reason to be involved in Declan's questionable business enterprises in the first place. It's pointless and I know it.

But I make a lot of stupid decisions.

"'Sup, guys?" Mark appears, munching on an apple.

He and Finn start talking about the football game they watched last night as we all head for the front doors of the high school.

I pull out my phone and scroll through the messages I didn't have time to read this morning. There are a few new ones from my dad. He's good about checking in with me and Sydney regularly. Of course, my angel of a sister has already sent him a lengthy response to his texts, telling him all about her wholesome weekend doing homework and hanging out with her best friend.

I type a short response and shove my phone back into the pocket of my fleece as we walk inside Pembrooke High School. It always smells the same in here—like cleaning supplies and paint. The high school is new. They finished building it four years ago, right before the start of my freshman year.

Every surface gleams, the tiled floors and the lockers that line the walls. Our school colors are blue and yellow, so the short strip of plaster above the navy lockers is painted a sunny shade.

The hallway is busy. We're only a few minutes away from first bell. Finn and Mark follow me to my locker. I grab the green notebook I use for English.

I slam the door shut and hear a distinctive laugh. Like a magnet, my gaze snaps to Cassia. She's standing across the hall at her locker. Sydney is right next to her. And Cassia…Cassia is talking to Spencer Barnes, who looks likely to shit himself over having her undivided attention. Over having made her laugh.

The pulse of possessiveness is expected.

Familiar.

Annoying.

I look away before anyone in the hall catches me staring. To them, Cassia and Spencer probably look like an obvious pairing. They're both smart and strait-laced and *nice*. They are the ones teachers like and parents adore.

There's more to Cassia, though. Or there used to be. I don't spend enough time around her anymore to tell for sure. I do everything I can to make sure our interactions are limited, which is harder than it should be.

We go to the same school.

Live on the same street.

She's best friends with my little sister.

And then there's this stupid draw to her that I've never been able to fully shake despite my best attempts. Some compulsion to stare. A burning curiosity about whether she's interested in the guy who's beaming at her right now, even though I shouldn't care. Shouldn't have even noticed how he's looking at her.

"See you at lunch, Adams," Mark says, then splits off from me and Finn.

"Yeah. See you."

Finn gives me a weird look as Mark heads to the left. "You good, dude?"

"Yeah. Fine."

"You've barely said anything this morning. Is your dad back yet?"

"No. He's not supposed to get back 'til Thursday."

I'm not holding my breath, though. My dad works as a long-haul truck driver. He's away from Pembrooke more than he's home. I know he feels guilty about being gone as much as he is. I also know me and Sydney were unplanned, and a burden he was saddled with when our mom split years ago. He racks up a lot of miles trying to make up for that. Or maybe trying to drive away from that.

His lengthy absences take a toll on us as a family. On Sydney, especially. She tries to be perfect, churning out good grades and attending play practices instead of parties so he never has anything to worry about. Her future is a lot more certain than mine.

College is a long shot for me. My grades are average at best. My only chance of going is a basketball scholarship. Even if I do get one, I'm not sure leaving is a possibility. It will be the biggest shock to our family dynamic since my mom left twelve years ago.

"Is your dad going to cause problems next weekend?" Finn asks.

I shake my head. "Nah. He spends most of his time home sleeping."

And if Finn is right about the amount of money Declan is offering, I won't take no for an answer. I'll sneak out if I have to.

If I'm not going to college, I need a back-up plan. And I enjoy fighting. I know it's reckless—that's part of the allure. More importantly, I'm good at it. Undefeated good.

Finn follows me into Mrs. Berwick's classroom for first period. Grace is seated in the second row, talking with her best friend McKenzie Howard.

Both girls give me flirty smiles. I'm not surprised by Grace. But last I knew, McKenzie was hooking up with Jordan, one of my teammates.

I couldn't care less about keeping up with current *who likes who, who hates who* drama. But basketball is one of the few things that matters to me. I won't pursue anything that might negatively affect that. I pass both girls and head for the back of the classroom without a word.

Grace glances back at me, her arms crossed, and her eyes narrowed. I assume she's irritated I never responded to the million texts she sent me this past weekend asking where I was and what I was doing. Questions I'm as unwilling to answer as she is to stop asking, apparently.

I slouch in a seat in the very back row and tap a pencil against the desk as the principal drones through the morning announcements. Finn kicks my chair from his spot next to mine as Principal Stevens starts reading off the day's birthdays. "What are we doing for yours?" he asks.

"It's during the senior trip," I reply. "We'll be in New York."

"Exactly. You only turn eighteen once, man. We're going all out." Finn waggles his eyebrows. There's a hell of a lot more to do there than in Pembrooke.

I shake my head and smile.

Mrs. Berwick begins taking attendance. "No hats inside, Mr. Adams," she tells me when she reaches my name.

I toss my baseball cap on the desk and run a hand through my short hair. Lacie Williams is sitting on my other side. Her brown eyes widen as she spots the bruise on my cheek. I wink at her. She blushes before looking away to focus on the class discussion about some Shakespeare play.

I slide down lower in my chair and yawn, wishing the day was over already.

The final bell rings. It's a loud, annoying chime. But right now, it sounds like the sweetest sound in the world.

I shove the paper we just got back into my textbook and slide it into my backpack. Stand and sling one strap over a shoulder before heading toward the door.

"Holden. Wait a minute."

I sigh and stop, playing with the strap of my backpack as I walk over to Mrs. Golden's desk. An ironic last name if you ask me. Everything about her is dark. The navy dress. The black hair. The stern expression on her face.

She has the decency to wait until the last student files out of the room, at least.

"A D was generous," she states. "You were three thousand words short of the word count and didn't cite a single source."

The strap digs into my palm as my grip tightens. "I was in a rush. I'll do better on the next one."

"You know what the student athlete policy is. You're close to failing this class, Holden."

I hold in a gush of air before exhaling. This was the first essay of the semester, meaning it's currently the bulk of my grade. "I know the policy, yeah."

"I haven't seen anything to give me the confidence you're capable of making improvements on your own. If you want to be eligible to play, you'll need to work with another student and hand in a new copy of this paper."

My molars grind. "I don't need a tutor. I'm not stupid."

"I don't think you're *stupid*, Holden. I think you're unfocused and unmotivated. The student I have in mind is one of the brightest I've ever taught. I have full confidence she'll be able to help you manage a passing grade."

I don't miss the pronoun. I sigh, annoyed Mrs. Golden is insisting, but the girls at this school generally are falling all over me. If it will get Mrs. Golden to pass me and allow me to play, I can handle it. "Fine."

The classroom door creaks open. I glance over automatically, then do a double take. Cassia gives me a small, tentative smile before shifting her gaze to Mrs. Golden. "Sorry to interrupt. I can wait in the hall."

"No need," Mrs. Golden says. "This is perfect. I was just letting Holden know you'll be helping him out on the essay."

My head whips back toward Mrs. Golden so quickly my neck cracks. "What?"

Mrs. Golden isn't paying attention to me any longer. She's handing Cassia a folder and pointing out lines on a document. The haze of surprise starts to lift. The papers she's giving Cassia are the syllabus. The prompt for the paper I just got back. "…let you decide where to start," she's saying.

And then we're being dismissed. Another student shows up— some wide-eyed freshman asking for help on a European history quiz.

Blindly, I follow Cassia into the hallway. It's half-empty by now. The final bell rang about ten minutes ago. If practices had started up yet, I'd be running late.

Cassia turns to the left. Without thinking, I grab her arm, stalling her in place. She spins around, eyes wide and expression stunned.

I avoid touching her.

I have no good reason to touch her.

The last time I did…it didn't end well.

"I don't need help," I tell her.

"You don't." She says it like a statement, not a question.

I take it as an agreement. "So…we're good here?"

"Sure. We'll meet in the library after school tomorrow."

The muscles in my jaw pop and tense. "I don't need your help."

"Mrs. Golden obviously disagrees."

"I didn't want to write the paper. That doesn't mean I *can't*."

"I don't care." Her hazel eyes flash with an edge of defiance Cassia rarely shows. The only times I've seen glimpses of it have been with me. It fucks with my head. "She asked me to help you. I said I would. I'm not lying to a teacher. And if you don't let me help me, you'll probably keep failing."

"I'm not failing. I just don't care about what happened a hundred years ago. When am I ever going to discuss the impacts of the Industrial Revolution?"

"Oh, I don't know…" She taps her chin with one finger. "Maybe when you're flunking American history?"

I shake my head, but some tiny part of me wants to smile at her sass. "Touché, Little Miss Perfect."

"Don't call me that."

Cassia says it like she means it, but she's never once told me not to call her flower. That fucks with my head too.

"Yo! Adams!"

I look away from Cassia, at Finn. He's standing with his hands cupped around his mouth, calling me from the other end of the hall with a bunch of the guys on the team. And a group of girls. "Let's go!" he adds when I don't move.

"Write a new outline for the paper tonight," Cassia says, drawing my attention back to where it wants to be. "I'll look at it tomorrow."

"I have plans tonight." I do. It's not a lie, but I mostly say it to be a dick. To test her on how seriously she's planning to take this.

"Your schedule will be wide open when you get benched."

I narrow my eyes at Cassia, then startle when I feel a hand wrap around my forearm.

The apple scent of Grace's shampoo hits me first, cloying the air with artificial sweetness. "Come on, Holden. Everyone's waiting for you."

I shrug away from her touch. I've made it very clear to Grace I have no interest in a relationship. That there are hard limits. Yet she insists on continually testing them. Touching me to mark her territory. Pouting when I won't kiss her.

When I glance at Cassia, her eyes are on my arm. Focused on the one spot where Grace was just touching me. Her expression is blank, no hint of the obstinance she just aimed my way.

Because she doesn't care what I think? Because she *does* care? I can't figure her out, can't read her intentions, and it bothers me more than it should.

Grace follows the direction of my attention. "Oh. Hi, Cassia."

"Hi, Grace," Cassia responds, polite as ever.

Her sugary sweet tone makes me want to shatter that poise, which is a good reason to walk away.

I glimpsed more emotion from Cassia in the two-minute conversation Grace just interrupted than in the past few years combined. Instead of ignoring her the way I've done, it makes me want to push her. To peel back more and expose whatever she's hiding.

"Let's go," I say to Grace.

I don't want to continue my conversation with Cassia in front of her. Grace nods. Her expression is bright and eager, happy I'm agreeing to go with her. After flashing Cassia another fake smile, she begins walking down the hall without looking back, obviously expecting me to follow her. I start to, until I encounter an unexpected obstacle.

Cassia grabs my arm, the same way I did to her. The same way Grace did to me a second ago.

Grace's grip was an irritation. Cassia's touch sears my skin like a hot brand, sending a rush of heat flooding through my veins.

I wasn't expecting her to touch me—to stop me. Surprising me further, she rises up on her tiptoes, so she's closer to my six feet two height. So I can read the determination in her hazel eyes.

"I'm not lying for you," she states. "You'd better show up."

"You've lied for me before," I remind her. When we were kids—when we were close—it was a regular occurrence.

Cassia's face hardens into an impenetrable mask. That affected her more than anything else I've said, it seems. "I also learned my lesson."

She drops my arm and walks away, leaving me standing here. I head for my friends, ignoring the curious stares most of them aim my way.

Once I reach the group, we head for the double doors that lead out into the parking lot.

"What?" I ask Finn as he falls into step beside me.

He nods down the hall behind us, in the direction Cassia left, a smirk pulling up one corner of his mouth. "What was that about?"

"Nothing."

"You finally tapping that?"

"None of your fucking business."

Finn's smirk grows as the rest of the group strains to hear what we're saying. "You're never possessive over girls."

This. This is one of many reasons I stay away from Cassia Nolan whenever possible. Because I can't think straight around her, and it results in predictable consequences, like me getting protective and defensive. Which, like Finn's made it his business to point out, is not my normal behavior.

I say nothing, hoping he'll drop it.

He doesn't.

"She's single, right? Maybe I'll—"

I act, then speak. The force of my shove sends Finn shoulder first into the lockers. Everyone else looks at us, but no one asks. They're used to me and Finn fooling around.

"Don't," I snarl.

And Finn, for once in his life, makes a wise decision and shuts up.

CHAPTER THREE

CASSIA

The soft patter of rain is the first sound I register, immediately followed by the sound of Sally's screaming. My youngest sibling at age four, is also the loudest. Thumps sound on the other side of the wall my bed is pushed against, indicating the twins are up. A door slams down the hall.

I glance at the alarm clock. It's set to go off in five minutes anyway.

I toss the covers off. Rub a palm over my face and run a few fingers through my tangled curls before standing and walking over to the window to pull open the curtains.

Droplets of water splash against the panes of glass, blurring my view of the front yard and the gray sky. But I can still make out the sole figure standing in the driveway across the street. He shoots the ball over and over again, making every shot.

The sharp ring of my alarm startles me. I abandon my spot at the window and rush to the bedside table to shut it off. Before heading to the bathroom, I pull on my usual uniform of jeans and a hoodie. I turn the handle, and…locked.

"Maggie!" I shout, banging on the wood. My oldest sister doesn't answer. I call her name again.

"Five minutes, Cassia. Jeesh!"

I continue down the hall into my parents' room. My mom is getting Sally dressed. My dad is gone, probably already at the office. Most of the time, I wake up well before my alarm and make it to the kitchen before he leaves. Miraculously, I almost made it to my alarm going off this morning.

"Maggie is in the bathroom," I say by way of explanation as I duck into the en suite. I catch my mom's sigh just before I shut the door behind me.

I run through my short morning routine and walk back into the bedroom. My mom and Sally are both gone. Likely downstairs, working on breakfast.

Predictably, the bathroom door is still shut when I pass it. "I'll leave without you, Maggie," I threaten before heading downstairs.

It's chaos, like always. Sally is crying again. My mom is making coffee. The twins are fighting over a baseball mitt. Regan is coloring at the kitchen table. On the kitchen table, partially.

"Can you get the twins some cereal, please?" my mom asks, handing Sally a banana that temporarily stops the screaming.

I nod, filling two bowls with Cheerios and milk and setting them on the table. "Charlie! Chris! Come on, breakfast!"

The twins abandon their argument and come eat breakfast. I grab a bowl for Regan as well, confiscating the markers and paper before wiping off the table with a paper towel. My mom gives me a grateful smile as she hands me a toasted bagel and a thermos of coffee. I'm addicted to caffeine, same as her. Most days, I limit myself to one cup in the morning. I have enough trouble sleeping as it is.

"Tell Maggie I'll be in the car, okay?"

She nods. "Have a good day, sweetheart."

I grab my lunch off the counter and shove it into my back-pack. Shrug on my raincoat and head out into the drizzle.

The soothing scent of rain fills my lungs as I inhale deeply, dodging the puddles that have formed along the front path. I pop the trunk and toss my backpack inside, allowing myself one glance over my shoulder.

Holden is gone. So is his truck.

I climb into the driver's seat, my wet jacket squeaking against the leather. I turn on the car and some music.

My phone buzzes in the cupholder. A few seconds later, the passenger door opens and Sydney climbs in. Her blonde hair is soaked, small droplets flying everywhere as she drops her back-pack in the footwell and looks over at me.

"Maggie running late?"

"Of course. I should leave her here."

"You won't."

"I know." I tap at the steering wheel, impatient.

"Graham Warner texted me last night." The sentence bursts out in a rush, betraying the eagerness that's also splashed across her expression.

"Really?" I ask.

"Uh-huh. Asking about a history assignment."

"He's president of the Honors Club."

"Right? It's an excuse, don't you think?"

"Sounds like one to me." I don't have any other boy advice to offer.

Sydney—everyone—thinks I have no interest in a high school relationship. That I'm focused on nothing besides getting into the best college I can and pursuing my dream of becoming a veterinarian.

I *am* focused on that.

But the real truth behind my perceived disinterest? There's

only one guy whose actions I'm interested in analyzing, and they haven't indicated any interest in *me* for years.

That's nothing I can admit to Sydney, though, since the guy in question happens to be her older brother.

"He's more realistic than Harrison," Sydney says.

She's had a crush on Harrison Baker—the star of the football team—ever since she started high school. Right along with most of Pembrooke High's female population.

"Reality is good."

The statement rings with sincerity. Fantasy has broken my heart more times than I'd ever admit.

Maggie streaks out from the house, her yellow raincoat a stark contrast to the gray sky and brown grass. She dives into the backseat and tugs her hood down. "You couldn't have parked in the garage, Cassia?"

"You couldn't have taken less than twenty minutes in the bathroom?" I counter. "I had to use Mom and Dad's."

"I don't see the issue. We both got ready on time. Problem solved."

I glance at the clock on the dash before I back out of the driveway and roll my eyes. On time is a stretch. "I figured you'd be eager to get to school. Don't you have Ceramics first period today?"

"Yes. Which is exactly why I couldn't show up to school looking like a troll."

I roll my eyes again. I wasn't nearly as dramatic as Maggie when I was fourteen. At least I don't think I was. But we are alike in other ways. I can be just as stubborn as she is. I also make too many boy-centered decisions.

"You're dressing up for Ceramics?" Sydney asks. "Isn't that kind of pointless?"

"She's dressing up for Ben Howard," I reply, flicking on a blinker before I turn at the end of our street.

"Who's Ben Howard?"

"Basketball player," I mumble. Maggie and I also have similar taste in guys, it seems.

Maggie leans forward from the backseat and holds her phone screen out to show something to Sydney. "That's him. Isn't he cute?"

"Super cute," Sydney agrees.

"Maggie! Seatbelt!"

My younger sister lets out a long-suffering sigh. "You're no fun, Cassia."

I know I'm not.

I'm bitter and jaded and set in my ways—at seventeen.

Sydney gives me a sympathetic look as I turn off the main road into the high school's parking lot. Rain is falling faster now, in rapid rivers of water that stream down the windshield quicker than the wipers can keep up with. I flick the control to a higher speed before navigating into an open spot toward the middle of the lot.

Maggie is out of the car before I've even turned it off, a cursory goodbye tossed over one shoulder.

Sydney laughs at her hasty departure. "To be young and in love and eager to make pottery."

I laugh too. But inside I'm wondering what that would be like —being bold enough to chase after who you want. To have the person you want to see be excited to see you back.

I search the parking lot as we hurry inside the school, even though I know I shouldn't. Searching out Holden never ends well. He's either surrounded by girls or talking with friends. Never paying any attention to me.

His truck isn't in the lot, which means he went somewhere

else before school. I tell myself not to care, but that tactic has never worked before. I focus on Sydney instead, listening to her describe the conversation she had with Graham last night in more detail. Watch her face beam with excitement and anticipation.

Like me, Sydney veers toward what's expected. Our motivations are similar, which is probably part of why we're such good friends. Her mom left when she was young and her dad works for a shipping company, logging hundreds of miles driving every week. Her father's sister used to come and stay with Sydney and Holden when they were younger, but now they mostly stay home alone. Holden took on the role of the reckless sibling and so I think Sydney feels an obligation to be the responsible one.

My parents have five other kids to worry about, so I adopt a similar mentality. Plus, it's been my dream to become a veterinarian for as long as I can remember. Doing well in school is necessary to pursue that path.

Spencer is next to my locker when I reach it, fiddling with his own combination a couple doors down.

"Morning, Cassia."

"Hey, Spencer," I reply.

"Made it through the deluge okay?" He gets his locker open and then pushes his glasses up his nose.

I laugh. "Yep."

Spencer is a nice guy, plain and simple. A little awkward, a lot nerdy, but nice. Sydney likes to tease me about his crush on me. How we could study together and discuss animal documentaries, which I love to watch, and Sydney finds boring.

But unfortunately, I've never felt the slightest attraction toward Spencer. And I've experienced firsthand how crushing false hope can be. I refuse to do that to him, so I've always kept our interactions completely platonic.

I finish getting everything I need out of my backpack and shut my locker. Say goodbye to Spencer and to Sydney, who's heading to her own locker. Since she's a junior, hers is in a different wing.

Holden walks in the front doors as I'm heading toward the science wing for first period. He's dripping water everywhere. His hair is soaked, rivulets of water dropping down his face. His stupid navy varsity jacket is soaked as well, the fabric so wet it looks black. Holden is surrounded by his group of friends, all of them clamoring for his attention.

I look away before he catches me staring.

He showed up to school. Whether he shows up this afternoon in the library is another story.

I can't decide whether I want him to or not.

That's the problem with Holden. I can lie to myself about my feelings all I want.

But they're still there.

———

The library is mostly empty when I walk inside. I hurried here from my last class, eager for reasons I'm choosing not to analyze but start with a H and end with a N.

I take a seat at an empty table, pulling a couple of folders out of my backpack as I settle in the wooden chair. I pop in a pair of earbuds and start working through my Calculus homework. If he shows, I want to look busy, not like I'm waiting for him.

Movement across the table startles me.

Harrison Baker smiles. I fumble as I drop my pencil and pull out my headphones.

"Hey."

"Hey," I repeat.

"How's it going, Cassia?"

I'm mildly shocked that Harrison knows my name.

Pembrooke High isn't huge. But people tend to stick to their own crowd, and I'm most definitely not part of the popular one he is. I know hardly anything about football, but from what I hear, he's one of the better players on our generally abysmal team.

It takes me a second too long to respond to his question. "Uh, good. You?"

"Pretty good. Football practice got canceled because of the rain, so I figured I should get some work done."

"That's, uh, that's smart." I pick up my pencil and fiddle with it, trying to figure out what is going on. I'm not sure if Harrison and I have ever spoken before. Maybe freshman year? We had Algebra together, I think.

"What are you working on?"

"Calculus." I try to think of something else to add to my answer and come up empty. I feel like I'm being rude by doing nothing to carry the conversation, when really I'm just too shocked to come up with anything substantive.

"Do you have Mr. Danvers?"

"Yeah. You?"

"Uh-huh. Seventh period."

"Did you guys do that derivatives competition last class?"

Harrison laughs. He has a nice laugh. It's deep and husky. Genuine. "Sure did. It was probably—"

"You're in my seat, Baker."

There's surprise on Harrison's face when he glances up at Holden, who's suddenly standing next to the chair opposite me. I'm sure there's some on mine as well. I really wasn't sure if he would show up. And despite everything I said yesterday, I think he knows I *would* lie for him.

"Your seat, huh?" Harrison replies. "You could just find another table, Adams."

"Cassia's helping me with something."

Harrison glances at me, seemingly for confirmation. I give him a small smile but say nothing to endorse or deny Holden's story.

I'm surprised Holden admitted to that much. Linked us together in some way, when he's tried to separate us as far as possible ever since we started high school.

"All right, I'll leave you guys to it. Good luck with those integrals, Cassia." Harrison smiles, surprising me again.

I manage a "Thanks" before he stands and walks away. Immediately, the seat is filled again.

Unlike Harrison, Holden doesn't bother with any small talk. He rifles through his backpack and pulls out a few crumpled papers, placing them on the table between us.

I study his face, trying to catch one emotion in the shifting kaleidoscope. Holden is hard to read. He always has been, and it's made the few times I've caught a definitive glimpse seem more meaningful.

We stare at each other.

Holden speaks first. "You into him?"

"He was just being nice."

That response earns me an eye roll. "Don't be naïve, Cassia."

"I'm not. Besides, I wouldn't do that to—" I cut myself off, remember who I'm talking to.

Sydney and Holden aren't close. Not in a confrontational or resentful way, but a distant one. They're just two very different people, despite sharing DNA. When we were younger, it often felt like I was the strongest connection pulling them together. That string was severed a long time ago—by the boy sitting across from me.

"I know Sydney has a thing for him." Holden leans back in his chair and stretches. His shirt rides up a few inches, revealing the dusting of brown hair below his naval and the distinctive V that makes my mouth go dry every time I see it. Ridiculously ripped isn't even a quality I'd look for in a guy. It's that they're *his* abs.

His arms drop, and so does his shirt.

I quickly avert my eyes back to the papers. "You actually wrote the outline?"

"Yup." He pops the P, leans forward, and shoves the papers closer to me. The spicy tang of cinnamon fills the air between us.

I skim the first couple of pages. Holden was right; he doesn't need a tutor. Not that I thought he did. His lackadaisical attitude about school has never been because he's incapable or daunted by the work. He's just indifferent.

I jot a few comments in the margins, then shove it back toward him. "Did Mrs. Golden give you a deadline for the rewrite?"

"Nope." He pops the P again, and I grit my molars in response to the irritating sound.

"How long will it take you?"

"An hour, probably."

I scoff. "Yeah, right."

"Start a stopwatch," he tells me. Then pulls his laptop out of his backpack and opens it.

I drop my gaze back to my Calculus homework, trying to refocus on the derivatives I was working on before. But I keep stealing glances at Holden. At the piece of hair that continuously flops onto his forehead. The focused expression on his face. The way his nose wrinkles and his mouth quirks while he types.

We work in silence. The library is mostly cleared out by the time Holden closes his laptop. I look up as he stands and walks over to the printers. He returns with a neatly stapled stack he drops in front of me. The pages are still warm when I pull them closer.

"Here you go."

I glance at the clock hanging above the circulation desk. Mrs. Henderson, the librarian, is sitting below it, knitting. "It hasn't been an hour."

He shrugs. "I know you've got somewhere else to be."

I blink at him, surprised he knows I volunteer on Tuesdays.

"Your room probably needs to be cleaned. Maybe there's some homework you already did but could redo just to see if there's—"

Holden shuts up when I grab his essay off the table and shove it in my backpack, rough enough to make it wrinkle. More so when I push my own work on top of it. I stand and sling my backpack over one shoulder. It lands with a heavy thump against my spine, exacerbating my irritation.

"I'll get it back to you tomorrow," I say, then start striding toward the double doors that lead out of the library and into the hallway.

My body weight slams into the bar, shoving the door open with enough force it clangs when it swings back into place. I stomp down the hallway, unable to find it in myself to care.

Steps sound behind me, echoing off the linoleum floor, and I *hate* how my traitorous heart picks up double time in response.

"No rush."

I don't look over at the figure easily keeping pace beside me. The hallway is empty besides us. There's no one around to stare or speculate. "There is. The sooner I do, the sooner this little arrangement is over. That's what you want, right?"

"I never said that."

Holden's voice is measured and calm, a stark contrast to the fact I'm basically speed-walking to shorten our interaction.

"Whatever."

We walk side by side down the empty, locker-lined hallway,

and it's too similar to the fantasies I used to entertain. When we were younger, I'd picture something exactly like this. Me and him in high school. Hanging out, even if we weren't dating.

It's a special sort of painful—experiencing something you wanted but has turned distorted. This isn't how I thought it might happen.

Holden and I aren't dating. We're not even friends anymore. A teacher arranged this; he didn't even ask me for help himself.

"What are you getting out of it?"

He speaks right as we reach the doors that lead out to the student parking lot. A gust of cool air replaces the heat of indoors.

"What?"

"This paper. What are you getting out of it? Extra credit? College recommendation? What's in it for *you*, Cassia? Or are you really that selfless?"

I swallow. "Are you calling me selfless? Or heartless? Maybe I just wanted to help another student out."

"Another student? Or me?"

Damn him for always knowing which questions to ask. Which questions I don't want to answer. Mrs. Golden told me it was him before I agreed, but I'm not going to admit to that.

"Finally!"

I look away from Holden at Maggie. She's easy to spot in the parking lot that's close to empty, leaning against the side of my car and wearing a scowl that disappears when she sees who's standing next to me.

"Hey, Holden." Maggie flips her hair in a flirty move I'd look ridiculous doing. My younger sister manages to pull it off effortlessly.

"Hey, little Nolan."

My parents stuck with the flower theme for their first two children, then abandoned the idea when the twins were born. But despite the fact magnolias are also flowers, I've never heard Holden call Maggie *flower*.

It's stupid—how much it matters to me. Yet another thing Holden does that shouldn't affect me, but somehow consumes me.

Maggie preens like he paid her a compliment before turning her gaze to me. "What took forever? I've been waiting out here for like twenty minutes."

"I told you I had something after school this morning," I reply. "I thought you were taking the bus."

"It left early."

"Right," I drawl. "And you *never* run late."

"Whatever. Can we go?"

"I'm volunteering today. You'll have to come with me. I don't have time to go home first."

Maggie rolls her eyes. "Are you serious?"

"Yes, I'm serious. Let's go, unless you want to walk."

"I can drive you," Holden offers. "I'm headed straight home."

Maggie's expression instantly transforms from annoyed to elated. Mine creases with an irritation I refuse to name.

He's doing me and Maggie a favor. I won't have to deal with Maggie asking if we can leave yet every few minutes throughout my whole shift. But I'm not relieved by the offer; I'm bothered. "You don't have to do that."

"It's no big deal," Holden replies. "You guys literally live across the street." He glances at Maggie. "Come on, my truck's this way."

"Okay!" Maggie straightens and grabs her backpack off the front of my car. "Bye, Cassia."

"Bye." My voice sounds flat, even to my own ears.

"You're welcome."

I glance at Holden, who's still standing next to me. "You think I owe you a thank you?"

"You're usually pretty polite."

Anger courses through me. He's right; I'm usually amenable. It's just simpler to be easy-going.

The ugliness heating my blood is jealousy. I'm jealous of my little sister because he's offering her more than he's offered me in years.

"I don't need you to do me any favors." I stalk toward my car, tossing my backpack in the passenger seat before starting the engine.

I pull out of the lot without once looking back in the rearview mirror.

CHAPTER FOUR

HOLDEN

Wind rips through the hoodie I'm wearing, chilling my skin as I cross the quiet street. No one else is out running fool's errands.

I hesitate, glance at the bold B- on the top of the paper Mrs. Golden handed back last period, and then continue up the Nolans' front path for the first time in…years.

I ring the doorbell and wait, listening to the commotion inside. Shouting, banging, followed by what sounds like a war cry.

The red door swings open a minute later, revealing Mrs. Nolan. She looks a lot like Cassia. Same curly brown hair. Same friendly smile.

There's a little kid hugging her legs. The last time I was over here, she was hugely pregnant.

It's a pointed reminder of how long it's been since I last stood on this stoop.

I submitted a new paper and aced it, bringing the average of the two up to a B-. My history grade is passing—no longer in jeopardy. There's no real reason for me to be here.

I doubt Cassia actually cares how I did on the re-do, based on how she handed me her suggestions for improvements for the essay without so much as a smile. But here I am anyway—because otherwise there's no guarantee I'll see her anytime soon. I'm not sure she'll be standing in the kitchen when I get home tonight.

"Hi, Holden. How are you?"

"I'm good, Mrs. Nolan. Thanks."

"Haven't seen you around here in a while." There's no accusation in Cassia's mother's voice, only curiosity.

"I know. I had a question—a school question—for Cassia. If she's home?"

Mrs. Nolan nods and opens the door wider. "Come on in."

The inside of the Nolans' house hasn't changed since I was last here. It's comfy and cozy and overstuffed. Filled with toys and games and stick figure drawings and family photos. Everything my home isn't.

Cassia's sister Maggie is lying on the sectional couch that takes up a large chunk of the living room. She sits straight up when I follow Mrs. Nolan into the room. "Holden! Hi!"

I smile, mostly in response to her pink cheeks. "Hey, Maggie."

"Maggie mentioned you gave her a ride home on Tuesday," Mrs. Nolan says. "I really appreciate it, Holden."

"It wasn't a problem," I reply, which is exactly what I told Maggie when she thanked me profusely during the drive.

The only person who *hasn't* thanked me is the one I did it for.

I know volunteering at the local animal shelter is important to Cassia. She's helped out there since her family moved in across the street from mine when we were both in elementary school. I figured she would be happy not to have her younger sister tag along, especially since Maggie clearly didn't want to go. Instead, she seemed mad at me about it.

I can't figure her out. I shouldn't care. Shouldn't be here. I'm the one who forced distance between us in the first place. That had consequences I'll have to live with.

"I'll go let Cassia know you're here." Mrs. Nolan departs with a smile, leaving me and Maggie. And the little girl, who's now busy knocking down blocks. The twin boys come scrambling downstairs a minute later, hitting each other with foam swords. They rush by and out into the backyard, screeching the whole way.

No wonder Cassia is an insomniac.

I shove my hands in my pockets and nod toward the television. "What are you watching?"

"It's called *Twenty-Five to One*," Maggie replies. "They fight over this one guy—or girl—and all go on group dates and stuff."

"Sounds like high school."

Maggie leans forward. Her eager expression makes me apprehensive. "You know Ben Howard, right?"

"Uh, yeah." My answer sounds uncertain, even though I'm not unsure about knowing him. I'm wondering where this is possibly going. Probably nowhere I'll want to follow. "He's a freshman on the team."

"We have Ceramics together."

I'm not sure how to respond to that. "Okay…"

"I like him."

Maggie's frankness makes me smile. Mostly because it's so different from her older sister, who constantly makes me second guess every word she says. "You're interested in Howard?"

"Yeah. Well, I'd rather date *you*, but Cassia would hate me."

I chuckle uncomfortably. She's not wrong.

Cassia doesn't think much of me. I'm sure she'd be horrified if I expressed any interest in her younger sister. Plus, Maggie is a freshman. Three and a half years younger than me. In some stages of life, that's nothing. In high school, it's a lot.

I've also found it hard to focus on anything else when Maggie's older sister is around since we were kids.

So…there's that.

"Cassia picks up Regan from dance on Thursdays. We always have to wait around for a little while. Roxbury Diner is right across the street from En'Lair. I'll tell Cassia I'm hungry, we'll walk over, and you guys will be there." Maggie clasps her hands, eyes pleading. "Come on, Holden. *Please*. It'll be perfect!"

I'm taken aback by how much thought Maggie has put into this plan. Do all girls go to these extremes?

I'm also surprised by the realization I'm actually considering it. I was named captain this year, more as a testament to my role as the team's leading scorer than any proclivity toward responsibility on my part. I like winning more than I hate responsibility, I guess.

It would be easy to spin some story for Ben. Tell him it's team bonding or some shit to get to know the new players.

Annoyance replaces surprise, as I realize I'm considering doing exactly what I just judged Maggie for. If I agree to this, it wouldn't be as a nice guy doing her a favor just because I can. Or *actually* getting to know one of the freshman who will likely spend the season riding the bench.

It would be because I want to spend time around Cassia Nolan. And that's a dangerous compulsion I thought I'd successfully squashed. Apparently not.

I think of sitting across from her in the library on Tuesday. Watching her run the tip of her pen across her lower lip and twirl a curl around one finger.

Footsteps sound on the stairs. Maggie stares at me, eyebrows raised and expression imploring. I don't usually think she and Cassia look much alike. But right now, it's all I can see.

Damnit.

"Yeah, fine," I tell Maggie. "Okay."

She beams at me. "3:30."

Mrs. Nolan walks into the living room. "Cassia's in the shower. I'm sure she'll be out soon."

"It's fine." I unzip my backpack and pull out the essay I got back earlier, folding it in half and handing it to Mrs. Nolan. "Can you just give this to her?"

"I—of course. But are you sure you don't—"

"No. I need to get going. Thanks, though."

"All right. Don't be a stranger, Holden."

I glance at Mrs. Nolan. There's something knowing in her expression, some conclusion about why I'm here and why I've stayed away. I don't know if it's the correct one, and I'm not all that interested in finding out.

I give her a smile and a small nod before turning and leaving the room.

———

A haze of weed smoke drifts by as I climb out of my truck. The old court usually smells like pot. They leveled the old high school when the new building was finished, but someone decided it wasn't worth tearing up the rectangle of asphalt and two metal hoops. The tennis courts survived as well.

"He's here, bitches!" Finn ensures no one misses our arrival, bounding out of the passenger side and toward the group gathered on the periphery of the woods. The *large* group.

What started as a small gathering has grown every week. I see more and more familiar faces as I walk closer, and it fills me with unease.

This was meant to be low-key—a way to blow off some steam and make money in the process. The more people who know, the messier it could get.

Finn reappears at my side, slinging an arm around my shoulder. "Casper is already here."

"Fine," I respond, shaking him off.

He reeks of vodka. Just about everyone here appears tipsy.

I'm entirely sober.

I'm stupid enough to fight, but I'm not suicidal.

Casper Wallace is a stereotypical football player. Solid, beefy, and broad. If he pins me down, I'll be in trouble. And I'm sure those massive fists of his pack a wallop. But I'm taller and faster than he is. Plus, the way Casper is shifting tells me this is unfamiliar to him. He probably ended up here the same way I did— needling from Declan. An offer of easy money and an ego boost.

Declan swaggers over to me right as I think his name, a broad grin stretching across his freckled face. He's as Irish as his name, down to the red hair. Not to mention the morally gray business ventures. According to him, his grandfather was in the Irish mafia and so it runs in the family. He deals drugs too, which is how I met him in the first place. Finn uses him as his main supplier.

Declan's smile impossibly widens when he sees me, taking over his whole face. He lives for this shit. "Adams! You ready, man?"

I meet his exuberance with monotone. "Yeah. I'm ready."

I am. My body is conditioned to know what takes place here by now. Adrenaline starts to pump through my system as I analyze Casper. Memorizing how he moves and where his weaknesses might be as he stands with a few other guys from Ridgemont.

Restless rage simmers and spreads, heating my blood and combating the chill in the air. I could probably trace the source of it if I really tried. Instead, I embrace the recklessness. It feels like driving down a deserted road with the windows down and the accelerator flat on the floor. Moving too fast to worry about consequences.

I know this is stupid and pointless. I know my dad would be disappointed and Sydney would be worried.

Sometimes making bad decisions feels really good.

Focusing on this cuts through the mess in my head, the worries about the future and the uncertainty about what my life should look like. I'm floating, and it's an anchor to grasp. The only other time I can tune everything out like this is when I'm on a basketball court.

My teachers call me lazy. My friends call me wild. My dad isn't around to call me anything.

The only thing I want to be called right now is a winner.

I pull the roll of tape out of the pocket of my hoodie and start wrapping my hands. It's a move I learned online watching boxing videos. As an intimidation tactic, more than anything.

I've always had a short temper. But I can control it. Most of the time when I'm pissed, I let it roil inside of me and don't let it out. When I do, it's because I choose to.

There are only a handful of times I've lost control. Most of them were when peers would pick on Sydney when we were younger. The most recent time was when Finn mentioned dating Cassia. I knew he was talking shit the way he often does, and I still lost my cool.

I rip the end of the tape off with my teeth and then shove the roll back in my pocket. Whip my sweatshirt and the t-shirt I was wearing off in one practiced move, smirking at the catcalls from the girls gathered round.

Casper steps up to the makeshift ring, lines drawn in the dirt. He's trying to hide the apprehension on his face, but it's there if you look hard enough.

Declan starts listing off the rules. The only important one is that the first man down loses. So far, it's never been me. That's why Declan is so desperate to keep finding me new opponents. But as I stand here, feeling the cold nip at my bare skin, I know I'm done.

The thrill is gone.

I'm used to this bored feeling. It happens all the time. With girls, with drinking, when I'm at parties. My life feels predictable in the worst way.

Swinging for sport isn't exciting—the way it was the first few times. And if I get seriously injured and can't play this season… I'm not sure I could live with myself, knowing I blew my one shot at a future. My dad makes a decent living, but there's no way he could pay for me and Sydney to go to college without any assistance. Not to mention, I want to play in college. Basketball is the one thing that's always remained fresh—that's never lost its luster no matter how many years pass or how many times I step onto the court.

Actually, that's a lie. There's one other thing.

I study Casper. He's listening to Declan, his hands swinging at his sides. Large muscles shift in his chest. I should feel apprehensive. I'm feeling nothing.

I've never even met this guy before. A punching bag would summon more emotion. So I do what I always do. I pretend he's someone I can't stand. Sometimes that means I'm swinging at myself. Tonight, I'm picturing Harrison Baker before me. Seeing him smile at Cassia and her smile back. Fury courses through me. My fingers twitch, ready to form fists.

For all of high school, I've never really considered the

possibility that she might date someone. I've done my best to tune out Sydney's babble whenever it concerns her best friend, to ignore the gossip, to not know what's happening in Cassia's life.

Maybe there have been lots of guys, and I've just been blissfully oblivious.

Maybe it was just shitty timing I had to watch another guy ogle her during the one encounter I couldn't walk away from.

I was there to meet with her. I couldn't *not* show when she was doing me a favor.

Although, with anyone else, I probably wouldn't have had an issue. I'm cold and selfish.

Sydney is like our dad.

I'm like our mom. I've never pretended otherwise, never bothered to battle the destructive inclinations.

The annoying bell Declan bought goes off. Casper swings. I duck. When I stand again, I picture Harrison leaning across the library table and kissing Cassia. I land an uppercut on Casper's jaw. He rears back, then lands a punch on my ribs that hurts like hell, followed by a smack to my jaw that stings.

I imagine them walking down the hall together. Her wearing his football jersey.

Casper grunts from the force of the next blow. Blood flows from his mouth freely, mixing with saliva and spilling out. He spits and it lands somewhere in the grass. The crowd around us cheers.

I don't hesitate. Don't bask in the glow of adoration or the thrill of victory. I land another punch before Casper has fully recovered. He goes down, wobbling at first and then his knees hit the grass as he grabs his jaw. Declan blows his whistle. One of Casper's buddies kneels to check on him.

I stand still, registering the cheers but not really hearing them.

This moment feels distended, like something I'm watching on a screen but not experiencing firsthand.

Finn jumps on me, screaming in my ear. Mark is right behind him and so are a bunch of the other guys. I spot Grace and a few of her friends standing behind them.

Declan approaches. "Holden! Amazing, man! You're—"

I cut him off. "Send me the money, okay?"

"Yeah, sure. Just—"

"And I'm done."

His smile falls. "What?"

"I'm done."

"Holden, we could make a ton of money. Don't—"

I turn around and walk away. Finn is the only one who follows me. "Want some?" He holds out a Gatorade bottle I'm willing to bet doesn't contain any Gatorade anymore.

"No. I'm driving."

"Driving? We're partying, Adams. You knocked him down in a few minutes, dude! Come on, let's—"

"I'm leaving, Finn. Do you want a ride or not?"

He studies me for a minute, then shakes his head. "Nah. I'll catch one with Mark."

"Okay. See you." I open the door.

"You sure you're good?"

"I'm good. He barely grazed me."

It's not true. My ribs ache. But I'd rather deal with it at home, not here. My dad ended up extending his current trip. Once he's out on a route, there are always extra deliveries to pick up, and he took advantage once again.

"Okay. You don't usually dip out so early, though."

"I'm tired. You get in the ring next time, see how you feel after."

Finn raises his hands as he starts to walk backwards. "Okay, fine. Text me tomorrow, yeah? I got that new video game."

"Yeah, sure."

I climb into the cab of my truck and exhale. Slam my sore hand against the steering wheel.

I'm tired, yeah. But I'm going home, hoping to see her. Wondering if she saw the essay and cared at all.

That makes me feel pathetic, not victorious.

CHAPTER FIVE

CASSIA

The digital numbers on the stove change, displaying the start of a new hour. I glance down at the glass of water that's been my sorry excuse for standing here for the last twenty minutes, annoyed with myself.

I'm not sure why I was so certain he'd be home by now.

Why the fact he isn't feels like a personal affront.

I stick my glass in the dishwasher and head for the stairs. My hand brushes the banister just as I catch a flash of movement out of the corner of my eye. I hesitate, my foot hovering in mid-air as I look out the living room window and watch as a tall shadow moves across the asphalt driveway. Warring with myself. Torn between what I want to do and what I should do.

There's a blue hoodie hanging from the row of pegs by the front door. I shrug it on before heading outside. It does little to temper the chill in the air, despite hanging halfway down my thighs. Based on the size, I'm certain it's Holden's.

I wrap the cotton tighter around me as I walk down the front steps and veer to the left, toward the driveway.

I hear the rhythmic smack of rubber against asphalt before I round the corner of the house. The basketball hoop is attached to the front face of the garage, which is tucked between the side of the house and the row of bushes that separates the Adamses' yard from the neighbors.

There's an exterior light affixed above the hoop that casts a dim light over the asphalt. Over the figure who's sitting on the asphalt now, instead of standing and shooting.

I walk over and sink down beside him. The driveway is cold and hard. But I'm more focused on the guy next to me than the fact it feels like I'm sitting on an ice cube.

"B minus, huh?"

The graded rewrite of his essay was waiting on the kitchen counter when I came downstairs after my shower, along with curious looks from my mom and Maggie.

Holden Adams doesn't casually stop by my house—not anymore. I have no idea what him dropping off the rewrite of the essay I helped him ace means. His version of a thank you?

"Yeah." One word, yet it conveys a lot. It tells me Holden is testy and annoyed. That our conversation tonight won't resemble the predictable pattern of past Friday nights.

I glance over, watching as he takes a drink from a glass bottle that was hidden in the shadows. The light is dim, but it's enough to illuminate a purplish bruise blooming just above the sharp line of his jaw. "What happened to your face?"

"Game tonight…devolved."

"Into a brawl?"

Holden scoffs. "You should see the other guy."

"You actually got into a fight?" My voice rises an octave, surprise and concern sharpening the words.

"It was nothing."

"Doesn't look like nothing." I glance at the long-sleeved shirt he's wearing, wondering if it's covering other bruises.

"Why do you care?"

"I…care. Getting drunk and fighting? You're more than that —you're better than that, Holden."

He snorts before grabbing the whiskey bottle and taking another sip of the amber liquid. "You can spare me the wasted potential pep talk."

"Fine. I will." I lean over, intending to snatch the bottle. If he wants to throw a pity party, at least I can save him from getting alcohol poisoning while he attends it.

Holden moves too. To stop me or grab the bottle, or maybe he's equally uncomfortable sitting on the hard asphalt. He straightens as I reach, and somehow I end up mostly in his lap. Closer than we've been since…I know *exactly* how long it's been since we were this close, actually.

I should move away. Far, *far* away, from the scent of cinnamon and the heat of his body. But I don't. I remain frozen in place, watching our proximity register on Holden's face. The haze of liquor leaves his eyes, and the false humor disappears from his face.

Holden tilts his head back, looking up at the sky. I can see more of his face than I could before. Not just the bruised jaw, but the freckle beneath his left eye. The small bump on the bridge of his nose from when he took a basketball to the face in fifth grade gym class. The small crease in the corner of his mouth where a dimple rarely appears.

His throat bobs as he swallows. Once. Twice. "Only you." He whispers the words, then laughs. "Only you could get me hard right now."

Unconsciously, I shift. Seeking. Or maybe it's conscious. Maybe I know *exactly* what I'm looking for. Maybe the past few years have all been leading up to this moment, to some acknowledgment there's more between us than a forgotten friendship. An abandoned friendship he walked away from.

Holden groans when I brush against the bulge in his joggers. It fuels something rising in me. Some urge, a primal motivation.

The words *Only you could get me hard right now* are echoing in my head.

A secret, sincere confession. And also an acknowledgment of what we've avoided. Well, what *he* avoided and I accepted, to protect what little of my heart he hadn't already broken.

"Fuck," he rasps, as my hips move closer. Faster.

From the outside, this looks entirely innocent. All our clothes are on. We're not touching anywhere except our laps. But nothing feels innocent about the sensations swirling inside me—the excitement and the arousal. They overwhelm me, adding to the thrill I always get around him. The inner giddiness is amplified to a degree that threatens to drown me, that overrides every instinct except one.

His erection thickens and hardens as I grind against it, chasing the bolts of pleasure that keep appearing when I nudge against him just right. His body is responding, but Holden hasn't moved. He's leaning back on one palm, blue eyes fixed on me straddling him.

I don't know what the hell I'm doing. He's drunk and experienced, and I'm neither of those things. The only guy I've kissed, much less humped in a dark driveway, is him.

A warm palm slides beneath the hem of my borrowed sweatshirt. His sweatshirt, technically. If he registers that detail, he doesn't comment on it.

Holden's hand slides higher and higher, over the curve of my ribs until it reaches the swell of my breast. He cups it and squeezes gently, taking advantage of the fact I'm not wearing a bra.

I moan, biting on my bottom lip to try to contain it. I wasn't expecting his touch to feel so good. I imagine his mouth and his tongue replacing the warmth of his hand, and heat creeps across my skin.

His eyes flare at the sound.

I'm disappointed when his palm slides back to my waist. His other hand does the same, so he's gripping my hips and guiding my movements. Immediately, the pleasure intensifies. I drop my head into the curve of his neck, inhaling the scent of laundry detergent and cinnamon.

There's a hint of weed too.

I try not to focus on that, choosing to ignore the reminder he's been out tonight doing who knows what with who knows who. I focus on him, which is easy to do. *Too* easy to do. Especially now, when we're doing things I've only fantasized about ever happening.

Our movements fall into a deceptive rhythm. Turn into a familiarity I thought was broken between us a long time ago. I can feel him—hard and thick and hot—between my thighs, and it fans the flames lighting between us.

Me.

He's reacting this way to *me*.

I feel the pleasure building inside of me. My hips move faster, chasing the high that's rapidly approaching. It explodes inside of me in a rush of euphoria, a thousand times more powerful than when I touch myself. I feel wetness soak my underwear as I muffle my moans in Holden's sweatshirt. He jerks beneath me, finding his own release.

We're both breathing heavily. Harsh, ragged inhales and exhales are the only sounds filling the still night air. My body feels loose and languid. Relaxed. I don't want to move. I want to sink into this moment, the way you snuggle beneath a blanket on the couch.

Anticipation of what awkwardness could be coming propels me into action.

Holden is still holding my hips, but his grip has loosened. His hands fall as I pull away from him and stand up. He's watching me move away while wearing an unreadable expression. There's no sign of pleasure or satisfaction on his face, even though I felt him come.

And rather than ask if that meant anything, if *I* mean anything to him, I turn around and walk away. Non-confrontational, nice Cassia doesn't demand answers.

Also, I'm embarrassed. *I* initiated things. *I* crawled into his lap and got myself off. Do guys turn girls down in that position? Especially when they're drunk?

I close my eyes to the reality of what just took place, only opening them when I reach the front door. I fumble with the handle, eager to get inside quickly on the off chance Holden is coming after me and wants to discuss what happened.

It's unlikely, considering he's made a habit of ignoring me most of the time. But I know for sure he won't barge into his sister's bedroom for answers.

There are no footsteps behind me as I yank off the hoodie with shaky fingers and hang it back on the hook. I don't want to wake up wearing a reminder of tonight.

Silently, I creep up the stairs and slip into Sydney's bedroom. She's fast asleep, like always. Hair fanned across her pillow and a peaceful expression on her face.

For a moment, I wish she wasn't Holden's sister. That I could wake her up and tell the closest friend I have what just happened between me and the only boy who's ever given me butterflies.

The guy I've had a crush on since before I could identify what one was.

Instead, I crawl onto the air mattress and try to fall asleep.

It meant nothing, I tell myself.

Lie to myself.

CHAPTER SIX

HOLDEN

I should have kissed her.

That's the main thought that keeps circling around in my head, instead of listening to Mr. Watson drone on about different types of seaweed and how to easily identify them. I thought Oceanography would be an easy senior year science elective. It's equally boring, unfortunately.

I tap my pen against the metal rings of my open notebook, my thoughts chaotic and my knee bouncing.

When the girl who's always been *the girl* ends up in your lap, humping your dick, you kiss her. Right?

I don't know what the hell I was thinking. I *wasn't* thinking, really. I was swimming with residual adrenaline, sore as fuck, more than buzzed from the whiskey I picked up on the drive home, and in no way prepared for Cassia to make any sort of move toward me.

I thought any interest on her part had long since fizzled, dispelled by years of barely exchanging trivial conversation, let alone anything meaningful. I thought, at most, there was maybe some physical attraction lingering.

Cassia isn't a random hookup girl. She's the girl you kiss on the front porch after a date, not the one you take upstairs to a spare bedroom at a party. But I didn't think she was the girl who climbed on a guy's dick to get herself off either, so maybe I misjudged her.

Based on the way she's gone out of her way to ignore me ever since it happened, she regrets that it did. That grates at me, even more irritating than the possibility Cassia is not as inexperienced as I assumed.

She was brazen and bold around me when we were younger. But I hadn't seen that side of her in years, the girl who goes after what she wants without second-guessing. Sure, she's driven, especially when it comes to school. But I think that's more about pleasing her parents than anything else.

And once again, I don't know. I have no idea when or if she still seizes control. It shouldn't bother me as much as it does, considering I'm the one who ensured I wouldn't—that I don't. But it annoys me anyway, itches my skin like an irritation that can't be scratched.

Finn keeps pace with me as we leave class and head toward the cafeteria. He's still talking about my victory on Friday night, describing what he considers my most impressive moments. Completely oblivious to the fact I'm not paying attention to a single word he's saying. More of our friends join us the closer we get to the cafeteria, and that distracts him.

I'm busy scanning the hall.

Mark asks me a question about the start of practice next week, which I focus on until we reach our typical table and sit. Grace and McKenzie appear, joining the group. Grace takes the seat next to me. Her hand finds my thigh under the table, stroking the denim.

"You okay?" she asks. Soft and quiet, not trying to draw attention to the question. Still, everyone else at the table is surreptitiously watching us.

Grace and I are primetime entertainment. Most of the guys have bets going on how long before we hook up again.

They're going to lose.

Maybe before Friday night, those odds had a decent chance. Before then, Grace was a hot blonde distraction who was happy with casual and no strings.

A possibility when Cassia was nothing but a fantasy. But now I know what the reality with Cassia is like. Know what the breathy moans she makes when she comes sound like.

I was in control, up until Cassia instigated things. I've never wanted to resist her, and I'm sick of trying. The problem is, my selfish tendencies have never extended to Cassia.

She's been the exception, always.

I'll hurt her, even if I don't mean to.

Me staying away is in her best interest and so I've tried to do exactly that. Not drag her down into my uncertain future. Into my destructive tendencies and volatile decisions.

The problem is, how I *actually* feel about her has never changed, regardless of how I've acted. It was much easier to keep that façade up when I figured all Cassia Nolan wanted was to become a veterinarian and meet a nice, reliable guy one day.

But then she came on my dick like she was desperate for me, and that assumption shattered like fragile glass.

"Holden?"

"I'm fine," I answer, then take a long pull of water as I watch the entrance.

Cassia walks into the cafeteria, talking to a girl with a blonde bob who I've never noticed before. They both walk over to the table of girls that includes my sister. Instead of her usual spot facing me, Cassia sits on the opposite side of the table so her back is toward me.

I sip more water, eyes fixed on the back of the gray sweatshirt she's wearing. She sits in the same spot, always. This is purposeful, her making a point.

She won't even look at me.

Fuck it.

I stand, ignoring Grace asking me where I'm going. Cross the linoleum floor of the cafeteria, pretending not to see the curious glances aimed my way. I stride straight toward Cassia, not bothering with any semblance of *I just happened to be walking by* casual bullshit.

Purposeful strides eat up the distance between us quickly.

I don't hesitate once I reach her, either. "I need to talk to you," I announce.

The table of mostly juniors falls silent. Her friendship with Sydney means most of Cassia's friends are a year younger. I was her strongest connection to our grade, up until I stopped inviting her to hang out.

I ignore the lingering guilt associated with that decision and focus instead on the prime view of Cassia's shoulders rising and tensing before her head turns around. I keep my gaze on her, leaving no question about who I'm talking to.

"Why? What's going on? Is something wrong?" Sydney fires the questions at me rapid fire, glancing between me and her best friend with an expression of concern.

"Everything is fine, Syd. I need help on a Calculus assignment, is all." I keep my eyes on Cassia the whole time, not missing the way hers narrow as I offer that made-up explanation.

It sounds plausible, at least. I've never been an honors student. Always been purposefully lazy when it comes to school. When it comes to a lot of things.

"Ask the teacher."

Everyone else at the table looks surprised by Cassia's curt answer. I'm not. I already figured out she's avoiding me. That she's regretful or embarrassed or both. And I already knew there's some fire hiding beneath her nice girl exterior.

"It's due next period," I lie, banking on her not knowing my class schedule. I already had math this morning.

"He needs to pass to play…" Sydney says.

Sweet, understanding Sydney, who looks confused by the fact Cassia is so reluctant to help me. Seconds tick by, the number of eyes on us multiplying with each one that passes.

Finally, Cassia stands, abandoning her half-eaten sandwich. "Fine."

She starts toward an empty table across the aisle. I rest a hand on her lower back and guide her toward one of the doors that leads out to the senior courtyard instead. It's getting too cold to eat out here. There are only a few people sitting in the courtyard, all bundled in coats neither of us are wearing. But I'm not worried about anyone overhearing us, which was a concern in the crowded cafeteria.

"Was that really necessary?" she asks as soon as we're outside.

I shove my hands in the pockets of my jeans, leaning against one of the empty picnic tables. It's chilly out here, but it's peaceful too. Fresh air and open space. "You tell me. How was your *nap* yesterday?"

Cassia scoffs as I mention the excuse her mom fed me when I tried to have this conversation yesterday, looking away at the massive oak planted in the center of the courtyard. The wind picks up, pulling a few pieces of hair out of her ponytail and dragging leaves off the branches.

"You needed help with Calculus then too?" she asks. Her tone is mocking. Annoyed.

It makes me want to smile. I like her like this. Raw and real.

"Nope. Did all my homework yesterday, actually."

She meets my gaze. "You always were a good liar."

"You wanted me to tell Sydney what happened Friday night instead?"

Her cheeks flush. Maybe from the wind that's still blowing, but I'm betting it's from the mention of what took place between us in my driveway. "There's nothing to tell."

"No?" I take a step closer, forcing her head to tilt back in order to hold my gaze. "You climb into a lot of guys' laps? No big deal?"

I'm hoping the questions are rhetorical. A part of me is really wondering, though. I don't know her as well as I used to. Maybe I'm a fool for thinking she wouldn't have instigated any sort of intimacy between us unless it meant something to her.

Cassia's front teeth sink into her bottom lip, chasing away the pink until she releases it to speak and color rushes back. "So what if I do?"

"Now who's lying?" I ask, unprepared to deal with the possibility she's not.

Cassia shrugs. Indifferent. Maddening. There's no trace of duplicity on her face, and it pisses me off to a degree I'm not expecting.

She's not yours, I remind myself.

Never has been.

Never will be.

"And you always just walk away after?"

"Mad I stole your move?"

I inhale sharply, surprised she's bringing that Halloween up.

Am I proud of it? No. But I thought it was settled history. Part of the past. Irrelevant moving forward. "Cassia…that wasn't—"

"I lost interest in an explanation four years ago, Holden. Don't bother."

Her tone is acerbic. Cutting. The complete opposite of uncaring, and a masochistic part of me wants to grin in response to that small victory.

"Yeah, *clearly* you're over it, since you just brought it up."

She sighs, long and irritated. "I'm cold and hungry and there's no point to this conversation. If you didn't want it to happen, you would have stopped it, since you've never had any issue being honest. It happened, it won't happen again. Now you can go back to ignoring me."

"Cassia…"

"I mean it, Holden."

She turns and walks away from me.

Again.

Leaving me standing here, a whole lot irritated and just as conflicted.

Because, the problem is, I *want* it to happen again.

I can admit that to myself. I'm just not sure it's anything I should tell her.

CHAPTER SEVEN

CASSIA

I'm shoving the last of my books into my locker when Sydney appears.

"Hey."

"Hey," I reply, shutting the door and spinning the combination. "You ready?"

"Uh-huh."

Most days, Sydney stays after school in one of her various roles as part of the theater elective she takes every semester. She's never acted in any of the productions, but always takes on some sort of managerial position as a stagehand. I've tried to talk her into performing for years, but I'm not really one to talk. Most of the time, I hang out in my comfort zone right alongside her. The only reliable pull toward the uncharted in my life has been Holden Adams, and I can't exactly pass that along to Sydney as solid advice.

We walk side by side down the hall. The final bell only rang a few minutes ago. Almost every locker is open, and the hallway is packed. I wave at London Jackson as I pass her. We share a lot of the same classes and usually pair up on projects when we can.

"So…that was weird earlier. At lunch?"

I barely register London's returning wave, too startled by Sydney's comment. I manage some vague hum that Sydney takes as me not knowing what she's talking about.

"Holden coming over to our table at lunch?" she prompts. "That was weird, right? He's never done that before. And he looked annoyed. So did you, actually."

My eyes stay focused straight ahead as we navigate the busy hall, headed toward the main doors.

Holden isn't a taboo topic between us. Sydney talks about him a lot. Worries about him a lot, more specifically. Most of the time, he's the only family she has around. But we don't discuss *me* and Holden. Not since Sydney noticed the space between us. She asked me, once, if something had happened. I said no—unwilling to dredge up painful details with anyone, including her—and that was that. All the years of the three of us hanging out were easily erased.

"I *was* annoyed," I answer. "You know how he can be. He asked me for help and then didn't listen to what I said."

I'm sticking with Holden's Calculus help story. No way am I telling anyone—especially Sydney—what we really discussed. Although it's absolutely a situation where I could use some guidance. Where it would be helpful to have a best friend who isn't related to the only guy I've ever been interested in.

"Holden hates asking for help."

I don't respond to the true statement. I figure the less I say about this subject, the better. Holden saying anything to Sydney is unlikely, but I'm not going to wade any deeper into this lie.

"Do you think he's failing? Maybe he's really struggling and he's too stubborn to say anything."

"I'm sure he's doing fine."

Sydney sighs. "I know he's worried about college. He's got a lot riding on this season, on getting a scholarship."

I grit my teeth together and grip the straps of my backpack. Analyzing Holden—sympathizing with Holden—is the absolute last thing I feel like doing right now.

I'm trying to hold on to my anger toward him. It's easier than exploring the emotions hovering underneath.

He represents my own weakness.

I want him—even though I shouldn't. Despite the many reasons he's given me not to. And now he knows that truth.

"He's doing fine," I assure her. "He figured out the homework pretty quickly."

I didn't tell Sydney about helping Holden with his history paper, and apparently he didn't mention it to her either. All the secrets I've ever kept from my best friend have involved her brother.

"Hey, Cassia."

I automatically slow at the sound of my name. Glance at Harrison, who's leaning against the cinderblock wall, filling his thermos.

"Hey," I reply. Clear my throat and remember how he carried our last conversation. "Heading to practice?"

He smiles before answering, "Yeah." Pleased I asked, I guess.

Harrison's smile is warm and genuine. And I hate—absolutely despise—that all I can picture is the annoyance on Holden's face when he saw Harrison sitting opposite me.

"This is Sydney," I say, once again at a loss for anything else to say to him.

Harrison dips his chin in greeting as he screws the top on his water bottle. "Hey, Sydney."

"Hi, Harrison."

He smirks a little at how she addresses him without an introduction, but he doesn't call her out on it. It makes me like him more.

"I'd better run. Coach is in his sadistic playoffs phase, so practice will be brutal. See you guys."

"See you," I say.

One final smile, and he's gone.

"He likes you," Sydney tells me as soon as he's out of sight.

"He was being nice," I reply as we walk outside.

Sydney gives me a look that's remarkably similar to the one her brother did when I said the same thing. "Cassia."

"What? He's a nice guy. And you think he's hot."

"What does that have to do with anything?"

"Girl code, Syd."

Sydney laughs. "I've never even talked to him until just now. He's fair game. If you like him, go for it."

Unfortunately, that's the problem. I *don't* like Harrison—not in that way. When I look at his blond hair and brown eyes, I imagine them dark brown and blue.

Crushes can take time to develop, I guess. I don't know anything about Harrison except that he plays football and is good at math. Maybe we have lots of shared interests that would make him more attractive and spark more of a connection.

I think those are the logical, sensible kinds of crushes, though. Where you really get to know someone and understand what they have to offer. Like a pro/con list for the heart. You form a conclusion first and then romantic feelings start to develop.

The problem is, I've experienced the illogical, consuming kind of crush. The *can't sleep, can't eat* sort. The *stay up for hours to talk to him for minutes* madness. Butterflies that keep flying. Giddiness that doesn't fade. Holden hijacks my brain like there's a part of him inside of me I can't ignore.

I'm not sure how to explain that to anyone without sounding crazy.

We reach my car and Sydney gets distracted by putting on a playlist as I pull out of my spot and join the long line of cars waiting to leave the high school's parking lot.

It's a fifteen-minute drive to the local animal shelter from the Pembrooke High campus. I volunteer here as often as I can. Sydney is not as much of an animal lover as I am, but she comes with me whenever she can. The shelter is always understaffed for the amount of work to be done. She usually helps with filing paperwork and cleaning, while I focus more on assisting with the animals.

Susan, a middle-aged woman who also volunteers, is out in the fenced run that juts off from the right side of the shingled building when I park in the small lot. The three puppies that were brought in last week are running around her ankles in circles, yapping playfully. I wave at her as Sydney and I head into the shelter.

There's no one at the front desk when we enter. I walk through the lobby and down the hallway, passing the rooms where potential adopters can play with the animals available for adoption.

The rest of the building is dedicated to housing the cats and dogs living here. I peek into the cat room first. All but one of the twenty cages are filled. The bowls are neatly stacked on the table for feeding later and the play area in the center room looks freshly cleaned.

Sydney follows me across the hall, into the dog room. Eileen, who manages the shelter, is sitting in the center of the room, cross-legged. Patch, the shelter's longest resident, is lying next to her, wagging his bushy tail as he gets brushed.

Eileen looks up and smiles, the corners of her eyes creasing as some gray hair falls out of the perpetually messy ponytail she has it pulled back in.

She's been in charge of everything for as long as I've been coming here. Now a retired veterinarian, she left a practice a few towns over to open up a shelter instead. Rumors around Pembrooke suggest she left a messy divorce behind, but I've never pried into her past and she's never offered any details. Her life is the animals, and she's been the largest inspiration for my planned path.

I walk over and crouch down beside Patch, rubbing his head and setting off a fresh wave of wags. Eileen always says the point of the shelter is to find new homes for the pets, not to have them all end up in her house, but I wouldn't be surprised if Patch ends up a permanent resident.

Eileen gives me a sheepish smile. "I'm behind with the rest of these guys." She gestures to the kennels around us. Most of them are empty right now, the dogs choosing to be outside in the sunshine instead of indoors. "Was just giving this guy a little extra love."

"He deserves it," I say, giving Patch another pet before standing. "I can get started on the rest of the crew."

"I'll get back to the filing," Sydney says, heading toward the door that leads to the office. "Same system, Eileen?"

"Yes! Thank you, Sydney."

Sydney smiles and disappears into the office.

"I'll be lost next year without you."

"Next fall is still a ways away." I force a smile, trying to ignore the twinge of anxiety the mention of college prompts. It sparks apprehension about where I'll end up and how different it might be from what I'm used to.

I've looked forward to leaving for college for years. It's a step forward, a chance to meet new people and have new experiences. Finally embarking on my planned path.

I feel stuck in Pembrooke. Everything about my life is expected and confined. Ever since my family moved here back when I was in elementary school, I've been the nice, quiet, smart girl. The girl who gets good grades and doesn't get drunk. I didn't realize how claustrophobic that was until recently, when I experienced the rush of the unexpected. And somehow, it made me more conflicted about leaving Pembrooke. Reticent, almost.

Especially since I discovered on Friday night, I don't have to leave to feel a thrill. To me, it feels like the thrill is tied to a person, not a place.

Cleaning out cages and measuring kibble keeps my hands busy, but my mind has nothing to do but wander. I know the mountain of paperwork Sydney is working on will take the couple of hours we usually spend here. Eileen left to help Susan with the puppies and then to feed the cats. I'm alone in the cavernous space, stuck with my thoughts.

I run through the list of assignments I need to finish tonight. Brainstorm ideas for my college essay. The prompt is *Describe an experience that is essential to who you are.* I can't come up with anything that doesn't sound boring or average. Getting good grades and volunteering here are what were supposed to help me get into college. It didn't allow for many memorable experiences. Humping Holden Adams is the most memorable thing that's happened to me lately.

Memorable, and also an experience I'm actively trying to forget. He's making it harder than I thought it would be. I thought pretending to be asleep when he came over yesterday would be enough of a deterrent. I had been trying to take a nap, I just exaggerated my breathing when I heard my mom open the door. Her knowing gaze at dinner last night was distracting. But the kicker was Holden himself.

Despite my best efforts, I've heard the rumors about him. He's a star player off the court as well as on it. In addition to being the hottest guy who attends Pembrooke High, he has *it*. That tangible charisma where you're drawn to someone even when they're doing nothing. He has a pull around him, a confidence that stands out regardless of where he is. Regardless of whatever he's doing.

Maybe it should make me feel better about my perpetual weakness, seeing how girls throw themselves at him based on that appeal alone. I have some measure of history with him, back when we were close friends. There were also ten thrilling minutes during eighth grade when I was certain he felt the same way about me as I felt about him.

I was sure Friday night would lead to the same indifference that rapidly followed our eighth-grade kiss. History is often an accurate predictor of the future.

Instead, Holden sought me out—twice—when he could have very easily pretended it never happened. He seemed…affected. He also acknowledged me at school, which he's never done, aside from the discussions involving the essay that were forced upon him.

It felt like people were giving me side glances all afternoon, and I don't think it was just in my head. It's part of the effect Holden has. There's no way he didn't know pulling me out of the cafeteria would draw attention.

He isn't as egotistical as he could be about the level of interest in him, but he's not oblivious either. I can't figure out why he did it. The only explanation I can come up with is that he's worried I'll say something to Sydney, and that pisses me off.

It would cause strife between them, and that's nothing I'd purposely encourage. I never told her how he ghosted me at the end of middle school. And he was the one who kissed me. I'm the one who initiated things between us this time, and that alone is enough to assure I'd never tell Sydney. Not only is the guy in question her brother, he's also the only boy who's broken my heart. If the roles were reversed, I'd be warning her far away from him.

Holden is synonymous with heartbreak. He's the highest of highs and the lowest of lows. I'm still not sure what force compelled me to act on my attraction after years of mirroring his indifference, but it's nothing I need to justify.

Me and Holden are one of those fantasies with flaws. A possibility that you can picture so clearly it seems perfect. But then life gets in the way somehow. Nothing works out exactly the way you imagined it might. Usually it's for the worst, in a way you make do with by saying it wasn't meant to be.

I need to stop allowing for the possibility we are meant to be. To focus on the reality of what we are—what he *made* us. There are certain things I can control. My own future and my own decisions are two of them. Holden is the furthest thing from controlled. He's unpredictable.

College and veterinary school will get me where I want to go. Speculating—wishing—won't get me anywhere. Focusing on my work here and my planned path will.

I finish rationing all the food and start setting bowls down in cages with fresh resolve. All the dogs run in when they hear the clank of the metal, eagerly gobbling down their portions. I mark off everything on the master chart, make sure all the plastic canisters are closed, and walk across the hallway into the cat room. It's empty, with no sign of Susan or Eileen.

I step back into the hallway. There's a laugh, followed by the murmur of voices. Someone must be here.

Most of my hair came out of its bun while I was working. I

yank the elastic out as I follow the sound of commotion, letting my curls fall freely. I run a hand through the tangled mess, turn the corner that leads into the lobby, and freeze.

Susan, Eileen, and Sydney are all gathered by the front desk, staring at…Holden. He's standing just inside the doorway, holding a stuffed monkey.

"All set?"

It takes me a minute to register Eileen is talking to me. An embarrassing long stretch of time, actually. I'm too busy blinking at Holden like he's a hallucination that might disappear. But no matter how many times I do, he's still standing in front of me.

What the *hell* is he doing here? Holden hasn't been by the animal shelter since we started high school. It fell away with all the other things we used to do together, becoming nothing but a bittersweet memory.

"Yeah. Dogs are good." I finally answer Eileen's question.

I glance from her to Susan to Sydney, looking for clues about why Holden is here. I would just ask him, but Sydney's questions earlier are fresh in my mind. The last thing I want is for her to have more for me. That will require lying or telling the truth, both of which have lasting consequences. I'd rather not have to come up with any answers.

"Great. Do you have time to help me with Snowflake's worming before you head out?"

"Yeah. Of course." I focus on Eileen as I answer her, but I'm totally distracted. I lean against the edge of the reception desk, trying to focus on the dig of the wood trim against my hip instead of the blue eyes that are too easy to get lost in.

He's here and he's looking at me. And I can't say a word—because I'm too worried about what might come out. My emotions are raw, and my judgment is shot, where he's concerned.

Holden tosses the monkey up in the air and catches it. The

stuffed animal squeaks. "I've gotta go. See you later, Syd."

"Be careful, Holden," she replies.

He grins, hasty and carefree. "I always am."

A scoff escapes my mouth before I can stop it. Sydney has never been awake to see him stumble home, drunk and bloody. As opposite from careful as one could be. I cover my disbelief with a cough, but the way Holden's grin widens suggests he sees right through it.

"Good to see you, Holden. Don't be a stranger. Bring Lily by sometime." Eileen is all friendliness and ease with Holden, which is rare. She's not a people person. She prefers animal company, obvious as she suggests he brings their dog by.

"Yeah, I will. She'll love this." Holden holds up the monkey.

The sentences should be aimed at everyone, but he's looking right at me as he says them. I inhale, sharply. Once again, I'm sure Holden is the only one who catches it. Knowing he is paying attention to me is a heady sensation. It's giddiness and butterflies, the secret thrill of coveted attention.

I stand still for too long as he says goodbye and walks out the door. Eileen and Susan disappear into the back to set up the worming, leaving me and Sydney in the lobby. She dives back into filing the stack of folders on the desk.

I deliberate for thirty seconds, then ask, "What was Holden doing here?"

"I left some scripts in his car this morning. He thought I might need them and knew I was here."

"Oh." That's all I can come up with to say in response.

I had a dentist appointment this morning, so Holden drove Sydney to school. Not a hardship on his part, considering they were leaving from the same place and headed to the same destination.

But driving all the way here to drop off something Sydney

might or might not need? That's something middle school Holden would have done. The boy who was rough around the edges but fiercely loyal.

That's part of what hurt the most when our friendship abruptly ended. I didn't choose to change things. He did. And then once he had, he backtracked so quickly it was like we were always distant acquaintances. Like he'd never shoved other kids on the playground for making fun of my braids phase that lasted through most of elementary school.

"I guess he's going to Grace's and won't be back until late."

"Oh," I repeat. Once again, nothing else comes to mind. But this time, I'm preoccupied by the sharp prick of jealousy.

I hate him.

The vitriol behind the thought surprises me. It's also a welcome relief from the uncertainty that's plagued me all day. From the small sprig of hope, when he didn't act like it never happened. When he acted like it might have mattered to him.

I figured he spent every Friday night with a girl in his lap. Part of me was relying on him viewing it as a nonevent, I think. I know better than to expect Holden to wake up and think we're meant to be.

I've been burned before.

"I'm going to go help Eileen with the worming. Then we can head out?"

"Sounds good," Sydney answers, already refocused on the filing.

I turn and head down the hallway.

Not only have I been burned before, I know that only fools play with fire. It has nothing but the potential to burn.

To eviscerate.

To devastate.

And Holden has already done enough damage to my heart.

CHAPTER EIGHT

HOLDEN

A country song croons on the radio. I don't really even *like* country music, but it beats sitting in silence. And I'm not really listening to what's playing, anyhow. I'm stuck in my own head, thinking about how I'm enduring this to spend time with a girl I'm certain doesn't want to spend time with me.

Cassia has continued to make a point of ignoring me ever since I pulled her out into the courtyard last week to force a conversation.

It's a clear signal—but it's also one I want to ignore. I'm not sure when this switch flipped. When it became such a challenge to continue pretending she doesn't exist.

Maybe it was the first time I came home on a Friday night and found her in my kitchen wearing pajamas that revealed a lot more than they covered.

Maybe it was when I saw a familiar flash in her eyes when she told me she wouldn't lie for me.

Maybe it was when I saw the way Harrison Baker was looking at her.

Whatever the cause, it's fucking annoying. I thought I had

moved past this. Sure, I think she's hot. I doubt there's a guy at Pembrooke High who doesn't. But I've spent years telling myself that's *all* it is between us—attraction.

Telling myself that the connection we share isn't anything special. That it's something I can easily ignore and that it doesn't mean anything.

If that were true, I think it would have *actually* faded in the past years. It wouldn't be this burrowing under my skin, this voice whispering I fucked up worse than I thought.

"This is a nice truck."

"Thanks," I reply to Ben's fourth version of the same compliment. This outing is awkward so far. There's no other accurate way to describe it. From Ben asking if I'd already met with the three other freshmen who made the team—which I'll now have to do—to him accidentally hitting the parking brake at a stoplight.

I pull into Roxbury Diner's parking lot, park, and turn the ignition off. I'm apprehensive about encountering Cassia. When I agreed to this, things between us weren't volatile.

It's got me tense and agitated, walking into a set-up. It was one thing to ignore Cassia when she acted ambivalent toward me. Another to respond when she initiated contact between us. It's different to pursue—to seek her out when she's actively avoiding me. Something I told myself I'd never do.

I'm turning a favor for a neighbor into something selfish. But we're chaperoning a couple of kids, one of whom is her sister. Cassia won't cause a scene. I won't be able to do anything really stupid—like kiss her.

Resolved, I turn off the truck. "Come on."

Ben jumps out of the cab eagerly. Guy doesn't even know why we're really here.

I probably should have put some feelers out. Asked if there

are any chicks he's interested in. If he already has a girl, for God's sake.

I drag a palm down my face and exhale, realizing this plan is unfolding worse by the minute. But it's too late to back out now. I follow Ben over to the entrance and inside the diner.

Warm air saturated with the smell of grease greets me. It's not too busy in here. I spot Cassia and Maggie immediately. Maggie is leaning against the counter, tapping her fingers on the Formica anxiously. Cassia is staring out the window.

Maggie spots us first.

"Ben! Hi!" Maggie's voice is high and excited. But there's no trace of expectation. No hint she knew we were coming or that this was pre-planned.

I'm relieved. Maybe that will save me from a more permanent spot on Cassia's shit list, which would surely be earned by knowing I showed up here with the knowledge she would be too. To set her sister up on a date, no less.

"Hey, Holden." Maggie greets me as an afterthought, her focus on the gangly, sandy-haired teenager next to me.

"Hey," I respond, when it seems evident no one else is going to say anything. Ben is wearing a shy smile, and Cassia…well, I haven't looked at Cassia yet.

Awkward silence ensues.

I shove my hands in my pockets. "Funny seeing you guys here."

Okay, so Maggie's a better actor than I am.

Luckily, neither she nor Ben seem to notice. The kid finally got over his surprise and is now talking animatedly. They're slowly drifting away down the counter, leaving Cassia and me standing here.

I take a deep breath and finally look at her. She's standing with her arms crossed, her expression suspicious. "You set this up."

"Shhh." I grab her hand and pull her away, toward one of the empty booths.

"Stop manhandling me," she hisses.

"You didn't seem to mind it last weekend."

Pink spreads across her cheeks. "I told you not to bring that up again."

"Fine. I won't. Just take a seat. Let me buy you a burger."

"I'm not hungry."

"Then just sit while I eat."

Cassia scoffs but sits. "I can't believe Maggie talked you into this." Her gaze is on the couple now sitting on stools. I follow it, relieved to see that Ben is grinning, appearing as taken with Maggie as she is with him. One potential crisis averted.

"All I had to do was get the guy here. It was no big deal." I grab one of the laminated menus, even though I always get the same thing here.

Studying the list of options sounds like a more appealing option than meeting Cassia's accusing gaze.

"Still. There was nothing in it for you."

"Sounds like you and my paper." I glance up in time to see her lips purse.

"A teacher asked me to."

Resisting a crack about being a teacher's pet is difficult, but I manage. "Maggie asked me to."

"And you care that much about her feelings?"

There's accusation layered in the question, along with something worse—hurt.

"Don't think much of me anymore, do you?"

"Which should impress me more, Holden? The fact you don't bother to do your work to the point of almost failing? Or the way you come home in the middle of the night on the weekends, drunk and bruised?"

My jaw flexes and works. Before I can decide how to respond, a waitress appears. She beams at us, failing to sense the tension sparking between us like a live wire in a lightning storm.

"What can I get you guys?" she asks, flipping open her little notebook and looking at us expectantly, pen poised.

I look at Cassia. She glances away, pointedly.

"I'll take a double bacon cheeseburger with an extra side of fries. And a Coke."

The waitress nods, scribbling. "And you?"

"I'm fine, thanks," Cassia replies, folding her arms across her chest. All it does is draw my attention to her tits. But the ice between us is so thin I can hear it cracking, so I avert my gaze and don't say a word.

We sit in silence. For long enough, I lose track of the seconds —the minutes. The only interruption is when my food is delivered. When I sneak a glance at Cassia, she's already looking at me. She flushes, then glances at the row of stools where Ben and Maggie are sitting.

"I should go over there."

I roll my eyes and take a bite of burger. Swallow and sip some soda. "They're fine."

"Wouldn't you worry if Sydney was out with some random guy?"

"That would require Sydney going out, which seems unlikely to happen. She spends her weekends hanging out with you."

Cassia huffs an exhale, her irritation obvious even before she speaks. "Is that supposed to be a dig at me? Should I be out drinking and fighting and doing whatever else you spend your weekends doing instead?"

I suck in a deep lungful of grease-saturated air. "It wasn't a dig, just an observation."

Cassia snorts, glancing over at Ben and Maggie again. Her fingers shred a napkin in quick, efficient strokes.

"What do you think is going to happen, Cassia? They're just talking. We're sitting right here. What are you worried about?"

"I'm worried—" She shoves the pile of white ribbons to the side and starts playing with the straw in her water glass instead. "I'm worried he's going to turn into a player and break her heart."

Her gaze meets mine, hazel slamming into me with an intensity I wasn't expecting.

I know she's not talking about Ben.

She's talking about me.

I swallow. "That's not something you can protect her from."

Cassia scoffs. "Yeah. I know."

I wipe my mouth and ball the napkin up in my fist. I'm squeezing it so tightly I know an imprint of my fingers will be left behind. "Excited for the senior trip?" I ask. It's the only thing I can think to ask about and it's probably the lamest I've ever felt. I sound like a teacher or a parent.

Everyone I know is excited for the senior trip. It's an annual tradition that's one of the highlights of being at the top of the high school hierarchy. Two nights of limited supervision in New York City. The weekend is legendary.

Cassia makes a face. "Not really."

"Why not?"

"I'm not friends with any seniors, Holden," she tells me.

The ball of guilt reappears. We used to be friends, until I fucked it up. "I'll be there."

"Don't say it like it's an enticement."

It's a dig I should probably be offended by. Instead, I'm amused. I like her sass. Like how it feels like we're kids again. It also provides an opening. "If it's such a hardship to be around me, Cassia, what was last weekend?"

She looks back outside, but not before I catch her cheeks flush. Again. "I was just…" Her gaze darts back to me. "It was no big deal."

"Ri-ght," I drawl the word, adding more syllables than it needs. "You said that before."

"And I meant it."

"Did you?" I sound jealous, and I hate that I do.

I don't know what the hell is wrong with me. Of course other guys have been interested in her.

Usually, it's easy to tune girls out when they mention exes. But I'm suddenly furious with myself for not knowing if Cassia even has any. She's best friends with my sister, for fuck's sake. I should have set any misplaced jealousy aside and ensured no one was taking advantage of her.

"You don't want to know the answer to that."

Apparently, I'm being transparent with my feelings. My hand tightens around the napkin. "Got it."

There's a change in her face. It softens with something that looks like uncertainty. "You wouldn't—I mean, it didn't even mean anything to you, right?"

I stare at her, too confused to answer. Does she seriously think I go to these extremes to spend time around a girl on a regular basis? That I do it ever?

I went to her house later that weekend. I concocted a bogus story to have an argument with her in the courtyard. And now I'm sitting here under the pretense of helping out a fourteen-year-old's love life.

"Does it matter?"

We stare at each other, looking for tells and truths. At least, that's what I'm doing.

Most of the time, Cassia is the most even-tempered person you could imagine meeting. She treats everyone the way she looks after the abandoned animals she cares so much about—with respect and kindness. Around me, Cassia seems to run on extremes. She's cold and detached or she's grinding on my lap.

"Uh, Cassia?"

Cassia jolts, almost knocking over her water glass as she glances at Maggie, who's now standing at the end of our booth. "Yeah. Everything okay?"

"It's after four."

Cassia pulls her phone out of her pocket, glances at the screen, and swears. She hustles out of the booth, her movements so hurried and jerky that she almost upends everything on the table.

Just before Cassia slides off the end, she glances back at me. "I've got to pick up Regan."

"I know."

"Right." She glances at Maggie, like she'd temporarily forgotten this entire thing was set up.

"Okay. Bye."

I want to smile but I don't. I nod, then watch as Maggie and Cassia walk out of the diner.

Ben takes Cassia's seat opposite me. "That was funny."

I glance at him, sure he's calling me out for setting this up. But he looks serious.

"Yeah. A real coincidence."

Ben misses my sarcasm. I hope I wasn't as oblivious as a freshman.

"You know Maggie's sister?"

"A little."

"You like her or something?"

I raise one brow at the ballsy question. I'm a senior, and his captain. Maybe I misjudged Howard as shy and awkward.

Ben hastily backtracks. "Not that—you don't have to tell me. I'm not… You do you, you know."

I crack a smile. "Yeah, I will. Thanks."

Ben orders a burger while I polish off the rest of mine. We make small talk as we sit. But the whole time his question echoes in my head.

You like her or something?

I like shooting hoops. Like beer and pizza. What I feel for Cassia has always been stronger. The tug of the tide, not just a passing wave.

Like is unassuming and casual.

Something is vague. It can encapsulate a whole host of emotions. Including ones bigger than like.

Ones big enough to break hearts.

CHAPTER NINE

CASSIA

The credits start to roll. "Did that ending make sense?" I ask. "I'm not sure if—"

I glance over at Sydney. Fast asleep. Rolling my eyes, I crawl over her and off the bed. This Friday night was Sydney's choice of movie. She still didn't make it through the whole film.

I stretch, check my phone, then tiptoe into the hallway. It's almost midnight.

Ever since last weekend, I've been resolved about how tonight is going to go. I even considered telling Sydney I wasn't staying over tonight, which would have broken our tradition of me sleeping over when her dad isn't home for the first time in years.

But then Holden showed up at Roxbury Diner with my sister's crush so they could have a pseudo date. Maggie hasn't stopped talking about it since. Holden has been elevated to deity status in her mind. And honestly, it meant something to me too.

I'm still not sure what his motivation for getting Ben there was, but he showed up. There were a million other ways he could have spent his afternoon yesterday, but he was there.

I don't know how to act around him. If I'm being too forgiving or not forgiving enough.

That's the problem with Holden—he skews my reactions.

If any other guy had made me come and then sat there silent, I never would have been able to look him in the eye again.

If any other guy had set up a date for my sister with the guy she likes, I'd agree with Maggie about the pedestal.

When it comes to Holden, I can't figure out his motivations about anything.

He very easily could have stopped anything from happening between us—he's done it before. But he didn't.

He very easily could have said no to Maggie. But he didn't do that either.

Lily is curled up in her plush bed when I reach the bottom of the stairs. Her yellow tail taps against the hardwood floor as I approach and crouch down beside her. She's mostly lab but with some other breeds likely mixed in too. The monkey toy Eileen gave Holden is lying on the floor next to her, already bearing evidence of teeth marks.

I stroke her soft fur gently, lingering on the white hairs around her muzzle. She was brought into the shelter right after I started volunteering there in elementary school.

My parents set the volunteering up as an attempt to stop me from begging for a pet of my own. They'd just had the twins and were firm our house was crazy enough as it was. That a dog wouldn't be happy listening to screaming infants all day.

When Lily was brought in as a puppy, I instantly fell in love. I became obsessed with finding her a good home.

She ended up right across the street. Sydney wanted a cat. Holden was the one who begged his dad for the dog until he relented. He's the one who walks and feeds her too. It's one of the reasons I've never been able to see him as the villain he should be in my mind.

Sure, he broke my heart without warning or explanation. But he follows through on other responsibilities—obligations he actually cares about.

Lily whines when I stop petting her. I smile as I relent, moving my hand back to the soft fur and rubbing the top of her head. She lets out a satisfied sigh. "What a good girl," I croon.

"Lucky dog."

I startle at the sound of his voice, nearly falling on my ass as I spin around while squatting.

Holden smirks. He's leaning against the opening that connects the living room to the kitchen. Arms crossed, but his pose is relaxed, not confrontational. Lily stands and pads over to him. He leans down to pat her head, keeping his eyes on me the whole time. I stand, twisting the hem of my t-shirt so I have something to do with my hands.

"You're home early." It's not even midnight yet. I'm used to encountering him later.

He straightens. Lily continues into the kitchen once she's no longer receiving attention. I hear her lie down with a sigh.

"It's raining."

I allow myself to study him a little closer. Note the darker droplets on the red flannel shirt and gray sweatpants he's wearing.

"Okay," is my creative response.

Holden saunters over to the sectional couch that takes up most of the living room. Sprawls out on the cushions.

The white t-shirt he's wearing under the half-buttoned flannel rides up. My eyes are drawn to the strip of skin exposed like a magnet. To the line of hair and glimpse of abs.

Based on the grin that's spreading across his face, my ogling isn't all the subtle. Holden tucks one arm behind his head, the damn dimple that rarely appears indenting his left cheek. "Come here."

I don't even hesitate. My responses are skewed when it comes to Holden. Always have been. And it's come into starker contrast these past couple of weeks. I thought I'd gotten over him—thought high school was enough time to move past a childish crush.

If the thundering heartbeat in my chest is any indication, it wasn't. Heartbeats don't lie the way heads can.

Holden is taking up most of the couch. There's nowhere to sit next to him. So, in a move that surprises the both of us, I crawl right on top of him, only stopping when my chin is resting on his chest. His hands slide up my bare legs to cup my butt, pulling me snug against his body.

I bite my bottom lip, excitement and apprehension warring within me. This is him winning our battle of wills left over from the courtyard. Me admitting that last weekend meant something, that it wasn't a momentary lapse.

"Sydney is asleep?"

"Yeah. She passed out during the movie."

"Were you waiting up for me, flower?"

The nickname sounds different when I'm lying on top of him. When I can feel his dick against my thigh. Not just familiar or teasing. Intimate.

"I couldn't sleep."

"Not what I asked." Holden shuffles us, moving me to the side and then rolling over me. We've swapped positions, him hovering over me while I lie on the soft cushions.

I open my mouth to ask what he's doing. Nerves and giddiness swirl inside of me as his hands slide up from my waist and under my shirt. Words exhale on a gasp as his lips lower, teasing the skin just beneath my jaw. His hot tongue licks a stripe along the skin before he sucks it into his mouth.

"Don't—I can't—my parents—Maggie—Sydney."

Holden understands my mostly intelligible sentence. My shirt moves up, the bare skin of my stomach rubbing against the cotton and flannel he's wearing. "What about here?" His mouth moves lower, following the trail of his hands up my abdomen until cool air covers my whole chest. "Will anyone see if I mark your tits, Cassia?"

All I can manage is a head shake in response. I'm adrift in a sea of sensation, savoring the feel of him touching me. Above me. There's a pulsing throb between my legs.

I shift my hips, searching.

He smiles against my skin, lips light and teasing. "You want to come, Cassia?"

"Yes." The word is a breath.

I'm expecting him to move his leg so I can rub against it. Maybe use his fingers. When he sits up and moves back, I rise up on my elbows. "What are you—"

"Lie back."

I hesitate before listening, rolling my head to the side so I can watch him. He tugs my sleep shorts down, leaving me in my underwear. They're boring and blue, not what I would have chosen to wear if I'd had any idea he'd see them.

Holden smirks as his hand moves from my hip and between my thighs. I realize why when he traces the strip of fabric.

I'm soaked. There's no way to hide how affected I am.

His amusement disappears when I undulate my hips, trying to chase some stimulation from his fingers. They fist around the blue fabric, and then it's jerked away. All of a sudden, I'm basically naked. My pajamas and underwear are on the floor and my shirt is up around my shoulders.

"Holden…" I'm not as embarrassed as I thought I would be, spread out under him like this.

There's a part of me that feels powerful, watching his gaze darken to navy as his eyes linger on all the bare skin beneath him.

But I feel vulnerable too. He's fully dressed and I'm on display.

And I have no idea what he's thinking. How far he wants to take this. Based on his comment earlier, he believed me about being more experienced than I actually am. About last weekend being a regular night for me. If he'd bothered to pay any attention to my stark lack of a social life, the idea is laughable.

"Fuck, Cassia. Just…fuck." His mouth lands on my inner thigh, and I figure out what he's planning to do. Anticipation and excitement streak through me, followed by the fizzle of nerves.

"No one has ever…"

I regret the admission as soon as it leaves my lips. That's the problem with lying. It's a web that spirals and expands, drawing you in and then twisting around you. It snags the truth and complicates it.

Holden's expression softens, his fingers tracing the curve of my hipbone. "Let me make you feel good."

I nod and wriggle, craving his touch as much as it intimidates me. I'm not sure how people do this with strangers. I've never been more aware of the years of shared history between me and him. The fact he raced me on the monkey bars and used to watch movies with me after Sydney fell asleep. He's also the only guy I've ever fantasized about, the face I picture when I touch myself where his mouth is heading now.

When his tongue swipes my clit, it feels like a bolt of electricity. It's a thousand times more powerful than my own fingers. A hundred times stronger than rubbing against him with two layers of fabric between us. It's pleasure like I've never experienced, so potent and hot it wipes away any uncertainty instantly. I bite the inside of my cheek and dig my fingers into the couch to keep from crying out and possibly waking Sydney upstairs.

My legs fall open as wide as possible, allowing him full access. My hips lift, begging for his tongue. I'll never, ever forget the way he looks right now. Hungry and focused—on me.

"Take off your shirt." I barely recognize the rasp of my own voice. It sounds hoarse and needy. Desperate.

Holden sits up, lips glossy. He unbuttons the flannel slowly, teasingly. I hook my knee over the back of the couch and bite my bottom lip, teasing him right back.

His white t-shirt disappears much more quickly, and then he's back between my legs. This time, I can see the powerful bunch of his shoulders. The bulge of his bicep, as he grips my thigh.

An orgasm hits me suddenly, with the force of a tsunami. I can't contain the moan that escapes as a hot flush works its way across my entire body, accompanying the pleasure rushing through my system. It goes on and on, wringing me out until I slump against the cushions, limbs loose and limp.

I'm not tired, though. And I'm very much aware of Holden on the other end of the couch, running a hand through his hair as he watches me with a satisfied smile. If he had any doubts about the fact I'm insanely attracted to him, I don't think he does any longer.

I sit up slowly, enjoying the lingering buzz humming through my body. Holden looks like a fantasy, leaning back with his legs spread, wearing just a pair of sweatpants. My shirt falls down as I move toward him, the brush of cotton against my sensitized skin impossible not to notice.

Holden's eyes turn hooded as my fingers trace the ridged muscles that cover his abdomen.

He says nothing. Doesn't guide my movements or tell me

what to do. He just lets me explore the impressive topography of his chest, running my fingers over the hot skin. The only hair is a small patch just below his belly button. After I've traced the V that points between his legs, my hand ends up there. I swallow, then move lower, dipping beneath the elastic hem of his sweatpants.

"You don't have to."

The gravel in his voice heats my blood. Tells me he *wants* me to. "I know."

I slide my hand into his sweatpants, tugging the gray cotton down. He's not wearing anything underneath. The heavy weight of his erection bobs free. I close my fist around it, exploring the hard length the same way I did to his chest. Tracing the flared head and the throbbing vein.

His abs clench, and I can tell he's holding himself back. I've never done this before, never even seen a guy's penis in person. It's bigger than I imagined, but I don't have anything to compare it to.

I swallow, then lean over and suck the tip into my mouth. He tastes salty. Groans when I run my tongue around the head. I gain some confidence, taking more of him into my mouth. I want to please him, want to give him pleasure the same way he crazed me.

His fingers thread into my hair. It's a gentle, light touch. A caress, almost.

I pull back for a breath. Stand. There's a flicker of something —disappointment, maybe—on Holden's face. It disappears when I sink to my knees between his legs, tugging his sweatpants down farther.

"Take off your shirt," he tells me.

"Because I asked you to take off yours?"

"No. Because I want to look at your tits while I fuck your

mouth."

Electricity zings between us. It's not a total surprise to learn Holden has a dirty mouth. He's always had a colorful vocabulary. It's one of the reasons people were surprised we were such good friends when we were younger. Holden would be the kid dropping swears during recess while I was the one insisting everyone follow the rules when we played Capture the Flag. Me and Sydney make more sense. She's as much of a good girl as I am.

But there's something in me that craves the rebellion. That hates how people think they always know what to expect from me, who think I'm always sweet and polite.

Holden sees that in me. Draws it out of me.

So, I put on a show for him. I lean back on my heels and drag my shirt up slowly, revealing my skin to him inch by inch. His eyes grow hooded and heavy as I push my breasts together, his hand falling and stroking his dick.

"Cassia," Holden whispers.

I lean forward, and he feeds the length of his cock into my mouth. I take more than I did before, but he's too big for me to suck completely. He doesn't seem to mind, though. His hands fist at his sides, tendons tensing in his forearms.

Holden's jaw hardens and his breathing quickens. He groans. "I'm going to come," he warns. "Cassia. I'm going to…"

I suck harder, and he trails off with another groan. This is stupid. I know what he's telling me. I should take the out. What am I trying to prove? But I keep sucking, resolute in my decision.

He grunts, and my mouth fills with hot, salty liquid. I have to swallow twice before rocking back on my heels, wiping my mouth with the back of my hand. Holden tracks my movements like an opposing player on the court, focused and intense.

I don't know what to do. Movies and television shows don't show this part. There's a suggestive shot of clothes falling to the floor or a door closing or a light turning off, and then it's the next day. There's no awkward moment when you have to face the guy across the street slash your best friend's brother slash your former crush after rounding third base on his couch.

Do people even still use baseball analogies to equate sexual experiences? Sydney is just as inexperienced as I am—was—and she's the only person I'd consider asking, knowing she wouldn't laugh at me.

Holden doesn't make any move to cover himself. To move. He just sits and stares at me while I hold his gaze. In some ways, it feels more intimate than what just took place between us.

I've heard the stories at school. Seen the girls hanging all over him. Holden Adams is a notorious player. It's a large part of the reason I've avoided high school parties. I don't want to witness it. And that pisses me off, that I've allowed him to dictate so many of my decisions, while telling myself it was so that I could get into a good college and not have to worry about what to wear or what to say around my peers.

Right now, I'm equally annoyed that he's giving me nothing to go on. No lead to follow. He's supposed to be the certain one.

I reach for my t-shirt and pull it on. Then stand and slide my underwear on, followed by my sleep shorts. My limbs still feel shaky, the lingering memory of pleasure loosening my movements.

Holden pulls his pants up and then leans forward, resting his elbows on his knees.

"Um, I'll head to—"

"You tired?" He cuts me off before I can get *bed* out.

I shake my head.

He stands and grabs the remote resting on the coffee table. Tosses it on the couch. "Put something on. I'll be right back."

I stare at him after he enters the kitchen and disappears from sight. He wants to watch something together? We haven't done that since middle school. And I definitely had no idea what size his dick was then. I should be mature enough to move past it…but I'm not sure I am.

If it was some other guy, I probably would be happy he wanted to spend more time together.

With Holden, I'm worried I'll say or do something to embarrass myself. If I haven't already.

I'm not comfortable or relaxed around him. I'm butterflies and heart palpitations.

Despite my apprehension, I take a seat on the couch and turn on the television. Because I'd rather be around Holden than not, and that's always caused conflict where my head and my heart are concerned. I scroll through the movie options until I land on some action thriller.

When Holden walks back into the living room, he's holding a bottle of beer. I twist the hem of my shirt, trying to act oblivious as he settles next to me. The cushions dip with his weight, and my stomach swoops as well.

"I was sober as a non-priest, flower."

I don't react to that statement. For one, I don't want Holden to think it matters to me that alcohol had no influence during what just happened between us. Or that I care he listened to what I said about priests and drinking, that we have some sort of inside joke about it now.

Holden raises his eyebrows, then takes a sip. The muscles in his throat contract and shift, and I avert my gaze, trying to ignore how there's something masculine and mesmerizing about the motion.

More than not wanting to give Holden a reaction, *I* don't want to react. I don't want telling myself I'm not affected by him to be a lie…but it obviously is.

Something cold touches my arm and I jump. He chuckles, something in the sound rattling around my chest like spare change in a car cupholder. I glance down and watch a bead of condensation roll down the green glass bottle being offered to me.

"No thanks."

"You'll swallow my cum but not swap spit?"

A hot flush starts in my cheeks and spreads. I guess we're not pretending earlier didn't happen.

I clear my throat once. "Maybe I'm not thirsty."

Maybe I like the taste of you.

No way am I saying that out loud. I'm treading on uneven ground. Unexplored terrain. I don't know what is happening or what to say or how to act around him right now.

Holden's eyes scrutinize my expression, his gaze hot and probing. It sears my skin like a physical touch. "Okay," he finally says, turning back to the television that's affixed above the fireplace mantle on the opposite wall.

The movie I clicked on is up on the screen. I hit play and lean back against the cushions, trying to figure out a way to avoid spending more time with him. I need a minute—alone—to internally freak out about what just happened. I can't do that when he's next to me, smelling good and looking relaxed and acting like this is no big deal.

Should I pretend to fall asleep?

Go use the bathroom?

Act like I heard a noise and am worried Sydney woke up?

Finding me sitting on the couch with Holden would be less shocking than seeing us half-naked, but she'd still have questions. Holden and I don't hang out together. Especially alone, in the middle of the night.

"Why did you pick this?"

I startle again when he speaks, lost in my own head. "What?"

He looks over and quirks a brow. "This movie. Why did you pick it?"

"Um…" Honestly, it looked bloody and action-packed and something a guy would like. That he would like.

Somehow admitting that feels difficult.

Holden leans forward without waiting for more of a response, grabbing the remote and clicking back to the main menu. He hasn't put his shirt back on. The muscles in his back roil and tense as he moves, his body more man than boy.

It's unfair, really, how my childhood crush grew up to be the hottest guy in town. Why couldn't he look like most of the boys in our year? Uncertain and lanky and unsure? He looks how he acts—assured—and I love it and loathe it in equal measure.

I wonder how cocky he'd get—if I asked him to put a shirt on. It's as distracting as the smell of cinnamon swirling in the air.

It's not until he settles back against the cushions that I realize he put something else on the television. I glance between him and the screen, too surprised to speak at first.

"Why are we watching this?"

He sips more beer, lifting his legs and resting them on the coffee table. "It's what I thought you'd want to watch."

The words I was too nervous to say when he asked are delivered simply. Easily, like it's no big deal.

Holden looks at me. "Was I wrong?"

"No."

"Okay then?"

I clear my throat. "Can I have some?"

He nods, then holds the bottle out to me again. I hesitate before sipping, rubbing my finger against the wet label until a few pieces of paper fall in my lap.

"I liked the taste." I drink, then muster the courage to look him in the eye.

"You'd never swallowed before?"

"No."

Something pleased and possessive washes over his expression, a response that makes my heart race and my blood warm. I wonder how he'd look at me if he knew my only sexual experiences have been with him.

I'm not brave enough to find out. I hand the bottle back and rest my head against the soft cushions. Focus on the screen, because this documentary about polar bears is one I've been wanting to watch.

"Why are you sitting so far away?"

I glance at Holden, then at the foot of space separating us. "Far away is a misnomer."

"Stop talking like a nerd and move closer."

"Wow. Such a sweet talker."

He rolls his eyes. And then he *moves*, which I'm not expecting.

Holden is suddenly everywhere. A hot thigh presses against mine. A warm arm wraps around my shoulders, pulling me closer to him.

I don't resist. I melt against him, feeling the ice around my heart thaw and crack. I tilt my head back, staring at the side of his jaw. The bruise there is faded now, nearly gone.

He doesn't need to be sitting here, watching this. And he definitely didn't need to glue our sides together.

"This is weird," I whisper.

Holden rolls his head to the side so he's looking at me. "Is it?" he asks before returning his attention to the screen.

And for the first time—ever—I consider that maybe he's imagined this—us—too.

CHAPTER TEN

HOLDEN

Finn laughs, and it pulls me back to the present when I was just zoning out. The hard metal door I'm holding. The guys huddled around me. But then she appears, and I'm distracted again.

It was one thing ignoring Cassia at school before. It's very different now. Knowing how she looks naked. How she tastes. How she looks on her knees. The sounds she makes when she comes.

Fuck.

I stop that line of thought in its tracks, scrubbing a palm across my face and forcing myself to focus on the books I'm looking at instead. I grab the two I think I'll need tonight and shove them into my backpack.

Today is a day I've been looking forward to for months. It's the start of the basketball season, the first practice of what will be many before we win a state championship or lose trying.

I've barely spared a thought about basketball all day. Cassia has more power over me than I realized.

I wasn't planning for things between us to go as far as they did. I was planning to kiss her, since I hadn't the Friday before. Prove to her the past weekend was more than a one-off.

Confirm that there's something still between us, even if she wants to pretend otherwise. Ironic, since I've spent a good chunk of time pretending too.

I wasn't expecting her to crawl on top of me. To be so responsive. I'd never gone down on a girl before. I'm not a total asshole in bed—I always make sure she gets off—but I've never prioritized someone else's pleasure.

Cassia said I don't want to know what she's done with other guys—but she's wrong. I do. Some masochistic, caveman part of me wants to replace every experience she's had with memories of me instead.

"You good, Adams?" Finn asks as we enter the locker room. "You've been distracted all day."

"Yeah. I just… This season is *it*, you know?"

It's not the only thing I'm thinking about, but it's not a lie. I am stressed about it. What it will mean for my family if I have options—my dad changing careers to come home or my sister left alone. What it will mean for my future if I don't get a college degree.

Finn's expression turns serious for a minute. "Yeah, I know."

But he doesn't, not really. He doesn't have to worry. His family is loaded. I don't think Finn even *wants* to play ball in college. Whatever comes from this season won't have the same consequences for him as they will for me.

The locker room is already full when we arrive. I see all the guys on the team regularly. At parties and in shared classes. Most of them show up to the old court for pickup games on the weekends too. But there's something different about being gathered together during the season, a heightened sense of comradery and anticipation.

I nod to the teammates I pass as I head toward my usual locker. It's right next to Jordan Eaton's. He bumps fists, then turns back to telling a few of the guys about the girl from Ridgemont he hooked up with this past weekend.

Ben Howard is part of his audience, and I hope he isn't listening to any of Jordan's advice too closely, especially if he's got a thing with Cassia's little sister. The protective urges I have toward Maggie are nowhere near as strong as how I feel about Cassia or Sydney, but they're there. In my head, Maggie is still a little kid.

I finish changing into my practice gear and head straight into the gym. Coach Benson is already standing with Mr. Williams, who is officially a teacher in the arts department and unofficially our assistant coach. He helps out when he can, running a second set of drills for the JV guys and assisting with scheduling our season.

Coach Benson gives me a nod of acknowledgment that I return. Mr. Williams is busy writing something on a clipboard. I head straight for the rack of basketballs, feeling better once I have the familiar weight of the rough rubber in my hands. I dribble down the court to the opposite end, savoring the rhythmic smack of the ball against the hardwood.

There's still a prickle of anxiety in my chest. A reminder that the sphere I'm bouncing is my ticket to something else. Rather than just excitement to be playing, there's apprehension as well. Pressure.

I stop at the foul line and start shooting, sending the ball through the hoop over and over again. I haven't missed one, when Coach Benson calls us all over to the bleachers. He's the type of coach who encourages dedication out of his players, rather than demands it. He takes the sport seriously but doesn't insinuate the sun won't rise the following day if we lose a single game.

I take one half-court Hail Mary shot as I follow the rest of the team over to the blue and yellow bleachers that take up one wall of the gymnasium. I make it, prompting awed looks from some of the younger guys. Mark rolls his eyes as I drop down on the bleachers beside him.

Coach Benson begins by introducing the new members of the team, all of which I met. Then he launches into his expectations for the season. It's a speech I've already heard three times now. I zone out, more focused on playing with a stray thread on the hem of my mesh shorts.

Once Coach starts discussing the start of the season, I perk up. He outlines the schedule I have memorized, including our practices and weight sessions. Team dinners and away games. We'll have a couple of weeks of straight practice before our schedule picks up, just before winter break.

My dad promised he'd be back for Thanksgiving and the week after, meaning he'll have a chance to see me play for the first time in over a year. He isn't the most athletic, his lifestyle of long hours on the road not really allowing for any sort of regular exercise routine, but he's always been supportive of my pursuits. And despite maintaining college is a possibility regardless of whether or not I get a basketball scholarship, I know it will be a big relief to him if I do.

Coach's talk ends and the guys scramble to stand, all eager to actually get out on the court. Today is sure to be a test, a rigorous workout to let us all know what is expected during the season. The most accurate shot in the world won't matter if the other team maintains possession the whole game because you can't keep pace.

"Adams. One minute."

I sit back down, watching the rest of the guys follow Mr. Williams over to the center of the court and start stretching. It looks like we'll be running first thing. Suicides, if I had to guess.

Coach studies me, rubbing one hand across the gray stubble that always peppers his jawline. "Ready for this, Adams?"

"Yeah, I am, Coach."

He nods. "Grades are good?"

"Yep."

"Laura Golden mentioned you turned in one hell of a paper."

I smile. That was nice of her. Mrs. Golden very easily could have told Coach about my D instead of the subsequent averaged B- that trying to impress Cassia earned me. I resolve to pay closer attention in History tomorrow.

"I've already got a few scouts lined up for the Covington game. If you're still wanting to play in college, I'll make sure to get everyone here I can."

I nod. "I am. Thank you."

"All right. Get out there." He jerks his head to the left, toward the circle with my teammates gathered in the center of the court.

I stand and walk down the bleachers. They squeak under my weight.

"Oh, and Adams?"

I glance over at Coach, right as I'm about to pass him. "Yeah?"

"I made sure to mention the special attention you're giving to the freshman when I talked to Dan Rivers and the other scouts. That's exactly the type of leadership these schools are looking for. Keep up the good work."

Special attention? What the hell is he...oh. He obviously heard about the outing with Ben. I followed up with hangouts with the rest of the freshman the next few days, so it didn't look like I was playing favorites. Plus, Ben asked if I was going to, so I didn't have much of a choice.

I nod and keep walking toward the team. If I get a basketball scholarship, it looks like I might have Maggie Nolan and her scheming to thank.

———

As soon as I walk inside my house, I beeline for the fridge. Practice was exhausting and I'm starving. I yank out a container of yesterday's leftovers and spin toward the microwave. Then freeze.

"Hi."

"Hi," I repeat, watching Cassia fiddle with the sponge she's holding.

It's not uncommon for her to hang around my house, but I wasn't expecting it either. I'm usually home later, closer to dinnertime. And there's a new dynamic between us—one I'm not sure how to navigate. Cassia says nothing, giving me zero clues about what she's thinking or expecting out of this interaction. There's no sign of Sydney.

I glance around the kitchen, which is much cleaner than it was when I left in a hurry this morning. All of the dishes have been washed and put away. The counters have been wiped. "You don't need to clean when you're over here, you know."

"I know."

"Okay." I walk over to the microwave and pop the glass dish inside, not sure what else to say.

"How was practice?"

I raise one brow at the question, mildly surprised she knew today was our first day. It suggests a level of interest in the basketball team I wasn't expecting her to have. "It was fine."

She sets the sponge down on the counter. "Ben and Maggie

talk a lot. *Maggie* talks a lot about what they talk about," Cassia explains.

"Guess that means I'm excellent at match-making."

Cassia rolls her eyes. "You think you're good at everything."

"Do *you* think I'm good at…everything?"

I don't mean it as an innuendo, but it comes out that way. I don't think I'm imagining the way her pupils dilate. How her breaths quicken.

"Okay, what about this top?" Sydney's voice announces her entrance a few seconds before she waltzes into the kitchen.

She barely spares me a glance, but I do a double take when I see her. Sydney's usually straight hair is curled in long spirals. She's wearing a full face of makeup, jeans, and a sweater that exposes an inch of her midriff. Most of the time when I get home, she's in sweatpants and a ponytail that's busy falling apart.

"It's cute," Cassia replies, looking Sydney over and nodding.

"Too little boob?"

"Jesus, Sydney," I say, running a hand through my hair. There are some things you don't want to hear your sister say, and that was definitely one of them.

"What? I didn't ask *you*, Holden."

"I'd definitely go with that sweater," Cassia states, drawing my sister's attention back to her.

Sydney nods and heads back upstairs.

"How many options have there been?" I ask.

Cassia laughs. I want to bottle it up, how that genuine amusement sounds. Tuck it away like a secret only I know.

"A lot."

I smile, then clear my throat. "Look, about Friday night…"

She straightens, all the amusement immediately falling off her face. "We're good. We don't need to talk about it."

Jesus, this girl. Maybe this is karma for how I've handled hook-ups in the past. The difference is, I made it clear to those girls I wasn't looking for anything serious. Cassia is far more complicated. "I know we don't *need* to talk about it. I *want* to talk about it."

Sydney bounces back into the kitchen. She looks at Cassia, ignoring me as she pirouettes. "You sure this is what I should wear?"

Cassia nods. "Yeah. You look hot."

The words are aimed at Sydney, but she looks at me as she says them. I quirk a brow at Cassia, trying to figure out what *that* means. If my sister wasn't talking a million miles a minute, it would be a lot easier to figure out.

The microwave beeps. I pull out the steaming pasta and dig in, not even waiting for it to cool.

"What is all that"—I wave the fork at Sydney—"about?"

"Graham invited me to a party tonight."

"On a Monday?"

Sydney glares. "It's a study party."

"What the hell is a study party?" I glance at Cassia. She shrugs.

"It's just a casual thing," Sydney tells me. "He invited me and I'm going."

"Who?"

"Graham! Keep up, Holden."

"Graham who?"

"He's not on the basketball team, so you wouldn't know him."

I smirk at that. This is more snark than I've seen Sydney display...ever. She must really like this guy. "What is not-on-the-basketball-team Graham's last name?"

"Warner."

"Never heard of him."

"Shocking," Sydney drawls.

"So, you're going to some random guy's house?"

"You do it all the time, Holden."

"Yeah…but it's different."

"Why? Because I'm a girl?"

Sydney's tone makes it clear *yes* is the wrong answer here. Unfortunately, there are things that happen to girls at parties— even study parties, whatever the hell that really means—that guys just don't have to worry about. I don't feel like getting into an argument about that reality. "Because I'm older," I say instead.

She huffs and flounces out of the kitchen.

I glance at Cassia. "What's wrong with Sydney? She's acting weird."

"She's *nervous*, Holden. She really likes this guy. I'll keep a close eye on her tonight. We'll be fine."

"*You*'re going?"

"Yes…"

Cassia is looking at me strangely, which makes absolutely no sense. I'm not the one acting differently. Sydney has never gone out to a party because a guy invited her.

Most of the time, it feels like she's the older sibling. But I'm suddenly very aware of the fact our dad is hundreds of miles away. If anything happens to Sydney, I'm the one who is responsible.

And I'm equally unenthused by the revelation Cassia is going. But I have no right to be. She can spend her night however she wants. One look at her was all it took for me to forget everything I told myself this weekend about her being a dangerous distraction. I tore up the mental list of reasons to pretend nothing happened on my couch as soon as I caught a glimpse of her brown curls in the hallway this morning. Some space is probably a good idea.

"Do you know this Graham guy?" I ask before polishing off the rest of the pasta.

"Yeah, sort of. We've had a few classes together."

"Sort of?" I shake my head and set the empty container in the sink. Then, realizing Cassia just cleaned, I rinse it and stick it in the dishwasher. "I'm going."

"You're *what*? Why?"

When I turn around, Cassia is looking at me with a bewildered expression. "Because *sort of* isn't good enough. What if he's a total creep?"

"He's not a creep, Holden." She rolls her eyes. "He's president of the Honor's Club, for God's sake."

"Sociopaths are always super smart."

Another eye roll.

"Whatever. I'm going. What time are you guys leaving?"

"Eight."

I snort. It's an eight on a Monday party? Maybe there really is nothing to worry about.

"You don't have to come, Holden."

"I know," I say, then walk out of the kitchen. I need to shower and attempt some homework before leaving. And text Finn, letting him know I won't be coming over to play video games tonight.

I run into Sydney in the upstairs hallway on my way to the bathroom. "I'm coming with you guys."

She halts in place, aiming a confused expression at me. "What? *Why*?"

"Because you've never gone to a party and you're my sister. I don't want anyone messing with you."

"No one is going to mess with me. Cassia is already coming with me."

"Even more reason."

Sydney stares at me and I realize I just said more than I meant to.

"Cassia doesn't go to many parties either."

"What makes you think that?" There's an edge to my sister's voice. I'm not sure if it's sticking up for her friend or something else. "Because they weren't parties *you* were at?"

My jaw flexes. "I'm going to shower."

"Holden. Seriously, you don't have to come. It's…sweet, I guess, but I'll be fine."

"Dad is in Minnesota. I'm responsible for you when he's not here. If you want me to sit outside in the car, I will."

Sydney scoffs and heads for the stairs. I hope that means I won't be stuck sitting in the car.

———

Cassia and Sydney are standing by the door when I walk down the stairs just before eight. Despite obvious surprise about my choice to come, they're clearly waiting for me.

"Okay, let's go," I say once I reach the front door. I grab a fleece out of the closet and look at the girls expectantly.

"What about your homework?"

I raise a brow at Cassia. "I did most of it."

"I mean, you're supposed to bring it."

"Bring it?" I glance between her and Sydney, noticing they're both wearing their backpacks. "Seriously?"

"It's a *study* party, Holden," Sydney says.

"I have no idea what that means. It's a group homework session. What about that says party?"

Sydney looks annoyed. Cassia hides a smile.

I sigh and trudge back upstairs. I didn't make much progress on my assignments earlier; I showered and then watched basketball highlights for a while as I scrolled through social media. But sitting around doing homework with a bunch of strangers does not sound like my idea of a good time. Maybe I can feel the "study party" out and then head to Finn's until the girls are ready to get picked up. I could even ask Cassia to come with me.

It's a bad idea, I know. Not only is it a direct violation of everything I promised myself I wouldn't do, where she's concerned, but I'm positive at least one of the guys will hit on her. I'm not sure I'm capable of handling that well.

Sydney and Cassia are waiting out on the front porch when I descend the stairs for a second time. It's dark and chilly out, signaling fall's creep toward winter.

Sydney is quiet as we walk toward my truck, all of her babbling earlier, noticeably absent. The lamps lining the street cast a white glow over her anxious expression.

"He invited you to his study thing, Syd. He must like you."

"It's a group thing," she replies. "He invited Meredith Lowe too."

And…I'm out of my element. I have no idea who Meredith Lowe is. I can't even picture this Graham guy. My level of experience with relationships is the same as Sydney's: zero.

I'd be better at this if I had a younger brother. I'd know how to teach him to unsnap a girl's bra or roll on a condom. Sydney's interests have never merged with mine.

We're more like roommates on good terms than siblings. I'd kill anyone who hurt her, but as far as casual chitchat goes? I've got nothing.

The only advice I have to offer pertains to casual sex, and that's not something I want to encourage Sydney to partake in. If she's this nervous about going to the guy's house, I'm assuming —hoping—that step is a long ways away.

"It's a group thing, Syd. Of course he invited other people. He probably didn't want to single you out or make you feel uncomfortable."

Sydney nods, appreciating Cassia's response far more than mine. I'm grateful for it too, until I start to wonder whether she's speaking from personal experience. Her smiling at Harrison Baker is suddenly all I can think about. Cassia suggested she wasn't interested in him, but that was in context to Sydney's crush.

It seems safe to say Sydney is over that, based on her reaction to Graham's invite. Will that change Cassia's mind about Harrison?

The possibility bothers me a lot more than it should. Harrison is a good guy, as far as I know. His friend group overlaps with mine some, and I've never heard about him getting into trouble. I'm certain he's never fought someone for money. He gets good grades. Has two present parents and a picket fence in front of his house.

"You sit up front, Cas," Sydney says.

My sister doesn't appear to notice the way Cassia glances at me as I unlock my truck, but I do. This is the first time she's ever ridden in it. I bought it last summer with money I obtained legally, stocking groceries at the local supermarket, plus years of birthday money from distant relatives on my dad's side.

It's too easy to pretend it's just the two of us sitting in here. After giving me Graham's address, Sydney is totally quiet in the back.

"Your truck is nice." Cassia isn't as willing to sit in silence.

"Yeah?" I glance over at her before taking a left-hand turn, surprised by the choice of comment. Her car is at least a decade newer than mine. There's a lingering tobacco smell in the cab and the brakes squeak. I'm not sure *I* would call it nice. More like functioning.

"Yeah. It seemed like it took a lot to get it running."

It did. I spent weeks fiddling with the engine in the driveway.

Mark helped some and so did his dad, who's a mechanic. But I did the bulk of the work myself, watching videos online and reading manuals to make sure it runs reliably.

"It seemed that way, huh?"

Cassia's house is directly across the street from mine. I'm not sure if she meant to insinuate she watched me work on this truck last fall, but that's what I got out of what she said just now.

The dim light and fact I'm driving make it difficult to tell for sure, but I think she's blushing. At the very least, I watch her shifting in the seat, fiddling with the strap of the seatbelt and looking out the window instead of me.

It only takes another five minutes to reach Graham's house. It's a two-level Colonial, well-maintained and modest. I eye the basketball hoop visible to the left of the driveway. Maybe I'll just hang out here instead of heading to Finn's. My muscles are sore, but it doesn't take much effort to just stand and shoot.

There's no one stumbling down the front steps. No flashing lights or music.

"Looks like a rager," I say, as we walk up the brick front path.

"I told you, you didn't need to come," Sydney says.

The door opens before we reach it. A tall, skinny guy with a mop of curly blond hair is standing in the doorway. Graham, I'm assuming.

"Hi, Sydney!" He beams at my sister, making no attempt to hide his excitement about seeing her. It's cute, watching them exchange shy smiles. He greets Cassia next. His tone is just as friendly, but it lacks the same eagerness, making my opinion of him rise a little more. Treating Sydney well while having no romantic interest in Cassia are the two best ways to endear himself to me.

"Graham, this is my brother, Holden," Sydney says. "He wanted to come."

Wanted is a stretch. But I did choose to. I wasn't dragged along, so I don't dispute it as I hold out a hand to Graham. "Nice to meet you, man."

"You too," Graham says, as he shakes it. His grip is firm, but not tight. "Although we've, um, we've met. We had Physics together freshman year. Mrs. Liberman, third period. Remember?"

No. I barely remember taking Physics, let alone anyone in the class. But Sydney and Cassia are watching me closely. If bonding with Graham over sitting in the same classroom for an hour three years ago will make this "party" easier, I'm fine with lying. "Right. Yeah."

"Come on in," Graham says, stepping to the side so we can enter the house. The open floor plan is similar to the layout of my house, with the living room to the left and the kitchen back behind it. About a dozen people are sitting in the living room, most of them spread out on the fluffy rug covering the floor. Everyone has textbooks or notebooks spread around them.

A few faces look familiar. Probably people I've shared classes with over the years slightly more memorable than Graham.

Everyone stares as we enter.

"Grab a spot wherever," Graham says. "And help yourself to anything." He gestures toward the coffee table covered with snacks. "I'm just going to grab some more chips from the kitchen."

Graham heads deeper into the house, leaving us standing here. Cassia and Sydney start talking with some of the "party-goers." I'm not sure who came up with the term study party, but I think study *session* would be the more accurate descriptor.

I smile at the two girls who make eye contact with me but don't engage anyone in conversation. I head toward one open corner of the living room and take a seat on the rug, leaning back against the bookshelf covering the wall.

My muscles protest the movement and the sitting on the ground. I'm going to be sore as fuck tomorrow. Practice was rough and lounging on the hard floor isn't helping.

I unzip my backpack and pull out my laptop. While I'm stuck here, I might as well be productive. Whenever I've done work at a friend's place, there's always been a lot going on in the background. Finn is usually playing video games or smoking weed. Mark likes to tinker around with his dad's old cars when we're at his home.

Graham's house is silent and clean. There's not even music on. It feels like working in a library during study hall.

I glance up from the essay I'm typing when Graham walks back into the room. He takes a seat on the edge of the couch, right near where Sydney has settled. They smile at each other and then both start on homework. I want to laugh but don't.

Cassia is standing near the opposite end of the couch. She's whispering with the same blonde girl she walked into the cafeteria with on the day I approached her table.

I refocus on my essay before she catches me staring. I very much feel like the outsider in this studious group. Cassia and Sydney were right—there was no reason for me to come. If Sydney hadn't been acting so strangely and the word party hadn't come up, I wouldn't have.

Movement catches my attention out of the corner of my eye, right as I hit submit on the essay. Cassia is sitting down next to me, instead of staying near the couch like I expected her to. It feels like a show of solidarity of sorts, and it's also distracting.

I haven't checked on Sydney and Graham once, mostly because there's nothing they could be getting up to, sitting right here with everyone, but Cassia just a few feet away? Yeah, I won't be getting any more work done.

I pretend for a little while, pulling out my history textbook and skimming the assignment chapters, then stand and stretch. "Where's your bathroom, Graham?"

"Um, down the hall to the left. I can show you…"

"Nah, it's fine. Thanks."

I follow his directions, walking through the kitchen and easily finding the half bath located next to the pantry. Rather than head back to the living room, I walk out the back door and down the deck, ending up beneath the basketball hoop I spotted when we arrived. I shove my hands in my pockets and scuff a sneaker against the asphalt.

"There's a ball in the garage." I turn to watch, as Graham ducks into the garage and reemerges holding a familiar orange sphere. He hesitates like he's considering tossing it, then walks over and hands it to me instead.

"Thanks." I tuck the basketball under my arm, studying Graham as some hair flops in his face and he brushes it away. As far as high school guys go, Sydney could do far worse. But I still feel obligated to say, "You seem like a nice guy, Graham. But if you break my sister's heart, I'll break your face. Got it?"

Graham nods like a bobblehead. Based on the sallow pallor of his skin, he took my threat seriously. As he should. I'm pretty sure rumors about the fights by the old courts never made it past the popular crowd because I'm certain Sydney would have said something to me if she had any idea.

"I'm not much of an athlete," he tells me, nodding to the hoop. "So I'm going to head inside."

I chuckle. "Okay."

Graham walks toward the house. I spin and start to dribble.

"That was…sweet?"

I pause to glance over one shoulder, squinting at the shadows until Cassia appears, zipping up the jacket she's wearing. I palm the basketball as she approaches, rough rubber rolling against my thigh as I move the ball back and forth. "Just making sure he knows where we stand."

"I'm pretty sure you scared the shit out of him."

I shoot, smiling at the satisfying *swoosh* as the ball sinks through the basket. I jog forward to retrieve the basketball, then tell her, "Good."

She rolls her eyes at me—again—and it makes me want to kiss her. So I suggest the only thing that might distract me right now.

I nod toward the hoop. "Want to play?"

"With *you*?"

Her voice is comically shocked. I make a show of looking around the empty driveway, just to be a dick. "Good guess."

"It's just—I—we haven't, in a while."

"I know." *My fault*, I think, and she's probably thinking the same. "Want to?"

Cassia glances around like she's looking for the right answer. Or maybe she's just stalling for time.

"Nevermind."

"No." She unzips the jacket she just zipped and pulls it off. The shirt she's wearing underneath clings to her stomach and breasts, and I realize this probably was a terrible idea.

Desire pools in my stomach. Getting turned on is not normally something I need to worry about while playing.

"Let's do it."

I know exactly what she's referring to, but my mind still goes straight to the gutter. I need to focus before my body starts thinking for me. "You start."

She catches the pass I bounce to her. "You think I'm rusty?"

"Are you?"

The last time I saw Cassia play basketball was in middle school. She didn't try out for the high school team, even though she easily could have made it. Not asking her why she hadn't was the biggest test of my resolve back then.

In answer, she sends the ball flying. I track the movement as it arcs and falls directly through the basket.

It hits the asphalt driveway with a loud *smack*. When I glance at Cassia with a brow raised, she smiles.

"Thank God. It would have been really embarrassing if I'd missed."

Laughter spills out without permission as I retrieve the ball and pass it to her again. "Why did you stop playing?"

I regret the question instantly. Cassia's expression turns somber as she rubs her fingers against the rough rubber, pressing hard enough tiny circles are probably indenting into her skin. "Just outgrew it, I guess."

I scoff. She might as well have told me it's none of my business. "Sure."

Her eyes narrow. "It's true. Sports take up a lot of time. I knew I needed great grades in high school to get into a good college."

"Colleges also like admitting student athletes," I point out. Digging the hole I'm in deeper, based on her annoyed expression.

"Why do *you* think I stopped playing?"

"I don't know. That's why I'm asking."

"*Years* later. You must have drawn conclusions at the time."

I exhale, looking away and running a hand through my hair. "You want me to say I thought it had something to do with me, Cassia? Fine, I thought it might have had something to do with me."

"You think I make my decisions based on *you*? I'm not that

pathetic, Holden." She spits the words, and I realize I've colossally fucked up by bringing this subject up. There's no satisfaction that I've cracked her sweet exterior. She's mad and hurt, and it's my fault. The realization sits in my stomach like a lump of lead.

"I don't think you're pathetic."

"Gee, *thanks*."

I inhale and exhale deeply, trying to release some frustration. Trying to come up with some way to salvage the conversation. But Cassia isn't done.

"You think the fact I gave you a blowjob means I *want* you? Means I've *forgiven* you? God, you've got a lot of nerve, Holden. But you always did, didn't you? You've always done whatever the hell you want. Fuck the consequences. Fuck other people's feelings." She shakes her head and drops the ball. It bounces a couple of times and then rolls away toward the bushes. "Just don't talk to me. We're not even friends, *remember*?"

Cassia storms past me and inside. I listen to her and say nothing. I'm not sure what I would've anyway. Do I try to explain? Tell her the distance between us was my fucked-up way of trying to look out for her? Or do I focus on basketball, on my future, and go back to doing my best to ignore her?

I grab the basketball and slam it against the backboard so hard the whole hoop rattles.

CHAPTER ELEVEN

CASSIA

I'm scrolling through my music library, looking for a playlist to listen to, when someone takes the seat next to me. I gape at Holden, watching as he adjusts the seat and pulls a water bottle out of his bag.

"What are you doing?" I hiss, glancing around at the surrounding empty seats.

"Sitting."

"Why are you sitting *here*?"

"It was open."

"So is half the bus," I tell him.

The PTA chartered ten coach buses for the senior trip to New York City. There are tons of other seats available. Most people are taking advantage of having a row to themselves to stretch their legs out or set their bags on the seat instead of the floor. Yet Holden—six foot two Holden—is folded into the cramped seat next to me, so close I can smell cinnamon and feel his body heat.

He swallows a sip of water and then turns toward me. "I'm sorry."

"For invading my personal space?"

His lips quirk. "Two seats are meant for *two people*, you know."

Whatever expression I make in response coaxes a full-blown smile out of him.

"That's not what I'm apologizing for, though. I'm sorry about Monday night at Graham's. I shouldn't have asked about why you stopped playing. It's none of my business. It wasn't then, and it isn't now."

I *hate* that he's apologizing. Not only because it's uncharacteristic, but because he looks like he actually means it. Earnest and sincere. But what I *really* hate is that it forces me to acknowledge that I overreacted, and the only reason I did is because Holden has a much stronger hold on me than I would like.

The truth is, he *is* the main reason that I stopped playing. I associate the sport with him. But that's not something I planned to ever acknowledge, and I hated that he was asking me to.

"It's fine." I look out the window at the high school's parking lot.

We haven't even left yet. There's a four-hour drive ahead before we're in the city. Four hours is a long time to sit next to someone you were hoping to ignore.

This trip is mandatory, otherwise I wouldn't be here. It's a final attempt to impart wisdom on the graduating class; to give us a glimpse of freedom before we're set loose on the world next spring. That's the school line, at least. Every student knows it's an opportunity to let loose under limited supervision. Rumor is a girl got pregnant on the trip a few years ago.

A warm hand grasps my chin and turns it away from the window. I suck in a sharp breath at the contact, and I know Holden doesn't miss the inhale. His thumb runs an inch across the edge of my jaw before dropping. Awareness trickles through my bloodstream from the one spot he was just touching.

"I mean it; I'm sorry. It's just something I've wondered about for a while. That seemed like a good moment to ask. It wasn't —obviously."

My stupid heart latches onto *something I've wondered about for a while*. To the indication that Holden has given some thought to me since he all but ended our friendship.

"I overreacted." I don't elaborate on why and he doesn't ask.

"I'll move, if you want."

"It's fine."

"Okay." He leans back in the seat and then picks up my phone and starts scrolling through the music app I have open.

I'm flustered and frazzled. He's too close. Too much.

"What are you doing?"

Holden doesn't answer at first, continuing to scroll down the screen. Finally, he looks up. "You have good taste in music," he tells me. "Guys, not so much."

I take that comment to mean he saw Harrison talking to me before we boarded the buses. "What does that say about you?"

He blinks, like he can't believe I said it. I can't believe I did either.

"Maybe I'm talking about me."

We remain locked in a stare-off until the bus's loudspeaker crackles to life. "Last call, everyone! We'll be departing in the next few minutes. Please make sure you have everything and that all bags are stowed properly. Mr. Harris will be distributing folders closer to our arrival to the city. Those will contain an updated itinerary for the weekend, along with your room assignments. Those are final. No room-swapping."

There's no grumbling. Switching rooms is a notorious part of this weekend. Nothing much the chaperones can do to prevent it, really, once keys are handed out. I'm apprehensive about sleeping in a strange place I'm sharing with a stranger, but, with the exception of Holden, virtually everyone in the senior class feels like a stranger.

There's some saying about doing something every day that scares you. It sounds like a stressful way to live, but there's probably some truth to it as well. Leaving your comfort zone is healthy, and this trip is definitely far beyond mine.

"Wake me up when we get there, okay?"

I glance over at Holden, who's dropped my phone and is now reclining his seat as far back as it'll go. His long legs get stretched under the row in front of us and he tugs the brim of his ball cap down, so it covers most of his eyes.

"Okay."

I study his relaxed profile for a few seconds, then turn to look out the window again. The bus pulls away from the high school, the familiar brick façade fading from sight as we turn onto the main road headed toward the highway.

I want to ask Holden what he's doing next to me. I want to ask him what this means. I want to ask him why he kissed me in eighth grade and hasn't acknowledged it in the four years since.

Back then, I did nothing to drive him away. I never told him I had a crush on him. But Monday night, I was very clear about asking him not to talk to me again. I overreacted, as I just admitted, and I regretted the harsh words, but I didn't give any indication of that to him. We haven't spoken since. But he's still here, next to me.

My phone buzzes in my lap. It's a text from Sydney asking how it's going. With not one but four question marks. I laugh under my breath before responding, letting her know we left the high school's parking lot about thirty seconds ago.

This will be the first Friday night we haven't spent together in a long time. But I associate the day of the week with Holden more than her.

I see Sydney almost every day. Aside from occasional glimpses at school, the nights Holden makes it home before I've fallen asleep used to be my one guarantee of time with him. My weekly hit and also my chance to show him I was just fine without his friendship.

And I am. I have Sydney, and there are plenty of girls at school I'm friendly with. That friendliness just rarely translates outside of school hours. Maybe it would if I did things that scared me more frequently.

But I miss him.

I was reminded of just how much on Monday night, when we were going to play basketball together. And when we watched the documentary.

Sydney hates sports and prefers watching comedies over anything educational. I've missed playing basketball and staying up late watching television shows with him. Things that I haven't done with anyone else since middle school. The reminder was a large part of why his question about basketball upset me so much. It dredged up all the resentment from the past years of nothing but some small talk.

I'm not sure I'm brave enough to ask him what happened. I was a confused thirteen-year-old harboring a crush and couldn't figure out if it was reciprocated or not. He kissed me and I thought it was. But then any confirmation was swiftly shut down when weeks, months, *years* of mostly silence followed.

Confusion turned into hurt. Hurt morphed into anger. And my pride kicked in. If he didn't want to be friends, then I wasn't going to *beg* him to be. We were navigating puberty and all that comes along with early adolescence. I thought we'd drift apart and then back together.

I gave up on that happening a long time ago. Or I thought I had, at least.

I can't figure out how we got here. Sitting side by side as two people who have barely spoken in years but know a lot about each other. Who have seen each other naked.

Holden appears to be fast asleep when I glance over at him. He's obviously not affected by my proximity the way I can't seem to ignore his.

The bus turns onto the highway. Fall foliage is out in full force, the trees lining the interstate boasting a broad array of red, orange, and yellow. They pass by like a watercolor as the bus picks up speed. I press play on a playlist and lean my head against the cool glass of the window. Close my eyes and try to fall asleep.

———

"Cassia. Cassia. *Cassia*!"

I blink. My eyelashes flutter, torn between sleep and waking up. The surface I'm leaning against isn't hard and cold. Nope, it's warm and smells like cinnamon.

Shit. Even before I open my eyes, I know what I'll see.

Not only did I manage to fall asleep, I also traveled from leaning against the bus window to resting on Holden's shoulder. I sit up straight, focusing on fixing my ponytail as an excuse for not looking at him.

"You kinda suck as an alarm clock," he comments.

"Set one next time, then."

I don't look over, but I can feel his eyes on me. Weighing my irritation. Trying to figure out its cause.

A glance out the window reveals we're already in the city. Miles of asphalt and multi-colored leaves have turned into skyscrapers and yellow cabs.

I play with the hem of my sweater, twisting the knitted wool.

"What's wrong?" he asks softly, like it's a secret between me and him.

I drop my hands. "Nothing."

"It's not *nothing*. If you don't want to tell me, just say so."

"It's just…overwhelming, I guess."

"What do you mean?"

"The city. It's big and busy and…I don't know. I prefer not to have people on top of me when I walk around."

I also have some apprehension about spending the next couple of days with the senior class. But Holden knows who I hang out with. Mentioning that will only make me look like more of a loser.

He half-smiles. It disappears quickly, like he's worried about offending me. "Does that mean Columbia is out?"

"I'm not expecting to have a lot of options."

"What do you mean? Of course you'll have a lot of options."

"My parents have five more kids to put through college. I can't afford to be picky."

"You're exactly what Admissions Offices look for, Cassia."

"Well, I'm not a student athlete, so there's that."

Holden shifts beside me. Clears his throat. "I didn't mean—"

I cut him off with a laugh. "It's fine, H."

He stares at me, clearly shocked. I haven't called him that since we were kids. Since we were friends.

Now, I'm the one flustered. Thankfully, we stop in front of the hotel a few seconds later. We're instructed to disembark quickly so the other buses can pull up and unload as well. Activity erupts around us, everyone eager to get off the bus, eat dinner, and get our room assignments. Holden and I are both silent as we follow the other students off the bus.

There are a few side glances and double takes. Our class is around five hundred students. Out of them, I doubt a single one doesn't know who Holden Adams is. Who he's friends with. And since at least half of them went to a different middle school, before the new high school was built and districts merged, they've never known Holden and I to have any familiarity.

Or maybe I have dried drool on my face. I swipe both cheeks once we're on the sidewalk, just in case.

Mr. Malone, one of the teachers chaperoning this trip, is waiting, passing out folders with schedules and envelopes with room keys. According to the planned itinerary that was sent out to parents a few weeks ago, we're supposed to have dinner delivered to our rooms tonight in preparation for an early morning tomorrow.

I see Mark and Finn disembarking from the next bus, along with the rest of the crowd Holden usually hangs around with. They all rode together, and he rode with me.

Because he knew I wouldn't have anyone to sit with?

Because he feels guilty about how our last conversation ended?

I have no idea, and I can't ask him without looking pathetic.

"Night," I say, then follow the stream of students being directed toward the elevators. Once I'm caught up with the group, I risk a glance back.

Holden's friends have all caught up to him, huddled around as they talk intently. Probably planning how and where to sneak off to tonight.

It's an important reminder. There might be some familiarity between us, but there's also a separation. Most of what Holden and I share is history, and it's supposed to stay in the past.

I don't look back again.

CHAPTER TWELVE

CASSIA

The light above the handle flashes green, and I push the door open. I glance around, pausing when I realize it's not empty like I expected. "Hey."

"Hey." McKenzie Howard, my roommate for this trip, is studying me closely. I try to think of the last time I talked to her before this trip and come up blank. Most people think going to a smaller school means you know everyone.

Truthfully, I think it segregates people more. Once you're associated with a certain group, that's your group. You can't "meet" new friends, they're technically peers you've known for years. Blurring boundaries becomes awkward.

Last night, it was late enough for conversation between us to be limited. *You use the bathroom first* and *Okay if I turn out the light?* was straightforward.

Now, it's more awkward. There's another layer of uncertainty between us that's fueled by the fact that there's nothing to do. Today was exhausting, endless stops around the city scheduled closely together.

I hung out in the lobby with London and a few other girls I'm friendly with for a couple of hours after dinner, expecting to come back and find McKenzie gone. This is our second and final night in the city, so I'm sure some—most—seniors are planning to sneak out.

I assumed McKenzie would be one of them. I was banking on it, actually. It's awkward, being in here with her.

After changing into my pajamas, I take a seat cross-legged on the bed. McKenzie is still settled on the couch, busy on her phone.

I pick up the remote and start flipping through the channels. It's mostly news and sports. I stop on an action thriller with an actor who looks familiar, but it's halfway through and the plot is hard to follow. At least the gunfire and explosions keep the room from total silence.

I'm barely paying attention to the movie when there's a knock on the door. McKenzie stands and walks over to open it.

Grace is standing in the doorway. She's wearing a low-cut top and tight jeans, her blonde hair curled and her makeup flawlessly applied. "You ready?"

"Yeah, I, um, I thought we were meeting at the elevators?"

Grace spots me. Her expression flares with surprise. Obviously, her best friend didn't mention she was rooming with me. "I got bored," she tells McKenzie. "London fell asleep."

I already knew London was staying with Grace. She mentioned it when we were hanging out earlier.

There's nothing malicious about Grace's words themselves, but there's a superiority seeped into her tone. Some judgment of London that seems like it's really a slight at me.

It's lingered in her voice every time she's ever spoken to me, and I've never understood it. Her fake niceness is like an artificial sweetener. She's insistent on acting nice toward me but wants me to know it's not genuine. I suspect Holden has something to do with it. Grace *did* go to middle school with us. She knows we were once friends.

I raise a hand in a small wave. "Hi, Grace."

"Hi, Cassia," she replies, looking me and my pajamas over. "You look…cozy."

I smile, the expression tight.

Grace glances at McKenzie. "You have the tequila?"

"Yeah." McKenzie walks over to her suitcase and pulls a glass bottle out. I avert my gaze back to the television.

A male voice draws my attention to the doorway again. "Come on. You ladies ready to…" Finn's voice trails when he sees me. "Cassia. Hey."

I raise a brow. "Hey, Finn."

Finn and Mark, Holden's two closest friends, used to be guys I considered friends as well. Up until Holden stopped inviting me to hang out—with them, at all.

I wonder if Holden gave them a reason for distancing from me. I'm guessing not. He's not the type to explain himself. And he was the common thread—the reason I was friendly with either of them in the first place. I've barely spoken to Finn since we started high school.

Finn takes a few steps into the room, acting like that's not the case at all. "Whatcha watching?"

I shrug, since I'm not really sure. Finn seems to recognize the movie, though, because his eyes light up with excitement as he studies the motorcycle chase taking place on the screen. "Oh! I love this part."

Well, that makes one of us.

"Finn!" Grace snaps. "Let's go."

She and McKenzie are waiting in the doorway. Impatience radiates from Grace. I'm surprised she's not tapping her foot.

He jerks his attention away from the television, aiming it at me instead. "Wanna come, Cas?"

I'm shocked, both by the casual use of the nickname and the invitation itself. Questions fly to the tip of my tongue.

Why is he inviting me?

What are they doing?

Will Holden be there?

I swallow them all, forcibly. It's after curfew. Whatever they're doing, it's not school-sanctioned. If I decline, I know exactly how this night will end. And for once, that bothers me. I'm a couple hundred miles from Pembrooke. If I stay out late, I won't have to worry about my parents noticing.

So I nod and stand. "Sure."

None of them expected me to agree, that much is obvious. Finn is the first to shed his shocked expression. "Cool. You ready?"

I nod again, turning off the television and pulling a sweatshirt on to hide the fact I'm not even wearing a bra. I feel silly asking them to wait for me to change, and I'm not sure what I would put on instead. The warm clothes I brought—sweaters and fleeces— are nothing like the cute tops Grace and McKenzie are wearing. None of them are wearing jackets.

All I do is slide on a pair of sneakers, leaving my sleep shorts on. At least I'll be comfortable.

Finn doesn't comment on my attire as I slide my phone and room key in the pouch of my sweatshirt and walk out into the hallway. He doesn't say anything at all, and neither does Grace nor McKenzie.

Apprehension swells, asking me what the hell I'm doing. I could be snuggled under the covers right now. As far as I know, Grace and McKenzie don't get in trouble, but Finn is a wild card.

Debauchery on this trip might be expected, but it's certainly not condoned. If we're caught, we could be suspended. My whole future could be gone in a flash. Nerves wriggle in my stomach, tightening into a ball of dread.

Finn stays silent as we walk down the carpeted hall, which must be a record for him. Usually, he won't shut up. In addition to not distracting me from my anxiety, it makes me worry what he's concerned about. Does he regret inviting me along?

There's audible commotion behind several of the doors we pass, and it relaxes me some. Obviously, Holden's friends aren't the only ones flouting the rules. If the chaperones decide to check on anything, that lowers the odds we'll be caught.

Finn finally speaks as we're nearing the elevator bank. Unfortunately, his choice of topic makes me wish he had stayed quiet. "So you and Holden…what happened there?"

I tense, I can't help it. I knew coming was a bad idea. "What do you mean?"

"Come on, Cassia. You and Holden used to be tight. Then one morning he's telling me and Mark not to talk to you."

I barely suppress the flinch that wants to surface. I could tell him the truth—that I'm just as much in the dark as he is. That Holden chose to end our friendship without consulting me, and I was too confused and heartbroken to consider confronting him until it felt too late and like too much time had passed. To the point that it felt pathetic to still be affected by it, to want to know answers.

The truth makes me look sad and discarded, like a used toy cast aside in pursuit of shinier objects. I'd rather Finn—not to mention Grace and McKenzie, who are eavesdropping—think that I played a more active role in the separation.

It's none of their business anyway. If I have to wonder, so should they.

"Ask Holden," I suggest, pressing the down button for the elevator and feeling all three of them looking at me.

Finn scoffs. "Yeah, I tried that. He didn't tell me shit."

"There's your answer then," I say as I step inside the elevator.

The descent to the ground floor is silent. So quiet I can hear the elevator's gears shifting, which is disconcerting.

I trail behind Finn, McKenzie, and Grace once we exit. They veer to the left of the lobby and down another carpeted hallway. They all seem confident in wherever they're going. I resist the urge to ask. I'm not sure it matters; I'm along for the ride at this point. *Expect the unexpected* needs to be my motto for this trip.

Finally, we stop. Finn knocks three times on the door, and I roll my eyes at the exaggerated cloak and dagger routine. No wonder he liked the spy movie I was watching so much.

Mark opens the door. His eyes skate over the group, land on me, and widen before he aims a questioning look at Finn. Finn is already walking past him, with Grace and McKenzie close behind. Mark's stare moves to me instead.

While Finn is easy to read, Mark is not. He's not as impenetrable as Holden. But he's serious and expressionless most of the time, like he is right now.

"Hey, Mark."

"Hi, Cassia."

"Uh, cool if I come in?"

"Wha—oh yeah. Of course." He holds the door open wider and I slip past him, into what I realize is the hotel pool. Hot, humid air swirls the scent of chlorine around. There's a group of people clustered around the far end where the lounge chairs are set up. Otherwise, the pool deck is empty.

Finn, Grace, and McKenzie have already melded into the group. I feel very much the outsider as I approach the loose gathering. McKenzie sets the glass bottle she brought down on the tile with a clang. I'd like to think that sound is what causes the pause in conversation, but I'm pretty sure it's my approach.

I scan faces I know by name but wouldn't consider friends. These are the popular kids, the people who never had to wonder about where to sit at lunch or whether they would have a date to a school dance.

I ate in the library more than a few times freshman year before Sydney joined me at Pembrooke High. I've gone to Homecoming with a group of girls each year. To say I don't fit in here is no understatement.

But I attempt to act otherwise, walking forward with a confidence I don't feel.

Holden isn't here. It incites a strange mix of relief and disappointment. I'm relieved he won't witness how out of place I am, my inability to fit in with his friends.

But he would have been a lifeline of familiarity. I probably shouldn't trust him to look out for me, but I do. And if he's not here, I can't help but wonder where he is instead. I seriously doubt he's asleep, obeying curfew.

Conversation starts up again right before I reach the group.

I settle on a chair, tucking my legs up underneath me. It feels like the temperature has risen, sticky warmth coating my skin and curling my hair. It makes me glad I kept my shorts on. The other girls here are dressed similarly to Grace and McKenzie. I'm guessing they're all sweating in the tight clothing.

I rub a finger against the hard plastic edge of my room key, safely tucked away in the pocket of my sweatshirt. It feels like an escape route. I'll stay here for a little while and then head back upstairs.

My phone buzzes. I pull it out to see a message from Sydney. It's a photo of Lily, sitting outside of Holden's bedroom door with the stuffed monkey that's become her favorite toy. *She misses you guys*, she adds in a second text.

I stare at the photo. Zero in on *you guys*. It chafes. I know Sydney—of all people—doesn't mean it to sound like a coupling, but it's so easy—*too easy*—to imagine a me and Holden.

I like both messages right as a door slams. Everyone looks toward the pool entrance. A jolt of adrenaline runs through me, wondering if it's a school chaperone or hotel employee here to bust us.

Holden walks into the room instead, with Jordan Eaton right behind him. A different sort of anxiety floods my system.

"You're late," Mark calls out.

"And you're supposed to knock three times," Finn adds.

Holden rolls his eyes as he walks over. He scans the group, looking for somewhere to sit. But then his eyes land on me.

I drop his gaze like it burned me, then immediately chastise myself. Not only does it make it seem like I'm unsure or embarrassed about being here, I can't read his reaction to the fact that I am.

These are his friends. I blame my inability to maintain eye contact on the way I'm in his element.

I obviously didn't look up the pool hours and policy, but I'm confident they're flouting both. I'm amongst people I don't know well in a situation that could blow up in my face.

There's no avoiding Holden, though, when he takes a seat at the end of the lounger I'm perched on. I know it's him before I look up, based on the glimpse of flannel I catch out of the corner of my eye and the hum under my skin.

When I glance over, he's already looking at me.

"Hey."

I clear my throat. "Hey."

The talking around us sounds muted, almost like I jumped in the pool and am listening to it from underwater. I hope it's in my head, not that they've actually quieted to listen to our conversation.

I wait for him to ask what I'm doing here.

He doesn't. He glances down at my phone, which is displaying the photo Sydney just sent.

One corner of his mouth lifts. "She's up late."

I check the time. Just after midnight.

Something else occurs to me. "Happy Birthday."

Holden glances up, and our gazes lock again. It's not light enough in here for me to read the emotion swimming in his eyes. Only the emergency lights are on, emphasizing the fact we're not supposed to be in here. The planes of his face are shadowed, all harsh angles and sharp lines. "Thanks."

"I'm rooming with McKenzie," I say. "Finn and Grace came to get her. Finn invited me." I shift so I'm sitting cross-legged after offering the explanation he didn't ask for. My knee hits Holden's thigh, but he doesn't move away. Neither do I.

He says nothing in response. His placidity emboldens me.

"Finn asked me what happened between us. Why we stopped being friends."

A noncommittal hum is the only response I get.

"I told him to ask you, and he said he has. That you wouldn't tell him."

This time, Holden raises a challenging brow. "So?"

"Would you tell *me*, if I asked?"

"I'd ask why it took you four years to."

Outrage courses through me, heavy and hot. *He* breaks my heart and then has the gall to ask why I didn't confront him about it sooner?

Not that he knows about the heartbreak—I hope. But regardless, he had to know distancing himself would hurt me. Would lead to insecurity and second-guessing.

"I can take a hint, Holden. If you didn't want to be friends, that was fine by me."

"*Want* has never been part of the problem, Cassia." He sounds irritated with *me*, which I don't understand. Almost offended that I'm questioning him, that the subject that used to be taboo between us has come up.

It makes no sense to me, but most of me and Holden since high school started has been a puzzle. I should give up on collecting pieces. But it's hard to do when he's sitting next to me, when I'm enjoying his proximity. When I keep replaying what happened between us that Friday night. If I had pushed for more, would he have had sex with me?

"Holden! You playing?"

I look away from Holden—probably for the first time since he sat down—to see that everyone else has gathered into a tighter circle. The bottle McKenzie carried down has been set in the very center, suggesting they're recruiting for some sort of drinking game.

"Yep." He stands, and I assume he's walking over there. Instead, he jerks the lounger I'm sitting on closer, so it's part of the periphery of the circle.

I fall back against the cushions, not expecting the sudden movement and unprepared to stay upright. "You *dick*." I speak without thinking, embarrassment coursing through me as everyone looks at me with shock.

Holden grins as I sit up. Amused by my outburst, not contrite.

"Truth or Dare, Holden?"

I scoff, both with annoyance that Grace is choosing Holden to start with and because of the irony we're playing a game that involves the word truth when there are so many lies stacked up between us.

Predictably, Holden chooses dare.

Grace jerks her chin toward the pool. "Take a dip."

There's murmuring amongst the group. Guys grumbling the choice of dare is lame. Girls excited about the prospect of Holden stripping to swim. Maybe I would be too, if I hadn't already had a private show.

But I doubt it. There's always been an innate possessiveness when it comes to Holden. Some claim that I can't make or resist. Watching other girls ogle over his abs is not my idea of a good time.

I focus my attention on anything but Holden as he stands. Jordan Eaton is sitting directly across the circle from me. When he catches my eye, he smiles. I smile back, hesitantly.

Jordan is on the basketball team with Holden. He moved to Pembrooke sophomore year, though, so I don't even have the distant history that I do with some of the other people here.

I startle when a ball of fabric lands in my lap. *ADAMS* is spelled out on the back of the gray sweatshirt, but the fact the guy next to me is now shirtless is really the only clue I needed to know the sweatshirt is Holden's.

I don't think his aim was off. Holden is the star of the basketball team, for Christ's sake. He's making a point. I make one too, shrugging the sweatshirt off my lap.

"Actually, I don't feel like swimming," Holden says.

He walks to the center of the circle, unscrews the top of the tequila, and takes a long pull from the bottle. I watch the shift in topography on his stupidly muscular back before he turns around and returns to my side.

When he sits, he doesn't pull his sweatshirt back on. His presence next to me is impossible to ignore. His knees are spread, and he's leaning back on his palms. It's like he's trying to encroach on as much space surrounding me without actually touching me anywhere.

I swallow. Glance at Jordan again. He's not looking at me this time, and it feels purposeful. Grace is having the opposite issue. Her gaze is direct and annoyed—and aimed straight at me. She's clearly irritated I'm here, and I'm assuming Holden's choice of seating arrangement has only amplified it.

"Eaton. Truth or Dare?"

I look at Holden, surprised by the edge to the question. He's friends with Jordan…right? I see them at school together. They showed up here together. But there's a challenge and maybe a warning laced in the words that don't sound very friendly.

Based on the nervous way Jordan clears his throat, he notices it too. "Uh…"

Jordan glances at Mark, who's sitting next to him. Mark shrugs.

"Truth, I guess," Jordan decides.

"Did you cheat on Lacie with McKenzie?"

There's a rumble of whispers around the group. Obviously, this is a well-known rumor or a poorly kept secret.

Jordan rolls his eyes. I think it might be a bit of false bravado, based on the flush to his face. But it could also be attributed to the temperature in here. If I were wearing a bra, I would have taken off my sweatshirt a while ago. It feels like the humidity has saturated everything I'm wearing, and I can only imagine what my hair looks like.

"Lacie and I were already over. And you're one to talk, Adams."

I don't need to look at Holden. I feel him stiffen beside me. "What the fuck does that mean, Eaton?"

"Just, I mean…you know." Jordan smirks, then glances

around the group. Interestingly, no one else seems interested in engaging in the conversation.

I glance around, literally in the middle of Pembrooke High's inner circle. It appears less leaks out than I thought, since I never heard any rumors about Jordan and Lacie. Or involving my current roommate.

"Know *what*?" Holden challenges.

Jordan is silent, seemingly trying to figure out how to back-track under Holden's glare.

"I think he's referring to how you *play* off the court." It takes me a second, and Holden turning to stare at me, to realize that I'm the one who said that. There are a few muffled chuckles around us, but Holden looks serious. Surprised.

His intensity is focused on me now. I don't shirk away from it the way Jordan did.

"I'm not a cheater."

"I know. That requires commitment."

Someone whistles, long and low. A muscle jumps in Holden's jaw, but he says nothing in response. Jordan is the one who speaks next, choosing someone to keep the game going. I miss who he selects and whether they pick truth or dare, too fixed on holding Holden's stare. It seems important, somehow, that I don't drop eye contact.

He looks away first, without giving me much of a glimpse of what he's thinking. I play with the ends of my hair, trying to figure out how I can extricate myself and head back upstairs.

I don't regret coming. Based on the curious glances I'm getting, I might have successfully disabused some ideas about me being the senior class's goody two shoes. There's a thrill to that.

"Cassia."

My head snaps up at the sound of my name. I focus on McKenzie.

"Truth or dare?"

I deliberate for a few seconds, then decide. "Truth." I think—hope—there's less that can go wrong there.

"Who was the last guy you kissed?"

At first, I'm relieved she didn't ask anything more invasive. Then I realize it's probably because she doesn't think I've done anything more than kissing.

And *then* I realize I was very wrong about truth being the less damaging choice. The honest answer to that question is not one I want to share. I don't want Holden to know he's the last guy I kissed.

We haven't kissed during either of our recent…lapses.

Which means the last guy I kissed was him—nearly four years ago. Admitting that will give Holden the impression I've never gotten over him.

While I know there's some truth to that—more than I'd willingly admit—it's nothing I want *him* to know. He'll read into what happened in his driveway and on the couch—think it meant something to me instead of being hormone-driven. That it wasn't about what we were doing, but rather that it was him I was doing it with.

If I answer truthfully, everyone else here might not know *when* we kissed, but they'll know we have at some point.

Holden has spent the past few years acting like I don't exist, especially while we're at school. I'm certain he doesn't want everyone knowing we've kissed, even if it was before high school started.

The longer I'm silent, the more oppressive the humidity around me feels. Everyone is waiting for my response…and I can't make myself speak the two syllables of his name.

I untuck my legs from under me and stand, feeling the blood rush down and heat my skin further. Eyes follow me as I walk over to the glass bottle. The only other person who has chosen to drink as a penalty was Holden.

The cap of the tequila comes off easily, and I take a healthy swallow. Smoky alcohol burns my throat and pools in my stomach. I want to gag or make a face, but I do neither. I enjoy the surprised expressions around me. Me drinking is almost as shocking as me sharing the truthful answer to that question would have been.

Mark is grinning, which feels like an accomplishment in comparison to his usual stoicism. He was always my favorite of Holden's friends. Less self-centered than the rest of the popular crowd.

I set the bottle back down. For a second, I entertain the idea of sitting somewhere else. I don't *want* to sit next to Holden. I'm trying to get him out of my head, which is especially hard to do when he's inches away.

Everything he does confuses me. He sat beside me on the bus yesterday. Didn't talk to me at all today. Then sits next to me now. It feels like a game of tug of war.

And I want to walk away. To not care what he does and why.

But feelings aren't a switch you can turn on and off. Love doesn't have to be requited in order for it to feel real. If it were easy to get over someone, there wouldn't be millions of songs about heartbreak. If it were simple to not care about someone by sheer force of will, moving on wouldn't be a monumental task.

So I know, even as I glance around, I'll end up right where I was. Literally and emotionally.

I zone out as the game continues. The whispering over seeing me drink is annoying, but it also distracts from the fact I neglect to choose who goes next. Truth or Dare skips on without me, full of side chatter and inside jokes.

I mostly stare at the smooth surface of the pool, inhaling chlorinated steam and feeling warmth slowly trickle into my bloodstream thanks to the sip of tequila.

Finn comes up with a dance routine for his dare. I take the opportunity to stand and head into the attached locker room. The air is cooler and drier in here. I inhale deeply as I use the bathroom and then wipe my face with a damp paper towel. I linger for a little while, trying to decide what to do next. Should I leave right away or wait a little longer?

When I walk back into the pool area, I'm expecting for nothing to have changed. It has. Instead of a crowded space, there's only one person left by the pool.

Holden is sprawled out on the lounger we were sharing earlier, hands tucked behind his head as he stares up at the ceiling. I glance up, wondering if there's something to see besides white plaster. There isn't.

I walk over toward him slowly, scanning the space like everyone else might be hiding and about to leap out. "Uh, where did everyone go?"

"Game got old. They went out to a club." He keeps his eyes on the ceiling as he answers.

"A club?"

"Yep. New York has a lot of them, I hear."

I'm expecting a mocking, sarcastic edge, but instead he just sounds matter of fact. "And…you didn't want to go?" Nothing about his answer explained why he's still here.

"No."

I consider that. Stick my hands in the pocket of my sweatshirt and rock back on my heels. "Okay. Well, I'm gonna…" My voice trails when Holden suddenly stands, still shirtless, and now he's tugging down his sweatpants. "What are you doing?"

He straightens, tossing his sweatpants on top of the hoodie he shucked earlier. I force my eyes to stay north. "Relax, flower.

Nothing you haven't seen before, right?" And then he walks over to the edge of the pool and jumps in.

Whatever expression I'm wearing when he surfaces makes him smile.

"Water is warm," he comments, spreading his arms.

My front teeth dig into the soft flesh of my lower lip. I shouldn't. I know I shouldn't, and yet I'm embarrassingly tempted. There's no one else around to wonder or speculate. I don't have to worry about what anyone is thinking about me—what judgments they're making about me—except for him.

Maybe that's who I should be most concerned with. I'm giving him more and more ammunition against me. Providing more and more evidence that he still has power over me—lots of it. When—and I'm sure it'll be a when, not an if—he breaks my heart again, I'll only have myself to blame.

But I know I'll agree anyway. "They're not coming back?"

"They're not coming back."

I exhale. Step out of my shorts and toss them on top of his clothes. It's an unexpectedly intimate sight, seeing our clothing mixed together in a discarded heap.

I grab the hem of my sweatshirt next, maintaining eye contact the whole time. He's seen me naked before, same as I've seen him. But twice feels more momentous than once. Smart people don't make mistakes twice, and I like to think I'm a smart person. Not an intelligence that's measured by your grades, but simple sensibility.

When my hoodie and tank top drop onto the lounger, I drop eye contact. I run toward the edge of the pool and leap, taking a deep breath before oxygen disappears. Warm water saturates my hair and surrounds my skin, sliding over me in a sensuous glide.

I remain underwater until my lungs begin to burn, breaking the surface and facing him.

For seconds—minutes, maybe—we stare at each other. Water drips out of his hair in small streams, traveling over the bridge of his nose and the angle of his cheekbones. Our strokes are lazy, just the bare minimum necessary to stay afloat. The pool isn't very deep; I brushed the bottom easily when I jumped in. But the motion of treading water is something to focus on, rather than him.

"Why didn't you answer?" That's all he asks, but I don't need to ask him to clarify what he's wondering about.

I drag my fingers through the silky water, focusing on the smooth glide instead of his intense gaze. "Doesn't seem like any of their business—who I've kissed."

"Is it mine?" One corner of his mouth tugs upward. "You know, as someone you've kissed."

It's the first time he's ever acknowledged it happened. He's made comments or references to the past here or there, but he's never outright stated what immediately predated the end of our friendship. I've always assumed he was worried I got the wrong idea. That he kissed me on a whim—as a dare, maybe—and regretted it right away. That he panicked and put as much distance between us as he could—an impressive amount, honestly, considering my friendship with Sydney and how we live across the street from each other, not just in the same town.

I stare at the wall of windows, wishing they displayed something besides foggy darkness. "You."

"Huh?"

"That's the answer. *You*. I didn't answer because I didn't think you'd want everyone to know."

There's a *long* pause following that confession. I'm not brave enough to look over and try to read his reaction.

"So…"

"I haven't kissed a guy in four years. Yeah." I tilt my head back. Partially because the sensation of warm water soaking my scalp feels really good. Mostly because I don't want to meet his gaze when I admit that.

"Why?"

"Herpes, mostly."

His laugh echoes across the surface of the water. But then it fades, and we're left in oppressive silence again. "You said it was a regular occurrence. Made it seem like there were other guys." His voice is quiet, not accusing. But there's no mistaking the undercurrent of irritation.

"Yeah, I lied. You might have heard of it?"

He scoffs, almost a laugh, but not quite. "Yeah. I'm familiar with the fucking concept, Cassia. I'm just not sure when *you* started lying to *me*."

"Probably around when you started ignoring me."

Holden swims closer. Everything inside me sings at the proximity. He reaches out, fingering one of my wet curls and tugging on it gently. "So *everything* we've done…was your first time?"

If I wasn't blushing before, I definitely am now. "Disappointed?"

He laughs, but it's humorless. "No. I'm definitely not disappointed." His hand moves to my jaw, tilting my head so I'm forced to look at him.

I can't read anything but sincerity on his face, and it soothes something inside of me that was convinced guys like him desire girls who are experienced and bold and know exactly how to pleasure them.

He kisses me, deep and hot and desperate. I sink into the kiss, everything inside me craving his touch. Holden is tall enough to stand. Water rushes by as he moves us closer to the edge of the pool. Rough cement rubs my bare back as I'm crushed between him and the tile.

His hands run up my thighs until they reach my butt and slide over my hips. I wrap my legs around his waist, heat sparking in my stomach when I feel him reacting.

He chose to stay behind instead of going out with his friends.

He followed through on the dare after they'd left.

He kissed me first.

I'm responding to those decisions just as much as his touch. For the first time in a long time, it feels like he's choosing me.

Prioritizing me.

It shouldn't undo the past few years when he's chosen differently, and it doesn't. But it means *something* to me. Makes me feel sexy and desired and all the ways I want to feel around him. Makes me feel more than I wish it would. But I've never had any control over how I feel around him—about him—and that's always been most of the problem.

I'm sure Holden is aware of the way his erection is pressed against me, but he doesn't attempt to do anything more than kiss me. His hands remain on my hips, holding me in place as he plunders my mouth.

I love kissing him. I missed it more than I thought you could miss something you'd only experienced once.

Kissing him chases away all the chatter in my head.

Happy thrills patter in my chest. If I were braver, I'd ask Holden if kissing always feels like this.

Sydney's first kiss was last fall, with a guy from her English class at Homecoming. The adjectives she used to describe it were wet and awkward. Kissing Holden has never felt that way, not even back when we were far younger and even more inexperienced.

I'm disappointed when Holden pulls back, but I work to hide it.

"We should get out of here," he says. "Someone might look in at some point."

I blink rapidly, recalibrating with reality. For however long we were kissing, I completely forgot we're in a hotel pool after curfew, naked. "Right. Yeah." I'm flustered. Turned on and confused. How does he keep doing this? Keep surprising me? Keep consuming me?

I swim toward the stairs. Holden hauls himself right out from the edge. Water sluices off his body and his muscles ripple, which does nothing to alleviate the ache between my legs. I watch as he adjusts himself and then pulls on his sweatshirt and sweatpants.

I hurry to put on my clothes too without bothering to dry off, not wanting to be the one of us left naked.

Water drips from my hair, soaking the hood of my sweatshirt immediately. I can feel droplets sliding down my skin beneath the fabric as I pull on my sneakers and confirm the room key is still in my pocket, along with my phone.

Holden holds the door for me, surprising me again.

"Thanks," I murmur as I pass him and start down the hall toward the elevators. The lobby is empty and there's no one at the front desk. I jab the up button twice, gnawing on my bottom lip as Holden catches up and stops next to me.

The doors slide open a few seconds later. I step inside and hit the button for floor 8. Holden shoves his hands in his pockets and leans back against the wall, making no move to hit another button.

When a seven flashes on the screen above the buttons, I glance over my shoulder at him. He's already looking at me, and my heart flips right as the doors open with a ding.

"I'll see you tomorrow?" I phrase it like a question, even though I know I will. We're visiting the September 11 Memorial and Museum tomorrow morning and then leaving the city in the early afternoon.

"It is tomorrow, flower." He straightens and walks past me into the carpeted hall. I hurry after him before the doors can close.

"You don't have to walk me to my room. McKenzie might be back."

"I'm walking to *my* room." Holden pulls out a key identical to the one tucked in my pocket.

"Oh." For some reason it didn't occur to me he might be staying on the same floor of the hotel.

He sleeps across the hall from me every Friday night. But this feels different. Maybe it's the lack of Sydney's presence.

"Who are you rooming with?" I ask, trying to distract myself —and him—from my wrong assumption.

"Jordan. But he's sleeping in Claire's room tonight."

Once again, "Oh" is the best response I can come up with.

Claire Scott is friends with McKenzie and Grace. She was at the pool tonight. I'm curious how *that* dynamic works, especially if what Holden said about Jordan and McKenzie is true.

My conversation with London and the other senior girls I'm friendly with centered around classes and college visits and the latest Taylor Swift album. Not backstabbing or cheating or sex.

But what I'm really absorbing is that Holden just told me he has a hotel room to himself tonight. Would he have mentioned it if I hadn't asked about his roommate? Is he expecting Grace or one of the other girls always hanging on him to show up after she gets back from the club?

Holden kissed me in the pool, but he was also the one who suggested we climb out. He was still hard when we got out, so I don't think I did anything to turn him off.

I don't *know*, though. Do other people just know what to do in situations like this? Was there some guide I missed? A tutorial I could have taken? My only reference is how my peers act at school.

My parents don't police my social life because they've never had to. I go to school and I volunteer at the animal shelter and I spend time with Sydney.

There's no way they would allow me to go to any of the parties Holden frequents. My dad works for a local law firm that's handled plenty of drug and DUI cases involving teenagers. He's always made it clear to me and my siblings what standard of behavior he'll accept.

Most of the time, it's one I have no problem adhering to. I'd rather watch movies and make chocolate chip cookies with Sydney on Friday nights than get drunk at a crowded party where I'm sure I'd feel just as out of place as I did earlier.

Holden stops walking. I glance between him and the closed door, deciding what to say.

He solves the dilemma for me. "Want to come in?"

My response is quick. Maybe too rapid. "Yeah."

Holden swipes his room key and opens the door. I walk in first, feeling his presence right behind.

The door closes, and we're alone.

CHAPTER THIRTEEN

HOLDEN

The water in the bathroom shuts off. I flip the remote in my hand, then start spinning it in circles.

I'm nervous. I haven't been nervous around a girl since... well, since Ginny Davis's Halloween party in eighth grade.

I can trace exactly how I got here, easily. The simplest place to rest the blame is on Finn. He was the one who invited Cassia to the pool, according to her.

It's Jordan's fault as well. He's a good friend and a decent basketball player, but when it comes to girls, he's the worst guy I know.

I saw the way he was looking at Cassia earlier. Somehow, he keeps drawing in girls who know he's fucked over their friends, and there was no chance I was going to sit back and watch him do that to Cassia. Watching Harrison talk to her before we left Pembrooke on Friday was bad enough.

But none of that required me to invite her into my hotel room.

We're in this situation squarely because of me. And I'm caught in a strange state of excitement and uncertainty. This is *exactly* what I've gone out of my way to avoid ever happening.

I don't trust myself around Cassia.

This isn't a drunken fumbling at a party. And even if it were, I'm pretty sure I'd be feeling this same way.

The bathroom door opens and Cassia appears. She asked to use the bathroom as soon as we walked into my room. Part of me thought it was her way of taking some time to figure out how to backtrack out of this situation. Then the shower started running. I figured she wanted to wash off the chlorine. I was planning to turn on the television so I could suggest we watch a movie or something.

I didn't consider this possibility.

Cassia walks out of the bathroom wearing nothing but a fluffy white towel. She didn't bother to put on any clothes. She didn't even dry her hair. Dozens of tiny rivers run down her arms, dripping onto the generic, patterned carpet.

I swallow. Watch her walk toward me. Her face is neutral. Her hands are gripping the towel so tightly I can see the whites of her knuckles.

Cassia doesn't stop the way I'm expecting. She comes closer and closer, until her legs are bumping against my knees. "You're sure Jordan isn't coming back?" she asks.

"I'm sure." My voice is the consistency of gravel.

She asked me something similar at the pool. It twists my insides, knowing that Cassia doesn't want anyone else but me to see her this way. It fuels the possessiveness she's in full command of.

A drop of water falls from her hair and lands on my thigh, darkening a spot of the gray cotton. I should have turned on the television. The only sound in the room is the gentle whoosh of the heating system as it exhales warm air. If anyone in the rooms on either side of mine is still awake, they're impossible to hear. It sounds like—feels like—the world has narrowed down to just me and her.

I'm startled by how much I like it. How right it feels.

Cassia stares at me. Girls don't usually look right at me like this. They want my attention, sure. But once they have it, they turn shy. Sly. Quick glances, then looking away. Slight brushes, then pulling away. Part of it is probably an act. Maybe they think I want uncertainty or are playing hard to get.

Ask most of Pembrooke High, and Cassia Nolan wouldn't be considered bold or brazen. But right now, she's both. One knee lands on the bed, then the other. She takes a seat in my lap, directly on top of my hardening dick.

It's the sexiest sight I've ever seen. Maybe—probably—because it's *her*. Cassia's hair hasn't dried in its usual curls yet. It's dark and wild, falling over her pale shoulders in messy waves. The white towel hugs the very top of her breasts, teasing at the cleavage beneath. Her legs are on full display, parted and pulling the towel up to the top of her thighs.

"What are you doing, flower?" I don't mean for the endearment to come out, but it falls out of my mouth anyway.

Somehow, it adds to the anticipation. It's an acknowledgment. I can't treat Cassia with any of the separation I should. I can't pretend she's just another girl in a bedroom.

Rather than answer the question, she shifts. The towel pools around her waist, and her tits are right in my face. I'm sure she can feel how hard I am. How much I want this and how desperate I am to be inside of her. To be the *only* guy that's been inside of her.

I've never slept with a virgin before. In the past, it's been an unpalatable option. Extra work with added potential for a messy separation, which I know makes me sound like a dick. I know it's a big deal to some girls, and it's never been something I've felt equipped to handle.

Sex is a physical release for me the same way fighting is. I don't attach any emotion to the act itself, I just enjoy the resulting adrenaline and endorphins.

But the thought of being the first guy that Cassia will be with? There's something primal about it. Incendiary. It heats my blood and makes my cock so hard it's painful. Destroys the indifference that's usually unshakeable.

I grip the towel that's the only barrier blocking her body, warring with myself. She shouldn't be offering this. Because I'm selfish enough to take it.

Years. I've spent *years* trying to resist this pull between us. We landed here anyway.

"Are you sure?"

This time, she answers. "Yes."

I scan her face. Features I know better than my own. I turned on the overhead light when we came in here. I wasn't trying to set any sort of romantic atmosphere. Its bright glare reveals everything. I can see everything, from the green swirl in her hazel eyes to the freckle just below her jawline. The small scar just below the dip of her chin from falling off the monkey bars in sixth grade. The generous swell of the breasts I've jerked off to way too many times.

"Are *you*?" she asks. Her confident façade falters, insecurity saturating the two words. She's not sure if I want this—want her. It's a misconception I'm suddenly desperate to correct.

And that's all it takes. The battle inside me ends. There's a chance this was always inevitable between us. In some ways, capitulating feels like another failure on my part. But the sense of victory—of relief—is much stronger.

I don't believe in destiny or fate. I'm not even sure if I believe in love. The romantic sort, at least. The kind where you *choose* to love someone without the link of any obligation.

But there's something that feels right, feels settled, about Cassia being naked in my lap. I fall into the pull, yanking the towel away and looking my fill. She lets me stare, holding my gaze every time it flickers back to her face.

I pull my sweatshirt off and shift so she's more on the bed than my lap. Kick off my sweatpants and boxers, leaving me as naked as she is. I consider turning off the lights but don't.

I like this—like seeing her. It's such a contrast from every other time I've had sex, there's no comparison.

Cassia bites her bottom lip as I lie down beside her. There aren't words that explain how this feels. Some combination of confusion and euphoria. Her hair is a dark tangle spread out on the sheets. She rolls on her side, facing me.

"I've never done this before."

"I know."

She's looking to me to take the lead, but it feels like I've never done this before either. It's never felt like this before with anyone else.

Her body moves closer to mine, until our bare skin is brushing. "I want to, Holden. I want you to fuck me."

Some of my confidence makes a sudden return. I don't know what it is about Cassia that disarms me so thoroughly. But I know those aren't words she could have uttered easily. She's putting herself out there—for me. Trying to entice me, as if I need any encouragement.

I reach out and brush some hair away from her face. "I'm going to, baby."

Her body stiffens. I still, just as surprised. I've never—not once—called anyone by that pet name. Based on the uncertainty that flashes across her face, Cassia doesn't think that's the case.

I roll above her, searching for any hint of reservation. There's none. I lean over, fumbling for the condom Jordan left on the bedside table.

He brought a box and passed them out when a bunch of the guys were hanging out in here last night. I left the one I rejected yesterday by the hotel phone.

I don't ask her again, but I give Cassia a minute to watch me. A chance to change her mind, if she wants to.

She doesn't look uncertain, but she does scoff as I toss the wrapper in the trashcan. "Prepared, huh?"

"Jordan brought them. I wasn't planning on doing anything this weekend."

Another scoff, this time louder. I crawl back over her body, easily shifting her into the position I want her in. The irritation disappears as I hover over her, apprehension appearing instead.

"I *wasn't.*"

I never justify my actions to anyone. Don't ever explain myself. Not to my friends, not to girls. But it feels immensely important for Cassia to know this wasn't my plan—for us to end up in a situation like this. Or even worse, for her to assume I figured I'd get my dick wet regardless, and she's just a stand-in for someone else.

"It doesn't matter. I don't care. I know you're not a virgin, Holden."

Cassia is saying exactly what would normally prompt a sigh of relief. Coming from her, all it does is piss me the hell off.

I grab both of her hands and hold them above her head with one hand, using my other palm to spread her legs. She's so wet I can see her arousal. Smell it. It eases some of my annoyance, but not all of it.

The tip of my dick brushes her clit and her hips jerk, instinctively seeking more contact. I slide my hand up her thigh. Slow. Teasing.

She writhes beneath me, a red flush working its way across her body. Her breathing quickens into desperate puffs.

I hide it, but I'm just as affected. There's nothing I want to do more than push inside her.

"You don't care, Cassia? This could be any dick you're so desperate to get inside you? If I'd had a different girl right where you are last night, that wouldn't bother you?"

Anger overtakes her expression. I'm playing with fire, just begging to be burned. I'm also walking a line so thin I can't even see it.

This thing between me and Cassia, it won't last. It's lust. She and I are about to head in two very different directions, and we both know it. We're satiating curiosity that's been there since puberty before the opportunity is lost for good. I can't lose sight of that.

But at the same time, I know it means something. To her, and to me. I can't *not* acknowledge that.

I lower my hips, letting her feel all of me. Cassia gasps, her back arching. Her breasts are right in my face and I finally give into the temptation, swirling my tongue around one nipple and then gently sucking.

She swears loudly, her whole body jerking against me.

"Do you care, Cassia?"

"Do *you*?" she spits, turning my own question around on me again.

"If I didn't care, I wouldn't ask."

There's a pause. Then, "I care."

The words are annoyed and rushed. But they're all I was looking for. I push into the wet clench of her pussy, watching her react to the intrusion.

I let go of her hands so I can grip her hips with both hands, holding her in place so I can control the speed and the angle.

Cassia's head falls back as her eyelashes flutter. Her teeth sink into her lower lip. I brush her clit with my thumb, worried she's in pain. Her inner muscles tighten around me as I slide deeper.

For the first time, I'm worried how long I'll last. I can't distract myself from what's happening between us, can't focus on anything but her looking like every fantasy I've ever had. It's too easy to get lost in the moment, to become fully consumed by her.

Cassia watches where we're connected. It's every intimacy I thought I'd shirk away from. I feel laid bare, every flaw and fear exposed, just from how she's looking at me sliding inside her. I'm barely inside. She's so *tight*, and I'm nervous to exert much more pressure.

"Can you kiss me?" she whispers.

In answer, I do exactly that. It's messy and heated. Nips and sucks without any finesse or pattern, like a dance we're making up as we go.

Cassia wraps her legs around my waist. I slide deeper, taking advantage of the way her body naturally opens. She stretches around me, her lips parting against mine.

"You okay?" I whisper.

"Uh-huh. It's just…weird. It feels weird. Huge."

Usually, girls commenting on the size of my dick is a nice ego boost. It's what every guy wants to hear. But right now, I'm more concerned with the grimace in her expression. "Bad weird?"

She shifts under me. "I'm probably not going to come. Most girls don't their first time. Just…move. You can, you know?"

It's so Cassia, turning her pleasure into some sort of statistic.

"*Of course* you're going to come."

Does she think I'm so callous I don't care if she enjoys this?

The thought pisses me off. Irritation helps me regain some of the control the novelty of being inside her shook.

I pull out, almost completely, and then push back inside. This time, there's less resistance. I still go slow, fighting the urge to thrust hard and deep.

This is what Cassia will forever remember as her first time. I'm determined to make it memorable for her. Good memorable, not painful or awkward. Fuck how it feels for me. I kiss a line down her neck as I rub circles right above where I'm entering her.

Cassia moans when I rock into her for the third time and a different sort of satisfaction rushes through me. I didn't think I could be more turned on or more affected than I am right now. But hearing her pleasure—knowing I'm the one inciting it—is the most powerful aphrodisiac I've ever experienced.

I rock in deeper on the next thrust, gripping her hips and guiding her to meet my body when I fall into her.

It's…indiscernible. Intense and consuming. Every time I shove my cock a little deeper, inching closer and closer to release. I hang on with everything I can, determined to make her come first despite being right on the edge and barely in control.

Her moans come faster and louder, interspersed by the sound of my name spoken like her favorite swear.

I move faster, continuing to play with her clit and breasts. "You take me so good, baby. You feel that? Come for me, Cassia. Come on my cock."

Her pussy flutters around me, responding to the dirty talk. A familiar feeling begins to build. It starts in the base of my spine and spreads throughout my body, electric and consuming. I keep talking, part of me wanting to shock her, part of me hoping it will make this more memorable in her mind, and all of me praying she'll come so I can finally let go.

When she does, it surprises both of us. I feel it around me. Hear it echo in her moans. See it explode in her expression.

My dick swells as I empty inside her, coming longer and harder than I ever have before.

We're both breathing heavily as I roll off her and yank off the condom. I toss it and lie back down, my heart racing and my skin sticky with a mixture of sweat and chlorine.

I search for something to say and come up totally empty. I'm grateful; it felt like a gift, but telling her thank you sounds lame. Asking if she's okay is redundant.

Cassia climbs off the bed and walks into the bathroom without saying a word. I sit up and pull on my boxers, a strange mixture of relief and regret filling my chest.

There's no party downstairs to disappear into, which is what usually follows sex. Should I offer for her to sleep here? I wait for the trickle of dread to appear, but it doesn't. Sleeping next to her sounds...nice.

She reappears, dressed in the same sleep shorts and sweatshirt from the pool. "I won't mention you to McKenzie if she's back yet," Cassia says.

Apparently, she doesn't want anyone to know we slept together. Or maybe that's what she thinks I want?

"Because it's none of her business, or because you think that's what I want?"

Her eyes widen, like she expected me to just nod along. "Both."

I scoff. "You're wrong."

She hesitates before speaking again, and I hate it. I want her to be honest with me, not be weighing words.

"I knew what this was, Holden. You're not—we're not—it was just sex, right?"

I can't figure out what part of that chafes. Why it feels like I should be shaking my head in response instead of nodding. Once again, she's saying exactly what I should want to hear.

She nods too. "Okay. Good night."

Without consciously deciding to, I'm standing and walking over to her. I'm still not sure what to say, so I act instead. I tilt her chin up and kiss her. Deep and heady. Thorough and consuming.

Her eyes scan my face once our lips separate.

"Good night."

Whatever she's wondering, she doesn't voice it. Cassia smiles and walks away, out of the room and into the hallway. The door shuts behind her and I sink back down onto the bed, resting my face in my palms and then scrubbing them over my face.

Trying to reconcile how that felt right and wrong.

Like everything and nothing.

CHAPTER FOURTEEN

CASSIA

The familiar shape of Pembrooke High School appears. I rub at the condensation that's formed on the inside of the window. The trees that separate the main brick building from the football field are nearly bare, just brown branches waving in the wind with only a few orange leaves stubbornly clinging to the bark.

The bus comes to a stop along the curb. Immediately, the rustle of activity picks up around me as my peers stand and stretch. Grab belongings and say goodbyes.

I stand and pull my backpack on before following the flow of traffic down the few steps and onto the sidewalk. The leaves that left the branches crunch beneath my boots as I scan the bags being unloaded from the luggage compartment beneath the bus. I finally spot my duffel bag and pick it up, slinging it over one shoulder.

"I got it." Suddenly, there's no weight on my shoulder.

I spin around, then take a step back.

Holden is close, closer than I expected him to be. He grips the handle of my bag since his own is slung over his shoulder.

I clear my throat. "You don't have to."

"I know." There's something warm and soft in his expression, an intimacy that makes my insides feel like toasted marshmallow.

I shift my weight from one foot to the other, not sure what else to say to him. We haven't spoken since I left his hotel room last night.

The night itself was perfect, everything I imagined and more. But it wasn't reality. I thought Holden and I were fated before. That fantasy crashed and burned. My expectations are rock bottom this time. I wanted Holden to be my first, and he was. Maybe—hopefully—that was the closure I needed.

The butterflies in my stomach say otherwise.

"You saw my text?"

"Yeah. I did."

His message saying he was riding with the guys because they had to go over something for the team was unexpected. It felt like something you'd send to your girlfriend, not the girl you had a one-night stand with.

"Sorry I, uh, forgot to respond. I fell asleep." I didn't know what to say in response either, but that feels harder to admit.

"Did you not sleep well last night?" Holden asks innocently. For anyone eavesdropping on our conversation—which I hope is no one—it's innocuous.

But I catch the teasing glimmer in his eyes. The upward curve of his mouth.

I want to be the girl who's suave and unaffected. Who has a flirty, clever response ready for any teasing. Instead, I'm the girl with warm cheeks and a tied tongue. Who's spent all day replaying parts of last night, worrying about what I might have done wrong.

I smile, then look at the ground. I'm so far out of my depth here, it's not even funny.

My familiarity with him is a double-edged sword. There's the scrawny six-year-old I moved in across the street from and used to play H-O-R-S-E with. Then there's the eighteen-year-old version who avoids commitment and who was inside me last night.

I know him and I don't.

Sometimes I hate him and I also might be in love with him.

Complicated doesn't begin to cover it.

A warm hand lands on my chin and tilts it upward. Blue eyes search my face. "Are we good, Cassia?"

"We're good."

Holden doesn't look away or drop his hand. "Are you sure?"

"I knew exactly what it was, Holden. Or rather, what it wasn't."

He studies me, and I have absolutely no idea what he's thinking right now. His expression is a blank page with absolutely no words on it. It's strange—how you can feel so close and familiar to someone in one way, yet so distant in others.

Eventually he nods, then looks away. "Your ride is here."

I follow his gaze to the blue minivan parked in one of the first rows.

My family is here. My *entire* family. The twins are both in soccer jerseys, so they must have all come from their afternoon game. My dad waves when he sees me, and Regan is holding a sign that reads *Welcome Home Cassia.* I smile at the sight. My family is crazy and loud, and I can't imagine my life without them.

I sneak a peek at Holden. No one is here for him. His mom walked away, and his dad is gone most of the time. Sydney put off her permit test since she had me and Holden to drive her around, so she won't get her license until this summer. With both of us out of town, she's stranded at their house.

"It'll be noisy and you'll probably have to sit on some Gold-fish crumbs, but if you want a ride…"

He glances at me, smiles, and it hits me square in the center of my chest. It looks like a special smile. A secret smile. A *you get me* smile. The sort that wreaks havoc on my heart and has me replaying parts of last night in my head without the filter of uncertainty. "I told Finn I'd come over for a bit," he says.

I nod. "Okay. See you later."

I reach out to grab my bag back from him, but Holden just chuckles and keeps walking toward my family.

They all watch us approach curiously. Me and Holden—together—aren't an expected sight, at least not anymore. The twins are arguing over a soccer ball and Sally is drinking from a juice box. Otherwise, everyone's attention is solely on us. My mom and Maggie's gazes feel especially probing.

"Hi, sweetheart." My mom is the first to speak, stepping forward and giving me a hug as soon as I reach them.

"Hey, Mom." I hug her back but drop my arms quickly.

It's stupid, considering he's known me since my family moved in across the street in first grade, but I don't want Holden to see me treated as a kid anymore. Especially after last night.

I glance at Holden and discover he's talking with my dad. About basketball, by the sound of it. My dad has always been an avid fan, and I was the only one of his kids to stick with the sport for longer than one winter.

"Did you guys lose this?" a familiar voice asks. Harrison is approaching, a soccer ball in his hands.

My mom glances between it and the twins. "Boys! What did I tell you about playing in parking lots?"

"Sorry, Mom," they both mumble.

"Thank you," my mom tells Harrison, taking the soccer ball

from him and tossing it into the minivan. "It was very nice of you to bring this over."

"No problem. I've got younger siblings too." Harrison smiles at my mom, then shifts his gaze to me. "Hi, Cassia."

"Hey, Harrison."

I can feel eyes bouncing back and forth between me and Harrison, but I resist the urge to look over and see who is paying close attention to us.

"Have fun on the trip?" he asks, in that easygoing way of his.

"Yeah, I did. The Met was cool."

"The Met was a highlight for me too." His tone is light. Flirty. We were part of the same group for the museum tour.

I smile, not sure what else to say. Harrison smiles back, but it drops off his face quickly.

"Baker." Holden's voice is close. Right behind me.

"Hey, Adams." Harrison mirrors Holden's polite, detached tone.

I play with the zipper of my jacket as he glances between the two of us.

"I'll see you guys later." He gives me another smile, one that looks more forced, before he walks off.

"Your bag is in the car."

I glance over one shoulder, meeting Holden's gaze. "Thanks."

A small nod and then he leaves as well. I can see Finn waiting on the opposite side of the lot, along with Mark and Jordan and a bunch of his other friends.

My parents start piling all the younger kids into the van. Maggie walks over and nudges me in the side. "So really, how was it?"

It's rare my little sister is interested in what I have to say. Most of the time, it feels like our roles are reversed. Like she's the wiser one between the two of us when it comes to life experience.

"It was fun."

"Did you—y'know—do anything?"

"There were tons of trips. We went to the Empire State Building and the Met and—"

Maggie snorts a laugh. "Yeah, okay."

Belatedly, I realize what she was actually asking. The senior trip debauchery is legendary, and she was asking if I partook.

For a split second, I indulge the idea of telling her I drank tequila, went skinny-dipping, and then had sex with Holden Adams.

Would she even believe me? She'd probably consider it a joke. Even if she did believe me, Maggie is notoriously terrible at keeping secrets. She spoils group gifts for our parents every year.

"I think he likes you."

My head snaps to the side. "What?"

"Harrison Baker. I think he likes you."

"He was just being nice." I fall back on my standard answer, smothering the disappointment Maggie wasn't talking about a different *he*.

"He came over here, Cassia."

"So did Holden."

"Yeah, but he's *Holden*."

I have no idea what that means, but I think it's a slight at me. As in, Holden would never be interested in me, but Harrison might be.

"Let's go, girls!" I turn around to see my parents, Sally, Regan, and the twins, have all piled into the minivan. I climb into the way back and move a few toys off the seat before buckling in. My dad pulls out of the lot, and I keep my gaze firmly fixed on the road ahead, not the group gathered in the corner of the parking lot.

It was fleeting between us. Temporary. I knew that all along.

But I admit to myself, just for a moment, that I wanted it to be more. Want it to happen again.

———

"This tastes funny." Sydney holds a spoon out to me.

I take a bite of the chocolate chip cookie dough she's offering and chew. Swallow. "Did you add salt?"

"I think so?"

"Syd," I groan.

Sydney is usually as fastidious as I am. But when it comes to certain things—namely baking—she's totally scatterbrained.

"I'm sure they'll be fine."

I'm less confident, but I continue rolling balls of dough anyway. The trays of cookies get slid into the oven and then we end up at the kitchen counter, sipping on the hot chocolate Sydney made when I first arrived. I lasted about an hour amidst the chaos at my house, unpacking and finishing one assignment that's due tomorrow, before crossing the street.

"So…was it wild?" she asks.

I've been preoccupied with rescuing her baking project since I crossed the street to her house an hour ago. We haven't discussed the senior trip beyond the few texts we exchanged while I was gone.

"It was different," I answer. "It felt grown up, you know?"

Sydney bobs her head. This feels very different than talking about the senior trip with Maggie. Sydney is more similar to me. She's not expecting any crazy stories and she would be shocked to hear I have any.

"I roomed with McKenzie Howard, so that was interesting."

"Was she nice?"

"Yeah. I think so. She wasn't trying to become best friends, but she didn't ignore me or anything."

"So you guys talked?"

"*Do you want to use the bathroom first?* Was most of it."

Sydney laughs. "How was the city?"

"It was a little overwhelming. But energetic. It was like you stand there and can just soak it all in." I fill her in on all the sights we saw and all the places we went to, then admit, "I played Truth or Dare."

"Really?" Sydney's tone is a mixture of shocked and excited.

"Yeah. Finn invited me when he came by the room to get McKenzie."

"Finn? Was Holden there?"

"Uh, yeah. He was."

"He wasn't rude to you, was he? I know you guys are…"

Sydney's voice trails. This is the closest she's gotten to addressing the rift between me and Holden in years, and it's incredibly ironic it's happening now.

"No. He wasn't rude."

That's all I say, and I watch Sydney forcibly shove down her curiosity. I show her some photos I took around the city and brainstorm a plan regarding another hang out with Graham until the cookies are done. By the time they're cooled, it's dinner time.

"I should head home. Dad wants to look over my college essay tonight." I finally managed to finish a draft right before leaving on the senior trip.

Sadness crosses Sydney's face like a cloud passing in front of the sun, the same expression she wears every time that the topic of college comes up. I nudge her shoulder. "It's still a year away."

"Eight months," she grumbles.

I haven't asked—and she hasn't said—but I know Sydney's

apprehension when it comes to the topic of college isn't just because of me.

Holden leaving will mean she's all alone. Their dad's schedule has gotten busier and busier in recent years. I've barely seen Mr. Adams in months. I have no idea if he plans to be home with Sydney once Holden leaves, and I'm not sure she knows either. It's not my place to ask.

Our goodbye hug is tighter than usual before I grab the plate of cookies and head for the front door. I slip on my jacket and step out onto the front porch, pulling the door shut behind me.

I turn and freeze. "Oh. Hi."

"Hey." As per usual, Holden meets my awkwardness with ease. He leans against the railing that runs the length of the stairs, totally relaxed.

"I was just, um, cookies." I swallow. Blush. "Sydney and I made cookies."

Holden smiles. "You're acting weird."

"No, I'm not." I can't keep eye contact through the three words.

He takes another step up the stairs, which doesn't help. Holden is closer now. Even more consuming. "Yeah, you are." He sounds amused about it, and I have no idea what to make of it.

"I…I just came to see Sydney. I don't want you to think *I think* things have changed between us. I know they haven't."

"You were right, when you said I avoid commitment."

"I know," I blurt.

He laughs. Slowly, the amusement slips away. "Probably have my mom to blame."

I still. Sydney has never, not once, mentioned her mom to me. My mother was the one who told me their mom left when Holden was five and Sydney was four. She also warned me it was a sensitive topic, so I've never asked. Never brought it up.

Holden takes another step. Now he's less than a foot away.

"Eighth grade? Ginny's Halloween party? I didn't mean to kiss you. I'd never kissed a girl before." He clears his throat, and it's the closest I've seen Holden to being embarrassed.

I don't think he meant to say that—to admit that to me.

"Anyway, I just, I knew I wasn't the right guy for you. I knew letting you think we possibly had that sort of future would just hurt you more in the end. So I thought avoiding you for a while would help draw boundaries. I didn't think—I didn't mean for it to totally end our friendship. But we started high school and had different friends. And then Sydney was a freshman, and you two were always together. You seemed happy. It didn't seem like you were stuck in the past. I had no idea it still bothered you until last night."

"I was closer with you than Sydney back then. You kissed me and then acted like I was invisible. *Of course* it bothered me, Holden."

"I'm sorry, Cassia. Truly." His blue eyes are sincere. I know he means the words, but they're not enough to completely wash away years of resentment.

"Thanks for…explaining," I say awkwardly.

Holden inhales. "Do you—do you regret last night?"

I'm thrown by the fact he's bringing it up. I thought what happened in his hotel room would stay in New York, never to be discussed again. I was banking on it, actually. Holden bringing it up is unexpected.

It makes me wonder if *he* regrets it. Is he worried I'll tell someone? That Sydney will find out?

"No." I answer honestly. "I don't regret it."

He exhales. "Okay. Good."

"Do, um, do you?"

"Nope." He grins, unexpectedly. "I enjoyed it."

Heat floods my cheeks, a mixture of embarrassment and pleasure fueling the blush. I was worried he was too busy treating me with kid gloves. "Me too."

"I know. I felt you come on my cock." He says the sentence casually, but I'm certain my face must be flaming red. It was one thing to hear him talk dirty in a hotel room when it was the middle of the night. His front porch in broad daylight is very different.

Holden smirks, confirming my suspicion my complexion resembles a tomato. He takes the last step, putting us at the same level, then tugs at a loose piece of my hair. His smile transforms from mocking to sweet as he tucks it behind one ear. "You look beautiful when you blush," he tells me, then keeps walking.

I hear the front door open and close, and know I'm standing on his porch alone now. My blood is buzzing, and my stomach is giddy.

Getting under Holden to get over him? Undoubtedly the worst idea I've ever had. Any closure between us feels non-existent.

I'm totally screwed.

My arms burn but I keep forcing them to move. Up. Down. Up. Down. It feels like it takes hours to reach fifty.

Finally, I drop the bar with a *clang* and sit up. I drink some water and wipe my face with a towel, rubbing away the sweat until my breathing evens. Around me, guys are starting to stand and head for the locker room.

Thursdays are our easiest day. We have a team meeting to go over specific strategies for tomorrow's opponent and then a weight session. Tomorrow's game is against Covington, one of our main rivals. The meeting lasted later than usual, then we still had weights.

I stand and head for the hallway. Finn meets me in the middle of the weight room and punches my bicep. "Fellini's?" he asks.

The local pizza parlor is a popular hangout after practice. I nod, my stomach grumbling.

I shower and change, remembering to text Sydney, letting her know I won't be home for dinner before I leave the gym. We eat separately most nights, especially now that basketball has started and taken over most of my schedule.

Most of the team is already gathered just inside the door when I arrive at Fellini's. It's seat yourself, so they're waiting for me. I stop next to Finn and glance around, looking for a couple of empty tables. And *freeze.*

I'm totally immobile and it's involuntary—completely outside my control. I just...can't move. Blinking, but can't process what my eyes are seeing.

Betrayal slashes my chest, hot and harsh.

"Adams?" Finn asks. "What are you—oh." He laughs. "Dude, she's a junior. She was going to start dating eventually. And that's the honor club guy. I doubt he's going to get her into hard drugs or knock her up."

I manage a grunt in response. Finn thinks I'm focused on Sydney, who's sitting in a booth next to Graham chatting away. I'm not. I'm looking at the girl with a brown ponytail and a *Pembrooke Animal Shelter* sweatshirt sitting across from my sister. Sitting *next to* Harrison Baker.

Cassia is on a double date with another guy—and my sister.

I can't figure out the flare in my chest, can't rationalize why I want to walk over and kiss her. Mark my territory and make it clear she's off-limits.

I've slept with several girls. Not as many as the school gossip mill speculates about, but she wasn't my first—the way I was hers.

That's the only reason I can think of to justify the way blood is whooshing in my ears. I want to look away, but I physically can't. It's like driving by a car crash. There's some morbid fascination, except the only person I'm hurting is myself. Everyone around me is oblivious to the hot spike of anger in my chest.

"Wanna go over there and mess with him?" Finn asks.

I clench my jaw and finally jerk my gaze away. "No."

I'm not worried about Graham. Between the talk I had with him at his so-called study party and the fact he seems to be every bit the nice guy he acts like, he's not a threat. I want Sydney to have fun. To branch out.

I just don't want Cassia to have any part of that growth if it involves other guys.

We end up sitting across the restaurant from the booth where Sydney, Graham, Cassia, and Harrison are sitting. I'd have to crane my neck to the side to catch a glimpse, and it's a good deterrent.

Mark ends up sitting next to me. "You okay?" he asks me quietly.

I glance at him. "Of course."

"It's not just Baker. I've heard other guys talk about her."

My look turns into more of a glare. "I don't know what you're talking about. I'm thinking about the scouts coming tomorrow."

He nods, but it's more of an *I'll drop it* than an *I believe you* gesture. As far as I know, Finn has always been oblivious to my feelings for Cassia, but Mark doesn't miss much. I saw him glancing between us at the pool last weekend.

Conversation about tomorrow's game dominates the rest of dinner. As soon as the last slice is finished, I announce I'm leaving, making up an assignment as an excuse.

I'm eager to get out of here. To clear my head. Maybe I should text Grace, but I doubt I actually will. As much as I want to wash away the memory of me and Cassia right now, I know it will haunt me for a long time.

I shouldn't have slept with her. I don't regret it, but it was a mistake. It's made the possessiveness I've always felt toward her a million times worse.

"You're not actually worried about Covington, are you?" Finn asks. "You didn't say much at dinner."

"No," I reply as we walk toward the door. "I'm not worried."

I *wish* basketball was the source of my anxiety right now. Covington is one of the biggest threats to our undefeated season and playoff rankings. To my chances of getting a scholarship. A bunch of scouts will be at the game tomorrow night.

But right now, my head is too full of Cassia to care if we lose tomorrow. And that freaks me the fuck out. When did she start to affect me more than basketball?

"Holden!"

I swear under my breath before pausing. If it was anyone else besides Sydney, I would keep walking and pretend I hadn't heard her. But I know it's not easy for Sydney, being my sister. I know girls have tried to befriend her in an attempt to get closer to me.

Whenever I'm with friends and see her—which isn't very often, since Sydney mostly hangs out at home or in the school's theater department—I always make a point to acknowledge her.

I don't want anyone thinking I'd tolerate any disrespect toward my sister, especially if I go anywhere next year and I'm not around.

Sydney is walking straight toward me. Graham is right behind her, with Cassia and Harrison a few feet behind. My hands form fists, then relax. I keep my gaze on Sydney as they approach. She has her coat on, so they must have just finished eating.

If I'd allowed myself to look over there once during dinner, I could have timed this better. Left sooner or later. Instead, it couldn't be worse. I'm stuck acknowledging them. Interacting with them.

"Hey, Syd."

My sister is smiling, her cheeks flushed and eyes bright. Despite my resentment of this outing, I feel myself smile in response to hers. Sydney looks happier than I've seen her in a long time.

Reluctantly, I glance at Graham. My mood improves further when I notice he's looking at me with obvious apprehension.

Finn chuckles under his breath beside me, probably noticing the same thing. "Hi, Graham."

"Hi." His response comes out as a squeaky syllable.

Mark muffles a laugh with a cough. "Haven't seen you all week, Cassia," he says. "One time hanging out with us was enough?"

Everyone looks at her, and I reluctantly do the same. Cassia glances away as soon as our eyes meet, a pink flush spreading across her cheeks.

She was already looking at me, and it eases a little of the tightness in my chest. At least she's not making googly eyes at Baker.

"I've just been busy," she says, twirling the end of her ponytail. "College applications and stuff, you know."

Another necessary reminder of why I've stayed away from Cassia—why I need to keep staying away. We're on very different paths. She'll have lots of options for college. I'll be lucky to have one next year.

"I'm headed out," I announce, more forcefully than I meant to.

"Dude, what the hell has gotten into you tonight?" Finn asks, chuffing my shoulder. "I've never seen you this eager to do homework before."

"You must be a good tutor," Harrison tells Cassia, laughing.

I hear him. Unfortunately, Sydney does too. She looks at Cassia, then glances at me. "Tutor?"

I tense. The last thing I need is for Sydney to start getting suspicious about me having feelings for her best friend. Or to start worrying I'm flunking out of high school again. As far as Sydney knows, Cassia and I haven't spent any time together alone in years.

"I just helped him with that one thing," Cassia says. "We should head out, right?"

Apparently, I'm not the only one more than ready to get out of here. Thankfully, Sydney drops the tutoring topic as we walk outside.

There's a sharp chill to the air, the closest to winter's bite we've gotten this fall. Every inhale burns my lungs and I can see my breath when I exhale.

"You good to get home, Sydney?" I ask.

Sydney glances at Graham.

"I can drive you," he offers.

It's obviously what she was hoping for, based on her broad smile, so I keep my mouth shut. I'm not expecting for Sydney to look to Cassia next.

"Can you give Cassia a ride?" she asks me.

I stiffen. It's obvious Sydney wants to be alone with Graham. But I assumed Cassia had driven here herself or came with Harrison.

"I drove," Harrison states. "I don't mind dropping you off."

Cassia smiles at him. My jaw clenches. Tightly enough, it's painful despite how numb my face is, thanks to the outside temperature.

"Thanks for offering, but Holden is right across the street. I don't want you to have to go out of your way."

It's obvious to everyone Harrison wouldn't consider it to be any sort of inconvenience, but Cassia turns and walks toward me before he can say a word. "Ready?"

"Yeah."

She chose me over him.

I'm not expecting for that to matter to me the way it does. There are plenty of girls who have ignored other guys in favor of getting my attention, as arrogant as that sounds. In the past, I've found it amusing or irritating, depending on my mood. It's never incited this warm feeling in my chest before.

I say goodbye to the guys and give Graham a glare that conveys Sydney better make it home safely. It's a ten-minute drive to our house from Fellini's, so I'll know if he makes any detours.

Cassia follows me down the street toward my truck. The farther we get from our friends, the tenser the silence between us becomes. The easier it is to imagine we were just the ones having dinner together.

I make it one block before glancing at her. Cassia's arms are wrapped around her midsection. She's wearing a sweatshirt but no jacket over it.

Impulsively, I shrug mine off. It's my letterman jacket, which I hardly ever wear. We're supposed to have them on for game days, though, so I grabbed it from my locker after I showered. It's not that warm, but better than nothing.

Without saying a word, I drape it over her shoulders. She looks over at me, then sinks her teeth into her bottom lip. It's the worst possible thing she could do because I can't think about anything except seeing her do that same thing when I was buried inside her.

"Thanks."

I nod as we continue walking.

"You're acting weird."

An involuntary smile tugs at my lips as she parrots the words I told her last week on my front porch. "I'm just…we're playing a rival tomorrow."

"I know. Covington, right?"

I glance at her, surprised. "How did you know?"

She shrugs, tugging my jacket closer around her. It looks good on her. Really good. I look down at the sidewalk, trying to think about something else.

"My dad follows the team pretty closely," Cassia says after a beat of silence. "It's sort of our thing, if I'm up before he leaves for work. Sometimes I feel guilty for not playing in high school. I guess it's my way of making up for it."

I hesitate before speaking. For one, I'm processing the fact that Cassia and her father follow my team. That it's their *thing*. Also, the last time the topic of her not playing high school ball came up, it wasn't exactly a relaxed conversation. I'm treading carefully.

"I'm sure your dad wouldn't want you to feel guilty," I finally say. "If you didn't want to play, you didn't want to play."

"I started playing because of you," she states. "So…in high school…there didn't seem like much of a point anymore."

I steal a glance at her. Cassia is staring straight ahead, obviously not interested in discussing the topic any further.

"You're not in a big rush to get back, right?" she asks.

"Uh…" I'm not sure how to answer. I was in a hurry to leave Fellini's. Now that it's just the two of us, I have no sense of urgency, honestly.

"I kind of want a waffle."

"You and Baker didn't split a dessert?" I huff a breath as soon as the question is out, thoroughly annoyed with myself for bringing him up.

"I voted no on dessert. I was sick of third-wheeling."

"It looked more like a double date."

Her eyebrows pull together as she stares at me. "I went to Fellini's with Sydney and Graham right after school. There weren't any open tables. Harrison was already there with some of his teammates and invited us to sit with them. They left before us and he stayed."

I swallow. *Fuck.* I'm relieved. I'm worried by *how* relieved I am.

"And even if I was out on a date with him, you have no right to—"

I kiss her, cutting off the rest of her indignation. Cassia freezes. Familiar electricity arcs between us, snapping and crackling with its potency and power.

When Cassia starts kissing me back, I groan. Wrap my arms around her and haul her closer to my body, right here on the sidewalk.

I tighten my grip on her jacket—my jacket—and that knowledge mixes with the desire circulating through my body. I've never kissed a girl wearing my clothes before. She was wearing my sweatshirt the first time we got off together in my driveway. It added an extra layer of intimacy then, and it does the same now. There's never been another girl I *wanted* to wear my clothes before. Just her.

She's so responsive, so eager. I just know, somehow, that it wouldn't feel like this with anyone else. I knew it when I kissed her in eighth grade, and I feel the same way now.

Her expression is dazed when we separate. It makes me want to start kissing her all over again, to keep that expression on her face and know that I was the one who put it there. I wait for the questions. The *What did that mean?* and *Why did you do that?*

Instead, she simply smiles. "Is that a yes on the waffle?"

I grab her hand and pull her toward the waffle place. It's warm inside and smells incredible. I haven't been here since last winter. There's a young family sitting by the windows, but the shop is otherwise empty.

Cassia walks right up to the counter and rattles off her order.

I raise my eyebrows when she looks to me. "You come here a lot?"

"It's on all my siblings' chore charts as a reward. So…yes."

I shake my head at that, marveling over just how different our families are before ordering one of their premade options.

Cassia argues when I go to pay, but I elbow her out of the way. Thanks to the illicit Friday night fights I spent the last couple of months participating in, I've got a decent amount of money set aside. And it occurs to me, as I hand my card over, that there's nothing I'd rather spend it on than her.

"I'm super excited for the game tomorrow night." It's not until the girl working the register says that while handing back my card that I aim any focus at her. She's on the younger side, probably a freshman or a sophomore. "I traded shifts just so I could go."

"It should be a good game," I say.

"You're playing so well this season. It's amazing to watch."

I'm no stranger to flirting. There's always been a reliable thrill to saying something suggestive or teasing to a girl. It's a dance, a tease, a push and pull. But all I'm feeling now is uncomfortable. There's nothing wrong with what she's saying, but the tone is unmistakable. And it feels wrong that she's talking that way to me in front of Cassia.

"Thanks," I reply, tucking my card back into my wallet.

I know this isn't a date and I know Cassia knows it isn't a date, but that's exactly what I assume it would look like to anyone else.

Our waffles are prepared and handed to us, along with a few napkins. Cassia heads for one of the tables, and I follow her over.

She dives into the dessert immediately. I can't help but smile, my bad mood totally forgotten, as I watch her annihilate the mound of waffle and ice cream. Some whipped cream gets left in the corner of her mouth. I want to lean over and wipe it away, but I pass her a napkin instead.

The second napkin in the stack has a number scrawled on it.

Cassia glances at the series of neatly written digits. Scoffs. "I guess she assumed I was your sister."

I clench my jaw, tempted to walk back over to the counter and ask for a new stack of napkins. I'm irritated by her presumptuousness.

But I don't hate the way Cassia is close to snapping her plastic spoon. Another girl giving me her number bothers Cassia, and I like the glimpse of possessiveness far more than I should.

"You didn't tell Sydney about me tutoring you."

I smirk. "I wrote the paper while you did your math homework. You call that tutoring?"

Cassia rolls her eyes. "I made suggestions."

"You didn't tell her either."

"I know." She plays with her spoon, dragging it through the small pool of chocolate that's all that remains of her dessert. I take the final bite of mine. "I was worried she'd think it meant something."

"Me almost failing history?"

"Yep." She smiles.

"I never thanked you properly."

"For what?"

"Helping me with that paper."

Her eyebrows rise. "You said you wrote it yourself."

"I did. But you…I wasn't going to waste your time."

Cassia studies me for a minute, then nods.

"There are some scouts coming to tomorrow's game." I share the information unprompted, which is unheard of for me. For some reason, there's an urge to share with her. To explain what I'm thinking and feeling.

"For schools you'd consider?"

"Yeah. One of them is my top choice."

"Top choice, huh?"

"I mean, they have a good program. I have a shot of getting in, Coach thinks."

"Which school?"

"Richmond."

She looks away. "In Vermont?"

"Right."

"That's on my list."

I stare at her. The possibility of us ending up at the same university has never occurred to me. "They have a good pre-vet program?"

"It's decent. I can take the classes I need pretty much anywhere."

The bell above the door rings. A large family walks into the store. Cassia consolidates her trash but leaves the napkins untouched. "You ready to go?"

"Yeah," I reply, doing the same with my bowl and spoon.

We stand and head for the door. I make sure Cassia sees me throw away all the napkins along with the rest of my trash.

My truck is parked another block down the street. I think of the trip to Graham's study party as we climb in the cab, the first and only other time Cassia has ridden next to me. It felt like we were alone then.

We *actually* are now. Rather than awkward, the silence sounds like possibilities. She hasn't brought up me kissing her on the sidewalk since it happened.

I war with myself as I pull out of the spot and start driving in the direction of our shared street. Should I mention it? Pretend it never happened? I had no plan for this encounter. I wasn't expecting to see her at Fellini's, and I definitely wasn't expecting to drive her home, just the two of us.

In contrast to my indecision, Cassia seems relaxed. She reclines against the seat and tucks one leg under the other.

Still wearing my varsity jacket, she's difficult to look away from. I like her like this. Wearing my clothes in my truck. Innocent and sexy. Familiar and new.

I stop at a red light. Fiddle with the heat and some music, so we're warm and not sitting in silence.

I tend to get lost in my own head while I'm driving. It's an easy way to think things through without overanalyzing them. But now, with her, I can't consider anything else.

"Can we do it again?" Cassia asks suddenly, right after I turn onto our street.

I glance over. "What?"

"Um, sex." The faint glow of the streetlights is enough to illuminate her blushing. "Can we have sex again sometime?"

I pull into my driveway and park, mind spinning.

"Nevermind." The momentary pause is all it takes for her to rethink things. "Forget it."

I turn off the ignition at the same second her seatbelt clicks. I look over to see her reaching for the door handle.

"Cassia." She keeps reaching, so I lean over and grab her hand. Then her chin, forcing her to look at me. "Yes."

"You don't have to say that," she whispers. "I just…last time was…I was so nervous." Cassia tries to look away, but I don't let her. "It felt really good, but I want to know what it's like when I know what to expect and you're not worried about hurting me…"

I brush her bottom lip with my thumb. "You don't have to convince me, flower. I'm fully on board, trust me." I'm getting hard at just the suggestion, but I don't go into that level of detail.

"I'm not expecting anything to change between us, Holden. If you're worried about that. We're not friends anymore. I know you don't want a relationship. I just…there's no other guy I trust to…"

"Make you come?"

She scoffs but doesn't dispute it. Trust feels especially important now that I know the truth behind her experience. I'm not just the guy she trusts. I'm the *only* guy who's touched her intimately.

Silence stretches between us. Silence with an *agreement*.

"So were you thinking a code word or a schedule or…"

Cassia rolls her eyes. "I was thinking I sleep over at your house every Friday night."

Today is Thursday, which means she's talking about tomorrow.

I've never scheduled sex. Never expected sex. It's always just happened. Planning it out is an idea I thought I'd hate, like a relationship. Like a box you're stuck inside. But instead…I'm excited. Anticipation is thrumming inside me, knowing that sex will happen between us again.

"Okay?"

"Yeah?" She looks excited, and it twists my insides further.

Does she care it's me, or is she just looking for a way to get off? I should hope it's the latter. That's always what I've been looking for when it comes to sex.

But instead, I'll be disappointed if it's not the former.

"Yeah."

"Okay. Night."

She lingers for a minute, and I consider kissing her again. But my thoughts are already a snarled mess. I thought once would be it for us. Not because I wanted it to be, but because that seemed like the reality of our past and our futures.

Cassia climbs out of the cab, giving me a small smile before shutting the door. I watch in the rearview mirror as she crosses the street and enters her house, still warring with myself.

I always viewed staying away from Cassia as non-negotiable. Also in her best interest.

But something leaped in my chest when she asked about us having sex again. Something more than just arousal or anticipation.

And I consider, for the first time, that maybe Cassia isn't the only one who will get hurt if things between us end badly.

CHAPTER SIXTEEN

CASSIA

The quiet murmur of voices comes from the kitchen when I walk inside the Adamses' house on Friday night. It's unexpected. Usually when I come over, Sydney is the only one home.

"Hello?" I call out. Maybe Sydney is talking to her dad? Or Graham? He's not supposed to come over until later.

As much as I like Graham, I'm dreading it. If not for the late-night plans I made, I would have come up with an excuse not to come over.

I know Sydney is trying to include me. She's not the kind of friend who would ever abandon you for a guy, especially not as part of a tradition we've had for years. I think she's also nervous about being alone with her crush.

"Kitchen, Cas!" Sydney calls.

I walk past the stairs and through the living room into the kitchen. Holden is leaning against the sink, arms crossed and smirking.

I focus on him first, my gaze sweeping over the sweatpants and t-shirt he's wearing. His hair is damp from the shower he must have taken after the game against Covington earlier.

Sydney is sitting on one of the stools at the kitchen counter, also dressed casually. I watch as she tugs at a hole in the knee of the yoga pants she's wearing.

"Uh, what's going on?" I ask, glancing between the two of them.

Sydney looks at me, a serious expression on her face. "Is Holden failing?"

Out of the periphery of my eye, I watch Holden roll his eyes and tuck his hands behind his head as he leans back against the edge of the counter. His shirt rides up, providing a very distracting view.

She takes my silent appreciation the wrong way. "Oh my God, he is."

"No. *No.* I mean, I don't think so." I glance at Holden. "Are you?"

"No!" His tone is exasperated as his arms fall back to his sides. "I'm tired from the game earlier, so I'm not going to Grace's party tonight. Sydney seems to think that means I'm either sick or flunking high school. She's settled on the latter, thanks to Baker's big mouth."

"Oh," I say. He's not going to Grace's party tonight?

I've spent all day replaying our conversation in his car last night. Preparing for the possibility he could change his mind while surrounded by hot girls and alcohol. Second-guessing ever asking him in the first place.

"You're hardly ever home," Sydney says. "And *never* on Friday nights."

Holden shrugs and takes a sip from the open Gatorade on the counter.

"Is this about Graham coming over? Because—"

He coughs a laugh. "Syd, I just want a quiet night. Stop reading into it."

Sydney glances at me. I avoid her gaze, hoping she'll drop it. I want Holden to stay, not only because of what I'm hoping will take place tonight, but because it will feel less like I'm third-wheeling.

Harrison joining us at Fellini's yesterday afternoon helped with that, but made it awkward in other ways. Namely, I wasn't quite sure what to say to him. I'm not worried about that with Holden. I mean, I am, but it's more in the context of being worried about saying too much. I'm not at a loss of what common ground to find in the first place.

"Cassia will be here. I don't need you to look out for me."

"Uh-huh. I'm sure Cassia is a very capable chaperone," Holden replies.

I roll my eyes at that, and he smirks in response.

"But for the millionth time, me staying home has nothing to do with you or with Graham."

He doesn't include me on the list, I notice. Probably because Sydney has no reason to think anything Holden does or doesn't do would involve me. But I read into it anyway.

Holden pulls his phone out of his pocket and glances at the screen. "See you guys later," he says, grabbing his Gatorade and leaving the kitchen.

———

I'm sitting on the couch, alone, almost as far away as possible from Sydney and Graham's whispering, when Holden walks back downstairs. It's been total silence upstairs since he left the kitchen a couple of hours ago. Part of me was wondering if he went out after all, without saying anything.

Based on how disheveled his hair is, I think he was sleeping.

He runs his hand through it again as he approaches the couch, smoothing some of the disarray.

Holden grins when he sees how I'm huddled at one end of the couch, then plops down right beside me, so close our arms brush. My cheeks flare pink, and I hope it's dark enough in here he can't tell.

All I can think about is the last time the two of us were on this couch together.

"What are you guys watching?" he whispers to me.

"I forget," I reply. "One of the goblin movies?"

He glances at me, one corner of his mouth curling up in a smile. "Lord of the Rings?"

"I guess? I didn't pick it. Graham would know." I glance toward the kitchen. "He and Sydney paused the movie a couple of minutes ago to make popcorn."

"Ah." He leans back, getting comfortable. I resist the urge to lean closer. We agreed to sex, not snuggling.

When I glance over, he's looking at me. It's a searching gaze. He's looking at me like it's the first time he's seeing me.

"Hi," I whisper.

He smiles. "Hi."

"Congrats. I saw you won."

"Yeah. Thanks." His fingers weave through the ends of my hair, combing through the strands falling across his shoulder. I tilt my head, allowing him more access.

I want to ask him why he's here. What made him decide to stay home instead of going to a party tonight like usual. But I'm worried it might fracture this moment, might not be an answer I'm hoping for, so I stay silent.

"You ever been to a game?"

I scan his expression, trying to read the subtext of his question in the curves and angles of his face. "Last season, I went to a couple."

All I get in response is a vague hum. Was that his way of asking me to come? I know Sydney goes to the ones she can, but I've always avoided them, aside from the few times she begged me to join.

The two I went to last season were uncomfortable for me. I already admitted I associate him with the sport. Connecting the lines between that and me not going seems simple, but he still asked.

"Are you cold?" Before I can answer, Holden is pulling an afghan off the back of the couch and draping it over my legs.

I wasn't cold, but the weight of the soft blanket feels nice.

"Um, thanks."

"Uh-huh." There's a twinkle in his blue eyes, a glint that makes my heart race.

Sydney walks out of the kitchen holding a big bowl of popcorn, with Graham right behind her.

Surprisingly, neither of them comment on Holden's appearance or seem to notice how close we're sitting together. Graham greets Holden with a nervous smile. I guess the threat I overheard is still fresh in his mind.

Sydney and Graham settle back on the couch, and the movie starts to play again. I relax back against the cushions, shifting a little closer to Holden and hoping Sydney doesn't notice. She seems totally wrapped up in Graham, giggling at something he's showing her on his phone. I'm happy for her. Slightly resentful they picked a fantasy film and aren't even watching it. There's an African cats documentary I've been dying to watch.

A warm hand settles on my thigh, and thoughts of television selections are suddenly irrelevant.

I tense, then glance at Holden. He appears focused on the screen, but one corner of his mouth is lifted.

His hand moves upward, slowly, and I realize why he draped the blanket over me. Sydney giggles next to me, right as he reaches the waistband of my pajamas.

I inhale sharply, glancing back and forth between him and the screen. He looks totally focused on the movie, but one finger plays with the drawstring. Every nerve ending in my body seems to focus on that one spot.

Breathing becomes difficult. I have to remind myself to take each breath and then let it loose in a gush, a simple reflex becoming a chore. I feel like I'm a kid playing Hide and Seek, trying to stay quiet and not be found. The quieter and more inconspicuous I'm trying to be, the louder each exhale seems to sound.

Graham and Sydney are still whispering to each other, but Holden is totally silent. His fingers dip lower, tracing the inseam of my pants. They brush my clit, sending a bolt of electricity through my whole system.

I bite my bottom lip—hard—worried I'll accidentally make a sound otherwise.

I've spent all day anticipating tonight. There's already a frenzy built inside of me. Each teasing stroke of his fingers sends me closer to the edge. My heart races and keeping my breathing even is a struggle. I slip one of my hands under the blanket and grab his, stilling his movements.

Holden finally looks away from the screen, at me. *I'm close*, I mouth. Heat flares in his eyes, turning them almost navy.

I'm expecting for him to pull his hand away, but he doesn't. We keep holding hands under the blanket. His thumb starts drawing circles on the back of my hand. That's all I focus on.

Not the movie playing.

Not Sydney giggling.

Just those circles.

———

When my eyes open, I'm on the air mattress. I sit up straight and glance around, startled. The last thing I remember is sitting on the couch.

Sydney is in her bed, sprawled out like usual. I scramble for my phone, finding it set next to the air mattress. It's just after one in the morning. Last I recall in the living room, it was ten something. I fell asleep, something I struggle to do under the best of circumstances. Passing out early and not in a bed is unheard of for me.

I glance at Sydney again before crawling out of bed.

I'm annoyed with myself. Disappointed. I spent all day anticipating tonight.

Once I'm in the hallway, I hesitate outside his door. Maybe he decided to go out after all. Maybe he's asleep. I have no sense of when the movie ended or when Graham left.

My hand closes around the knob and turns. Holden's room is dark; the only illumination is the moonlight streaming in through the gap in the curtains. I scan the room and my focus lands on the bed. There's a large lump in the middle.

I close the door and tiptoe closer.

"Holden?" I whisper.

He sits up. "Cassia?"

"Sorry. Did I wake you up?"

"No." A pause, where I hover and he stares. "Come here."

I walk across the cold hardwood until I reach the edge of his bed. He holds up the edge of the covers and I slip inside, sighing when the heat envelops me. His sheets smell like laundry detergent and cinnamon. I inhale deeply and snuggle against the soft cotton.

"I didn't mean to fall asleep."

"I don't blame you. The movie was terrible."

"Pretty sure you were the only one watching."

His chuckle is low. I feel it as much as I hear it. "Yeah."

"I'm glad you stayed home tonight." I second-guess the words as soon as they're out. I don't want him to think it's what I expect. Or that it matters to me he chose to. It's just another Friday night, but it feels entirely different.

Holden doesn't answer. He pulls me on top of him and kisses me. I sink into it, into him. This feels different from the hotel. More purposeful, more permanent.

We kiss and kiss. I get lost in the sensation, swimming through the depths of what it feels like to kiss Holden. I try to memorize it, to imprint every touch.

Our hands begin to wander. Mine slide lower and lower, tracing every dip and valley. All he's wearing is a pair of boxers. It's easy to slip inside of them and grip his erection. My boldness surprises me, and I think it catches him off guard too.

Holden hisses when I grip his cock. "*Fuck*, Cassia."

His breathing grows harsh and fast. Ragged, just like mine. I keep stroking, watching the pleasure play out on his face.

"We don't have to do this."

"Do you not want to?" I ask, worried he's changed his mind.

He laughs, low and unamused. "Of course I want to."

Holden rolls so he's above me and kisses me again. He doesn't seem in any hurry to skip to the sex. He kisses me like it's the destination instead of the journey. Like it's a privilege instead of an obligation.

It makes me think of his confession—that I was his first kiss.

He has all of my firsts.

At least I have one of his.

I close my eyes and kiss him back between ragged breaths. I let myself pretend this means something to him. That *I* mean something to him.

Most of the time, I'm careful to keep a close grip on reality. It's easier to avoid disappointment if you stick to what you know for sure. But I let myself drift, just for now. I pretend. I let my mind warp the situation into exactly what I want it to mean.

The longer we kiss, the more I experiment. I tug his bottom lip between my teeth. Suck on his tongue. Holden grinds his hips into mine.

"These fucking shorts." His hand fists the fabric as his mouth moves to my neck. "Drive me fucking crazy."

"Take them off."

"So impatient." His mouth travels lower, kissing a line across my collarbone. I arch against him, pressing our bodies as close together as possible. My body throbs, craving his attention.

There's a hum in my blood, a thrill skipping across my skin. Anticipation floods my system like an addictive drug. We're both breathing heavily, our mouths so close together the same air is being exchanged.

"Please," I whisper. My heartbeat is an impatient thrum, eager to have him inside of me. To be connected, not just touching.

His hand runs up my thigh and between my legs, slipping beneath the strip of wet lace I'm wearing beneath my sleep shorts. I left my clothes in his bathroom the last time we hooked up, mostly because they were damp and smelled like chlorine, but also because I was wearing comfortable cotton briefs that didn't add much to the moment.

I planned ahead tonight, knowing what was going to happen, wearing a pink thong that I bought at the mall last summer on a whim. This is the first time I've worn the lacy underwear with the intention of anyone else seeing them. Usually they're pulled out on days I need an extra confidence boost or a lack of panty lines.

One of his fingers sinks inside me. I moan and he groans.

"You're so wet."

"Your fault," I whisper.

His laugh is quiet. I feel it more than I hear it before he moves away and opens the drawer next to his bed. It's filled with a random assortment of stuff: a composition notebook, a packet of tissues, some gum, and a box of condoms.

He sits up to tug down his boxers and rip open one of the foil packets. I bite my bottom lip as I watch him roll on the condom, warring with my riotous emotions.

Of course he has condoms in his bedroom. This moment that feels so special to me is ordinary for him.

The more I get lost in this, the more it will hurt when it ends.

I'm chasing pleasure that I know will turn to pain.

I shouldn't have suggested this.

He shouldn't have agreed.

But I want it. So badly I can barely think straight. Call it lust or hormones or misplaced hope. But it feels like I'm in pain *now*, and he's what will bring relief.

Holden lies back down, holding his weight on his arms so he's hovering over me. I'm caged in by his body, and I've never felt safer.

"You good?"

"Yep." I run a hand down the side of his abdomen, exploring all the hot, hard skin above me.

"What's wrong?"

"Nothing." I lift my hips, trying to guide him inside me.

"Flower."

For some reason, the nickname draws tears to my eyes. I blink rapidly to chase the emotion away. "I'm fine. Just fuck me."

Holden laughs, but it's humorless. "Just *fuck you*? Maybe you should just buy a damn sex toy, Cassia. Is that all you're looking for? A way to get off?"

He moves, his arms lifting as he starts to shift away. I panic, wrapping my legs around his waist. His dick rubs right against my center, and the pleasure is overwhelming. Based on his expression, Holden is affected too.

"I want *you*, Holden," I tell him. "But I'm…nervous. I've thought about this all day and it's finally happening, and I just need it to *happen* so I can stop overthinking. You don't need to ease me into it." I swallow. "Just…just treat me like you would anyone else."

"I *can't*, Cassia. You're not anyone else. You think I fuck other girls in my bed?"

I say nothing. Because yeah, that's exactly what I thought.

Two firsts. Twice as many as I ever expected.

Holden sighs and drops his head so it rests in the crook of my neck. He's still supporting his weight, and I run my hands up his arms, marveling at the tendons and the muscles which are all sharply defined.

And then I feel him. He eases into me slowly but purposefully. I gasp at the intrusion. It still feels foreign, but there's no twinge of pain this time. I'm being stretched in a way that's satisfying instead of overwhelming.

He lifts his head. "Better?"

I roll my eyes. "You dick."

"Seems like you like my dick, flower."

Holden pulls out and then thrusts back inside. I can't contain the moan that slips out. Triumph flashes on his face. I tighten my inner muscles around his cock, and it quickly transforms into an expression of pleasure.

He grabs my knee and hooks it around his hip. I moan again

as he slips deeper inside me, hitting a spot that sends sparks skittering across my skin.

It's easier to find a rhythm this time, to meet each thrust and feel like I'm participating instead of just receiving. I clench around him every time he slides in fully, making him groan with each glide.

My world narrows down to Holden and the spot where we're connected. It's too much and not enough. I'm struggling to adjust and craving more.

Our mouths meet again. It's filthy and desperate. I spread my legs wider, savoring each slow drag and strong thrust. Any anxiety is slipping away, the hot wash of pleasure consuming everything else. He fucks me harder and deeper. The build inside me explodes, my inner muscles contracting around the hard length filling me.

"*Fuck.*" Holden's cock thickens and throbs, his eyebrows drawing together in an intense expression that borders on pain.

I relax against the soft mattress, watching him come. There's no guard on his face now, some combination of tenderness and satisfaction obviously displayed on his handsome features.

I run my hands over his back and into his hair, taking advantage of the final opportunity to touch him. Holden doesn't move away. I wait for the embarrassment or the shyness, but it doesn't appear.

He kisses me before rolling away and pulling off the condom. I don't move. My body feels boneless. Sated and sleepy.

But I force my eyes to stay open. Holden and I are already straddling a strange boundary thanks to our past friendship and how close I am to Sydney.

So I sit up and glance around, trying to locate my underwear and pajamas.

Holden lies down next to me, totally naked. My eyes skate

over every inch of him, soaking him in greedily, as if this is the last time I'll see him like this.

Maybe—probably, it is. His dark hair is messy—from my hands. The rows of abs that were just hovering above me are clenched and defined. My gaze moves lower, to the half-hard dick that was inside of me a couple of minutes ago.

He's ridiculously hot. The fuel for fantasies. And tonight, he was mine.

"What are you doing?" Holden tucks one arm behind his head. His bicep bulges and my throat goes dry. It feels like I'm becoming more attuned to him instead of less, which is not what was supposed to happen.

"Going to bed. I just need…" I spot my pink thong at the end of the bed and lean forward to grab it.

His free arm closes around my waist, pulling me back against him. I relax automatically, the smell of cinnamon reassuring and the heat of his skin relaxing.

"Stay," he whispers.

Smart is undoubtedly the adjective most people associate with me. It could be much worse. Of all the things you can be known for, being smart is better than most.

I might be book smart, but I think I'm lacking other forms of intelligence. Because I close my eyes and melt against the boy most likely to break my heart instead of inserting some distance.

This was only supposed to be about the physical. Giving Holden my body is much less risky than handing him my heart.

Can you choose who you fall for?

Or is it called falling because it's outside your control?

"Holden?"

"Yeah."

"Did you ever think about this—us—before last weekend?"

"Of course I did."

"What did you think?"

"I think that you're better off without me."

"Don't you think that's my choice to make?"

He's silent in response. Neither an agreement nor a dispute.

"When you thought about it, what was it like?"

"What do you mean?"

"People say fantasy doesn't live up to reality. So…I'm just wondering."

I'm glad I can't see his face and he can't see mine. It's much easier to make confessions or ask difficult questions under the cover of darkness.

"Wondering if you as a reality lived up to the fantasy?"

I can't see his expression, but it sounds like he's smiling.

"Yeah, I guess."

His lips brush my hair. "It was better."

I fall asleep with a smile on my face.

CHAPTER SEVENTEEN

HOLDEN

My dad yawns as he approaches. His shirt is on inside out and he's clutching the mug of steaming coffee like it's something precious.

When he's gone on a route, his sleep schedule is discombobulated. Returning home can involve a time change as well. Still, he does his best to be up when me and Sydney are, even if it means less sleep for him.

This is extreme, though. For both of us. I tossed and turned for an hour before getting out of bed and coming out to the driveway right as the sun rose.

"What's your read on this Graham guy?" he asks, then covers a yawn.

I grin as I dribble. "Sydney told you about him, huh?"

Last night, I went to Finn's place for an early celebration of Mark's eighteenth. I was wondering if Sydney might say anything when I was gone.

I'm not surprised, really. She's always been an open book with our dad. I'm the kid who keeps secrets.

My dad nods, then grimaces. "Sydney invited him over tonight."

"Graham is a good guy. A little nerdy, but nice."

He muffles his guffaw, but I don't miss it. It feels good, laughing with my dad out in the driveway. He's home for a little over a week. While I appreciate the freedom of having no parental supervision sometimes, I wish he was home for longer.

"What about you? Any girls catch your eye?"

My eyes flick across the street. It's involuntary. Startling. I don't think my dad notices, but internally, I'm reeling.

I've had sex with Cassia twice.

I've known her for over a decade.

Neither entirely explains how she's become a pivotal part of my world. Why she's the person I want to share good news with. Who makes bad moments feel better.

"I'm focused on basketball," I say instead.

It's true. I've made basketball a priority because it makes me happy. But it's gained a new importance this year, a fresh elevation.

"I spoke to Larry last week," my dad says. "Starting in May, I'll be cutting back. Shorter routes and longer breaks."

"You don't have to do that, Dad. Chances are, I won't get a scholarship. And even if I do, I don't have to take it."

"It wasn't a question, Holden. You're going to college, scholarship or not. We'll figure it out. That's part of being a parent—ensuring your kids have more opportunities than you did. It's an experience I want you to have."

I don't answer right away. We're dancing close to a topic we don't discuss—my mom.

She got pregnant with me in high school, then had Sydney just eleven months after I was born. I wasn't planned, and I'm pretty sure Sydney wasn't either. Our existence changed their lives. For the worse, even though I'm sure my dad would say for the better. He's done his best to compensate for our mom walking away, making do with the limited opportunities a lack of a college degree allows and working himself to the bone for the shipping company he still delivers for.

It's a large part of why Sydney and I have always gone out of our way to assure him we're fine with his long absences. And I know it's why my dad is so insistent on me going to college, even though it would make things easier for him and Sydney if I didn't.

"I talked to a scout after the Covington game," I state. "He said they might make an offer."

My dad looks elated. "Which school?"

"Richmond."

"That's amazing, Holden. Of course, if it doesn't work out, it'll just be their loss."

Something warm and soft swells in my chest. I'm not used to having these sorts of conversations with my dad. Usually, our discussions are a predictable back and forth. Him asking about my grades and groceries. Reminding me when Aunt Catherine is stopping by to spend a night with us. It's rare to delve deeper.

"Were you in love with Lana?" I haven't called her Mom since the day she left.

Sometimes my dad is hard to read. Right now, all I can see is shock. Shocked I brought her up. Shocked I asked about love. Just shock.

But then he answers without having to think about it much. "No."

"You weren't?" I'm surprised by his response and how certain it is, and I know it's reflected in my tone.

"Maybe I could have loved her. But no, I never did. She was an adventure. Excitement. You and Sydney came along. We could have grown into it. Instead, we grew apart." He sighs. "I wish it had worked, for you and Sydney. But for me? I think I always knew there was something missing. Probably more than you wanted to know."

He's wrong. It's exactly what I needed to know. I always assumed he and Lana were an epic love story with a sad ending. That they'd tried to make it work and failed spectacularly. Knowing it never was headed that way…it helps, actually.

"Thanks for telling me, Dad."

"I'll tell you anything, kiddo. Might not be what you want to hear, but…there's nothing I'll hide from you."

I smile. Shoot, and watch the ball sink with a swoosh.

"You hungry? I was going to make pancakes."

Suddenly, I'm starving. "Yeah. That sounds good."

He nods and smiles. We head toward the front porch, side by side. "So…who's the girl?"

"There's no girl."

My dad laughs. "Okay."

Sydney is already in the kitchen when we walk back inside the house. It turns into a lazy morning, typical for most families but unusual for us. We eat together. Clean up together. I help my dad with some repairs around the house while Sydney works on costumes for the spring play in the living room.

Around three, we start work on our version of Thanksgiving. Roast chicken instead of turkey. Baked potatoes instead of mashed ones. Barbeque sauce instead of cranberry sauce.

The doorbell rings while I'm cutting the ends off the green beans. Sydney goes to answer the door. When she returns, Cassia is right behind her.

I freeze for a second, soaking in her appearance. I saw her at school on Tuesday, but that was only a glimpse.

We haven't spoken since last Friday night. I woke up to an empty bed on Saturday morning, disappointed but not surprised.

Cassia has never given me the impression she's interested in anyone else knowing about us. I'm assuming that applies to my sister in particular.

I refocus on the green beans while Cassia exchanges pleasantries with my dad. She's carrying a pumpkin pie that her mom must have asked her to bring over.

Her conversation with my dad and Sydney seems to drag on forever. My dad is asking about her family, catching up on everything her siblings and parents have been up to during his latest trip. Sydney tells her about Graham's visit later and the costumes she finished.

I'm silent during the whole interaction. It's some form of torture, listening to Cassia talk and not reacting. Pretending like her presence has no effect on me.

I focus on each individual bean, trying to drown out the conversation.

"Holden?"

I glance up. "Yeah?"

Cassia is looking at me. So are Dad and Sydney.

"I was talking about that English assignment. Do you have the textbook?"

I stare at her for a second. We don't have English together. Don't have an English textbook.

Sydney laughs. "Come on, Cas. It's Thanksgiving. You'll be over here again before anything is due on Monday. And you know any teacher would give you an extension."

"Yeah, you're right."

"I have it," I blurt. "The textbook."

Cassia is looking for an excuse to talk to me alone, something I'm fully on board with. My dad will be home this weekend, the first weekend in many weekends. She won't be sleeping over, and there will be no opportunity to take advantage of her being across the hall.

I toss the rest of the green beans in the pan without bothering to trim the ends, then head for the stairs.

Steps follow me. Cassia's steps.

Once we're in my room, I turn. "We don't have English together. Or an English textbook, even."

"I know."

I wait for more of an explanation, but it doesn't come. And I don't need one. I've given up on fighting the pull toward her. It might last or fizzle. Be love or lust. I'm worried I could accurately predict each choice.

"Happy Thanksgiving."

She smiles. "Happy Thanksgiving." Cassia is wearing a dress with a sash.

I use the ribbon to pull her closer to me, so her lips are mere breaths away. "I wanted you to be in my bed when I woke up."

"I was worried Sydney might wake up."

"And you don't want her knowing about this."

Cassia's eyebrows rise. "I don't even know what *this* is."

I don't either.

I think about her constantly. I haven't been with another girl since she crawled into my lap in my driveway, weeks ago.

But all the reasons I decided to stay away in the first place still exist. I'm still selfish. She's still leaving for a brighter and bigger future.

I don't think love is supposed to hurt. To limit someone.

I don't *want* to love her if it will hurt her in the end.

So I step away, instead of closer. All of my school books are stacked on the desk. "You should take one of these. Dad and Sydney might notice."

Cassia nods, then reaches for the composition notebook next to the stack. "What about this? I can—"

I grab it before she can make contact. "This is for basketball."

"What? You record every box score?"

I don't answer. Don't lie.

The notebook I'm holding has everything to do with her and nothing to do with basketball. But that's the last thing I can tell her, when things are so uncertain between us.

"Here." I grab a random textbook and hand it to her. "Use this."

"Thanks." Sarcasm saturates the word, then she turns and walks out of my bedroom. I hear her steps echo down the stairs. Her goodbyes to my dad and Sydney.

When I return to the kitchen, my dad is the only one there. He's spinning the roast pan around and checking the temperature of the meat. "Sydney went over to the Nolans' for a bit."

I grunt an acknowledgment and head for the sink. There's a tall stack of dishes that's piled up from our cooking. I grab the sponge out from under the sink and start washing.

"It's Cassia Nolan, right?"

I still, my hands submerged in soapy water. "What?"

"She left with an Oceanography textbook, Holden. I'm thirty-six, not blind."

"It's just…it's not going anywhere."

Footsteps sound behind me as my dad walks over. He adds the meat thermometer to the pile of dirty dishes. "That's a damn shame. Because what you'd call nowhere? I'd say it looks like a place worth exploring."

Then he walks off, leaving me alone to question everything all over again.

CHAPTER EIGHTEEN

CASSIA

I 've never seen the main hallway as empty as it is right now. Staying after school on a Friday isn't a popular choice, unsurprisingly.

I shut my locker with a slam that echoes and head for the main doors, all of Mrs. Golden's advice whirling around in my head. I asked her to be my faculty advisor for my college applications. Her suggestions were useful. They're also stressing me out. They sound like more pressure. Everyone seems to expect perfection from me. Seems to assume I'll have no problem rising to the occasion and doing exactly what needs to be done.

Another figure appears up ahead, heading out toward the parking lot, same as me. I swallow a groan when I realize who it is.

Grace glances at me, her expression equally displeased. She waits until I reach her. We're an awkward amount of distance apart, where she has no choice but to stop and I have to hurry to close the space between us.

"Hi, Cassia."

"Hi, Grace."

I thought New York might have been the end of the forced pleasantries between us, but apparently not.

"Staying after?" She smirks a little, like it's a perceived weakness. I'm not sure what her point is. She's here too.

"Yeah. I had a meeting about college applications."

"Of course you did."

I say nothing. Non engagement has always been my preferred choice of tactic when it comes to Grace. If she wants to take subtle jabs at me, she can feel free.

"How are you? I haven't talked to you since the senior trip." There's a mix of annoyance and curiosity in Grace's voice. She obviously noticed Holden stayed behind with me.

I'm tempted to laugh. She's making it sound like us talking isn't the rare occurrence it is.

"I'm fine, thanks."

Grace stops just before we reach the double doors. "Look, Cassia. I know you're a nice person. So I just feel obligated to tell you...Holden will lose interest. You're his little sister's best friend. All innocent and sweet. You're a novelty, something a little different. But he'll get sick of you. A little friendly advice? Don't get too attached."

She follows the fake speech up with a sweet smile. Like she really only wants the best for me, and I might have no clue that Holden Adams is considered the school heartbreaker.

"I appreciate it," I say.

Grace smiles again, like she thinks that's all I'll say in response.

I smile back. Decide to abandon my non-engagement strategy. "A little friendly advice for *you*? Don't worry about my sex life. It makes you sound...attached."

Predictably, Grace's smile disappears, creasing into a scowl instead. Maybe she didn't think I'd ever call her out on her passive aggressive friendliness. Maybe she didn't actually think anything has ever happened between me and Holden. Either way, any forced niceties are officially over.

"Don't say I didn't warn you," she tells me before striding out into the parking lot.

I loiter in the lobby for a couple of minutes, hoping she'll be gone by the time I walk outside. Thankfully, she is. But there's a familiar truck parked near the entrance to the gymnasium. I veer course in that direction, walking along the concrete path and inside the set of double doors.

The rhythmic staccato of a bouncing basketball echoes as I walk into the gymnasium. It's a massive, empty space. Like a temple to five guys on a court.

Holden stands at the top of the key. Basketballs litter the honey-hued hardwood as he shoots over and over again. Shots bounce and roll, colliding like bowling pins knocking into each other.

I walk toward him slowly, studying the tense line of his shoulders and feeling the irritation radiating off him.

"Bad practice?"

He stills and spins, watching me walk toward him. "Bad day."

"Yeah. Me too."

Holden studies me. "Want to talk about it?"

"Not really." I hold out the Oceanography book I borrowed from him on Thanksgiving. "Here you go."

We haven't spoken all week. His dad is still in town, so I haven't been spending as much time over at the Adamses'. I want Sydney—and Holden—to have as much time with their dad as possible. And I'm perpetually confused about where Holden and I stand. Are we just sex? Does he want more? Do I want more? Should we try to salvage our friendship?

I miss him. Ever since that night in the kitchen where I stole a sip of beer from him, it feels like something permanently shifted between us. Like he finally noticed me again. It makes me feel weak and pathetic; the girl sitting around waiting instead of pursuing life.

But *Holden* doesn't make me feel weak or pathetic. I walked in here stressed and uncertain. And now, just from looking at him, there's a lightness in my chest that wasn't there before. A bubbly giddiness. Happiness.

Should you chase happiness if it's attached to a guy who broke your heart once before?

Holden takes the textbook from me and walks over to the bleachers, tossing it into a pile of his stuff.

I should go. Instead, I drop my own backpack and grab one of the abandoned basketballs, dribbling it a few times before shooting. It bounces off the rim and to the side.

"Lower your elbow."

I send Holden a glare. "I didn't ask for pointers."

He flashes me a smile. The smirk that makes me feel like I'm floating and flying and falling. The expression I'd do anything for.

Then he walks over, not stopping until he's standing right behind me. He smells good. Not like cinnamon today, but something masculine and musky. The heat of his body radiates, warming my back and flushing my cheeks.

His hands land on my hips, shifting me slightly so I'm facing the hoop head on. I pull in a deep breath, unable to think about anything but the last time he held my hips—while he was moving inside of me.

Goosebumps spread across my skin as his hands move upward, skating across my sides until he reaches and adjusts my elbows. My breathing is erratic now, frantic huffs and puffs as I try to focus on the basket I'm supposed to be making.

I sway back against him as Holden releases my arms and tugs at the bottom of my ponytail. He chuckles as our bodies brush, his own breathing deep and even. Unaffected.

But I don't think he is.

There have been enough moments between us where there's something more, when he's let his guard down a little. He'd do it when we were kids, but the secrets he'd share were breaking the garage window while playing basketball. Admitting to missing his dad. Staying up later than he was supposed to, watching television. Nothing like his hopes and fears now.

"You're supposed to shoot."

Instead of replying or taking the shot, I turn around and drop the ball. It bounces and rolls away, but neither of us look down or make any attempt to retrieve it. Holden stares at me, and I stare at him.

His blue eyes are stormy yet clear, taking me in with an intensity I wasn't expecting. He looks like he wants to consume me, and I want to let him.

I step forward, all but erasing the distance between us. I raise one hand, brushing the stubborn piece of hair that's usually flopped on his forehead away. Outside of our most intimate moments, I've never really touched him. Not like this, at least. Not when we're all alone, so purposeful and direct.

I'm proud of how I hold eye contact as I trail my fingers down and across his jaw, not shirking from his searching expression or worried what he'll find. I've gained confidence from our physical interactions. It's much easier for me to read how he responds to those than how he's feeling or what he's thinking. I don't think he'll reject me this way, and it emboldens me.

"What are you doing, Cassia?"

I slide my hand lower, fisting the fabric of his shirt. "I miss your cock."

His eyes flare, surprise and lust mixing in ocean-colored depths.

There. I did my scary thing for the day.

I could have easily said I miss him, and it wouldn't be any form of a lie. But I'm not sure I've ever experienced what *having* Holden is truly like. He was my first crush. Long before our friendship blew up, I hoped we'd become more. Instead, I got less.

I've never felt like he's given me much. Nothing to my everything. The moments when we've had sex are some of the few times it felt like we were equals, when it felt like he wanted me just as much as I crave him.

There's also a part of me that chases the boldness he pulls out of me. I do and say things around him I just know I'd never do or say around anyone else.

Like what I just did.

"Careful what you ask for. I could fuck you right here."

I think he's trying to shock me right back. Regain the upper hand. Holden is assuming the thought of having sex at school is unappealing to me.

And yeah, part of me is mortified by the prospect of a teacher or janitor catching us. But another part of me—a *larger* part of me —finds the prospect of having sex here incredibly arousing. It's the exact opposite of what anyone would expect from me.

"The locker room is empty, right?"

Holden raises a brow at me. I raise one right back.

He's looking at me exactly the way he used to when we were

younger. When he'd suggest staying up later to watch one more movie and I'd put on the second one. When I'd make a crazy shot from the street, and he'd miss. Half approval and half incredulity.

I used to think there was something else there too. Not love, but love-adjacent. Something more powerful than like or friendship.

I see it now, flickering across his face as he grips my waist and pulls me flush against his body.

"We could get caught," he teases, slipping his thumb under the hem of my sweater and rubbing it back and forth just above the edge of my skirt. "Suspended. People would talk. They'd know you aren't the good girl everyone thinks."

I lean into him, letting Holden support most of my body weight. "Make it worth my while, then. I'm not risking all that for subpar sex."

Holden's hand stills on my back. He laughs. "Baby, it's never going to be subpar between us."

There's affection and familiarity in his tone as he grabs my hand and tows me toward the locker room. My heart takes off at a gallop, excitement and anticipation coursing through me. I can't believe we're doing this. I can't believe *I* suggested this.

I've never been in the boys' locker room, obviously. The layout is the same as the girls'. I look around like there's something to see, fiddling with the hem of my sweater.

Holden glances at me as the door swings shut. "We don't have to—"

"I want to." I'm nervous, but it has nothing to do with second-guessing. For once I want to regret what I've done, not what I haven't.

I'm not sure I could ever regret anything involving him, though.

I reach down and pull off the boots I'm wearing. The tile is cold and hard but looks clean. I peel off my tights next, followed by my underwear, leaving my skirt on. Based on the way Holden is looking at me, he likes that I did.

He takes a seat on the scarred wooden bench that runs the length of the room, knees parted and expression serious. I walk closer and closer, not stopping until my legs hit the edge of the bench and I'm standing between his.

This isn't the frantic hook-up I was picturing. I thought we'd come in here and it would happen immediately. That drawing things out would have lost the appeal to him. That the novelty has worn off, like Grace said.

I startle when his hands land on my thighs and slide up, under my skirt. Staying upright becomes a challenge as he cups my ass and then slides a hand between my legs. My breathing becomes loud. Ragged. In the quiet room, it's all I can hear.

"Always so wet for me," he whispers.

I moan, everything else but him melting away. One of his hands moves to the waistband of the mesh shorts he's wearing, pulling out the long, pulsing length of his dick. I ogle his erection as it bobs between us.

I wasn't lying when I said I missed it. I lean forward and suck him into my mouth, swirling my tongue around the flared tip of his cock. Holden's hips jerk, his hand sliding into my hair as I pull him deeper into my mouth. His grip tightens as my lips slide along his length.

Abruptly, he pulls away. "You're too good at that."

I lean down and kiss him, and he pulls me into his lap. Our mouths set a rhythm that our bodies match. He's everywhere. A hot tongue in my mouth. A warm palm sliding under my sweater and into my bra. A hard penis rubbing between my legs.

I freeze when I feel the head probe my entrance. Holden stops kissing me, pulling back and studying me with concern. "What's wrong?"

"Nothing. You just—I'm not—I'm not on anything. Sydney said the pills made her feel weird." I fumble for words. He's always worn a condom. His parents had him when they were teenagers, and that story didn't have a happy ending.

Holden makes a face. "I really didn't need to know my sister is on birth control, Cassia."

"Graham hasn't even kissed her yet."

Holden glances down at our laps, then back up at me. "We don't have to…we can slow down."

I shake my head. "I want to. Just put on a condom."

"I was going to. I've never…not."

Part of me regrets bringing this up and ruining the moment now. But I'm also curious. "Never?"

He shakes his head. Probably wary of discussing other girls with me, which I appreciate.

"So if I did go on birth control, I'd be your first?"

Holden swallows. Nods. "Yeah."

I'm putting myself out there a little, even if it is just in the context of sex. He's not shutting the idea down or looking uncomfortable about me assuming we'll sleep together again.

"You have all of mine," I whisper.

"You have more of mine than you think," he tells me before turning and opening one of the lockers.

When he turns back around, he's holding a familiar foil packet.

I scooch back to watch him roll the condom on, biting my lower lip. "I know this is super convenient, so I'm glad you do. But seriously? You guys keep condoms in here?"

Holden smirks as he grabs my hips and pulls me back toward him. "I've never used one before. Never had sex in here." His lips move just below my jawline, kissing the sensitive skin there. "Another first, flower."

I shiver at the sweetness, the intimacy of the moment. "I like when you call me that," I admit for the first time. I've never commented on the nickname before. It was all that remained of our friendship for a while, the sole reminder of what we were. I was worried addressing it might make it disappear along with everything else we used to be.

"Yeah?" He murmurs the word against my neck.

"Why do you call me that?"

"Cassias are flowers."

"I know. I just…"

He didn't answer my question, but I'm not sure how else to ask.

Holden sighs. "I wanted to have a name no one else called you."

I'm not sure what to say to that, so I kiss him instead. Holden's hand slides under my skirt. There's no uncertainty. No hesitation, on my part or his. His hand returns to the spot between my legs, rubbing my clit for a minute before he guides his dick inside. The stretch as I slide down is nothing but pleasure.

He feels bigger from this angle. Pushes deeper. We fall into an effortless rhythm.

Moans fall out of my mouth as the pleasure sparks and spreads.

"Quiet, flower," he says. "Or else the whole school will hear how much you love taking me like this."

The taunt of the forbidden, delivered in Holden's husky voice, is all it takes. I come quickly, Holden groaning when I contract around him. He comes right after, our bodies totally in sync.

I don't move off him right away, wanting to live in this moment a little longer.

Our breathing slows and evens. Holden's hands are on my waist, covering the strip of skin between my skirt and sweater.

"Subpar, right?" he whispers.

I roll my eyes, but I'm smiling too. I move off him, grabbing my underwear and tights to get redressed. Holden tosses the condom and fixes his shorts. Tugging them down was as undressed as he got.

As far from subpar as the sex was, I wish I'd been able to explore his body more.

We're both silent as we walk back into the gym, but it's a comfortable one. The kind when you're around someone who already knows everything important. I'm not sure that's entirely accurate when it comes to me and Holden, but that's how it feels.

"Give me a sec," he says as I pick up my abandoned backpack. "I'll walk out with you."

I nod, watching as he retrieves the balls on the court and returns them to the rack. He grabs his backpack and gym bag off the bleachers and then returns to my side.

"Sydney asked me to come over tonight," I tell him. "There's a movie she wants to watch, and your dad is going out with some friends before he..."

"Before he leaves again." The words are flat.

"Yeah."

Holden sighs. "I hate how he still skips out. I know it's his job —know he's providing for us the only way he knows how. But it feels like abandonment too, you know? Like not sticking around the one place you're needed."

I don't respond right away. I'm floored, not only by what he's saying, but that he's saying it at all. Opening up to me, without me even asking.

"Have you ever said anything to him?"

"No. We're basically adults—I am one, legally. It doesn't matter anymore."

"It can still matter, Holden."

"I told him not to change anything next year. Chances are good I'll be here regardless."

"Why are they good?"

He glances over. "My grades are shit. Basketball is a wild card. I could get injured next game and never play again."

"You beat Covington last week by twenty points. Chances are *good* you'll have options."

He glances over, his serious expression turning into a smirk. "Twenty points, huh?"

I shrug. "I checked the school site."

"You do that often?"

"After every one of your games for the past three years." It's terrifying and relieving to admit. To give him a glimpse into the ways I've held onto him. How far from over him I really am.

His expression softens as we approach my car. It's one of the few left in the lot, aside from his truck.

"I won't be home tonight. I promised Finn I'd come over. He's having a party."

"Oh."

"It'll probably run past Syd's bedtime if you want to come."

"You're inviting me to Finn's party?"

He nods, sucking his bottom lip in between his teeth. "If you want to come."

"What would I tell Sydney?"

Holden shoves his hands into his pockets. "You could tell her the truth."

That suggestion is just as shocking as the invitation itself. She's my best friend and his sister. It involves permanence. Seriousness.

He smiles, probably in response to my shocked expression. "You can think about it. Totally up to you."

I nod, still numb with shock. He kisses me, deep and somehow sweet. Then turns and heads for his truck.

I stand in place, frozen and upright.

But it feels like I'm falling, too.

CHAPTER NINETEEN

CASSIA

Sydney lifts one hand from under the blankets to point at one of the characters on the screen. "Do you think he's lying?"

"Hmm?" I refocus on the movie playing on the television screen.

Sydney huffs. "You aren't even watching."

"I am. I'm just…" *Distracted.* "Tired."

"And yet you always stay up way later than me."

I say nothing, contemplating the segue. If I replied with "I was waiting up for Holden," what would she say? Would she be angry? Excited?

I'm not sure how to bring him up. *If* I should bring it up. I could mention the party and leave it at that. She'd have questions, but not nearly as many as if I admitted to why I'm wanting to go.

The house phone rings. Sydney pauses the movie and stands. "It's probably spam, but I'll check it and make some popcorn. Want any?"

"Sure. I'll help."

I toss the blanket off and stand, leaving Lily sleeping on the couch. I'm antsy, trying to decide what to say to her. Doing something is better than sitting and stewing. Thinking and overthinking.

I head into the pantry and grab the box of microwave popcorn. Sydney picks up the phone as I pop it inside and start the timer.

When I turn around, Sydney is still on the phone. "...my phone died," she's saying. "I didn't know you'd want to talk."

Her cheeks flush a pretty shade of pink as she glances at me, mouthing *Graham*. I nod and smile, right as there's a knock on the front door.

I'll get it, I mouth back, walking out of the kitchen and through the living room—couch still a jumble of blankets—toward the front door.

I glance through the peephole, and it feels like a heavy stone was just dropped in my stomach. I don't know *who* I considered as options for people standing on the front porch, but two uniformed police officers were not on the list. Two *grim* uniformed police officers. I've never seen an upbeat cop, though. Not even when members of Pembrook's police force have come to school for demonstrations or talks. They're always serious and stoic. Maybe you have to be whenever you're on duty in that sort of career field. Where you have to witness horrible things. Share horrible news.

My hands are shaking as I work to undo the deadbolt and turn the knob. The police don't show up—without you calling—to deliver good news. It's a universally dreaded sight.

I manage to get the door open, letting in whoosh of cold air that helps me stay in this moment instead of my mind racing with terrifying possibilities.

"Miss Adams?"

I clear my throat, worried no sound will come out otherwise. "Um, no. I'm a neighbor. A friend."

One of the officers nods. "Is there anyone home related to a

Joseph Adams?"

For an awful stretch of seconds, I thought they were here because of Holden. The rush of relief is dizzying, closely followed by the worry something is still wrong.

"Yes. I'll…I'll get her."

I go to close the door, then think better of it. I leave it half-open as I spin and sprint toward the kitchen.

Sydney is leaning against the counter, still talking on the phone.

"Sydney," I hiss. "Sydney."

Her eyes meet mine, the happy shine slowly fading as she registers my expression. "I have to go, Graham," she says, then hangs up. "What is it? What's going on?"

"There are police officers at the door. They—" That's all I manage before Sydney is hurrying toward the front of the house, following the chill spreading through downstairs as the draft expands.

The officers are still waiting on the porch. Part of me was hoping they'd disappear. That they would realize they had the wrong house, the wrong person. That this was all a terrible misunderstanding that would simply disappear.

But it's not.

"Miss Adams."

"Yes, that's me."

I linger in the background a few feet behind her, my pulse and mind racing. I'm an observer in this moment. It feels like I'm seeing this unfold as part of the movie we were just watching, not as someone experiencing it firsthand.

This isn't my house. This isn't my father police officers are discussing using phrases such as *head-on collision* and *killed instantly* and *identify the body*. That's all Mr. Adams has become. A body, not a person.

But this will have consequences for two of the people I care most about in this world. I barely register that thought, the realization that at some point I re-elevated Holden to the same level of status as my best friend. That I forgave his silence or moved past it, or accepted people make mistakes.

I step forward and squeeze Sydney's hand as the officers leave after a final round of condolences.

Sydney's eyes are wide and unseeing, the color mostly drained from her face. I shut the door, figuring the cold won't help.

"My dad is dead." Every word is coated in disbelief.

"I'm so sorry, Sydney." That's all I can think to say. I've been lucky enough to avoid tragedy in my life. All of my grandparents are still alive, even. I have two present, healthy parents.

Sydney has none now.

I don't think anything I say will ever make that okay.

Sydney steps back until her back hits the plaster wall of the entryway. There's a photo of Holden and Sydney with their dad hanging next to the bottom of the stairs. I'm glad her back is to it. Glad she doesn't have to look at those smiling faces right now.

She sinks to the floor slowly, studying the hardwood with a blank expression, like she's never seen it before.

I pick up the landline and dial one of the two numbers I know by heart. My dad answers after three rings. "Nolan residence."

"Dad?"

"Cassia?" Instantly, his tone changes into apprehension. I rarely call the home phone, and he knows I'm supposed to be sleeping across the street.

"Dad, I need you or Mom to come over. The police were just here." I glance at Sydney, who's still staring at nothing. "They… Mr. Adams was in an accident. He, uh, he didn't make it."

There's a sharp inhale on the other end of the line, followed by some commotion. I can hear Sally screaming. My mom asking a question and Maggie replying. I can't imagine getting the call Sydney just got. Can't imagine losing a member of my family.

"I'll be right over, sweetheart."

"Okay," I whisper, then hang up the phone. I stare at the number pad.

I have Holden's cell memorized. Should I call him?

"My dad is on his way," I say.

Sydney nods.

"Can I get you anything? Do anything?"

This time, there's a head shake.

We sit in silence on the floor until the front door opens. Both of my parents walk inside.

My mom rushes to Sydney's side, giving her shoulders a squeeze. "Maggie's watching everyone," she tells me.

My dad crouches down as well. "I'm so sorry for your loss, Sydney."

"Thanks," she whispers.

"I've got some contacts at the police station. I'll give them a call, see what needs to be handled."

Sydney nods. "Thanks," she repeats.

"Did your dad have anywhere he'd keep papers or documents?"

"I'm not sure. His room, maybe?"

My dad nods and stands. "I'll go take a look."

"Let's get you off the floor, sweetie," my mom says, helping Sydney stand and guiding her over to the couch. Lily stands from her spot curled up, walking over and sniffing at my mom's jeans. One of my siblings probably spilled something on her.

I trail behind them, then force the words out of my mouth. "I'll go tell Holden."

Sydney nods. She's in no shape to. She doesn't even question how I know where he is. My parents are handling everything that needs to be done here.

It feels like years, not hours, since our time at the gym. When Holden invited me to Finn's tonight, this is not at all how I imagined showing up.

"Are you sure, sweetie? Dad or I can go."

"I'm sure."

I don't want to do this at all, and especially not alone. But I need to.

"Be careful, Cassia."

I nod.

My feet drag as I walk outside, fingering the car keys in my pocket and relieved I left them there. I don't feel like going inside my house and facing my siblings' questions. I'm closest with Sydney and Holden because of our ages, but my brothers and sisters all grew up across the street from them too. There's a whole section of our fridge dedicated to postcards Mr. Adams would bring back from his trips around the country.

The drive to Finn's house passes too quickly, even sticking exactly to the speed limit. I need more time to think through what to say. How to tell him.

The roads are empty and quiet, no sign of any death or destruction. If the officers shared where exactly the accident took place, I missed it in my haze of disbelief.

Cars are parked haphazardly on both sides of the street. It takes me a little while to find a space to squeeze into. I lock the car and walk toward the house, shoving my hands in my pockets.

I'm dressed in leggings and a fleece. My hair is a mess and I'm not wearing any makeup. It's stupid to be focused on my appearance right now, but I still regret changing out of my outfit from school earlier as I step inside and register the number of skimpy tops and short dresses.

It's hot and sticky in here, the air filled with the scent of pot smoke and hormones. People bump and grind up against one another, laughing and spilling drinks. I push through the crowd, ignoring anyone who does a double take.

This plan was not thought through. I should have texted him first. What if I can't find him? What if he's high or drunk or with a girl?

I soldier on despite my misgivings. I make it to the kitchen and spot Holden immediately. He's standing by the fridge, talking with Mark. He appears sober and there's not a girl in sight. Relief and dread war within me as he glances up and spots me. Abandons Mark and walks right over.

"Hey! You're here!"

He looks thrilled to see me. My heart swells in size as I live the beginning of a fantasy I've had since freshman year.

Then I remember why I'm here. The reminder twists in my chest like a jagged knife. I wish I could enjoy this moment. Wish I could smile back and wish I could not know his whole world is about to be upended.

"I need to talk to you. Can we go outside?"

Holden's forehead creases with confusion. "Uh, yeah. Sure." His eyes skate across my face, looking for clues or hints.

I head for a back door that looks like it leads outside, hearing his footsteps follow and ignoring everyone looking at us. I keep walking until I reach the railing of the back deck. I take a deep breath and spin around. Cold air shocks my lungs.

He's right behind me, expression unsure as he shoves his hands into his pockets. Each exhale of air lingers in the air for a second before fading away.

I don't want to be the one who has to tell him this. Selfishly, I don't want him to associate this moment with me.

"You're acting weird," he states.

This time, I don't crack a smile.

"There was an accident, Holden." I pause, letting those words hang in the air between us with our breaths for a minute. "Your dad…he didn't make it. He's gone."

Holden stares at me, his gaze flat and unblinking.

"I'm so sorry," I whisper.

Still, he says nothing. He doesn't react. Doesn't ask questions. Definitely doesn't lean into me or seek comfort.

"Sydney's at your house with my parents. If you want, I can drive you." I hold up my keys, like he needs proof I'm capable of operating a vehicle.

I'm not sure what else to do or say.

Nothing.

Once again, he's giving me nothing. If our roles were reversed, I'd lean on him. I'd want him here. There's nothing on Holden's face to suggest the same.

"I have my truck."

I wait, but that's all he says.

"Okay. I'll, uh, I'll go."

I wait for him to say something else. All I get is more silence.

He's in shock. I'm not sure I should leave him, even if that's what he wants. But I'm not sure what else to do or say.

A few hours ago, it felt like we were on the brink of becoming something. All of a sudden, those possibilities look like ash. I'm not his girlfriend. I'm not even sure he considers me a friend.

So I turn and walk down the stairs. The whole time I wait—hope—he'll call me back.

But all I can hear is silence.

Once again, he's shut me out. Without warning and about something I have no control over. I see the parallels slide into place.

He kissed me. He forgot about me.

He slept with me. He's over me.

I glance back, once, as I reach the grass. Holden is no longer on the porch. I can see in the through the window, the lights in the kitchen a beam through the darkness.

He's standing right where he was when I walked into the kitchen. Back near the fridge, talking with Mark. McKenzie Howard walks over to them, and I watch him greet her with a smile. More than he mustered for me.

I feel thirteen again, watching out my bedroom window as the boy across the street leaves on bikes with a group of friends without glancing at my house once. Forgotten. An inconvenience.

I thought he'd changed. I thought I'd changed. I thought *we*'d changed.

Maybe I'm leaping to too many conclusions. Maybe this is the aftermath of shock, where he acts out of character. But the problem is, this *is* in character. This is exactly the way he's treated me for years. It's only recently that's started to shift and change. That I fell for his touches and smiles all over again.

Instead of smart, I feel like the stupidest person alive. Who lets the same person break their heart the same way twice?

My face is numb. I turn and walk toward the spot where I parked my car. I'm upset enough it takes a while. After five minutes of aimless wandering, I spot the sedan and slip inside. I slam the door shut and exhale, leaning my head back against the seat and letting one tear escape my closed eyes.

I love him.

I hate him.

One of those is a lie. You can't feel two such strong emotions for one person at the same time. Or at least, I didn't think you could.

If one's a lie...I'm not sure which.

CHAPTER TWENTY

HOLDEN

When I leave the gym, it's long after everyone else, which has become routine. Coach tried to talk me into not playing for a few weeks. Told me scouts would understand and so would my teammates, given the circumstances. But I *want* to play. It's the one escape I have.

I haven't even used my dad's death to get out of school assignments. All of my teachers have been understanding and accommodating. But I've turned everything in on time, despite knowing I'll pass regardless.

Tragedy is a funny thing. It can rock your world to its core and leave everything else untouched. My dad is gone, just like that. Forever, I'll no longer have a dad.

But my life looks the same. My routine is unchanged.

He was gone more than he was home. It's very easy to pretend my dad is still alive. That he's just driving an eighteen-wheeler through Kentucky and will be home for Christmas.

Sydney is having a hard time adjusting. But she *is* adjusting. She talks to her friends and still helps out with school plays and is now officially dating Graham.

I'm not in denial. I know he's gone. But I'm stalled in place. Stuck in a reality I don't want to actually face.

There's a female figure standing by my truck as I leave the sidewalk and cross the parking lot.

My sure steps stutter. For a second, I'm worried it's Cassia. I haven't spoken to her since she came to Finn's to tell me about my dad.

There was no funeral, just a cremation and a will reading. My dad kept his wishes simple and straightforward, just like him. He left me and Sydney everything. Since I'm eighteen and she isn't, I'm also technically my sister's guardian. A shitty one, so far. I'm too consumed by my own grief.

I've always felt like a mess in comparison to Cassia's poise. But that's especially true now. I'm scared to face her. I've always known she deserves better than me, but it's never seemed clearer than it does right now.

It's not Cassia next to my truck, though.

It's my mom.

She showed up about a week after a drunk driver swerved across the center line and took my dad's life. Fucking ironic. He logged thousands of miles on the road. Late nights and long hours all across the country. And then he died fifteen minutes from our house.

I stop a few feet away from her and cross my arms.

"What are you doing here?"

"I told you I'm living in Ridgemont."

Right. The first time she showed up, she dropped that bomb. She walked away from us, a whole two towns over. Didn't even leave the county.

"*Here*, as in the high school. You want Sydney to see you?"

I haven't told Sydney our mom showed up. I'm worried how

it might affect her. I don't trust any of my mom's intentions as honorable.

"I'm not giving you money."

I was shocked when I heard how much my dad had tucked away at the will reading. Enough I can afford college without a basketball scholarship.

It should be a relief. Instead, it's another thing I'm stressing about. I don't see how I can leave now. Abandon Sydney. She shouldn't have to stay home alone. Extended family offered to take her in—take both of us in—but that will require switching schools. No one lives close enough to Pembrooke High to make it a reasonable commute. I'm not asking her to do that, though I'm sure she'll offer. It's a conversation I'm dreading. A large part of me does want to leave, to get away from this town, and I'm sure Sydney recognizes that.

"You don't think much of me," my mom comments.

"Is that a surprise?" I ask, tone cutting.

"Not really."

I inherited my bluntness from my mom, I guess. I'm worried about what else I might have inherited from her too.

"It's easy to judge, Holden. It's hard to be home with two toddlers. Your dad was always gone."

"That's not an excuse for abandoning your kids. There *is* no excuse for that."

She shrugs. "I knew you were better off without me."

That sentence hits me hard, with more force than anything else she could have said. Because that's always what I've told myself when it comes to Cassia. It feels like I'm having a conversation with my own insecurities.

"I wasn't meant to be a mother," she continues. "I never wanted to be a mother. I was a kid, younger than you, when I had you."

"What's your point?"

"I don't have one. I'm sorry—sorry you got me as a mother. Your dad promised me he'd be there. Instead, he was out. Working. Doing God knows what with God knows who."

"Providing for us, you mean?"

"Your father wasn't perfect, Holden. I know I'm a low bar. But me leaving forced him out of some bad habits. If I hadn't, you would have ended up with two crappy parents, not just one."

Part of me wants to ask what she means. But most of me doesn't want to know. Delving into my parents' train wreck of a relationship won't bring my dad back or change who my mother is.

"You should go."

"Okay."

My mom doesn't offer any resistance, and that stings, even though it shouldn't. *She* abandoned *me*, and still there's some part of me that doesn't hate her. How can she feel nothing toward me?

She walks away, toward a black hatchback parked across the lot. I climb into the cab of my truck, not wanting her to see me standing here, watching her walk away from me again. Part of me wants to fling more questions at her, demand answers and apologies.

But I know none of them will be satisfying. She made a decision that can't be undone. Even if she did regret it, it wouldn't change anything. I don't think I'm capable of forgiving that choice.

For a minute, I stew. I don't want to go home. Can't deal with watching Sydney go through my dad's things or forcing smiles around me.

My emotions are swirling close to the surface. I need an outlet or some sort of release. If Declan hadn't paused fights for the winter, I'd be texting him right now.

I turn on my truck and head for the old high school. The only stop I make is at the seedy liquor store on the fringe of town.

The guy behind the register recognizes me. Knows I'm in high school and underage. But he just eyes me with pity as I check out, not even asking to see my fake ID.

I'm so sick of the pity. Sick of a lot of things.

There's no one else at the old courts when I pull up along the asphalt. It's a sad sight. Faded lines and frayed hoop strings. A few tufts of grass have managed to survive in cracks in the court, tiny spots of life in the midst of an unforgiving surface.

I grab the whiskey bottle and the basketball I keep in the back of my truck and walk out onto the court. The lights flicker on, contending with the rapidly dropping sun. One of them is permanently out thanks to a stray shot Finn took. As far as the town is concerned, this place is out of commission. No one has come around to fix it.

I start dribbling, ignoring the chill in the air as I weave across the court, pretending to dodge and block invisible opponents.

Then, I start shooting. Every shot I miss, I take a sip of whiskey. The more I drink, the more I miss. The more I miss, the more I drink.

Eventually, I stop. I'm breathing heavily. Lazy heat is swimming in my bloodstream thanks to the alcohol.

My body is already exhausted from practice earlier. I'm emotionally drained too, from the encounter with my mom.

I sink down in the center of the court, not caring the ground is cold and hard. There's no way I can drive. No way I could do that to Sydney or live with myself if I took a stranger's life the way someone took my dad's. I'm going to have to call someone to come pick me up.

I'm not sure how long I've been sitting here, when another car pulls up. I roll my head to one side so I can look and see, too lazy to actually turn my whole body around.

Finn climbs out, followed by Mark. Jordan. Grace. McKenzie. A second car arrives, spilling out more of my friends. Finn approaches me first. "Figured you'd be here."

I grunt, trying to decide how I feel about them all being here. I wanted to be alone. But I'm sick of it too.

"Started the party without us?" he asks, spotting the bottle.

I wouldn't call this much of a party. Graham's study thing was livelier. "I guess."

More of the group filters over. Jordan sets up a speaker and pop music starts blaring. It's better than sitting alone in silence, but I'm not really in the mood to party, either. Most of my friends respect that, smiling at me but not approaching.

Most of the guys start playing a pickup game. Grace comes and sits beside me. A few of the other girls follow her over.

"Hey," Grace says.

"Hey." I run a finger along the edge of the whiskey bottle.

"I'm worried about you, Holden."

"Don't be. I'm fine."

"You're drunk on a Monday night."

"I had a shitty day."

"Right." She sighs. Things between us were never good, but they've been bad as of late. No matter how drunk I get, I can't seem to stomach touching a girl who isn't Cassia, so I haven't had sex in weeks. I know Grace wants to think we were ever more than that, but we really weren't. She's stopped pushing anything physical and tried to be here for me as a friend. The problem is, we never were.

So I'm perpetually disappointing Grace.

Perpetually disappointing a lot of people.

Grace doesn't make any more attempts to talk to me. She

chats with the other girls instead, while I lean back on my palms and stare off into space.

I'm buzzed enough zoning out is peaceful, not boring. I tip my head back and stare up at the stars, trying to trace patterns in the constellations twinkling overhead.

It got completely dark out when I wasn't paying attention. That's how all the days have felt lately—like they're over minutes after I've woken up. A constant cycle with no clear start or end.

At first, I think the stars are falling. But then I force my eyes to focus. A snowflake lands on the back of my hand, melting as soon as it touches my skin.

Usually I hate snow. It's a pain to clean the truck and shovel the steps. Means I can't play out in the driveway and turns into a mess.

But there's something peaceful and mesmerizing about watching it fall. The ground isn't frozen, so it disappears as soon as it touches the earth, dissipating as if it was never there in the first place. Like magic.

A third car arrives at the court, headlights cutting through the darkness and illuminating the lazy drift of a few snowflakes before they shut out. I squint at the car, then glance at the court. No one is missing. Maybe they're kids from Ridgemont?

Two figures reach the edge of the court. Familiar figures.

This time, I sit up. My body is sluggish, my movements slow.

Fuck.

I don't want her to see me like this. Don't want either of them to see me like this. Sydney walks over first, with Cassia right behind her.

She crouches down beside me. "Hey," Sydney says softly.

"Hi."

Sydney glances between me and the half-empty bottle, her

expression tight. Disappointed. "I got worried. You weren't answering your phone, so I asked Cassia to drive me here."

I glance at Cassia. She's standing a few feet away, hands in her pockets, watching the guys play. Studiously not looking at me.

"I left my phone in the car," I tell Sydney. "Just needed a…minute."

I've been out here for hours, though, and I hate that I worried her. The last thing Sydney needs is to be stressing about me.

"I'm sorry. I should have texted."

"It's okay," she replies.

"I'll be home soon, okay?"

Sydney glances at the whiskey again.

"One of the guys will drive my truck," I add.

"Okay." She stands and walks away, passing Cassia.

I'm expecting Cassia to follow Sydney. To leave.

She doesn't. She walks right up to me and leans down. I have a clear shot down the front of her shirt. Despite all the whiskey I've drunk, I feel my dick twitch.

It's déjà vu to the night we sat in my driveway. I wonder if she realizes the same, especially when she grabs the bottle.

Last time, I stopped her, and she ended up in my lap.

This time, I don't move.

"What the fuck are you doing, Holden?" she asks.

For a second, looking at her, I forget how to breathe. The night air around me seems to stiffen and constrict, crowding in around me.

"Coping."

Her hazel eyes glance between Grace beside me and the bottle she's holding. She scoffs. "Yeah. I see that."

I stand so suddenly she has to take a step back. Grab her wrist and pull her away, off into the grass.

"Don't act like I owe you anything," I say. Because it feels like I do owe her something, and I'm not sure why. She's better off without me. I have nothing to offer her.

Cassia's eyes flash with brown-green fire. "Owe me? How is me *caring* inconveniencing you, Holden?"

I grind my molars. "You shouldn't have brought Sydney here."

"Well, I did. If you don't want people checking up on you, maybe you shouldn't disappear and get drunk."

"Whatever." I turn to leave. I shouldn't be having a conversation with her right now. I'm too drunk, too volatile.

I freeze when I hear the crack of glass. I glance between Cassia and the broken bottle, some disbelief breaking through the haze of whiskey as I stare at the two broken halves on the edge of the court.

"You're going to walk away from me? *Again*?" She shakes her head, anger twisting her expression. "Sydney wasn't the only one worried, you know. She isn't the reason I'm here. You made me think…" Her voice cracks, and it breaks something in my chest too. "It's been *weeks*, Holden. Not a fucking word from you."

I scoff, attempting to act unaffected. "Life doesn't work out exactly how you want it to, Cassia. I've had some shit going on."

"I know that, Holden. You think I don't know that?"

"I don't know. What has ever gone wrong in your life? You have the happy family. You know exactly what you want to do with your life."

"What's ever gone wrong in my life? Well, falling in love with you has been fucking inconvenient." She spits the words out. They sound more like a declaration of war than of love.

I freeze. I've wondered how she felt about me. We've been stuck in a cycle of lust and confusion. But for some reason, I never thought she'd say it. At all, and certainly not like this. "It was a waste of time too."

I say what I'm thinking, and she stills like I slapped her. I meant it as an apology, more than anything. I feel unlovable right now. She should have been falling in love with a guy who can handle hardship without falling apart. Who has a certain future and something to offer her.

"Don't talk to me again, Holden. We're *done*, you hear me? This thing between us, it's finished."

It's exactly what I wanted. Needed. For her to let go, so I can stop feeling guilty or like I'm letting her down. But I'm stunned by how much it hurts. How much I want to take everything back.

Instead, I force myself to keep going. Clean breaks are easiest to move on from, right? "Fine by me. We fucked a few times. You're not my girlfriend. I can do whatever the fuck I want."

That's what I thought I wanted. The truth is, I haven't touched any girl since the night she climbed into my lap and made me come fully dressed.

That's nothing Cassia knows. Nothing I intend to tell her.

"You think I'm so dick-whipped I won't do the same, Holden?" she snaps. "I *will*."

I let the alcohol in my blood temper the way those words feel like a blow. "Fine."

"You're an asshole."

"Yeah, I know," I agree. "Told you you have shitty taste."

Cassia shakes her head. "Wow. I thought you'd changed. I thought you actually cared." She spins and starts to head toward her car.

Everyone on the court is staring at us. I should let her walk away, but something in me can't leave things like this between us.

"Goddammit," I mutter. "Cassia!"

She spins around. "*What?*"

I take a step closer. "It's better this way, okay? There's not—I'm not—" I exhale. "I'm sorry. I'm sorry everything changed. But I'm not—I have no idea what the hell I'm going to do. I'm not going to drag you down into that with me."

I'm not expecting a smile and apology accepted. But I'm not prepared for the vitriol in her expression either.

Cassia looks like she wants to shove me. Maybe slap me. "Right. Don't ask me what I want. Don't talk to me about how you're feeling. Just decide—the same way you've decided everything else."

I inhale, bracing myself for what I need to say. Stare at the grass and scoff my sneaker against it. I can't keep waffling. Giving her false hope. "You should move on. Give Baker a chance. He's a good guy, Cassia."

She says nothing. When I finally man up and look at her, I realize there's a wet sheen covering her hazel eyes. My stomach drops.

"Cassia…"

"Bye, Holden." Those are two words she's said to me before. But there's a permanence now. A finality.

She turns and walks away. Just like I did to her four years ago, at Ginny Davis' eighth grade Halloween party, right after I kissed her.

I thought that hurt—walking away.

But it hurts just as much—maybe more—to be the one walked away from.

CHAPTER TWENTY-ONE

CASSIA

I prefer animals to people. No cat has ever made me feel excluded. No dog has ever broken my heart.

I stroke the soft fur of one of the unnamed puppies absentmindedly, barely registering the warm lick of her tongue. My thoughts are stuck on harsh words and broken glass. That's why I'm here on a Friday afternoon instead of sticking to my normal schedule. I'm desperate for some distraction.

"You okay, Cassia?" Eileen asks.

I give the puppy one final pat and stand, turning back to measuring the kibble. "Yeah."

"College troubles?"

"Uh, no." My applications are all submitted for early decision. It's a waiting game at this point. Nothing else I can do.

"How is Sydney doing?" Eileen's voice is soft. Pembrooke is a small town, and Joe Adams' accident was the subject of discussion for weeks after it happened. So was the man from Ridgemont who was drunk and also died in the accident. A tragedy all around.

My broken heart was another casualty. But that will heal. Repair itself. I'll move on, even if it hurts like hell right now.

It takes me too long to respond.

"Cassia?"

I clear my throat. "She's doing okay, I think."

"What about Holden?"

An innocent question with a lot hiding underneath. One most people haven't even thought to ask me. They associate me with one Adams sibling, and it's not Holden. But Eileen knew us before. She saw him volunteer with me here. Was there for the beginning and middle of us, and now she's asking about the end.

My elbow knocks one of the bowls, prompting a clang. "I don't know."

"I'm sorry to hear that."

I glance at her, something in Eileen's expression suggesting everything I've been too scared to say is obvious in the way I answered the question. "Am I that transparent?"

I try to pair the question with a wry smile, but I'm sure it falls flat.

"I have some experience with complicated love," Eileen replies, suggesting some truth to the rumors I've heard. "And…I saw the way you two were looking at each other when he was here last month."

"Pretty sure you misread things on his end." Despite my best attempts, plenty of bitterness saturates my voice.

Eileen hums. "It's harder to see love up close."

"There's definitely no love to see." If the radio silence of the last couple of weeks wasn't enough to tell me so, pushing me toward another guy sure was.

Eileen picks up a couple of the bowls that have already been filled. Gives me an understanding smile. "I hope you're wrong."

She takes the bowls toward the far kennel, starting to distribute dinner among the dogs.

The sad thing is, even after everything, I hope so too.

———

I'm close to home, running through a mental checklist of the work I need to finish tonight, when I realize I forgot my Calculus textbook in my locker.

I rushed out of school as soon as the final bell rang, eager to get to the animal shelter. Actively avoiding Holden. Not that he was trying to talk to me.

I turn around in a random driveway and speed back toward the high school.

The lot is almost empty. I forcibly shove back the memories of the last time I was here with so few cars as I park right in front of the school. Quiet hallways greet me as I enter the building and hurry toward my locker. There's no one else around. I grab the textbook I need and retrace my steps back outside.

I'm halfway to my car when movement catches my attention out of the corner of my eye.

My heartbeat stops and stutters before I realize the tall frame doesn't belong to the boy I'm avoiding.

Harrison smiles as he approaches, as friendly as ever. "Hi, Cassia."

"Hi, Harrison," I reply.

We haven't spoken since he stayed behind at Fellini's after his teammates left and hung out with me, Sydney, and Graham. Honestly, that's the last time I thought about him—until Holden brought him up at the basketball court.

"How've you been?" he asks.

"Um, okay."

Harrison nods, understanding. He knows I'm best friends with Sydney. Which is useful, honestly. I'd be just as affected by Mr. Adams's death if Holden had been his only child because it affected Holden. It's easier to hide how much I care about Holden under the guise of how recent events have affected my best friend, which makes me feel spectacularly shitty.

"You doing anything tonight?"

"No," I answer, honestly. Sydney is going over to Graham's. I was planning to watch a documentary and go to bed early, like a geriatric spinster.

"Jack Randall is having a party. If you want to hang out...I'll be there."

"I'll think about it," I tell him.

"Okay," he replies, smiling before he walks away.

I told myself to move on. Holden told me to move on.

But still...I'm conflicted.

———

Three hours later, I park in front of Jack Randall's house. After a twenty-minute speech on what I should be aware of at a high school party, my parents told me it was okay for me to go.

I was shocked. Part of me told them so I wouldn't be able to come. So it wouldn't be a possibility.

Instead, they endorsed it. Said they were happy I was going out. I guess I haven't hidden my heartbreak over Holden as well as I thought. It's a new low—when your parents think you're pathetic.

Maggie fussed over my hair and outfit. I'm wearing skinny jeans and a top I never would have picked out for myself, my hair straight and my eyes smoky.

I feel good. I'm also scanning the other vehicles parked as I walk toward the front door, looking for a familiar truck. There's still no sign of it when I reach the front door.

It's unlocked. I step inside, the scent of beer and sweat immediately reminding me of the only other high school party I've been to. I push away the memories forcibly.

Holden wants me to move on.

Told me to move on.

Living in the past won't do me any good.

I spot Harrison as soon as I enter the living room. He walks over to me right away.

"Hey!"

"Hi," I reply, tugging the hem of my borrowed shirt anxiously. I'm awkward and uncomfortable. Proud of myself for coming and also ready to leave.

"You want a drink?"

"I'm driving."

"There's soda, Cassia."

"Oh. Okay, sure."

Harrison smiles at me and then guides me into the kitchen. He grabs me a ginger ale, which I sip on as he introduces me around. *You know Cassia, right?* is a constant refrain.

It's sweet of him to include me. I try to relax and enjoy myself, nodding along like I get jokes and agree with what everyone is saying as I down the ginger-flavored soda.

I finish it about fifteen minutes after I arrive and immediately have to go to the bathroom.

As soon as the lacrosse player he was talking to heads into the kitchen, I ask Harrison where it is.

"I'll show you," he offers.

"You don't have to do that."

"I know. But it can get a little crazy upstairs, and the lineup there will be shorter."

I smile and nod, following him toward the staircase. I try to ignore the fact people are looking at me. It's a novelty I'm here, I guess. I also try to ignore how neither Holden nor any of his friends appear to be here. I didn't think Pembrooke was large enough to host multiple major parties in one night.

Maybe he's drunk at the old court again.

Not my problem, I remind myself. He made that clear.

Harrison leads me to a bathroom upstairs. There's only one girl in front of me, so it's a short wait. I use the restroom. Study my appearance as I wash my hands.

I hardly recognize myself in the mirror.

I look older. Adult. More like a woman than a girl. From the outside, you'd hardly know anything is wrong. On the inside, I'm a mess. I want to be here. Want to move on and be over him. Why can't *wanting* that be enough?

Harrison is waiting dutifully when I walk out of the bathroom. Leaning against the opposite wall, wearing a small smile.

I study him as I approach. His jeans and his Pembrooke Football sweatshirt.

And I will myself to feel something. Anything.

Nothing.

When I reach Harrison, I do something that shocks us both.

I kiss him.

It takes him a few seconds to start kissing me back. But once he does, it's hesitant. Tentative. At first, I think it's surprise. But we kiss and kiss and it's a long ways from consuming. Water lapping at my toes as opposed to being pulled under by a rip current.

When Holden kisses me, I have to remind my heart to beat. My lungs to breathe.

I pull back slowly, dreading having to explain my actions to Harrison. We stare at each other for a few seconds.

"Sorry," I say. "I shouldn't have done that."

"Don't be. I enjoyed it."

I'm blushing. I can feel the heat in my cheeks. "Oh. Um, good. You ready to go back downstairs?"

Harrison doesn't move. "Why'd you do it?"

I shift my weight from foot to foot. My fingernails dig into my palms.

"Why did you kiss me, Cassia?" he asks again.

His tone is kind, but it beckons an answer. One I don't want to give him. I kissed him because I wanted to break what is already battered. I wanted to destroy me and Holden beyond repair. Wipe away the past and prove I'm capable of moving on.

And that isn't me. I'm not the girl who uses one guy to make another jealous. And the worst part is, I'm not sure if Holden would even care if he knew I just kissed someone else. We fooled around, same as he's done with lots of other girls.

"I just...wanted to."

He nods like that was the answer he was expecting. Then he looks away, down the hallway. "It's obvious you're in love with him."

Harrison doesn't even specify who he's talking about. He says it like it's obvious—to him, to everyone.

"I...I don't want to be." I whisper the words, worried about what truth they hold.

Another nod. "I know. Adams is an even bigger idiot than I thought."

I flinch when he says Holden's name.

Something wry and knowing twists Harrison's expression. "I wish I could be your rebound guy, Cassia. But I like you too much. You're my first choice, and I'll always be your second."

"Holden and I are finished. There's too much...too much has happened. There's more hate than love there now."

"Hate and love are the two most powerful emotions. If you feel both for the same person…"

"You're saying I'm screwed."

He quirks a smile. "I'm saying, give Adams hell."

"He doesn't…" I look away, because it's embarrassing to admit. "Things weren't like that between us. We were just casual."

"He told you that?"

I nod.

Harrison swears under his breath. "Come on, let's go downstairs."

A moan sounds from one of the closed doors we pass. I glance at Harrison and he smirks.

"I'll set anyone straight who thinks that's what we were doing up here."

"You don't have to." I doubt Harrison is a crappy kisser. Which means my reaction earlier means my body is not ready to move past Holden. That doesn't mean he can't think that I have.

He smirks. "The basketball team is tight. You're putting a target on my back."

"Why would the basketball team care?"

"Because *Holden* will care, Cassia."

"I told you—"

"Yeah, I know. I'm sure that's what *he* told *you*. But he lied. Adams has always been a wild card. The fighting, the—"

"What fighting?"

Harrison exhales. "He used to fight for money, down at the old high school."

I think of all the Friday nights he came home with bruises or bloody. How I assumed it was an errant elbow or a trip or a game that got "heated."

I feel foolish. Oblivious. Inexperienced.

Did I ever really know him at all?

Right at the top of the stairs, I pause. Lean back against the wall and exhale. I feel the hot tears coming and let them loose. Here, where no one else but Harrison can see.

Harrison looks horrified. And uncomfortable. "Cassia, I—"

I wave his concern away, then swipe at my cheeks. "It's fine. I'm fine. I'm just…" I take a deep breath. Wipe away a few more tears. "He never told me. I gave him everything, you know? He gave me nothing." I sigh. "Sorry. Let's go."

"Don't apologize. Do you need another minute?"

"No. I'm good. I promise."

"Okay." He doesn't move. Neither do I.

"People went to these fights?" I ask, curiosity getting the better of me.

"Yeah. They placed bets. That's how it made money. Holden always won, so he drew a crowd."

"You went?"

"Yeah. Once. He fought a guy from Ridgemont's football team. Most of my teammates were going, so I did too. Adams kicked his ass."

I nod. I can't picture it. Can't fully register it.

We walk downstairs and head into the kitchen. It's more crowded than it was earlier, but I have no issue picking one face out of the dozens gathered.

Holden's expression doesn't change when he sees me.

But I catalogue the tiny changes in his posture. The way his fingers tighten around the plastic cup he's holding. The flex as he tightens his jaw. How his eyes bounce between me and Harrison.

There's no way Harrison hasn't noticed Holden is here. But he acts oblivious, guiding me over to the fridge and pulling out a chilled bottle of water, which he hands to me.

I shoot him a grateful smile as I take it, twisting off the cap and taking a long swallow. The cold water soothes my throat and settles in my stomach. I focus on the sensation, trying to tune everything else out.

"What the fuck did you do, Baker?"

Suddenly, Holden is near, close enough I can smell cinnamon.

"Ask yourself that same question, Adams," Harrison retorts.

The kitchen falls silent, all other sounds leaching away like water through a sieve.

Holden looks at me. "What happened?"

"None of your business. We're *done*, remember?"

Something flashes across Holden's face before he looks at Harrison. Something other than indifference, which is what I was expecting to see. He doesn't look peeved, like a little kid annoyed someone else is playing with his toys. He looks *hurt*, and the sad organ in my chest thumps pathetically.

Holden glares at Harrison. Harrison looks at me, wearing a *told you so* expression.

But I don't think Holden is jealous. I think he's mad he was wrong about me moving on. That what is pissing him off is seeing me at a party with another guy and not heartbroken at home.

There's no regret on his face. No resentment. Just rage—pure and strong.

Holden looks away from Harrison, at me. "What happened upstairs?" he asks again.

"Are you asking if I hooked up with him? Because that's not really any of your business."

His jaw tenses to the point it looks like it could snap in two. "You've been crying."

"So? Go do *whatever the fuck you want*, Holden."

His blue eyes blaze as I throw his words back at him. "I didn't mean—"

"Yes, you did. You did mean it. That's the problem."

I brush past him, heading for the kitchen island that's covered with a wide array of bottles. I grab a plastic cup from the stack and one bottle at random, pouring a generous splash. I tip it back and swallow, enjoying the burn as it slides down my throat. But it leaves behind the bitter aftertaste of regret. I promised my parents I wouldn't drink tonight.

"Leave it, man," I hear Harrison say.

"Don't talk to me, Baker," Holden responds.

I drink more after listening to that exchange. Heat trickles lazily into my veins as I sense him approaching me. I spin and stare him down, my gaze defiant as I drain the rest of the cup.

Awareness simmers and crackles between us.

"There you are, Holden. Why did you—oh."

Everything in me tenses as Grace appears, slipping her arms around Holden's waist. He doesn't lean into her touch, but he sure as hell doesn't push her away.

My eyes prick, exhaustion and emotion overwhelming me. I'm not going to cry again, though. Not here, not in front of him.

I set my empty cup on the counter. Take a step forward and rise on my tippy-toes. Holden inhales sharply as the space between us shrinks down to inches.

"His dick is bigger than yours," I whisper in his ear.

Then I walk away, out of the kitchen, not turning around once. Not even when I hear something crash behind me.

I need to get the hell out of here before I do anything else I'll regret.

I don't make it far, though. I weave through the living room and end up on the front porch.

I pull my phone out of my pocket and call my home number.

My mom answers. "Cassia?"

"Hi, Mom. Can you come pick me up?"

I wait for the disappointment, but all I hear in her voice is understanding. "Of course. Text me the address, okay?"

"Okay. Thanks."

I hang up and send her my location. Take a seat on the railing and stare up at the sky. It's a clear night. All the stars seem visible, sprinkled through the heavens as pinpricks of light. Beautiful and massive.

The front door opens a few minutes later. Harrison steps out.

I give him a sheepish smile. "I'm really sorry about all that."

"Don't apologize, Cassia."

"Bet you regret inviting me."

"No, I don't," he tells me, earnest. "Do you regret coming?"

"I haven't decided yet, honestly. I was hoping for some closure."

"I don't think closure is something to hope for. Either you want it, or you don't."

"Are you saying I don't want it?"

"I don't know. Do you?"

I glance up at the stars again. "I want to want it. Does that count?"

When I look at him again, Harrison is smiling. "No. It doesn't."

My phone buzzes in my lap. I look down to see a message from my mom. Our blue minivan is visible between two of the cars parked directly in front of the house. "My mom is here. I texted her after I started drinking."

Earlier, I would have been embarrassed to admit that. Now, I don't really care. I'm emotionally tapped, incapable of caring.

Harrison nods.

Impulsively, I step forward and give him a hug. He smells like laundry detergent and spicy cologne. Nice, but not cinnamon.

"Thank you—for tonight."

He smiles as we separate. "You know, the first time I noticed you was during the Homecoming assembly freshman year. We were seated alphabetically. Adams was in the row right in front of me. The whole time—when the principal was talking, when the cheerleaders were performing, when the team captain was giving a speech—he kept glancing over to the right. It took me a little while to figure out what he was looking at."

I wait. Raise an eyebrow.

"*You*, Cassia."

"If he cared—at all—I wouldn't be out here with you, Harrison," I tell him. "No offense."

Harrison grins. "None taken. But I've been at a lot of the same parties as Adams. He cares—a lot."

I sigh, too exhausted to keep arguing and not wanting to keep my mom waiting any longer. "Night, Harrison."

"Night, Cassia."

I walk down the front steps to the waiting car. My mom glances over as I settle in the passenger seat and snap my seatbelt. She starts driving right away, which I'm grateful for. All I want right now is to go home and go to bed. And hopefully wake up as someone better equipped to handle heartbreak. I'm not proud of the way I acted tonight, no matter how forgiving Harrison was. I shouldn't have said what I did to Holden, shouldn't have had a drink. My actions blurred the line into mistakes. I'm not sure how to move on without making them.

"Did you have fun?" my mom asks as she flicks on the blinker and makes a left turn.

"No."

She laughs at my candor, but it's brief. "I'm sorry, sweetheart."

I stare out the window. I can't see anything besides blackness. "It was my own fault."

"Did something happen?"

"I fell in love."

"Tonight?" I hear the attempt at levity in her tone. But there's also understanding. Acknowledgment.

"Ten years ago, when we moved in across the street."

There's a long stretch of silence, none of it sounding like surprise. She knew. "Love can take time, honey. Face obstacles. It doesn't mean it's not real. That it doesn't matter."

I look over at my mom's profile, surprised. I figured she was going to tell me to forget he ever existed. Girl power. Independence. Value your own worth. "He doesn't love me."

"Did he tell you that?"

"He said I was better off without him."

"Do you think you are?"

I don't hesitate before answering. "No."

"Maybe you should tell him that."

The rest of the drive home is silent.

CHAPTER TWENTY-TWO

HOLDEN

Grace gapes at me, shocked. My hand throbs like a motherfucker, but it's nothing compared to the anguish splintering in my chest. I storm past a shocked Finn and out onto the back deck. No one else is out here—it's freezing.

The cold feels good. Numbing.

I take a seat on the picnic table, trying to focus on the physical pain and nothing else. I don't realize I'm bleeding until some blood drips onto the wood beneath me. I yank down the t-shirt I'm wearing beneath my sweatshirt and wrap my split knuckle in the white fabric. It's immediately stained red.

My breaths come in ragged gasps, pain and fury roiling my insides. My eyes screw tightly shut, trying to force away the images my brain conjures easily. Harrison kissing her. Touching her. *Fucking* her. I'm tempted to punch another cabinet.

As angry as I am with Cassia, I'm even more furious with myself. I did this.

I pushed her away when she was only trying to help.

I made her hate me, when it was a miracle she cared in the first place.

And I knew there would be consequences. I didn't think they'd be her coming downstairs with some guy, hair tousled and lips swollen. Didn't know that sight would feel like a hot knife to my chest. I've fooled around with plenty of girls. I've seen most of them with other guys, and it never bothered me at all.

I should have known she'd be different. I *did* know, which is part of why I did it.

Masochism and self-sabotage are two of the things I'm best at. I knew she'd move on eventually; knew we were headed on two very different paths. If it wasn't Harrison, it would have been someone else.

I thought a clean break sooner rather than later would be better. Would hurt less.

Except, I can't imagine anything hurting more than this.

The screen door squeaks open. Mark steps out.

I look away, not wanting to see anyone. Definitely not wanting to talk. "Here." He holds a bag of ice in front of me.

"I'm cold enough, thanks."

He drops it in my lap. "For your hand, dipshit. We've still got a championship to win, remember?"

I can't summon anything in me to care about basketball right now. But I grunt a "thanks" as I drop the cold bag on my split knuckles.

"You love her, huh?"

I clench my jaw so tightly I hear a crack.

Mark sighs. "Baker said he didn't screw her."

"He's worried I'll come after him."

"Why would you do that, if you don't care?"

I scoff. I care, and he knows I care. He's trying to force me to admit it. Maybe I should. Pretending she doesn't matter to me hasn't accomplished a whole heck of a lot. It's landed me bitter and freezing out here.

Mark sighs when I say nothing else. "He doesn't look like a guy who just got laid. He looks like a guy who doesn't have a shot in hell with the girl he wants. *You* do." Mark claps my shoulder, then heads inside.

I sit for a while longer, letting the cold numb me. I'm sober, which I haven't been in weeks.

Eventually, I fish my keys out of my pocket and walk toward my truck. I'm not sure why I came tonight. Part of me wishes I hadn't. Now I have the sight of Cassia coming downstairs seared into my brain.

It was an attempt to return to normalcy, I guess. An acknowledgment the path I'm on is a destructive one. My dad would want better. Would be disappointed by the way I've acted since his death. That realization singes in a way little else has managed to affect me in weeks.

All the lights are off across the street when I park in the driveway. Cassia's car isn't there. The knowledge niggles against my skin like a rash, persistent and irritating. Maybe she went home with Baker. Maybe she's still at the party, dancing and drinking.

She's not mine. I have no claim over what she does or who she chooses to do it with. But yeah, it fucking stings.

Sydney is sitting on the couch, arms crossed, when I walk into the living room. I sigh, then drop my keys in the dish on the coffee table.

Of course this would be the night she stays up past eleven p.m. It's bad enough I feel like I'm disappointing my dad's ghost. I'm letting her down too.

"What happened to your hand?" she asks.

The bleeding has stopped, but my knuckles are still red and swollen. I debate lying, but she'll hear the truth at school on Monday. "I punched a cabinet."

Sydney's eyes widen. "What? Why?"

"Felt like it. I'm going to bed." I turn, heading toward the stairs.

"Was Cassia there?"

I still but don't turn around. "Yeah."

It didn't occur to me she would have told Sydney she was going to Jack's party. It should have.

"Did you apologize?"

I wince, recalling what I said to her. "She doesn't want to hear it. She hates me."

"*Goddammit*, Holden."

I flinch. Sydney never swears.

"She's my best friend. She's been there for me through everything. And I can't be there for her because you're my brother. She doesn't even want to come over here anymore. Won't talk to me about it, because I'm your sister and she doesn't want anything between her and you to affect our relationship. I have no idea what happened between you guys. Back in eighth grade, now, she won't tell me anything. Neither will you."

I close my eyes. "I'll go," I offer. "I'll spend a couple of nights at Finn's, and you guys can—"

"I don't want you to go, Holden. I want you to stay. To show up. To stop running away."

My jaw works. "I'm here right now. I'm here for you, Sydney. You're not alone."

"I'm not talking about *me*, Holden. Did you know Cassia has a cinnamon air freshener in her car? Those Lions tickets that her dad won last winter? I found a receipt for them in her room over the summer. The only day she drinks coffee in the afternoon is Friday, so she never falls asleep before me when she sleeps over. Those granola bars you eat every morning? She brings a new box over every week, for you."

The fist around my heart tightens.

"*Apologize*, Holden. Fucking grovel for her forgiveness. She might hate you right now but she's also in love with you. Has been since we were all kids. Anyone could see that, especially someone who knows you both as well as I do."

"She deserves better than me."

"You're right. She does."

I scoff at Sydney's hasty agreement.

"Better than this version of you, at least. But she wants *you*, Holden."

I tilt my head back to stare at the ceiling. "She hooked up with Harrison Baker at the party tonight."

"She told you that?"

"They came downstairs together."

Sydney stands and walks over toward me. "If you're not sure, let her go. If you are, *do something*."

"Sure of what?"

"You know what."

Then she walks up the stairs, leaving me standing here staring at the couch, where I first saw Cassia naked, with a mess in my head.

CHAPTER TWENTY-THREE

CASSIA

Everyone stares at me on Monday morning. It's the first indication that Friday night wasn't just a bad dream.

I hid out all weekend. I didn't answer any texts. Didn't go on social media. Didn't so much as glance at the house across the street.

Maggie and Sydney are silent as we walk inside the high school. It's a chilly, gray day that matches my mood perfectly. Maggie peels off to head toward the freshman wing. Sydney stays by my side as we walk down the busy hall.

It's not until we reach my locker that she speaks. "Did something happen between you and Harrison on Friday night?"

My muscles tense as I put my lunch away. "I thought you were over him. Especially now that you're with Graham."

"I am. That's not why I'm asking."

"Does it matter?"

"To Holden? Yeah, it does. I'd never seen him more upset than when he got home on Friday night."

My fingers turn white as I grip a textbook so tightly no blood can circulate. "Sydney…" This isn't a topic I want to discuss with her. Not under these circumstances.

I considered telling her how I felt about Holden when we were in a good place. I never considered it might come up now, when we're a broken disaster.

"You're the two people I love most in the world, Cassia. And you're both miserable."

I tense, wondering what the hell Holden told her in order for her to land at that conclusion. "That's not my fault."

"I know. I'm not taking sides, I swear. Holden said he messed up. But if there's a chance you can forgive him—"

"He hasn't *asked* me to forgive him."

Sydney sighs. "I know. He's an idiot. He's hurt, though. And angry."

My fingers start to feel numb. He must have shared a lot. Why? "He has no right to be."

"Would it have bothered you if you saw him coming downstairs with someone else?"

Yes. "Whoever told you about me and Harrison obviously left out that Grace was all over Holden."

"*Holden* is the one who told me about you and Harrison, Cas."

"He did?" I'm surprised, and it saturates my voice. Holden doesn't talk about what bothers him, usually. He holds it in until he lets it out with flying fists or harsh words. Illicit fights at the old basketball courts. Smashed bottles and secrets. "What, uh, what else did he say?"

Sydney shakes her head. "He's my brother, Cassia. Don't put me in the middle."

The problem is, I can't ask Holden. I *won't* ask him. I've folded when it comes to him too many times. My pride won't allow me to ask him for answers when he's given me no indica-tion he regrets how he handled things between us.

"I can't believe he said anything to you."

"Why?"

"He's just…it's not…I mean, we're not…" I fumble for words. "Does it bother you?"

"That you never told me how you felt about him? Not really. I figured it out a while ago."

I look away. "I would have told you if it became anything serious."

Sydney laughs. "Cassia. Holden punched a cabinet over what-ever he thinks you did with Harrison Baker. It's serious for him."

"He *told* me to date Harrison at the court that night." I feel obligated to defend myself. I'm also admitting to a lie. When Sydney asked me what we were arguing about, I said I was lecturing him about drinking. A partial truth, not the full one.

Sydney nods right as the first bell rings as the two-minute warning. "He cares too much, Cassia. It's not because he doesn't care *enough*."

She says *that*, then darts off. I want to call after her and demand more of an explanation. I trust Sydney. Rely on her. Harrison telling me Holden has feelings for me didn't have the same effect.

The second warning bell rings, and it prompts me into action. The rule-following part of myself won't allow me to be late.

I duck into first period right as the loudspeaker crackles to life for the morning announcements. I take my usual seat in the third row and flip through the pages of my planner, crossing off the assignments I've already finished.

"Are you going to the basketball game tonight?" London asks, leaning over. The low hum of chatter echoes around us.

"Um, no. Probably not." My voice is sharper than I mean it to be. Mostly because of *who* the captain of the basketball team is. My life is filled with reminders of him, and it makes me wish my acceptance or rejection letters had already arrived so I had a solid means of escape from them.

London's cheeks flush. "Oh. Okay."

I grip my pen tighter, trying to get my emotions under control. "Sorry. I'm super tired. Are you going?" I struggle to keep my voice light and unaffected.

"Yeah, probably. I mean—"

"Hey, Bobcats."

I freeze at the sound of the familiar voice. London stops talking. So does everyone else. The room I'm in is suddenly silent.

"This is Holden Adams. Tonight, we're playing the Edgewood Ravens, so make sure that you come out and show your support. As most of you know, my dad passed away a few weeks ago. A portion of the tickets sold tonight will be donated to an organization that works to prevent drunk driving. It's a worthy cause to support, even if you're not a basketball fan."

There's a long pause, and I think he's done talking. So does everyone else. The gossip starts up immediately, people muttering about Mr. Adams. About their plans to attend the game tonight.

"I also wanted to say…"

Silence falls again, everyone trying to hear what Holden is going to say, as if he's whispering instead of speaking on the loudspeaker so his voice is echoing around the room.

"I'm sorry, Cassia."

My heart takes off at a gallop. The whoosh of blood makes it hard to hear. My fingernails dig into the skin of my palm, hard enough they're probably leaving marks. I can't believe he's doing this.

Here.

Now.

At all.

Years of meaning nothing to him in the four walls of this high school. And now, this. An acknowledgment that confuses every instinct.

There's some noise in the background. The screech of feedback.

"Game tonight starts at seven. Be there or be lame."

The loudspeaker shuts off. And everyone turns to stare at me.

My locker looks foreign. I stare at the neat row of books like I've never even seen it before.

My mind is preoccupied. By the stares and whispers that have followed me around all day. By the words he said and the wondering about whether he meant them.

"Hi."

I bite on the inside of my cheek hard enough to taste blood before I turn to him.

Holden looks cool, calm, and collected as he leans against the locker next to mine. Relaxed, as he holds the strap of his back-pack and stares at me.

I swallow. "Hi."

"Are you coming tonight?"

"I haven't decided."

It's a lie. I know I'll be there. But it doesn't mean I forgive him, and I don't want him to think that it does.

Holden nods. "Okay."

"That wasn't much of a sales pitch." I speak without thinking, falling into the instinct to speak first and think second that's always been way too easy around him.

He grins, but it disappears quickly. "I'm not here to talk you into anything. I meant it when I said you're better off without me."

Everything in me tenses at the reminder of that conversation.

"I'm selfish, Cassia. I've always tried to protect you from that. But it doesn't mean I don't care about you. I gave you my heart a long time ago. You don't have to believe me. I won't blame you if you don't forgive me. You can punish me. Ignore me. Hate me. But no matter what, it will always be yours."

Weeks ago, this speech would have made me melt. Now, I challenge everything he's saying. "Was it mine when you were ignoring me for years, Holden? When you were with other girls? When you forgot about our friendship?"

Holden winces, looking away and running a hand through his hair before he holds my gaze.

"I would change things if I could, Cassia." He reaches into his backpack and pulls out a composition notebook. I recognize it. It's the same one he told me was full of stats when I reached for it in his bedroom.

I doubt that's what he's handing me. "What's this?"

"Things I never told you."

I start to open it. He stops me, holding a palm to the cover. "Don't read it here. Just…you don't have to read it at all, actually. But every time during the last few years, when I thought of something I wanted to tell you, I'd write it down. That's what's in here. So, yeah. Hate me, I deserve it. Mistakes, I've made plenty. But don't ever think I forgot about you. That I didn't care. That you've ever meant nothing to me. I know you won't believe me if I just tell you that. So here's the proof, if you want it."

Before I can say a word in response, he's turning and walking away.

I'm not the only one who tracks his movements down the hallway. But I'm the only one holding a notebook of his thoughts.

————

I end up in the library, which has been my sanctuary throughout all of high school. A peaceful, sacred space. I walk to my favorite table, spread my homework out, and then pull the notebook out of the laptop compartment of my backpack where I stored it.

Stare at it.

I glance around, like someone might be reading over my shoulder. There are a few other people around, but no one nearby. I open to the first page, smiling at the messy scribble covering the neat lines.

Made the shot from just past the marigolds Mrs. Lowe planted. You would have missed. That's the first entry.

My dad was only home for six days this time. Trips are getting longer. Sydney probably told you that, is the second.

They go on and on. Pages of increasingly neat lettering detailing comments about basketball. About his friends. About his dad. About Sydney.

There's never anything about other girls, but there's a lot about me.

You should wear your hair down more often.

Finn made a comment about dating you and I shoved him into the lockers. Probably wouldn't actually have told you that, is a recent entry.

It takes me a couple of hours to read through and reach the last page that has writing on it. It's close to the end of the notebook that contains years' worth of thoughts. None of the entries are dated. But there are small clues scattered throughout that hint at timing. Entries that mention prom and Homecoming. Holidays and certain classes.

The final entry is separated from the one before it by three lines, instead of one. The letters are large, like he knew there would be nothing after it.

I love you too.

I stare at them. Trace them. The pen strokes are harsh, cutting into the paper and leaving sharp indents behind.

I remain in the library until it's nearing seven, the start of the game. I try to do homework, but I mostly stare at the notebook.

Sydney texts me at quarter of seven, telling me she and Graham are going to the game and asking if I want a ride. I reply, telling her I'll meet her there before I pack up my books and leave the library.

There's a steady stream of people headed into the gym as I approach it. All the players are already out on the court, warming up.

I find Sydney and Graham easily. They're sitting front and center. Both of them eye me curiously but say nothing about this morning's announcements or anything Holden-related. I'm grateful, especially once I spot him on the court.

We're close enough to the sideline that he looks larger than life. He walks across the court like he's commanding its presence, the snug fit of his uniform impossible to ignore as he gestures and talks with his teammates.

My eyes trail him instead of focusing on anything else, absorbing every little detail.

Every now and then, Holden looks away from the court. It seems like he's looking for something, but he doesn't glance my way. Not until the very start of the game. He sees Sydney first and gives her a wave. Then spots me and freezes.

We stare at each other for what feels like far too long.

He gives me a nod of acknowledgment, and then the game begins. I barely pay attention to any of the plays taking place, too lost in the confusion of my own head. I came because I couldn't not come, and I'm not sure that's the right reasoning.

There's some part of me that is used to capitulating to him, to taking what little he offers, and I don't think that's a healthy instinct. He's too adept at pulling me in and then shutting his feelings down.

It's devastating for my head. For my heart.

The final whistle is startling. I was watching the whole game and missed every moment. I know they won, but still have to glance at the scoreboard to confirm.

Sydney stretches and glances at me as other spectators start to file out of the gym. It was a sold-out game, the gym fuller than I've ever seen it. "Are you staying?"

I know my answer before I say it. "Yeah."

Her smile eases any fears I had about her not accepting me and Holden, on the off chance that we became something *to* accept. "Okay."

She wants to say more, I can tell, but she doesn't, just giving me a hug before she and Graham depart.

I stay seated, watching everyone else filter out of the gymnasium. Through the lobby and outside into the parking lot.

Holden is the first player to walk out of the locker room, with wet hair and a serious expression. It seems like he rushed, and I suddenly can't think of anything else besides the four words he scrawled on that last page. I don't need to ask to know when he wrote them.

"Hey." He stops at the edge of the bleachers, his grip tight on his gym bag.

"Good game," I say.

"Yeah. Thanks." He kicks the edge of the bleachers. Exhales. "You read it?"

"Yeah." That's all I say. I'm not sure what else to. I can't keep up with how I feel about Holden.

I know there's love—a lot of it. That's why everything else is so amplified. Why, when he hurts me, it feels like my heart is being squeezed too tight. Why, when he kisses or touches me, it feels like the sweetest euphoria. He's the highest of highs and the lowest of lows. Only a masochist would willingly accept that exquisite torture.

But maybe I am one.

Maybe he made me one.

I stare at him, memorizing every detail. The letterman jacket he's wearing with his jeans. The way his brown hair is mussed, like he's been running a hand through it. The bob of his Adam's apple.

"You hungry?" He sounds nervous and uncertain—two adjectives I'd never associate with Holden Adams normally.

"Starving," I admit.

"We could go to Fellini's?"

Fellini's is where *everyone* will be headed, and he knows it. The two of us showing up there—together—would be a statement. One I'm shocked he's willing to make.

I fiddle with the strap of my backpack and then force myself to say exactly what I'm thinking. "I've always been here, Holden. Waiting. For years. You ignored me for *years*. Why should I believe you've cared all along? About any of it? What happens the next time you're angry or upset? The next time you tell me I'm just a fuck who means nothing to you?"

He winces. "I was drunk and pissed. It's not an excuse. It's just how I felt. My dad…it was a lot."

"I know." I manage to say, through a thick throat.

"You were trying to help. And I lashed out—because I was sad and angry, and I didn't know how else to deal with it. I didn't say it because I meant it. I said it because I'm in love with you, and I was trying to hurt *me*, more than you. Trying to take away the one thing that made me happy, so that I could just be miserable. It's not an excuse, just the truth. And you deserve to know it. Deserve better than me. I'm the cautionary tale parents tell their kids—the guy who could've been something but self-destructed instead. There are so many things I'd go back and fix if I could. But you and me? The good parts? Cassia, there's nothing I'd change."

I swallow. "Did you sleep with her? Grace?"

"I haven't been with anyone since you dry-humped me in my driveway."

Despite my confusion, my anger, I feel myself blush. I look away, studying the empty rows of bleachers. "I have no idea what the size of Harrison's dick is."

I hear him exhale. It sounds like relief.

Part of me is scared to trust this place where we're headed. The rest of me knows it's inevitable.

Knows I'll regret not falling into this far more than I'd ever regret not walking away.

I stand and walk down the bleachers. Don't stop until I'm standing right in front of him, under the blinding lights of the gymnasium that is entirely empty. "I gave my heart to you a long time ago, Holden. Stop breaking it, okay?"

Holden's smile is unexpected. Breath-taking. My heart thumps in my chest. Alive. Active. *Whole.*

"Those Friday nights when you'd come home, bloody and beaten up. Were you playing basketball?"

He holds my gaze as his head shakes. "Baker has a big mouth, huh?" There's no venom in his voice. Mostly resignation. Maybe some regret. "The fighting was stupid, flower. I needed—I *wanted* —an outlet. It felt good in the moment. I'm focusing on what makes me feel better all the time. What makes me want to *be* better. Basketball…and you."

I scan his face, absorbing his earnestness. "Stop doing things I'll have to forgive, okay?"

"Okay."

"No more fights and no more shutting down. Or I'm done, Holden. I mean it."

He nods. "I promise."

We stare at each other. Tentative feelings bloom in my chest. Hope and anticipation and lust and love.

"So…dinner?" he asks.

I nod and turn toward the door. I'm embarrassingly eager to go out with him. To take what he's offering and hope and pray this time will end differently between us. Holden grabs my arm before I can take a step. Stalls me in place and says, "You were wrong."

"What?"

"You said I'm good at everything, remember? I'm not, Cassia. I'm terrible at a lot of things, and I'm especially bad at this." He gestures between us, then tucks a stray piece of hair that's fallen out of my ponytail behind one ear. "You're easy to love. I'm just…really bad at loving."

"But…do you? Love me?"

It was one thing to read it. Another to look at him while he says it. "Yeah. I love you, Cassia."

The water in my eyes starts to overflow, dribbling down my face in thin streams. He brushes one tear away with his thumb. "Can I kiss you?"

"You've never asked for permission before," I say.

And then I kiss him. It's punishing and bruising. Desperate and deep.

But then something shifts. His mouth opens, his tongue

tangles with mine. Holden is kissing me like I'm oxygen and water combined—like I'm something he can't live without. Like he's desperate for it and miserable without it.

Like he used to.

When he pulls away, he grabs my hand. And then we walk off the court.

Together.

"Stop smiling." Mark says.

My grin stretches my cheeks.

Finn rolls his eyes. "It wasn't that good of a shot."

It was, though. I celebrate by raising my cold can of beer in a cheers motion before taking a sip.

Jordan takes his turn. We're playing a version of H-O-R-S-E with more letters. S-E-N-I-O-R-S. It seemed fitting, considering we graduated high school today. As of midnight, we'll be kicked back to freshman status.

I glance across the yard, scanning the faces gathered round. Finally, I find her.

Cassia stares straight at me. Her hair is down and loose, brown curls falling over the green t-shirt she's wearing. She smiles. Mouths *good shot* before Sydney says something and steals her attention away.

I resist the urge to walk over to her. The guys would give me shit for it, but I don't care about that. I want her to have time with Sydney. Come fall, she and I will be leaving for Richmond together. I got a full ride offer and so did she.

There were other schools she got into too. More prestigious schools. But she chose Richmond, and I'm not sure how to convey to her how much that matters to me.

My dad's younger sister, Catherine, requested a remote work option. She's moving to Pembrooke in September and will be staying with Sydney through her senior year, so she's not all alone and is able to finish high school in the same town.

Sometimes it seems silly, how much time I spent worrying about the future and all that could go wrong.

Other times I feel guilty for feeling so happy when my dad is gone and my mom doesn't care. I never told Sydney about her brief reappearance. I want to shield her from whatever I can. Maybe one day I will. Slowly, I'm learning that opening up leads to more good than bad. But I'm not sure anything good could come from mentioning our mom. She hasn't shown up since the school parking lot. Whatever obligation she felt to check in after our dad's death was short-lived at best.

Mostly, I'm grateful that my mistakes aren't permanent. That Cassia didn't kick me to the curb the way I probably deserved.

"Your turn, Adams." Finn bounces the ball to me.

I back up a few more feet, then take the shot. It swishes, and all the guys around me groan.

I'm the only one without a letter. Most of them miss from the spot, racking up another themselves.

Mark is the first to earn a second S. Rather than keep playing for other places, we abandon the game, spreading back through the party.

I beeline for Cassia, walking up behind her and closing my arms around her.

She leans back against me and glances up. "Did you win?"

I pull her closer to me and drop a blistering kiss on her lips. I pour everything into it—love and lust and vulnerability.

Cassia is an addiction—a healthy one. She soothes the darkness. Makes me want to be less destructive. Care more. Focus more. Matter more.

We don't separate until my lungs are burning for air. "Basically."

"I could have beat you."

I scoff. "Sure."

She rolls her eyes, but smiles.

I savor it—the feel of her in my arms and the soft expression on her face. "Finn wants to play Truth or Dare for old time's sake. He's been talking about it all morning."

"I'd rather play with just you."

"Oh, yeah?" I wrap one of her curls around one finger and tug. "Well, the truth is…I really want to fuck you right now."

Cassia's hazel eyes widen with surprise, then another emotion I recognize. Lust. "You asking me to go upstairs with you, Holden Adams?"

"Not asking. Just stating a fact."

Going upstairs at a party together comes with a label. Even though we've been officially dating for months, people will notice. Care. Talk. It doesn't bother me, but I don't want Cassia to be uncomfortable.

She grabs my hand and pulls me toward the stairs, in full sight of everyone. The kitchen is crowded and so is the living room. But people make way for us, most of them watching with wide eyes. I guess we're still some sort of novelty.

Once we're upstairs, I pull her into the first bedroom.

Everything I thought I'd hate about commitment is absent when I'm with her.

I love how familiar I am with her body. Love how there's no hesitation when she tugs down my shorts and grips me, familiar and eager.

We've done this many times before. But somehow, it never loses its novelty.

I'm especially impatient tonight. Aunt Catherine was visiting this week for graduation, meaning it's been days since I've been inside of Cassia.

"Lie down," I whisper.

She falls back on the bed, watching as I tug her jeans down and parting her thighs to accommodate me between them. I pull her thong down and thrust inside of her.

Cassia moans, wrapping her legs around my waist and pulling me closer. I lean over, resting my weight on my forearms.

I kiss her, slow and searching. Her nails dig into my back, and I start moving faster. We both come quickly, within minutes. I don't move away, though. I soak in this moment, and it feels like she's doing the same.

"We'll be able to do this for four years at Richmond," she whispers, running a hand across my shoulder. "No parents or siblings."

As busy as my house has been lately, it's nothing in comparison to hers. I've never even managed to kiss her without one of her siblings bursting into the room or one of her parents calling from downstairs.

I kiss her again. "Forget college, Cassia. I fully intend to do this for the rest of my life."

Something sparks in her eyes. Hope, I think it looks like. I know I've given her a lot of reasons to distrust my intentions. But I can't imagine my life without her in it anymore. All my intentions of ever walking away from her left me a while ago. I'll do whatever I can to make up for it.

"Do you promise?" She whispers.

"Yeah, flower. I promise."

TUESDAY NIGHT TRUTHS

CHAPTER ONE

CASSIA

Humidity hangs in the August air like heavy curtains, hot and suffocating. Coating my bare skin and curling my long hair. Making each breath labored, even though I've barely exerted myself.

And the stupid ball won't go in.

It hits the rim for the third time in as many tries. Teeters. Then falls toward me instead of through the net.

I let out a frustrated huff, my irritation having hardly anything to do with my abysmal scoring percentage. It's just an easier annoyance to focus on.

I retrieve the ball and dribble back to the top of the crease, the rubber surface of the basketball damp and sticky. The tiny circles rub against my fingertips with each bounce, the texture adding some force to each slam.

Pound. Pound. Pound.

I reach the line, turn, and shoot again. Rubber ricochets against metal as the ball bounces once on the rim and then falls in the wrong direction again.

A long, blown out breath doesn't release any of my frustration.

Four unsuccessful attempts later, I give up, abandoning the orange ball in the grass and grabbing my plastic cup. I carry it over to the bleachers, skirting the crowd gathered around center court. Someone set up a speaker next to the cooler of alcohol, a rap song with explicit lyrics splintering damp air that smells like weed.

I ignore the hub of activity and drop down on the metal still warm from the sun, kicking out my Converse and taking a long sip of water.

Grace and McKenzie are perched at the opposite end of the bleachers, talking and giggling with the group of popular girls I've never been a part of.

I could go over there. Could flip my hair and listen to the gossip about who's hooked up with who this summer like it's any of my business.

Instead, I tilt my head back to study the stars. The only reason I even showed up tonight is because it sounded slightly better than spending another night sitting at home.

I pull my phone out of my pocket, registering the lack of messages. Stare at it until the screen goes black.

Unsurprising that Maggie never texted me back. And thoroughly depressing, realizing my little sister has more of a scintillating social life than I do.

"Hey."

I startle at the sound of the unfamiliar voice, slipping my phone back into my pocket before it becomes obvious I was staring at a black screen. Glance up at a guy I've never seen before, who takes a seat on the bleacher below me and holds out a hand like we're attending a business meeting.

"I'm Brooks," he continues.

I clear my throat and straighten, leaning forward to shake his hand. His grip is firm, his palm cool and calloused. I'm sure mine is sweaty.

"Hi. I'm Cassia."

"Nice to meet you." He flashes a row of straight, white teeth at me, then drops my hand and picks up his red cup. "So, you play?"

"Play…"

Brooks raises his cup and tilts it in the direction of the hoop. "I was watching you earlier." He grimaces. "In a less creepy way than that just sounded. You're good."

The smile comes automatically. Not forced, the way so many have felt this summer. "You need your eyes checked, then. I didn't make a single shot."

He smiles back, the corners of his eyes creasing. He's cute, I realize belatedly. Tan skin. Tall. Blond, messy hair.

"Better than I can do," Brooks tells me.

"Yeah? Did you play?"

His long legs stretch out, his posture settling like he plans to stay put for a little while.

And it doesn't bother me.

I'm not looking for an escape route.

"In high school. But I sucked. I didn't make it to varsity until my senior year, and I'm pretty sure the only reason I got moved up was because the coaches felt sorry for me."

I laugh. His self-deprecation is oddly endearing. An indication I've spent too much time around guys way too full of themselves.

Brooks smiles. "You never answered my question. Did you play?"

"Up until high school, yeah."

"Why not in high school?"

I hesitate, and Brooks smiles apologetically.

"Sorry. I didn't mean to—"

"No, it's fine. I just decided to pursue other interests. Focus on school so I could get a good scholarship."

I push all thoughts of the other reason far, far away.

Instead of looking off-put by the revelation my family isn't rich and I'm a nerd, Brooks leans a little closer. "Where do you go to school?"

"Richmond College," I reply. "How about you?"

"Arlington University."

"Ah. So you know Finn?"

"Yep." Brooks takes a sip of his drink, then sets it down between us. "That's how I ended up here."

"Ah," I say.

"So, you wanna play?" He tilts his head toward the hoop. The few strings hanging from it are frayed. Bedraggled and worn. The town gave up on maintaining this place after the new high school was built.

"Um." I start to form an excuse, then decide not to bother. It's not exactly a blast, sitting here alone. Mark, who invited me when I ran into him at the gas station earlier, is clustered in the center of the court with the rest of the popular crowd. "Sure. Sounds good."

"Great." Brooks stands, then grabs his cup. "I'll meet you over there. Just going to grab a refill first. Want anything?"

"No, I'm just having water. Early morning."

"Me too. Can I grab you some?"

"Sure. Thanks." I pass him my cup.

Usually, I'd be wary of trusting a stranger. But Mark and Finn are standing right next to the cooler, and the large canister of water is sitting out in the open. Aside from me and Brooks, I doubt anyone is drinking any of it. I've been to enough of these gatherings to know it's usually reserved for later, once the beer is gone and pick-up play begins.

I stand and stretch as Brooks walks away, checking my phone again for messages. Only one, from my mom, wondering what time I'll be home. This is day five of my dad being gone on a work trip, and juggling my younger siblings is exhausting under the easiest of circumstances.

I respond, letting her know it'll be around eleven thirty. That gives me twenty more minutes here and means about seven hours of sleep.

After sliding my phone into the back pocket of my shorts, I head for the lone basketball. It's sitting in the same spot I abandoned it in earlier; everyone else is more interested in getting drunk and socializing than playing.

I dribble around aimlessly until Brooks returns with our drinks, accepting my cup from him and taking a grateful sip. The water I had left was lukewarm, and the icy, chilled liquid is far more refreshing.

"P-I-G?" I suggest, setting my cup down off to the side.

Brooks grins. "That'll be a short game, I'm guessing. H-O-R-S-E? Give me a chance?"

I smirk, then pass him the ball. "Sure."

He captures the bounce easily, making me think he's underselling his skills.

"Hey! Cassia!"

I turn, automatically smiling when I see Harrison walking over. "Hey!"

He opens his arms and I step in for a quick hug.

"How've you been?" he asks once we separate.

I keep the smile fixed on my face, aware he's studying me more intently than I'd like. "Same old. How about you? How was LA?"

He's been gone for the past month, staying with his grandparents in Southern California.

"Good. Flight took forever. I learned to surf." Harrison glances at Brooks, then holds out a hand. "Hey, man. I'm Harrison."

"I'm Brooks."

Harrison glances back and forth between the two of us, the question clear on his face. I'm relieved when Brooks elaborates.

"I go to Arlington with Finn. He invited me."

"Oh. Nice. You from the area?"

Brooks rolls the ball on his hip, shaking his head. "San Fran, actually."

"Nice. I've never been up that far north."

"It's a cool city."

An awkward silence falls. "Want to play H-O-R-S-E with us?" I ask Harrison. "We were just about to start."

"Nah, I'm good, thanks. Just wanted to say hi. Gotten my ass kicked by you before, Cas."

I roll my eyes. He's neglecting to mention that was a team's round, and most of the credit belonged to my partner.

"See you later," Harrison continues. "Nice to meet you, Brooks."

"You, too." Brooks glances at me, one eyebrow raised as soon as Harrison walks away. "Ex?" Then winces. "Sorry. I swear I'm not normally this nosy."

I smile. "It's fine. And no, we're just friends. It's a small town thing, I guess. Everyone kinda keeps track of each other."

His hum sounds a lot like a disagreement, but Brooks says nothing else. He takes his first shot, which is a near miss.

I retrieve the ball and take my first shot. My unlucky streak finally ends, the ball falling through the hoop with a satisfying *swish*.

Brooks groans. "Knew it."

I grin. "Good luck."

He misses making the same shot, but it's close. And he's a good sport about it, which is more than I can say for a lot of guys.

By the time he hits E, we're both breathless and laughing.

"Good game," Brooks congratulates. "Rematch?"

I smile but shake my head. "I should head out soon. Just going to grab some more water before I do."

My cup was drained a while ago. I might have won, but Brooks was a decent opponent.

I finished the game with H-O-R, a few lucky bounces deserving most of the credit for my victory.

Brooks pulls in a deep breath that strips me of ease even before he starts talking. "Can I get your number? I'll be here for a few more days, and I had a lot of fun hanging out with you. Would love to do it again sometime."

I could say yes.

Should say yes, probably.

My summer has sucked, and based on what little I know of him, Brooks seems like a genuinely nice guy. A unicorn, in other words.

It usually takes me a while to warm up to strangers, but I feel like I've known Brooks for a lot longer than however long it's been since he came over to the bleachers.

But my head is already shaking, which I don't realize until I notice his hopeful expression has shifted to embarrassed.

"Sorry, I didn't mean to—"

My head keeps shaking. "No, I'm flattered. I really am. You're great. It's just—there's this guy and it…" I exhale. "It's just *really* complicated. I'm not in a good place to start anything new."

That sounds slightly better than *I've been in love with the same guy for as long as I can remember, but I'm not sure where we stand right now.*

"I get it." A little of the disappointment has disappeared from Brooks's face. Then totally fades when he shoots me a small, cheeky grin. "If anything changes, Finn has my number."

I nod and smile, grateful he's not making this awkward. Hopeful there will be a day when this doesn't feel like such a monumental moment, and I don't feel like a cheater for even considering it. Wondering what's different about me, that's kept my heart loyal while everyone else seems to cycle through significant others.

"So, have you always lived in Pembrooke?" Brooks asks as we turn toward the center of the court.

It's still crowded with people, the sound of joking and laughter switching from background noise to loud activity the closer we get.

The bleachers are totally empty, everyone except us clustered in one spot. I've avoided most people since I arrived an hour or so ago, only talking to Brooks and Harrison on the court's periphery.

My stomach somersaults as we approach the commotion. I like Harrison and Mark. Finn has always been nice to me too. But they're not *my* friends. Not really.

"Yeah, I—"

I freeze.

Blink.

Once. Twice. Three times.

Nothing about the scene in front of me changes.

My heart free falls through my chest and lands on the cracked asphalt of the court with a silent splatter.

Holden is *here*, standing with Grace Harper and Mark, who's got one arm slung over Holden's shoulder and is grinning widely. Grace is standing just as close to him, her blonde hair skimming Holden's other shoulder when she tosses her head and laughs.

He looks good.

I hate that's my second thought, but it is. Our many issues have never included a lack of attraction, and as soon as I've registered Holden is here, his appearance is what catches my notice next. Wearing a faded t-shirt and mesh basketball shorts, which have been his summer uniform for as long as I've known him, he looks taller and broader and older than the last time I saw him.

And hotter.

There's an unmistakable tug of lust deep in my stomach, and I hate that it's there at all, let alone after months of silence.

We haven't spoken since he left for basketball camp.

He didn't text.

Didn't call.

Not a single. Damn. Word.

"Cassia?" Brooks is confused, glancing between my frozen self and the group huddled up ahead.

We're close enough to the center, a few other people look over as well, and that's what unfreezes me.

I don't want this reunion to take place here, and I'm pissed at Holden for putting me in this position. For showing up to socialize with his friends like all is right in the world.

Maybe it is—in his.

I'm not in the mood to fight, and it's probably past when I told my mom I'd be home.

So I choose flight.

"I've, uh, I've actually gotta go."

"What?" Brooks takes a step closer, his expression creasing.

I step back so quickly I almost fall over. And instead of answering Brooks, I glance over at Holden again, the realization he's now looking this way jolting me like an electric paddle to the heart.

Seconds stretch as we stare at each other.

Holden's expression is entirely unreadable.

No surprise.

No jealousy.

Just a blank face.

And it's so *familiar*. Not only his physical features, but the apathy.

It's always been small gestures instead of big moments with him. He opens up when we're alone, never when we're surrounded.

I know Holden grew up differently than I did. That love and affection weren't on display during his childhood in the same way they were in my family. And it used to make me feel special, knowing I saw a side of him no one else did.

Right now? It makes me feel sad. Empty.

That he's standing there and I'm standing here and I know, even as we hold eye contact, that neither of us are going to take a step to close the distance.

"Bye, Brooks," I say, then spin and start walking toward the line of cars behind the bleachers.

Silently pray no one blocked my car in, because I'd rather walk all the way home than have to go back over there and ask someone to move their vehicle.

I think Brooks might call my name, but I don't look back. I'm worried *he* might still be looking.

And even more scared that he won't be.

CHAPTER TWO

HOLDEN

"So...you wanna talk about it?"

"No."

Finn sighs but says nothing else. He glances at Mark, who's slouched on the bleachers with Jordan. Everyone else left a while ago.

I toss another can into the air, the crunch of aluminum connecting with the wooden bat not nearly as satisfying as I was hoping it would be.

The crumpled can flies about thirty feet in the air, landing right in the dumpster. I'm too pissed off to feel any satisfaction about my perfect aim. I chug the remnants of the beer in my hand and then that can goes flying too.

Three more.

Five.

I'm close to running out of projectiles when I finally ask. "Who the hell is he?"

"Thought we weren't talking about it?" is Finn's response.

I scowl as I pick up another can from the shrinking pile and send it flying into the field, making my lack of appreciation about his sarcasm known.

Finn sighs again. "His name is Brooks. We're in the same frat. He came back to campus early for some teacher's assistant training thing, so I invited him to come and hang out tonight."

So he's a non-awkward nerd. *Fucking fantastic.*

At least they met tonight. He hasn't been hanging around her all summer.

"You let your frat bro hit on my girlfriend?"

Finn doesn't ask the obvious question.

Is she my girlfriend?

"Harrison went over there, made sure she was okay."

I snort. "How noble of him, angling for a spot in line."

"I didn't say he did it *for* you." Finn sends a can flying into the field. "But he'd probably never do that to you."

I grunt, hoping he's right.

Probably, because it's practically an open secret Harrison has had a thing for Cassia since high school. If she indicated she was interested, I doubt any loyalty to me would be enough to keep him from acting on it.

"Are you coming on the trip tomorrow?"

"Are you asking because you invited Douchenerd?"

Finn rolls his eyes, which I take as a yes. "Fucking *talk* to her, Holden."

"I will."

I just need to burn off the anger about coming home to her laughing and playing basketball with another guy. And get a handle on the fear about what she might say when we *do* talk.

It's the same reason I didn't reach out to her all summer because I needed a possibility to keep me going instead of hearing it's over while I was a couple hundred miles away. Because she asked for space, and I didn't want not giving it to her to be another strike against me.

"And yeah, I'm coming tomorrow."

Finn nods. "Good. By the way, Jordan invited all the girls."

"What? Why?"

"Why do you think? He's hooking up with McKenzie again, and he didn't think McKenzie would go unless he invited Grace. And he didn't want to piss the rest of the girls off by inviting only McKenzie and Grace, so he made it an open invitation."

I groan. "It's supposed to be a *guys' weekend*."

"Didn't think you'd be back. Didn't think you'd care." Finn slants a curious look my way, likely wondering why I came home early without telling anyone. "You could invite her."

I'm very tempted to say I'm not going at all now that I know who all will be there.

My plan was to come back, talk to Cassia tonight, and then go off with the guys tomorrow to celebrate or commiserate.

Every summer since graduating high school, we've driven to the state park an hour away and camped out in the woods. Drunk beer, talked about nothing important, and gone fishing.

This year feels like it'll be our last chance. Next summer, we'll have graduated college.

That's the only reason I decide not to back out, even if the trip will most likely be filled with drama and complaints if the girls are coming. And possibly flirting, since my relationship status is ambiguous to everyone, including me. Everyone saw Cassia walk away from me earlier.

"Not her thing," I say, since that's easier than admitting the truth: I don't think she'll go. Not if *I* ask her.

Finn sighs again. He's always extra dramatic when he's drunk.

And being my best friend is probably an exhausting job.

We finish hitting the rest of the leftover cans, then toss the ones that didn't make it into the dumpster and head back toward the court.

Grass gradually gives way to the rectangle of cracked asphalt that marks one of my favorite places in the world. I've been coming here since I was a kid, riding my bike until I was old enough to drive. It's seen me through plenty of shitty times, and I wish it was totally empty now.

I'd love to stand and shoot.

Something about sending a basketball through the hoop over and over again soothes my annoyance like nothing else.

Maybe it's the repetition.

Maybe it's the purpose.

Maybe it's that I'm *good*, and there's a special satisfaction that accompanies success you've earned. Whatever the reason, I could really use that sort of therapy right now.

Mark, Jordan, Finn, and I played some two-on-two earlier, but it was a friendly game lacking all the intensity I'm craving.

I'm not as tired as I should be after weeks of pushing myself physically. There's a relentless buzz humming beneath my skin, one that amplified with each swing of a brown ponytail walking away.

I should have gone after her. Probably. Maybe. Fuck if I know the right move.

We didn't hammer out any details of our "break" or discuss whether the space she asked for extended to when we were in the same place again.

Cassia has always complicated my priorities. I fought falling for her; it happened anyway. Fought it for lots of reasons, but high on that list was not wanting to hurt her. She deserves better than me and my baggage. She's smart and kind and motivated, none of which are adjectives most people would use to describe me.

I'm driven when it comes to basketball, I guess. But that road is close to ending. Chances I'll wind up getting drafted to play professionally are slim. So I'm staring at a future without the escape I've always excelled at. And possibly without the one person who's my calm in the midst of chaos.

I might not deserve Cassia Nolan, but hell if I don't want her. Need her.

And it's always felt like she wanted *me*. Needed *me*.

Until now.

I talk with the guys for a few more minutes, finalizing plans for the trip tomorrow and catching up. I barely kept in touch this summer, using basketball and being away as an excuse.

"I'm headed out," I announce, pulling my keys out of my pocket and spinning them around one finger.

Finn glances over. "You're good to drive?"

He squints at me like he's in any shape to assess my sobriety. Mark's driving him and Jordan home.

"I only had one beer. I'm good."

We say our final goodbyes and then I head for the makeshift parking area. My truck and Mark's SUV are the only two cars left.

I have a longer trip home than most of my friends. The house I grew up in—the house across the street from the Nolans'—now belongs to a young couple with a toddler.

My aunt Catherine moved back to Pembrooke after my dad died, renting a condo in a newer development on the far edge of town so that my younger sister Sydney could finish high school here and to take in Lily, our family dog who died last year.

Both Sydney and I expected Catherine to leave once Sydney graduated, but she met a guy and chose to remain in town even once we were both in college. It's meant Sydney and I can come back here over breaks, and as a bonus, Catherine spends most nights at her boyfriend's, so the condo is usually empty.

I'm really hoping that'll be the case tonight.

I don't feel like talking to anyone.

Sydney stayed in New York for the summer, attending a theater program. I saw her briefly, before I left for basketball camp two months ago. And we've spoken sporadically since, mostly occasional texts checking in with each other. Mostly sent by Sydney.

I'm about as shitty of a brother as I am a boyfriend.

I near my truck, stumbling over tire treads and uneven clumps of grass in the dark. Feel my pocket for my keys and then curse when they slip through clumsy fingers.

Before leaning down to pick them up, I tilt my head back, staring at the dark sky decorated with the scattered pinpricks of stars. Suck in a few deep lungfuls of summer air to try to alleviate the suffocating sensation I'm experiencing. Any peace playing and hitting empty cans offered has dissipated like smoke in the wind.

Eventually I stop staring. Stop searching. I'm not sure what I'm looking for.

Driving through downtown Pembrooke feels strange. It's deserted, the storefronts dark and the streetlights casting long shadows across the pavement. The commercial section of town gradually gives way to residential neighborhoods.

The complex where Catherine's condo is located has about fifteen units. All the windows in the bottom unit are dark and empty when I park in the assigned spot and climb out of my truck. My shoulders burn as I stretch, my muscles sore from weeks of strenuous exertion.

I grab my duffel out of the back and then head toward the front entrance of the building. It takes a few minutes to get inside and flick on the lights. Everything is neat and orderly, like a show home.

Catherine, like everyone else, had no idea I was coming home today. And based on the sterile feel of the place, she hasn't been here in several days.

I stuff the contents of my duffel into the washing machine, start a load, and then take a quick shower.

My phone screen is covered with messages when I get back to my room. I flop down onto the bed in boxers with wet hair, exhaustion spreading through my body as I sink into the mattress.

I skim the first couple of texts—one from Grace, asking if I'm okay and another from Mark, wondering if I can fit a cooler in my truck—then switch to staring at the list of favorites.

She's at the very top.

The first fucking name.

I've called her hundreds of times. Maybe thousands.

To ask meaningless questions.

What time she was done with class. What food she wanted me to order. Saying good night.

Times I easily could have texted, I called her so I could hear her voice. So I could experience the effect she has on me.

And right now, when I really *need* to talk to her, I'm terrified to.

It wasn't just the laughing or the guy that threw me off tonight.

She walked away.

She's always walked toward me, and this time Cassia headed in the opposite direction.

It burns in a way nothing ever has before.

Through all our ups and downs, she's stuck around. I'm the one who avoids.

I toss my phone onto the comforter and roll over, hoping I'll fall asleep quickly.

But knowing I probably won't.

CHAPTER THREE

CASSIA

Milo wiggles around on his back, pink tongue lolling as he shamelessly begs me for more attention. I squat down to give his belly yet another rub, smiling when his tail begins sweeping across the concrete.

I'm a sucker for his big brown eyes. And when you're in a perpetually terrible mood—the way I've felt all summer—being around animals who don't know what a bad feeling is can be a bit of a balm.

Maybe today will be the day that optimism wears off on me.

I feed Milo a treat from one of the jars scattered around the room, then straighten and stretch. Yawn, before heading over to the folding table covered with containers of different kibble and supplements.

I was home by midnight, but I didn't manage seven hours of sleep. I tossed and turned until my legs were tangled up in the sheets, staring at the phone screen that never lit up.

If we hadn't made direct eye contact, I'd think he didn't realize I was there last night.

Holden's friends tiptoed around mentioning him to me on the

rare occasions I ran into any of them this summer. Sydney stayed in New York. And my family is too busy and too chaotic to have wondered why Holden never came back a single weekend to visit.

I wonder if anyone asked him about me last night.

Wonder what he said if they did.

"He's sure made a lot of progress."

I turn to look at Jackie, who's walking into the kennel with Cooper. He's a mastiff mix dropped off at the shelter two weeks ago by a couple who surrendered him because they didn't know how big he would get.

Susan handled his intake, which was probably for the best. She's more even-tempered than I am in those situations, saying it's better they brought their pet here than leaving them out on the streets.

True, but also a really low bar.

"That's great," I say.

Jackie puts Cooper into his kennel and focuses on Milo, who's taken a seat at my feet.

He was picked up on the street, young enough it's possible he's never had an owner. He arrived about a week after I got back to Pembrooke for the summer, and I've grown more attached to him than I have to any other animal at the shelter.

And the feeling seems mutual. He's much less skittish than when he first arrived but doesn't seek out affection from anyone else.

Susan calls him my shadow.

Jackie walks over to Willow's cage, tucking her short hair behind one ear.

I start stacking up all the silver bowls now that the morning feeding is done. They'll have to be washed, then the same process run through again tonight.

"I'll take Willow out next?" Jackie asks me.

"Sounds good," I reply.

Jackie's fifteen, about to be a junior at Pembrooke High. She started volunteering here last summer and has kept coming back ever since. Her mother is allergic to dogs, so she's never been able to have one of her own. Similar to the way I started working here. Her cheerful chatter breaks up the comfortable silence Susan and I usually share when it's just the two of us.

I'm halfway through washing the bowls when the phone starts to ring. I shrug out of the dish gloves as soon as I remember Jackie is out walking Willow and can't answer it, rushing through the door and down the hallway toward the reception desk.

I turn the corner and then my quick steps stutter, focusing on Jackie first.

She's standing by the front door, Willow sitting patiently at her feet. And Holden is only a few feet away, nodding along to something she's saying.

Jackie glances my way and then startles, like she's registering the ringing phone for the first time. She steps toward the desk, so I tell her "I've got it" and answer.

"Pembrooke Animal Shelter, how may I help you?"

The woman on the phone asks what our hours are tomorrow.

"Tomorrow, uh, Saturday?" I rub my forehead, conscious of the strands that have fallen out of my messy bun. Keeping my gaze on the desk calendar instead of anywhere else. Anyone else. "We're open from ten to four."

The woman thanks me, then hangs up.

I pull in a deep breath before doing the same.

My steps are slow and reluctant as I leave the barrier of the desk, wishing I wasn't wearing old athletic shorts and a ratty t-shirt. Thoroughly annoyed he managed to catch me off guard —twice.

Jackie is enthusiastically telling Holden the story of how Willow ended up here.

I recognize the way she's looking at him.

The same starry eyes I aimed Holden's way when I was her age. And when I was twelve. Sixteen. Twenty.

The same way I look at him now, even after everything.

"Cassia's done really amazing work with her."

I smile automatically in response to Jackie's comment.

It's an overstatement, since Willow was dropped off by loving owners moving to an apartment that didn't allow pets. She hasn't suffered the same trauma a lot of our other residents have, just confusion.

"So have you," I say.

Jackie blushes, then looks at Holden. "Are you here to volunteer?"

I tilt my head, curious what his answer will be. When we first started dating, he would come here a lot. Pick me up, drop me off, but also spend time in the kennels.

And then, gradually, things shifted. We left for college and there were different schedules.

Different responsibilities.

Different priorities.

"No. Not today." Holden shoves his hands into his pockets, gaze only on me. "Just here to talk to your boss."

"Oh," Jackie says, glancing back and forth between us.

And I realize that they've never met. That Holden hasn't visited me at the shelter since Jackie started working here.

I've been in a basketball arena countless times in the past year.

"Nice to meet you, Holden," Jackie says.

"Yeah, you too."

She rushes outside, like she's suddenly aware of the simmering tension in the air between us.

The bell above the door tinkles cheerfully, like it's not.

"Hi," he says.

I kind of want to snort at the unoriginality. Months of silence. Years of dating. All I get is *Hi*.

At least we're conversing, I guess.

"Hey."

"How's your summer been?"

Lame. Depressing. Boring. "Good."

Holden shoves his hands in his pockets. Glances around. "This place looks the same."

"Some things don't change."

His eyes are back on me. "You left pretty fast last night."

"I didn't know you'd be there."

"Yeah." He exhales. "Plans changed."

"Thanks for the heads-up."

A muscle jumps in his jaw. "I didn't know *you'd* be there."

"It might have come up, if we'd talked in the past two months."

He steps forward. "Listen, Cassia, I—"

"I'm working, Holden. I can't do this right now. Here. I'm done at four if you want to talk then."

He exhales, then glances away. "I won't be here. I'm leaving for Haryock in an hour."

I laugh with absolutely no amusement. "*Wow*. In an hour. You really budgeted a lot of time for this conversation, huh?"

If I hadn't seen him at the court last night, would he even be here? Or would he have just left again, without bothering to talk to me at all?

"When did you want to talk last night? While you were

hanging out with that guy or when you took off as soon as you saw me?"

My molars grind. "You know, the more you talk, the less I feel like there's anything left to say."

"So…I budgeted *too little* time, or *too much*?"

I look away, at the photo wall of smiling faces who've adopted animals from here. *I* don't know what to say. If he had approached me last night, I don't know where we would've begun. That and the attention from everyone else is why I didn't go over to him.

The best moments in my life have all involved Holden.

So have the worst.

He's the highest of highs and the lowest of lows.

He also has the ability to irritate me like no one else.

When I look back, he's still staring at me.

"I haven't heard from you in months." I try to keep my voice even, but some hurt manages to sneak in.

"Phones work both ways," he shoots back. "And the break was *your* idea, remember?"

"Because we were a mess, Holden! You can't fix something until you acknowledge there's a problem. And what did you do? You were gone all summer. You haven't even been back twenty-four hours, and you're leaving again."

"It's a camping trip with my best friends. I haven't seen them all summer."

"I'm not *surprised* that you're going, Holden. That's the worst fucking part. You get back, you go to the court to see your friends. Next day, you're off to the woods. I'm *surprised* you even bothered to come here at all. Clearly, you have other priorities."

All the ease leaves his posture as his jaw clenches tightly. His hands are still stuffed in his pockets, but his shoulders are rigid and tensed beneath the cotton material of his t-shirt.

"You're a priority."

I wait, but that's all he says.

I'm sick of him giving me inches and pretending they're miles.

"I should get back to work," I say, waiting for him to leave.

The soft *click* of paws on linoleum sounds. Milo appears, slinking around the corner and taking a seat by my feet. I rub the top of his head gently.

"New dog?"

That would apply to any canine we've received in the year it's been since he was last here, technically. But I know he's minutes —if not seconds—from walking out the door, and I simply don't have the energy to make that point.

"Yeah."

"He's cute."

"He is," I agree.

Holden is looking at Milo like he's expecting the dog to walk over and greet him, but he remains at my side dutifully.

My affection for Milo swells. Leaving him next week will suck.

"You're not giving me much, Cas."

I stiffen. At the implication the awkwardness between us is exclusively my fault, and at his use of the casual nickname.

"I don't have much to give."

I've known Holden since we were kids. I was in love with him for years before we officially got together. He was my first kiss. My first love. The first guy I had sex with.

I've given him *everything*.

My heart. My body. My loyalty. My love.

And I'm worried he's bored. That commitment isn't exciting.

Worried my standards sunk. That I started getting less and less, and just accepted it.

Worried we got too comfortable. That we're in a routine of a relationship.

Suggesting we take a break this summer was supposed to jolt us.

And…I'm not sure what it did.

"Does that mean you're done?"

Done.

Such an innocuous word for such a massive decision.

But Holden isn't indifferent, at least. There's emotion in the words that's echoed in his tense posture.

"It means we need to talk. And I can't talk now. Plus, you're about to leave." *Again*, I add silently.

He exhales. "You could come."

I scoff. "On the guys' trip?"

"Jordan invited McKenzie and a bunch of other girls since he's hooking up with her."

"Oh, even better. On the guys' trip with a bunch of your exes?"

Holden exhales. "They're not my…" Shakes his head. "Nevermind."

This is an ancient argument between us.

I've never been completely comfortable around his friends. Always felt like I was intruding. No matter how much time passes from when we were younger, it still feels like I'm on the outskirts. A plus one, but never a main character.

Last night was an unfortunate reminder of that. I'm not even sure why I went, besides boredom. Maybe part of me was hoping they would mention I was there to Holden.

I'm quite certain me fleeing wasn't the carefree update I was aiming to get passed along.

"Have fun on your trip."

He stares at me.

Stares, the intensity uncomfortable and unwavering.

Then lets out a long breath and straightens. I know he's leaving long before he turns toward the door.

But I'm not expecting him to glance back. I'm unprepared for the defeat on his face, like he had some fantasy of this conversation going differently.

"Camp was fine, and the rest of my summer sucked, in case you were wondering."

I was.

I've spent all summer wondering how he was doing. What he was doing. Who he was doing it with.

But I don't say so. Don't react at all, as I watch the door shut behind him.

I just focus on deep, even breaths, barely registering the sting of my nails digging into the soft flesh of my palms.

Fighting the urge to follow him.

———

The twins are wrestling in the front yard when I pull into the driveway.

"Hi, Cassia!" Charlie calls.

"Hi, Cassia!" Chris echoes.

"Hey, guys!" I wave as I step out of the car. My brothers are already back to rough-housing.

The soccer camp that took up most of their summer just ended, so they've literally been bouncing off the walls waiting for school to start.

There's a messy heap of shoes and sports equipment piled just inside the front door. I kick off my sneakers and sort through the mess, shoving everything back into its proper cubby based on who it belongs to.

Regan wanders into the entryway as I'm tossing shin pads into Charlie's cubby, sucking on a red popsicle. The sharp smell of chlorine follows her, blown around by the air conditioning.

"Hey. Where's Mom?"

Regan shrugs, continuing to slurp her popsicle. Her brown hair is wet, droplets of water dripping onto the tile floor.

"How was swim practice?"

"Fine. Maggie's hogging the bathroom. She has a date with Silas later."

I exhale. "Great."

Regan is clearly waiting to shower and I'm sweaty and covered with dog hair.

I finish cleaning up in the entryway and then head into the kitchen. Sally is sitting at the kitchen table, her expression pinched with concentration as she alternates between eating cheese crackers and stringing beads.

"Hey, Sally."

"Hi, Cassia." She's so focused on her crafts, she doesn't even look up.

"Do you know where Mom is?"

"Upstairs, I think."

I grab a banana off the counter and then head upstairs. The bathroom door is open, steam wafting out despite the heat outside.

I follow the sound of Maggie's raised voice into my parents' bedroom.

"Midnight!" Maggie tosses her hair over one shoulder, squaring off against my mom, who's folding laundry on the bed.

"Ten thirty."

"I'm starting college next week, Mom! I could come back to the dorms at four a.m., and no one would care! A little *trust*, please."

"You're not at school yet, Magnolia. You live here right now, and I don't want you coming home in the middle of the night. You'll wake everyone up. And I want to go to bed, knowing you're home and safe."

"Silas is taking me to dinner at a new restaurant in Blackford. If I have to be home that early, it'll ruin the whole meal."

"Eat dinner somewhere closer, then," my mom suggests.

"Ugh!" Maggie throws her hands up in the air, then spins and stalks toward the door, almost colliding with me. "Couldn't you have rebelled a little bit, Cassia?" she asks. "Made this a little easier on me?"

My mom sighs as Maggie disappears down the hall, then keeps folding laundry. "Hi, honey. How was work?"

I exhale. "Fine."

"Are you hanging out with Holden tonight?"

Oxygen stalls in my lungs. "What?"

She tosses some socks, then glances over at me. "He stopped by here last night. I let him know you were over at London's. I thought you two might be spending tonight together. He's welcome to come over for dinner."

"Oh," I say.

Fuck, I think.

Does it absolve him of everything? No.

But it makes a tiny difference knowing Holden came here rather than heading straight to the court last night.

My mom's waiting for more of an answer. "He didn't mention it?"

"Uh, no. He has a lot of other stuff to catch up on."

She smiles. "I'm sure. So, should I plan on you for dinner? Planning to start cooking as soon as I finish this load."

"Um, I'm not sure yet."

"All right. I'll just make extra."

"Will Dad be home for dinner?" His job has always kept him busy. But I've barely seen him all summer.

"I'm not sure," she says, dumping another clean load of laundry on the bed. "He had a busy day today."

"Seems like all his days have been busy lately."

"The firm is going through some changes."

"*Laying people off* changes?"

"No, no, nothing like that. More like they have so much business, your dad is handling the workload of three attorneys."

"That's good, I guess."

My mom nods.

"I'm going to go shower. I'll let you know about dinner."

"Sounds good, honey."

I head down the hallway, past Maggie's shut door. The bathroom door is closed again.

Regan must be showering.

I blow out a long breath once I'm inside my room, relaxing in the familiar surroundings. I strip off my sweaty shirt and toss it on the floor, padding over to the window in just my shorts and sports bra.

I stare at the house across the street. There are toys scattered across the asphalt driveway, which was never the case when the Adamses lived there. But the basketball hoop is still standing, the fading daylight casting a long shadow.

My whole life is filled with reminders of him. Ones I couldn't remove even if I tried.

I can't escape him when I want to.

But the main problem is that I've never wanted to.

I chew on my lower lip, barely registering the nip of pain as I accidentally bite down too hard.

You could come is not the most heartfelt of invitations. It's a small gesture. But it's something, and I was too surprised by Holden's sudden appearance to really register or consider it. Him coming to the animal shelter hadn't occurred to me as a possibility, and it's another small gesture. So was showing up at my house.

My options are to stay here and wish he'd made more of an effort, or I can go tell him I want him to.

I stare at the old hoop for a minute longer, then pull my duffel bag out of the closet and start packing.

CHAPTER FOUR

HOLDEN

It takes me eighty-seven minutes to drive from Pembrooke to Haryock State Park. I spend every one of them replaying the conversation with Cassia in my head. Trying to figure out how the hell we got here.

She blindsided me, asking for a break.

We only saw each other sporadically over the spring, but that was more because of her busy schedule than mine.

I took the fact we didn't have to be in constant contact with each other as a sign of strength in our relationship.

Cassia clearly considered it the opposite.

And instead of telling me that, she started this summer by telling me we should "take a break."

Neither of us clarified what that really meant. If it was a pause or an ending or a restart.

I was too stunned—and hurt—to ask her for details or fine print. I got drunk with Finn and Mark, then left for basketball camp early the next morning. And since she never reached out to me, I never reached out to her.

Childish, but it was easier at the time. My logic was she wanted the break, so I would give that to her.

And now? I have no idea what to do.

It feels like I'm losing her. That holding tight or letting go will have the same heart-breaking outcome.

Nothing is more terrifying.

I exit the highway and follow the signs toward the campgrounds' entrance. My dad and I came here a handful of times growing up, and it's become an annual tradition with my friends. One I almost missed this year because of my damn pride.

It's almost laughable that Cassia thinks she isn't a priority to me. It feels like all my decisions started centering around her a long time ago.

What isn't funny is that she doesn't see that.

I park next to Finn's Jeep, exhaling a long breath before opening the car door.

The smile comes automatically, like slipping on a mask. I've always been good at shielding my true emotions.

Maybe *too* good.

At a certain point, it became my first instinct.

Finn obviously told everyone I was coming because no one looks the least bit surprised to see me unloading my stuff from the bed of the truck.

Mark ambles over first, grabbing the cooler out after knocking fists.

I inhale deeply when a breeze kicks up, the scent of exposed earth and pine needles soothing. A little of the serenity fades when I catch Grace's eye. She winks at me, then goes back to sorting food supplies with McKenzie.

I haven't said a word to anyone about where things stand between me and Cassia. But everyone seems to know we're in a bad place, which makes me wonder what she's said or done this summer. If I had a little less pride, I'd ask. It seems like more than just us not talking last night. And I would have handled that differently if I'd had any clue she'd be there. Her mom said she was at London's.

Peacefulness fades a little more when I spot the guy who was playing with Cassia last night piling sticks in the fire pit. Brent? Brett? Some preppy name.

I shake off the annoyance and focus on unloading the rest of my stuff. This place isn't as rustic as most campgrounds. Each site has its own fire pit, grill, and water pump. Plus, there are a few outbuildings scattered around the park with showers, sinks, and toilets. But we still have to bring a bunch of equipment, plus food.

There's a sizable pile of luggage in the center of the clearing. About half the stack is pink or light purple.

Once I get all my stuff unloaded, I carry it over to the spot closest to the woods.

"Hey, Holden."

I glance at Camila Stuart as I shake the tent poles out of their bag. She's one of Grace's good friends, but I doubt we've ever exchanged more than a few dozen words.

"Hey."

Instead of moving along, she lingers. "How was camp?"

I've gotten used to people I barely know knowing details about my life, but it's still strange. At one point, it was because of my talent and notoriety. After my dad died, it seemed like it shifted to some pity.

"It was great," I say.

She nods, still not moving.

"How was your summer?" I ask, feeling obligated to reciprocate some conversation.

"It's been awesome!" Camila responds. There's a peppiness to her tone that was missing when I asked Cassia the same question earlier. And that my answer was probably lacking.

She still doesn't leave.

I'm uninterested in making more small talk, but I can't come up with any way to say that without sounding like a total dick.

"I've never been camping before," Camila tells me. "Neither has Grace. She set up our tent, so I'm hoping it holds."

I glance over at the green tent she points toward. "It looks sturdy."

Camila smiles. "Well, it won't kill us if it collapses in the middle of the night, right?"

"Doubtful."

"Comforting." Her grin widens. "It was nice of you guys to include us."

I've got nothing to say to that, since I wasn't the one who extended the invitation and my reaction to it was irritation. Harrison appears, saving me from a response.

"I'm going to see if McKenzie needs help," Camila says, then walks away.

Harrison watches her depart, hands shoved in his pockets and eyebrows raised.

I start connecting poles, waiting for him to talk first. We're better friends than we were in high school, when we shared some of the same social group but played separate sports. He goes to school close to Arlington and is usually there the times I've visited Finn.

We would be closer if he'd never shown any interest in Cassia. My right hand pulses with the memory of old wounds.

"Hey," he says.

"Hey."

"Camp good?"

"Uh-huh."

There's a pause. Then, "You couldn't just leave her alone?" he asks.

I'm well aware of who he's talking about, but I say, "She came over here."

Harrison shakes his head. "Don't you think you've done enough?"

"Mind your own business, Baker."

I drop the pretense and the poles, pulling out the fabric and spreading it on the ground. Focusing on the task of setting up the tent so I'm less tempted to forcibly shut Harrison's mouth.

Harrison has never made a secret of the fact he thinks Cassia deserves better than me, and he's probably right. Doesn't mean I need it shoved in my face.

"I would, Adams, but you don't seem to get the message. You saw her take off last night. And then you show up at the animal shelter this morning?"

I glance up, my annoyance building. "How the hell do you know that?"

Finn is about ten feet away, setting up his tent. He glances between us, then shakes his head, opting not to get involved.

"My sister is best friends with Jackie Hathaway."

I raise one eyebrow.

Harrison sighs. "Jackie volunteers at the animal shelter. She was there this morning and told Alexis that you showed up. So my sister's been texting *me*, asking if the two of you are back together."

I toss the half-assembled tent on the ground and turn around, giving him my full attention. "You're the messenger for a couple of high schoolers? You hear how fucking ridiculous this conversation is, right?"

"I'm just looking out for her."

"Cassia can take care of herself."

"Because you've made sure she had to."

Something in my expression must convey to Harrison how close he is to crossing a line, because a spasm of uncertainty crosses his face.

"*My* relationship with *my* girlfriend is none of your business, Baker," I growl. "Or your sister's."

"So she *is* your girlfriend?"

"Focus on your own relationship. Oh, wait…" I try not to follow gossip, but I know he ended things with his ex a few months ago.

Harrison shakes his head. "You're a dick."

"Says the guy who decided to stick his nose in my business. Did Cassia tell you she's single? Ask you to lecture me?"

He's silent and still, only his jaw twitching with irritation.

"Yeah, that's what I thought."

"We're friends. I care about her, that's all."

"And you think I don't?"

Harrison shrugs. "Hard to tell, sometimes."

His words make me pause. Because I can tell he means them, that he's not only trying to piss me off.

And if that's what a guy I grew up with thinks—someone who's been around us countless times over the past few years—I wonder what everyone else thinks. What *she* thinks.

"You didn't come back once this summer, and once you did, you left the next day. Everyone's thinking it, Adams. Don't get mad at me just because I'm the only one saying it."

That's *exactly* why I'm pissed at him, but it sounds small and petty to respond that way.

I refocus on assembling the tent instead, not-so-subtly letting him know I'm done discussing it. I was the last to arrive, so I'm behind on setting up.

Harrison exhales. "One burger or two?"

"Two." There's a subtle whiff of smoke in the air that suggests dinner is already in the works. "Thanks," I add reluctantly.

It's past seven by the time I've got the tent up and unrolled my sleeping bag. I change into a long-sleeved shirt and then head toward the fire pit, bumping fists with Mark and Jordan before grabbing a beer from the cooler.

Finn is grilling, the aroma of roasting meat mixing with wood smoke in the cooling air. I end up standing next to him, watching him flip patties while we talk basketball.

I'm relaxed and enjoying myself, so of course it's when his frat brother decides to come over. He's a good-looking guy, I guess. Tall, but I still have a couple of inches on him. His friendly, open grin reminds me of Finn's. Maybe amiability is a requirement for joining their shared frat.

"Hey, man. I'm Brooks."

"Holden." I shake his offered hand, my grip a little tighter than it needs to be.

Brooks doesn't wince. "Nice to finally meet you. Finn talks about you a lot."

Finn has never once mentioned Brooks to me, so I'm guessing that's an exaggeration. And we've never crossed paths when I've visited Arlington's campus, so I seriously doubt they're that close.

But I nod instead of stirring up shit. "Yeah. Nice to meet you too. Your jump shot needs work."

Finn rolls his eyes.

I could have said worse.

Brooks laughs once, then runs a hand through his hair. It's a few inches longer than mine, flopping across his forehead. "Yeah, I know. Probably why I lost. I warned Cassia I was terrible before we started playing."

I *hate* the casual way he says her name.

My hand tightens around the bottle I'm holding, but I don't

react otherwise. Don't say a word. I let the silence linger until it turns awkward.

I don't really care if Brooks is an oblivious bystander to the situation between me and Cassia or if he's mentioning her to test my reaction. I dislike him the same amount either way.

"Mind grabbing the burger buns, man?" Finn asks Brooks.

"Yeah. Sure." He's quick to leave us alone.

Finn glances at me, eyebrow arched. "Could you chill the fuck out?"

"I'm chill," I say, then sip more beer.

Finn rolls his eyes again.

Jordan walks over to us a minute later. "You didn't tell me Cassia was coming."

I tense as soon as I hear her name, the rest of his words taking another few seconds to register. Once they do, I turn, my grip automatically tightening on the bottle. I might break the glass.

Assuming Jordan was mistaken.

But he's not.

I recognize the sedan as soon as I spot it. Excitement and confusion war within me.

Nothing about our conversation earlier left me with the impression she might show up here.

I abandon my beer on the table by the grill, avoiding the questioning looks aimed my way as I walk straight toward her car.

Cassia climbs out of the driver's seat right as I reach it.

"Hi," is the only greeting I can come up with.

I know her better than anyone else. Know her intimately. And I can't seem to come up with a single interesting thing to say to her.

"Hi," she repeats, fiddling with her keys like she's nervous.

"You came." I state the obvious.

"Yeah." She reaches into her car and grabs a water bottle out of the cupholder, studiously avoiding eye contact as she flips off the lid and takes a sip. "Did the invitation expire after an hour or something?"

"No, of course not. I just… I didn't think you were going to take it."

She continues to avoid my gaze as she flips the lid back on. "I didn't come to fight."

"Me neither. I mean, I don't want to fight either." I push away from the hood and straighten. "Can we start over?"

"How far do you want to go back? High school? Middle school? Maybe the day you moved—"

I fight the smile that wants to appear in response to her heavy sarcasm. "This morning. I'm talking about this morning, Cassia."

She looks at me, her expression serious. Then something shifts. A lightening or relaxing. Some break in the clouds. "My mom said you came by the house last night."

"Yeah. Pop the trunk."

Cassia flips the handle on the door, opening the back of the sedan with a soft *click*. I round the back of the car, grabbing her duffel and sleeping bag out of the trunk.

"Were you going to tell me?" she asks.

"I don't know." I thought about it when she started surmising about my priorities earlier. It didn't occur to me Mrs. Nolan might mention my brief visit. When I stopped by, three of Cassia's five siblings were screaming.

"More people here than I was expecting," Cassia comments, glancing down the line of parked cars. Her fingers play with the hem of her shirt. She's definitely nervous.

"Is this everything?" I ask, closing the back.

"My backpack is in the middle."

She steps toward the door, but I beat her to it, grabbing her backpack and slinging it over one shoulder.

"So, where do your parents think you are?"

Cassia holds my gaze for a minute. Then exhales, nodding a couple of times. Admitting I know her. "My dad's working. My mom thinks I'm in the city visiting Sydney."

"You've been to see her?"

Sydney didn't mention it. Then again, we haven't talked much recently.

"Once." She glances at the campsite, then back to me. "I didn't tell her anything about us. I didn't want to talk about it, and I figured…" Cassia clears her throat and extends one arm. "I can carry my own stuff."

My grip on her bags doesn't loosen. "I know."

Her nod is slow and unsure.

"My tent's this way."

I head in that direction without waiting for her, needing a little space to decide how to act around her.

Does not fighting mean not discussing we spent the summer not speaking? Because I'm not sure I can do that. I need some answers from her. At this point, it sounds better than this ongoing state of uncertainty.

Plus, there's everyone else here. I haven't said anything about where things stand with Cassia to anyone, but my friends have drawn plenty of conclusions that this trip will contribute to.

I don't really care what they think. But I'm worried it'll play into the uncomfortable dynamic between me and Cassia right now.

"Snagged the coveted spot closest to nature," I tell Cassia when she stops beside me.

"It looks…nice."

There's an uncertain lilt to her voice that tells me there are other adjectives that came to mind first. Maybe small.

"It's assembled right," I assure her, setting her duffel, back-pack, and sleeping bag down in the grass.

Then shove my hands into my pockets so I have something to do with them while watching Cassia pull back the flap and peek inside. It's a two-person tent, the same one my dad bought years ago for our camping trips. But it's not roomy. We'll have a foot of space between us, maybe two at most.

"Need help with anything?" I ask.

Cassia shakes her head as she leans down to sort through her stuff.

"Okay. I'll be over by the fire pit." I hike a thumb over one shoulder, pointing to the spot that's impossible to miss. It's the very center of the clearing, a stone circle surrounded by logs and a few Adirondack chairs.

"Okay," she says.

I turn to go, then spin back. Cassia hasn't moved. She's staring at the contents of her duffel bag, wearing a blank expression.

"I'm glad you came."

I hold my breath in anticipation of the moment when our eyes connect. And it doesn't disappoint, the intensity of her hazel gaze making my lungs constrict in a way that's almost painful.

She nods.

I nod back.

Then I keep walking.

CHAPTER FIVE

"Hey."

My crossed arms drop as I turn to watch Brooks run a hand through his shaggy hair. He's smiling, a grin that's half-surprised, half-pleased.

"Hey," I echo, tugging on the hem of my shirt.

The sun is steadily sinking, the air chilling with its disappearance. I discovered my hasty packing didn't include tossing a sweatshirt into my bag. Continuing to rub my arms will draw unwanted attention to that mistake.

I'm not close enough with any of the girls here to ask them to borrow something. Asking Holden is…complicated. And taking another guy's clothes isn't an option.

"I was hoping we'd run into each other again," Brooks says. He's still smiling. "Didn't think it'd be here, out in the middle of nowhere."

His tone is light, but there's a question in his probing gaze. Possibly because I literally ran off from our last conversation. Probably because he's since heard some version of why I did that paints me as pathetic or cowardly or both.

"I, uh, I didn't realize you'd be here either." Realizing that sounded unfriendly, I quickly add, "Not that it's not nice to see you again. I just didn't realize camping is what you meant by sticking around."

His grin broadens. He's either one of those perennially optimistic people or genuinely happy to see me. "I came back to campus early for training with a professor. I'm supposed to be his TA for the fall semester. The day I arrived, his daughter was rushed to the hospital to have her tonsils removed. She's fine, but he's spending a few days at home. It was either sit on campus or come hang out with Finn. Basically just along for the ride of what he's up to."

I nod. "What class are you TAing for?"

"Organic Chemistry."

I blink at him. "Seriously?"

"Yeah." His smile turns sheepish. "I like a challenge."

"Sounds more like you're a masochist."

Brooks laughs. "Yeah. I've heard that before. It's not as bad as people say."

"I know. I took it."

"Oh, yeah? What's your major?"

"Biology. I'm pre-vet."

"What year did you take Org Chem?"

"Uh, freshman."

He blinks at me. "You passed Org Chem as a *freshman*?"

"Passed?" I grin. "Got an A."

"Impressive."

"Thank you."

We're drawing attention, I realize belatedly, registering the curious side glances aimed our way.

"I'm going to grab a drink," I tell Brooks.

He nods an acknowledgment before I continue walking toward the two coolers, wading deeper into an uncertain situation.

McKenzie Howard is already standing there, pouring liquid from a plastic pitcher into a cup.

She glances up and looks me over, one eyebrow rising. "Hey, Cassia."

"Hi, McKenzie," I reply, shooting her a smile I'm relieved she reciprocates.

My relationship with Holden's group of friends has always been uncomfortable. We might have gone to the same high school, but we definitely weren't part of the same social circle, so there was no natural integration to mirror our relationship. Most of the girls have some sort of history with Holden, and all of the guys are loyal to him over me.

During moments like now, when things between me and Holden are rocky, it's especially awkward. I'm afloat with no safe harbor to head into. But I knew that would be the case when I decided to come.

"Want some lemonade?" McKenzie tilts the pitcher she's holding toward me.

"Sure." I nod. "Thanks."

I watch as she pours a second cup and hands it to me. Then take a tentative sip, repressing the strong urge to cough.

The contents taste more like citrus-flavored vodka than hard lemonade. Alcohol burns my throat as I swallow, then sears my empty stomach. I skipped eating lunch earlier, my appetite nonexistent after Holden's brief visit.

I take another sip, then another, until I'm no longer chilly. Glance at the group standing around and half-listen to the chatter echoing around me. I'm undecided on whether or not showing up here was a mistake.

"You know Brooks?"

I glance at McKenzie, surprised she's striking up a conversation with me.

"Uh, not really. We met last night."

"He's cute."

I make a noncommittal noise in response.

I'm ninety percent certain that Holden mentioned Jordan invited McKenzie because he's hooking up with her. But I'm definitely not going to ask McKenzie what her interest in Brooks is.

"I'm surprised you came."

I take another sip, deliberating my response. "Why?"

"Doesn't seem like your thing."

"Ditto."

McKenzie laughs. "Jordan said there are actual bathrooms with running water. If we were squatting in the woods, it would have been another story."

I nod, not giving away I had no clue that was the case.

A little humbled and a lot depressed by the realization I barely thought this trip through.

How I jumped on the first sign of Holden giving a shit.

It's not like he hung around my front yard and waited for me to get home. Called or texted me to see where I was. He just stopped by, then quickly gave up.

Another large gulp of sweet lemonade chases some of the bitterness away.

I haven't forgiven or forgotten just by showing up here. I'm just refusing to keep avoiding, like I did all summer. Nothing would have changed or been resolved if I'd stayed in Pembrooke this weekend.

But I'm sick of that too—of always being the mature one. Of always making the effort first and him meeting me somewhere along the way. It's not an entirely accurate assessment, but the rational, logical, forgiving side of myself is overwhelmed by booze and bitterness at the moment.

"She's after him."

I startle when McKenzie suddenly speaks, so lost in my own thoughts I'd half-forgotten she's standing next to me.

"Not being very subtle about it, but just so you know. She's like a shark circling *Holden Adams is single* blood in the water."

I sip more, my head spinning and my appetite waning after that metaphor.

"Grace has always been a good friend to me, but that doesn't mean I'm blind to her flaws." McKenzie shrugs. "In her mind, she had him first."

"She didn't."

McKenzie raises one brow at the venom in my voice. "I always figured there was more to you than the good girl act."

I don't respond, opting to drain my cup instead.

"Should be an interesting weekend. Cheers." McKenzie tilts her drink toward me and then walks off, leaving me standing alone.

I refill my cup before heading toward the smoking grill. Everyone is either grabbing dinner or already seated around the fire pit.

I focus on the spread of food set out on the folding table next to the grill. A bowl of salad, bags of potato chips, and an array of condiments. More impressive of a meal than I was expecting, honestly. Holden never shared details of what they ate on these trips.

Finn is the one manning the grill, rubbing the dirty grates with an oversized brush that makes a horrible, nails-on-a-chalkboard screech.

"One sec, Cassia," he tells me. "I'll put another burger on for you."

I read between the lines.

I'm an interloper. No one expected me to show up.

Finn is being nice. But it doesn't erase the sliver of insecurity or the voice in the back of my head that whispers *outsider*. That makes me feel like an awkward add-on.

"Okay. Thanks," I say, picking up a plate and taking a pinch of salad.

My insecurities aren't Finn's fault. Holden didn't mention I might be coming, clearly.

A steaming burger lands on my plate. I glance over at Holden, but he's not looking at me. He's piling toppings onto the burger still sitting on his plate beside an empty bun.

"I can wait."

"Take it," he tells me, not looking over.

It's not worth arguing about, not when my stomach is rumbling with hunger and there are so many other things we could fight about.

So I silently add ketchup and mustard, pretending not to notice the way Finn keeps glancing between me and Holden.

The scrutiny doesn't really bother me, for once.

Maybe it's the vodka dulling my self-consciousness. Or maybe I've finally reached the point where I really don't care what other people think. What *these* people think, in particular.

I finish making up my food and walk toward the fire, balancing my plate carefully as I cross the uneven ground. There's more scrutiny aimed my way when I take an open spot on one of the logs, particularly from Grace's seat across from me. McKenzie is right next to her, giggling at something Jordan is whispering to her.

They look happy and carefree, and I briefly wonder if that's how Holden and I would appear right now if I'd never said anything about taking a break.

He's good at making me feel like a priority when we're together.

It's stretches of time apart that have always made me second-guess us. How we attend the same university yet hardly see each other on campus. How our separate social circles never over-lapped, even after years as a couple. How he never seemed to resent the distance, just enjoyed the reunion.

"I didn't know you were coming, Cassia."

Mark takes the open spot beside me, his plate balanced on one knee as he cracks open a can of beer.

"Was kinda a surprise to me too," I comment dryly, then take a bite of burger.

"Glad you were able to make it," he says. "Holden said you're super busy."

I read way too much into that comment.

Was it a slight against me? An excuse? An explanation?

"I wasn't the one in Michigan all summer."

I half-regret the hasty words as soon as they're out of my mouth, but it's also oddly freeing to say exactly what I'm think-ing. I can't spend this weekend pretending things are good between us, not when that's been one of our problems all along. It feels amazing to remove the filter of always second-guessing, to let whatever I want spew out of my mouth without weighing each individual word.

Mark obviously isn't experiencing the same sense of relief regarding my response. Based on his unsure expression, he has no clue what to say.

He's Holden's friend, I remind myself.

I saw them all grow up together, witnessed the hero-worship up close.

"Nevermind," I mutter, then sip some more of my drink.

"These burgers are great, huh? Always taste better outside."

Harrison takes the seat on my other side, appearing oblivious to the lingering awkwardness between me and Mark. He takes a hearty bite of his burger and then nudges my knee with his. "How's the animal shelter?" he asks once he's swallowed.

"Uh, good."

It's weird to remember I don't have to go in tomorrow. All summer I've worked on Saturdays. But Susan was thrilled when I called her to ask if it was okay to take the day off, saying Jackie would be happy to cover my shift and that she was happy I was "finally having some fun."

"Any new arrivals?"

"Not this week. Which is good. We're almost to capacity."

We've only run out of space a couple of times since I started volunteering at the animal shelter in elementary school, but it's extremely stressful. Not only does it make caring for the current residents more of a challenge, it means we can't take in any new animals. They get shipped to Morrisville instead, which is a kill shelter.

"Jackie really loves working with you."

I smile. "I love working with her too."

Harrison keeps asking me questions about the animal shelter, which gives me something to focus on as I eat the rest of my dinner. And when Holden walks by with his food, taking a seat on Mark's other side.

I can't discern anything in his expression that indicates how he feels about his friends sitting with me. Harrison has always acted like he's as much my friend as he is Holden's, maybe more. But Mark's behavior is more unusual, and I have no idea what to make of it.

Finn suggests playing 21 as soon as everyone finishes eating. I've participated in the numbers game before, but never this tipsy. It's much more of a challenge to keep track of what was last said and what leap was made. I miss the change in direction twice, but luckily I'm not up next either time. We're a large enough group, so it takes a few minutes to go around. I spend that time staring at the flickering flames and downing more lemonade.

Grace fakes a yawn after the sixth round ends. "I'm bored of this game. Let's play something different."

For once, she and I are on the same page.

I'd rather enjoy the sleepy buzz of alcohol than have to stay focused on numbers. My pride is the only reason I've kept up so far.

"Truth or Dare?" McKenzie suggests.

I roll my eyes behind the cover of my cup.

"Nah, let's do Two Truths and a Lie," Finn suggests. "Mark to Grace, you're team one. Everyone else is team two."

There's rumbled agreement around the campfire. I sip more lemonade, which chases the increasing chill in the night air away. A piece of wood shifts in the campfire, sending sparks flying upward toward the dark sky.

I'm *very* nervous about heading to bed. The sleeping logistics were another thing I didn't think through when I impulsively decided to show up here. Since I told my mom I was headed to the city for a girls' weekend with Sydney, dragging an old tent out of the basement wasn't really an option. Like pretty much everything about this trip, I decided I'd figure it out when I got here.

Scanning the faces surrounding the fire, it's obvious who my only option is. There's no one else here who I'm comfortable sharing space with, even with the awkward tension humming in the air.

Ridiculously, I'm anxious about sleeping next to him. We haven't been that close to each other in months.

Physically, at least. There will still be an emotional gap.

It's obvious in the way our eyes won't meet, how one of us

glances away as soon as they do. We haven't exchanged a single word since he gave me his second burger.

I'm almost as aware of how everyone else is tuned in to our distance, how McKenzie and Grace exchange looks after noticing Mark seated between the two of us.

I'm sure plenty of rumors about our relationship status are swirling amongst the popular crowd, but I still have no idea what —if anything—Holden has told his friends about us.

Another disadvantage on my side.

Equally maddening is the suspicion McKenzie confirmed earlier: it's all because of Holden. No one cares about my relationship status, much less happiness.

"Brooks, you start," Finn says.

"'Kay," Brooks agrees. His eyes meet mine across the flames, and I quickly drop my gaze down at the pine needles littering the ground. "I was born on Halloween. I'm left-handed. I've only slept with one girl."

There are a couple of giggles following that last one. Brooks looks over and winks toward the titters before focusing on Finn.

It's where everyone else is looking too. Finn is on the other team, and he's the only one who has known Brooks for longer than a day. It makes sense that he'll be the one who guesses.

But Holden is the one who answers. "First one is a lie," he says, then swigs from the can he's holding.

Mark rolls his eyes. "We're supposed to discuss it as a team before you answer."

"Was I wrong?"

Tension hums through the still air as Holden and Brooks stare at each other.

"No," Brooks answers. "That's right."

"One girl, man?" Finn laughs. "Come on…"

Guffaws and whispers swirl around in the night air.

Brooks shrugs, unbothered. "Wanted it to mean something."

My gaze moves to the interior of my cup. Something he and I have in common that probably isn't a popular viewpoint among people our age.

It's definitely not something Holden and I have in common.

I've never asked for exact details—who, what, or where— about Holden's experience before he and I got together, but we grew up in the same town. Attended the same schools. Had the same classmates.

So, I have a pretty good idea.

And I thought I'd accepted it. Thought I got past it a long time ago.

But right now it burns like a cut that scabbed over but never fully healed, reminding me the wound is there.

Maybe it's the alcohol.

Maybe it's that I'm feeling incredibly insecure right now and a reminder of our differences isn't helping.

I was *there* the whole time. If he loves me the way he claims to, why did it take me grinding on him in a driveway to set off the chain of dominos that ended with us in a committed relationship?

And maybe it wouldn't still bother me if I was fully confident in us.

But I'm not. Not right now.

Our different pasts feel like proof of how uneven our relation-ship was. Is. I'm not sure which tense is proper right now.

Camila goes next. She's one of Grace's good friends. She's also sitting on the other side of Holden, so I avoid looking at her as she shares her three sentences. No one on my team asks me for my opinion on her lie, so I focus my attention on draining the rest of my cup instead.

My stomach is churning, my skin warm and tingly from all

the vodka I've knocked back. I don't drink alcohol very often, so my tolerance is probably somewhere right around *extremely low*.

I'm stuck here.

It's dark and late, an hour plus drive back to Pembrooke.

Not to mention, I'm drunk.

So, the best solution seems to be to keep drinking. The next time the pitcher gets passed around, I top my cup off once again.

Jordan is the next one to go. Since he's on my team, I don't have to participate.

And then…Holden is up.

"I have five cousins. I eat cereal without milk. My favorite flavor of ice cream is cookie dough."

"Jeez, man. Too vulnerable," Harrison jokes.

A few laughs echo around the fire.

Then, one by one, everyone on my team looks to me. Brooks is the last to, a wrinkle appearing between his eyes as he follows everyone else's attention.

Maybe I was wrong. Maybe he hasn't heard Holden is the guy I was referring to last night.

I shouldn't care. I don't care. He's just one more witness to the rollercoaster that's my relationship with Holden Adams.

I take some petty satisfaction in taking a slow sip of my drink, pretending not to notice the expectant expressions aimed my way.

"Cassia?" Jordan prompts.

"What?" I reply.

"Uh…" He glances at Harrison, who's now studying the ground instead of making jokes. "I just, um, do you have any thoughts?"

"Nope, no thoughts. It's a *really* tough call."

"Um, okay." Jordan obviously has no idea what to make of my sarcasm.

Around Holden's friends, I'm usually easygoing and affable. I wanted them all to like me. To get why Holden liked me.

Right now? I don't really care. They probably all formed their conclusions about me a long time ago, and I've wasted my time ever since.

"His aunt doesn't have any kids, right?" McKenzie says, from my left. "Does his dad have other siblings?"

"No clue," Jordan replies. Then glances at Harrison, who shrugs.

"Straight cereal is criminal," Brooks comments. "I bet that's the lie."

"Two of them have to do with food and one doesn't," Jordan states. "I think that means something."

"Oh, I didn't think of that," McKenzie says. "Okay, yeah. I vote for the cousins one."

It doesn't escape my notice that the deliberations about Holden's clue have already lasted twice as long as everyone else's so far. The spotlight is always a little brighter when it's aimed toward him.

I drain the rest of my drink. Then stand. "He eats cookie dough straight but not in ice cream," I say.

Surprisingly, my empty cup lands in the trash. I wasn't sure, between my buzz and the distance. But it's satisfying to make the shot. One part of tonight that goes according to plan. A little mic drop moment.

Everyone's attention is on me.

"I'm heading to bed," I announce. "Night."

I grab my empty plate off the ground and climb over the log, tossing that in the trash too.

"Do you know where the bathrooms are?" Harrison asks, standing as well.

"I saw the signs, yeah."

"I can show you…" His voice trails, and my alcohol-addled brain takes a second to figure out why.

"If you don't want my fist in your face, stop fucking asking for it, Baker."

I glare at Holden, who's glaring at Harrison.

"He's just being nice."

A muscle jumps in Holden's jaw as he stares Harrison down. The only sound is the crackle of the fire, the scent of smoke flavoring the thick tension in the air.

I'm mad at Holden, but I'm also annoyed with Harrison now. He could have easily predicted this is exactly how Holden would react. That it would lead to this spectacle I want no part of. And I don't need or want Harrison's help, even if it's well-intentioned.

I shake my head and turn away, heading in what I think is the direction of the path that had signs pointing toward the restrooms. I really have to pee, plus I'm exhausted. Bed sounds wonderful, even if it's a flannel-lined bag on the ground.

There's a clink of glass, then the fall of footsteps following me. I spin to watch Holden walk my way, his strides easy and confident. All the anger just aimed at Harrison appears absent.

"What are you doing?"

"You know *exactly* what I'm doing."

I cross my arms. "One, I'm perfectly capable of finding the bathrooms by myself. Two, coming here was a mistake. Three, I'll be even more pissed at you than I am right now if you insist on coming with me. Which one's the *lie*, Holden?"

He mirrors my pose, and it makes his biceps bulge. I swallow, blaming the vodka for noticing that instead of focusing on my irritation. In my traitorous libido's defense, he's the hottest guy I've ever seen. Dating him for three years and knowing him since we were young enough to have recess at school hasn't dulled that attraction.

"You're drunk in the woods with no flashlight, no cell service, and no idea where you're going. There are wild animals around and who knows what kind of strangers. Does that sound *perfectly capable*, Cassia?"

I have no interest in going to the bathrooms alone after his little speech, and also no interest in admitting that to him.

So I turn around with a huff and continue walking.

"It's to the left."

"I know. I need to get stuff from the tent. Is that okay with you, *boss*?"

Holden doesn't reply to my sarcasm, just follows me over to the tent. Helpfully shines a light on where my bags are located so that I can grab my toiletries out of the duffel, but I don't thank him. Don't speak until I see him grabbing his toothbrush.

"You're going to bed?"

"Yep."

I glance at the campfire, still glowing brightly a couple dozen feet away. "No one else is…"

"I'm not sharing a tent with any of them. If you're ready for bed, let's go to bed."

"You can stay up," I say stupidly. Since I'm certain Holden doesn't need or want my permission. "I had an early morning, that's all."

"I know. Your Friday shift starts at seven. You work from eight to five on Tuesdays and Thursdays, seven to four on Monday, Wednesday, and Friday. Ten to four on Saturdays." He glances over, an unamused smile appearing as he registers my obvious shock that he memorized my schedule. "Years of history aren't that easy to erase, Cassia."

"I'm not erasing anything."

"Then what are you doing? Why did you bother coming if you weren't going to even talk to me?"

"You haven't talked to me!" I exclaim, well aware it's the most childish response I could have come up with.

In my defense, I'm drunk. And Holden has always affected me in a way no one else does.

Holden just shakes his head. "You got all your shit?"

I huff and straighten, my small bag of toiletries fisted in one hand. "Yes."

He nods, then starts toward the parking area. I trail behind him, grateful he keeps the pace slow across the uneven ground.

It takes about two minutes for me to realize Holden was completely right about me going alone being a bad idea, but he doesn't utter a *told you so*. Admitting he was right would be a decent olive branch, but I'm in no mood for building a bridge at the moment. More in the mindset of lighting a match.

We walk silently along the path, which is lined with spotlights every dozen or so feet. They're too dim to cast more than a subtle flicker, barely providing enough illumination to keep me from tripping repeatedly.

It takes us a few minutes to reach the brighter lights that glow up ahead. A small building appears. It reminds me of the structures you see off the highway at rest areas, a long, low building with multiple entrances and exits.

"I'll be waiting out here," Holden tells me, then heads inside one door.

I nod in acknowledgment, then follow a middle-aged woman inside another.

The fluorescent lights sting my eyes, reflecting off the glass mirror and shiny counters. The interior looks exactly like the girls' locker room at Pembrooke High did, with one section for changing and another for stalls.

I use the bathroom first, then carry my toiletries to an open sink to wash my face and brush my teeth. I study my reflection in the mirror as I get ready for bed, noticing the dark circles under my eyes and the permanent wrinkles in my forehead.

I feel older than twenty-one. And I look it too.

After stowing my toiletries and washing my hands, I head back outside. The scent of artificial cleaner is replaced by pine needles and fresh air. The buzzing lights fade, the ones out here swarmed by bugs.

Holden is waiting right where he said he'd be.

Neither of us speak as we retrace our steps back to the campsite, the entire trek taking about fifteen minutes. Everyone else is still gathered at the campfire, shouts and exclamations carrying easily across the clearing.

Part of me expects Holden to head for the fire after all. It's barely past eleven, much earlier than parties with his friends usually end. But he ducks inside after me, zipping the tent flap closed behind us.

Despite barely muffling the noise outside, it's enough to make me feel like we're completely alone.

Holden turns on the small lamp on the floor and shuts off the flashlight on his phone. The lamp flickers a couple of times, the orange glow brighter than I was expecting.

I toss my toiletries back into my bag, deciding to sleep in the shirt I'm already wearing. I unclasp the back of my bra and slip it off with a maneuver I perfected back in middle school, then step out of my denim shorts.

My eyes avoid his as I kick off my sneakers and then slip into my sleeping bag, the laundry detergent-scent of the flannel a comforting reminder of home.

I roll onto my side, staring at the flimsy material that makes up the side of the tent and trying not to imagine a bear's paw swiping through it. I might love animals, but I have no interest in encountering any wild ones on this trip.

I study the navy material, trying and failing not to listen for the rustle of fabric as Holden changes. Keeping my eyes open so I don't accidentally picture how he looks in his boxer briefs. Resenting the traitorous pulse between my thighs that reminds me how long it's been since I saw him naked in person.

The light turns off with a soft click, leaving us in darkness.

Ever since I arrived, I've vacillated on whether coming here was a smart move or not. And I'm still conflicted now, listening to his steady, even breathing a couple of feet away. Considering how easy it would be to roll over and kiss him, to lose myself in the way I've only ever felt around Holden.

But I don't move.

I'm scared to cave. Worried what might happen if I stop ignoring him.

Holden and I are a powder keg, one lit match away from exploding.

It's a thrill.

A high.

A problem.

CHAPTER SIX

HOLDEN

It's so silent that I can *feel* it.

There's an invisible hum in the air between us. Not unpleasant, but not pleasant either. Just…there. Inescapable, in the tight confines of the tent.

Cassia's awake too.

I'm not sure how I know in the darkness, but I do. Her breathing is steady and even, almost purposefully so. While I'm making no secret of my insomnia, shifting around in my sleeping bag as I try to get more comfortable.

She probably would have had a better chance of falling asleep if I *had* stayed up later. I can hear the occasional snippet of voices or laughter drifting in from outside, suggesting everyone else is still up.

I'm not trying to keep Cassia awake. But I am wanting her to know I am. I'm hoping she'll be the one to break the silence at some point.

Finally, after I fake cough a couple of times, she does.

"You weren't supposed to be back yet." Her voice is low and even, no emotion suggesting how she feels about my early return.

My hands tighten around the fabric I'm lying on. It's too hot to have the sleeping bag zipped, so I'm just lying on top of it. "I was pissed at you when I left. I knew Dave would be cool with me staying with him for a few days after camp ended. So that's what I was planning on. What I told everyone."

"Then why didn't you stay?"

There's no motion on her side. Cassia still won't look at me, facing the fabric of the tent instead. It's nothing but a stretch of navy, which she's studying like a puzzle.

"I missed you."

We're far past the point of quips and deflections. I'm under no illusions our relationship is in a decent place right now. That a summer of space hasn't resulted in anything but more distance. And based on how she's turned away, refusing to look at me, Cassia isn't closing the gap.

"You missed me." Her voice is flat. Unemotional. "I didn't hear anything from you for *two months*."

A swell of anger appears that I try to tamp down. "You asked me for space, Cassia. Now I'm the bad guy for giving it to you?"

"Nope." She pops the P, irritation translating through the syllable. "You just reminded me exactly where I fall on your list of priorities—at the bottom. It must have been a relief to you when I asked for a break."

She's baiting me. Basically begging me for a reaction.

This time, I don't try very hard to curb the anger. "It must be fucking nice, knowing exactly what everyone else is thinking and feeling all the time. You learn that in one of your animal behavior classes?"

"Yeah. Because I *go to class*, instead of partying and playing basketball all the time."

I scoff. "I'm going to college to play basketball. You knew I wasn't a nerd when we got together. *Before* we got together. Don't act like that's some surprise to you."

"We were kids, Holden. Now we're not."

"Yeah, people grow up. I've grown up. You said you weren't happy, and you needed time. So, I gave it to you. Listened to you, like an adult."

"That's part of the problem."

"So, you're mad at me because I listened to you?"

"No. I'm mad at you because you did exactly what I hoped you wouldn't."

"You blindsided me with the break shit, Cassia. I thought things were fine between us."

"Because we'd barely seen each other in months?"

"You were busy! You wanted me hanging around, distracting you when you were studying for finals and preparing to take the GRE and saying how exhausted you were? If you wanted to spend more time together, you should have said so!"

"I'm sick of being the one making an effort, Holden. I'm not going to *beg* you to make me a priority."

It's the second time she's said that. Told me that she's not a priority.

And I'm taken aback it's a thought that's even crossed her mind. I know that I'm selfish. I always have been. If there's something I don't want to do, I won't do it. There's a very short list of people whose feelings I care about hurting. If she wasn't a *priority* to me, we wouldn't be in a relationship to take a break from.

Another flaw of mine is that I'm not great at expressing how I feel. I prefer to show my feelings, but nothing in Cassia's tense posture suggests that she's open to physical affection right now.

So I offer her the same answer I did earlier. "You are a priority. You're making it sound like we hardly ever saw each other. We never went, what? More than a few nights?"

"Showing up for sex and then leaving to lift weights with the guys early the next morning is not prioritizing me."

"I'm the captain of the team, Cassia. I can't just not show up. And you were pushing me toward your bed, eager to get off those nights, not asking to talk."

She scoffs. "Isn't there another tent you can sleep in?"

"Aside from this one that I brought and set up? Nope, I'm good."

"Didn't Finn bring a tent? Mark? Grace?"

I laugh incredulously. "You're telling me to go sleep in *Grace's* tent?"

"According to McKenzie, she'd greet you with open arms. Open legs, rather." She snorts.

I'm having trouble keeping up with the conversation. And I have no clue what the right thing to say is anymore.

I know Cassia's drunk. I said nothing when she was tossing back drinks earlier, certain of exactly how badly that would go over.

I didn't see Cassia talking to McKenzie and have no clue why she would have said something to Cassia about Grace.

"So?"

"*So*, she's after you because she 'had you first.' Isn't that nice?"

Cassia's tone is the vocal equivalent of a land mine. There's a lot of emotion simmering beneath the flippant words, so I tread carefully.

"Nice? I'd call it psychotic. I'm not interested in Grace."

"But you *were*. You've had sex with her, right?"

I exhale. "Cassia…" I'm not sure what else to say.

Foolishly, I guess, I thought we were far past this. I haven't kissed another girl since the first time we hooked up—nearly four years ago.

Cheating on Cassia has never occurred to me.

I *love* her. There's emotion behind every kiss or touch we share. Before her, sex was mechanical. Another form of exercise that was all pleasure and no pain. An escape less destructive than flying fists or stolen whiskey.

I thought it was less destructive, at least. I was in no shape to be in a committed relationship back then, and based on where things stand between us now, maybe I'm still not. I faced two options—losing her or changing for her—and picked the one I could live with.

Again, I'm selfish.

And I thought Cassia seeing me with other girls in high school would take care of any feelings she had for me. She wasn't supposed to still want me after the fact.

"I can't change the past, Cassia." I blow out a long breath. "Grace means nothing to me. None of them did."

Things I've told her before.

Truths that didn't sink in.

Not like Brooks did. I saw her face earlier when he said he'd only been with one girl. When the other guys were teasing him about it. It meant something to her that they have that in common, and it's something I can never share with her.

I didn't cheat.

I didn't do it to hurt her.

But my past is there between us, and if it hasn't faded by now, I'm not sure if it ever will.

I look over, tracing the lump of her body lying a few feet away. It feels like she's a lot farther.

"I'm not a cheater, Cassia. I'm *committed*."

No response.

I don't make another sound. I pretend to fall asleep, the same way she is.

CHAPTER SEVEN

CASSIA

My eyes open to an empty tent. My mouth is dry, and my temples are pounding. I have one hell of a hangover.

I stare at Holden's empty sleeping bag for several minutes, my heart aching worse than my head.

Bits and pieces of our conversation from last night burrow into my brain, making me wince. I said more than I meant to last night. Some of it needed to be spoken. Some I wish had stayed thoughts.

With a sigh, I slide out of my own bed. I'm not sure how early it is. There's no sound of activity outside and my phone is dead, thanks to the lack of outlets.

I get dressed in shorts and a clean t-shirt, then grab my toiletry bag. The tent's zipper snags a couple of times as I open it, the flaps waving in the slight breeze.

The campsite is empty. All the other tents are still zipped shut, the center of the fire pit a pile of black ashes.

I'm relieved—and proud—when I successfully navigate to the bathrooms on my own. The trip is much easier in the daylight, sunshine exposing all the dips and valleys and crags in the path. It must be early because there's no sign of any activity on the trail or in the bathrooms.

I run through the same routine as last night, except this time I slather some sunscreen and concealer on my face after washing it.

After a split-second of deliberation, I apply mascara and lip gloss as well. I'm not sure if it's a good or a bad inclination, how I still feel the urge to look my best in front of Holden.

When I get back to the campsite, Brooks is standing by the table that serves as the "kitchen", stirring the contents of a cup. He glances up and catches my eye, giving me no polite choice except to walk over to him.

"Morning."

"Good morning," I reply.

"Coffee?" He tilts his head toward a glass canister. "It's instant, but not terrible."

"Um, yeah. Sure." I help myself to a plastic cup, reading the instructions on the coffee canister before measuring out a spoonful and adding bottled water. It tastes like crap and is luke-warm, but it's better than nothing.

We sip in silence as I wonder where the hell Holden went. There's no sign of anyone else being up yet. His truck is still here so he couldn't have gone that far.

"So…your complicated relationship."

I glance over at Brooks. "You don't want to talk about the weather or something instead?"

One corner of his mouth curves up. "We can, if you want."

"No, it's fine. You can ask."

"Still complicated?"

"Still complicated."

"You deserve better."

I exhale. "What we want…what we get…what we deserve? Those can all be different things."

Brooks raises one eyebrow. Maybe that made no sense. It's hard to boil down years of history into two sentences.

I want Holden. Being with him has never felt like settling. But I'm also scared he'll devastate me, if I let him.

"How long have you guys been together?" Brooks asks.

"We started dating our senior year of high school. But even before…" I shrug a shoulder. "It's sort of always been him. For me."

It hasn't always been me for him.

At least in some ways.

"Yeah, I get that," Brooks says.

I sip more coffee and immediately regret it. "Wanna talk about it?" I ask.

He shrugs. "There's not much to say. She cheated on me with my best friend. One of those cliches you hear about and think will never happen to you. We met in high school. Waited to lose our virginity to each other. Except…she wanted to know what it was like with another guy. The way she tells it, the 'other guy' just happened to be my best friend." Brooks scoffs. "I'm still a little bitter about it."

"I would be too."

"Did he cheat on you?"

I'm not a cheater, Cassia. I'm committed.

I hate him a little for throwing those words at me. For knowing exactly what would hit me the hardest. For bringing up that night.

"No," I answer. Reluctantly, I add, "He wouldn't."

In many ways, it would be easier if he had. It would be a clear betrayal with an unforgiveable outcome. A clean break.

It's much harder to explain what being overlooked feels like, even to myself. How it builds from a series of small moments.

Seeing him tagged in social media posts at parties I wasn't invited to.

A text chain of him answering my messages but never being the one who reached out first.

Watching him across campus, knowing his friends' conversations would end if I walked over.

Not sure how to tell him that and not able to bury it forever.

Brooks sighs. "She asked me to forgive her, and I tried. But in the end, I couldn't. It hurt us more than it helped."

"I'm sorry you had to go through that."

"Thanks. I hate talking about it but it also helps to."

We both turn at the sound of approaching footsteps.

I'm grateful for the interruption.

Finn and Holden are carrying armfuls of kindling into the clearing and stacking them by the fire.

"I'll go see if they need some help," Brooks says, setting his cup down.

I nod, my gaze dropping to the bins of food stored beneath the table. I'm impressed by the amount of provisions here. My assumption was Holden and his friends ate beef jerky and drank beer on these trips. But there are lots of snacks, including chips and dried fruit. Granola bars, which is what I focus on.

I squat to grab one out of the plastic bin.

"How'd you sleep?"

I pull in a deep breath as soon as I hear his voice.

"Shitty." I straighten, keeping my focus on ripping the wrapper. It tears to the side instead of straight down, and I grit my teeth with irritation.

Warm fingers close around mine, taking the bar and easily opening it.

A thrill sneaks up my arm in response to the contact. This is the first time we've touched in...unfortunately, I know *exactly* how long it's been. Could tell you down to the day. Which is just as embarrassing as the realization I'm this affected by his hand brushing mine.

"Thanks," I mutter, when he passes it back to me.

"You're welcome."

I finally meet his gaze, dreading and anticipating the moment our eyes connect. He's even closer than I was expecting, his blue gaze intense and searching.

My inhale is ragged and unsteady. "How did *you* sleep?"

"Great."

I huff a laugh. "Great. Good for you."

He continues talking like I never spoke. "You were a couple of feet away, instead of eight hundred miles."

My mouth goes dry, tongue turning to sandpaper.

I'm still mad at him—so mad.

Hurt—extremely hurt.

But those two primary emotions are beginning to wear through, revealing everything underneath.

Reminding me that the *reason* I'm so mad and so hurt is he was gone, and I missed him in a visceral, painful way that kept me depressed even when I wasn't consciously thinking about his absence. That scared me, honestly, because I've always known Holden has the power to devastate me but never experienced it to that extreme degree.

"You wearing a swimsuit?" he asks.

"Uh, no?" It comes out like a question, even though I'm certain I'm not.

"Well, unless you wanna skinny-dip, which I'm totally not opposed to..." His voice trails suggestively, my skin warming automatically in response to hearing that tone.

I glance away in an attempt to hide that reaction. "I'm not skinny-dipping."

"Then go get changed."

"What's the rush? Almost everyone is still asleep."

"They're not coming."

"What?" I look back at him.

"Unless you'd rather stay with the group?"

"Um, no." I don't have to think about it. Again, I'm not sure if that's a good or bad thing.

"Great. Get changed, and let's go."

I stare at Holden, trying to figure out exactly what's going on. After last night, I woke up with very low expectations of what today might look like.

The two of us going off by ourselves did not cross my mind as a possibility, and I'm stunned it occurred to him.

He's staring at me, one eyebrow raised expectantly.

"Uh, okay, yeah." I hesitate for a split-second longer, then head back toward the tent.

My bikini is at the very bottom of my duffel bag, thrown in on a whim. I undress to swap out my bra and underwear for the swimsuit, carefully tying the strings behind my neck and on my hips before pulling my shorts and shirt back on. I hunt around for my water bottle but can't find it.

Eventually, I give up.

Mark and Jordan have joined Finn, Holden, and Brooks by the fire pit by the time I climb back out of the tent. Another fire has been lit, the flames cracking merrily as they spread across the fresh kindling.

I approach the group slowly, the denim of my shorts a rough rub against my knuckles as I shove my hands inside of my pockets.

Mark notices me first, shooting a warm smile my way. There's a crease across one of his cheeks from a pillow and his hair is sticking up in three different directions. Jordan is in patterned pajamas. It's kind of nice, seeing this more relaxed side of the guys. Makes me feel more at ease around them.

Holden is talking to Finn, his expression serious.

There's a spasm of unease in my stomach, worried something is wrong. But it relaxes when Holden notices my reappearance, punching Finn's shoulder and then walking over to me. He stops to pick up his backpack, which I eye curiously.

"Have you seen my water bottle?"

"Yep." Holden pats his backpack. "I packed it. You want it?"

"No, that's okay. I just wanted to make sure I…had it."

He nods, tugging down the brim of his ball cap. "Ready?"

I swallow my nervous apprehension. "Uh-huh."

He glances back. "See you guys later."

His friends' expressions range from confused—Jordan—to amused—Mark.

"What time are we supposed to send out a search party?" Finn calls, as we start toward the far side of the campsite's clearing, in the opposite direction from all the tents.

Holden flips him off over one shoulder.

"Where are we going?" I ask as we start along a trail.

"You'll see," he replies.

"Very reassuring."

"Don't you trust me?"

"You're the one who freaked me out about wild animals and no cell service last night."

"That was you walking alone, not with me."

I scoff, and he suddenly turns.

"You trust me, Cassia?"

Maybe I should hesitate, after all that we've been through. But it's also why I don't. "Yes."

A small smile touches his lips. "Good." Then he turns around and keeps walking.

The trail is well-maintained but narrow. We walk single file across the leaf litter and pine needles scattered along the ground, shaded by the broad branches above. Small patches of sunlight permeate the canopy above, but the rest of the path is shaded, the fresh air damp and cool.

I inhale deeply, especially once the incline starts. Holden doesn't glance back once.

He's obviously paying attention to me, though, because he slows after I slip on a stray rock. I catch my balance, rubbing my palm against my shorts to wipe away the dirt before continuing to trek.

It's a peaceful, comfortable kind of silence, permeated by the occasional bird call or twig snap. The kind I wasn't sure we were still capable of. The kind that reminds me how tightly woven Holden Adams is in my life. That I'm not just attracted to him or in love with him, but I also consider him a best friend.

I feel more myself around him than I do when I'm alone.

And it's the reminder of the friendship that predated our relationship that makes me decide to strike up a conversation. "So was camp really that terrible, or were you just being dramatic?"

He huffs a laugh. "Both."

"Same guys as last year?"

"Yeah, for the most part. I hung out with the same crew, at least. Coach Jackson was there."

I nod, then realize he can't tell. "Nice."

A pause, before he asks, "Everything okay at the shelter?"

"Yeah. It's been busy. We're almost to capacity, which sucks."

"Isn't Eileen putting in a new kennel?"

"I thought so, but she's changed the subject every time it's come up. Guessing there's a money concern. She's paying me more than minimum wage and wants to start compensating Jackie for her time too."

"Did you know she's friends with Harrison's sister?"

"Um, yeah." I battle curiosity and lose. "She told you that?"

"No, he did."

"What? Why?"

"He was giving me some shit for showing up there yesterday."

My stomach jolts uncomfortably. Unfortunately, Harrison has always been a touchy subject between us. It explains some of the tension last night. "I didn't ask him to do that."

"I know."

"I'd rather you show up more, not less." It's easier to admit that while staring at Holden's back instead of his face.

His steps seem to falter for a half-second. "I thought it was the opposite. Your place where you didn't want distractions."

"I never said that. You used to come by and help out. Then you just…stopped. We never discussed it."

"You're right. I'm sorry."

I blink rapidly. Apologizing is not Holden's typical response.

"Thanks," I finally say, not sure that's the appropriate reply and equally uncertain what is.

The incline we're climbing steepens suddenly, tree roots sticking out at awkward angles. I focus on pulling deeper breaths into my lungs, feeling sweat dampen the back of my neck.

A few rock boulders appear ahead, and I'm very tempted to suggest we stop at one. But my pride pushes me ahead, focusing on Holden's back and continually climbing toward it.

Ten minutes later, the path evens out. Clumped earth turns to flat stone.

The view is impressive. Leaves flutter like a living, green wave, stretching down and around in every direction. A sloping slant of greenery that leads all the way to the sandy shore on the other side of the mountain. Just past it, the dazzling glint of sunshine off blue water.

"Wow."

"Careful." A warm palm wraps around my elbow, tugging me to a stop.

I glance down, belatedly registering the slope on the other side of the rock face.

"Thanks."

Holden doesn't drop his hand right away. Once he does, it feels like a loss.

My body is starved for attention. For *his* attention, specifically. I crave it like an addiction.

There's another couple up here, the first people we've seen since leaving the campsite. They look to be in their mid-thirties; the woman giving us a small wave while the man offers one of the nostalgic, indulgent smiles adults often give anyone younger. Sort of a *good luck you don't know what life is really like yet* grin.

Holden stops about halfway down the rock, dropping his backpack and bending over to unzip it. "Water?"

"Yeah. Thanks."

He passes me my canteen and I take a long pull, the bottle's insulation keeping the water cool.

Holden's pulling a beach towel out of his backpack, spreading it across the slanted surface and then taking a seat. I hesitate for a second, then sink down beside him.

"You hungry?" he asks, pulling a paper bag out and setting it between us.

I stare at the bag, both eyebrows raised.

"What?"

"I'm impressed," I admit.

One corner of his mouth tilts upward before he drinks some water. "It's just peanut butter and jelly."

It's not *just* anything.

It's him, electing to spend the day just the two of us. Waking up early to make us lunch. Asking about the animal shelter. Apologizing.

There are so many tiny moments that make up me and Holden.

Good and bad.

Ugly and beautiful.

No history is perfect. It's a collection of memories that time twists and warps. The break this summer was supposed to emphasize that. To let me look at us from a distance and decide who we are now.

Instead, we feel more entangled than ever, eating sandwiches side-by-side at the top of a mountain.

We feel familiar and right, like the last two months were only a short chapter in a much longer story. We seem bigger than hurt feelings and harsh words.

We mostly eat in silence, but it's not an uncomfortable one. It means something, I think, that there's a lot unsaid between us right now and we're still able to enjoy a peaceful quiet together. That we're drawn to each other even when we're pushing each other away.

Once we're finished eating, Holden leads me in the opposite direction from which we came.

"The way back is shorter," Holden tells me, sensing my silent question as the sun creeps directly overhead and then nearly disappears once we're back in the woods.

It's also downhill, which makes a big difference in our speed. The decline is challenging in its own way, sections of the trail shifting underfoot. But it's much faster than the climb.

By the time the ground begins to even out flat again, I'm coated with sweat. Even though sunrays aren't reaching us, the air temperature has risen. The muscles in my calves burn from remaining tense and ready to react to the changing topography. My neck is stiff from constantly looking around and down, keeping track of the surroundings.

And despite it all, I'm in a better mood than I can recall experiencing in a long time.

We're rarely alone, just the two of us.

Whether it's in Pembrooke or on campus at Richmond, there's usually a rotating door of people around us. His friends. My family. Sydney. Roommates. Other students. Even if we go out to dinner together, chances are one or both of us will run into someone we know. Someone in my family is always home, and his aunt Catherine's schedule is unpredictable.

Today feels special. Sacred.

Every possible distraction has been stripped away. We don't even have cell service. Which is stressful, considering all the catastrophes that could take place. But also a reminder I trust Holden with my safety—with my *life*—even if I'm disappointed when he doesn't text me. That big feelings matter too, not just small moments.

I notice the sand first.

It mixes with the brown earth gradually, then turns to light gray as soon as we break through the tree line. My steps slow as my sneakers sink into softer ground, glancing around at the sudden shift in scenery. Instead of tree trunks and leaves, there are shells and pebbles mixed in with the sand. The soundtrack of bird calls and snapping sticks is now waves crashing into the shore.

"This was my dad's favorite spot," Holden tells me.

"Oh," I say.

I never bring his dad up, and Holden rarely does.

He's been gone for almost four years, but the loss feels fresh and raw.

It was so sudden. So shocking. So…final.

The beach is more crowded than anywhere else we've hiked. A parking lot is visible on the far side, so some people must avoid the camping experience and drive here just to come to this spot.

There are several families who've staked out spaces in the sand, the piles of toys and chairs and coolers way more than anyone could carry via the route we just came. I'm carrying nothing, and I'm exhausted.

"Come on." Holden grabs my hand, our fingers twining together naturally as he tugs me closer to the water. A jolt of awareness trickles through me from the casual touch.

About a dozen feet from the ocean's edge, Holden drops my hand and his backpack. His sneakers get tossed too, then his shirt, leaving him standing in his swim trunks.

I just stare.

Holden grins, catching me checking him out.

He's always been in good shape from basketball. But now it looks like his muscles have sharpened, strong ropes of sinew lining his shoulders and arms. His abs are more defined, hard, stacked ridges with no sign of softness or fat.

"I, um, that camp took training seriously."

I'm not completely aware of what's coming out of my mouth. I just feel like I need to say *something*, rather than continuing to ogle him silently.

He laughs, and I smile automatically at the sound. "Most guys went out at night. I hit the gym."

"Why didn't you go out?"

"Was in a shitty mood and wasn't much fun to be around."

I nod slowly. Happiness probably isn't how I should be feeling, but I don't hate hearing his summer was as crappy as mine. And decide to offer up a little of my own misery in return.

"Sally renamed our family as the seven elves last week. I got

Mopey, who doesn't even exist. I think she meant Dopey, who isn't much of an improvement."

What I don't say is they all assumed my melancholy was because Holden was gone, not that we weren't talking. I also don't mention my dad should have gotten Absent instead of Doc and my mom has been more Stressed than Sleepy.

To Holden's credit, he tries to hide his smile. "What did Maggie get?"

"Grumpy."

"Are she and Silas still together?"

"As far as I know." I'm the lame older sister in her mind. If you ask Maggie, Holden is the most interesting thing about me.

I play with the hem of my shirt.

"You regret it, Cas?"

I glance up, meeting his gaze. "It?"

"*Us*. Do you regret us?"

"No," I say. Then shake my head because that doesn't seem like enough of an answer. "Do you?"

"You're joking, right?"

Slowly, I shake my head.

Doesn't anything get stale eventually? Doesn't the grass always start to look greener elsewhere? Especially when you're the popular, athletic guy who everyone wants to be with or around?

"You're the best part of my story. But…" He exhales. "I know I'm the villain in yours."

"You're not."

He half-smiles. "I don't believe you."

"I've been in love with you since the first time we met, Holden. You're the best part of my story too."

He stares at me, something intense and searching in his gaze. "You're overdressed."

I glance down at my t-shirt and shorts. Kick off my sneakers. Inhale deeply, before I flick open the button and let the fabric slip down my legs. I hold Holden's gaze until the material of my shirt hides him from view, then let that drop to the sand as well.

I resist the urge to cross my arms across my chest. Right now, it doesn't feel like he's seen me wearing even less. It feels raw and vulnerable, especially when his eyes stay focused on my face instead of dipping downward.

"Ready?" He holds out a hand.

I nod before taking it. Our palms connect as naturally as they did earlier, the rub of his skin against mine comforting and electrifying as we walk toward the water. Sunlight glimmers off the surface of the waves and catches the tiny crystals mixed in with the grains of sand.

The ocean is colder than I'm expecting, the contrast jarring after the sun-warmed sand. I haven't been to the beach once this summer. The only swimming I've done is at the local pool with my siblings.

There's a slight sting as the sea laps against the scrape on my shin courtesy of one of the wire cages at the shelter. The pain eases the deeper we walk, Holden's tight grip on my hand reassuring as the water rises higher around us.

We get caught right in the middle of an approaching wave, the crashing spray soaking most of my body. Droplets of salty water land in my hair, curling the sweaty strands even more.

"Go under the next one?" Holden suggests.

His blue eyes are sparkling and bright, the shade somewhere between the water surrounding us and the sky stretched overhead. He squeezes my hand as the next wave gathers on the horizon.

A silent gesture that I appreciate—that I need.

"Okay." I agree, and that's always my first instinct when it comes to Holden. An inclination that sometimes seems dangerous, but right now is natural.

He pushes me in a way no one else does, or maybe a way I just won't allow anyone else to.

There's a measure of trust between us that hums like a living presence. I know he feels it too, tightening his grip right before we dive under the wave when it crests, and it alleviates a little of my worry.

The water is cool and refreshing, immediately washing away all the sweat and dirt from our hike. It swirls around in a rush, muffling the outside world. I relax, Holden's hand keeping me anchored.

And then I'm above the surface again, feeling droplets drip from my soaked hair and roll down my face. A slight breeze raises goosebumps on my skin as the sunshine chases away some of the chill from the cooler water.

I look over at Holden, squinting at the sparkles reflecting off the surface of the water. He's grinning, a light, carefree expression that eases the fist squeezing my heart.

My feet brush the sandy bottom before another passing wave lifts me up like a bobbing cork.

"Pretty nice, huh?"

I glance toward the horizon, water spread in what looks like an endless stretch. It's a perfect summer day. There have been lots of sunny days this summer.

This one feels different, and I know the difference.

He's the difference.

And that terrifies me.

But I decide to lean into the fear instead of hiding from it.

"It's a little scary. Sharks, stingrays, riptides… All sorts of awful stuff happens in the sea."

Holden shakes his head, still smiling. "I'm right here. You don't have to worry about any of that."

"You're awfully cocky."

"Confident, you mean."

"I wasn't sure I could still rely on you." I'm no longer talking about the ocean.

The amusement slowly melts off Holden's face, as he registers the same.

"You can always rely on me. *Always*."

We're still holding hands. And in a move that surprises us both, I let go. Only to breach the foot between us and wrap my arms around his neck instead, so I'm clinging to him like a barnacle. He's so close I can see every freckle. See the water clinging to his eyelashes.

"I want to."

His hands find my waist beneath the waves, the water not muffling the feel of his touch sliding across my hips. My heart pounds so quickly I'm worried it'll beat right out of my chest.

I melt into his embrace, our chests pressing together so tightly there's no water between our bodies anymore.

"Do you still love me?" he whispers.

The question is saturated by the vulnerability he usually hides. I hear the loss in his voice, the boy who stopped celebrating Mother's Day before he understood what the holiday meant and who buried his father before graduating high school.

An immediate *yes* forms on my lips. But the single syllable doesn't sound like enough of an answer. "I don't know how to stop."

"What if you did?"

I exhale. "Then… I'd still love you, Holden Adams."

He smiles, then grazes his thumb along my jawline. "Are we okay, Cas?"

"We're better," I tell him. "I needed…this. Reassurance. *You.*"

"You have me."

"This is the first time it's felt like it in a while."

"Tell me that, then. Don't act like everything is fine and then suddenly say you need some time, and we should take a break."

"It was hard to tell you when I barely saw you." My voice is soft. I'm trying to explain, not to pick a fight.

Holden exhales. "This year is going to be even busier than last year was."

"I know."

"If you need more time or space or a break or whatever this summer was, that's okay."

"Uh…okay." I chew on the inside of my cheek. Something about him being understanding and accommodating more grating than any disagreement. Better than the way he shut down before, I guess. That stung.

"I'll wait, no matter how long it takes."

My inhale is sharp and surprised, but Holden's eyes don't waver. He stares at me, his attention consuming. Warmth blossoms inside of me, separate from the lust humming in my veins as our slick bodies rub against each other.

I love him.

Part of me hoped—*feared*—this summer apart would change that. Change us.

Now, I wonder how I ever thought we'd end up anywhere but here.

I decided he was *it* a long time ago.

And some things don't change.

CHAPTER EIGHT

HOLDEN

We're the last ones back at the campsite. Unsurprising, considering we covered about eleven miles and the spot where Finn was planning on fishing is only a half-mile away.

My skin is sticky from salt and sweat.

My shoulders ache from carrying a backpack all day.

My entire body is sore, actually. The weights and cardio routine I'm used to don't utilize the same muscles as hiking.

But I feel better than I have in weeks. The rock that's been sitting in my gut ever since I heard the word *break* has shrunken up and disappeared.

Things between me and Cassia aren't perfect, but they're a hell of a lot better than they were.

It casts a warmer, more positive glow over everything. I'm no longer pissed at Harrison's interference or irritated simply by the sight of Brooks's face.

I *grin* as we walk into the clearing. "We made it."

"Thank God." Cassia exhales dramatically, but she's smiling too.

Everyone else is gathered around the campfire. Tonight's

dinner is hot dogs, because meal options are pretty limited when you're cooking on a grill for a large group.

At this point, I'm hungry enough to eat just about anything.

I drop my backpack outside the tent and stretch. It wasn't *that* heavy but carry anything all day and it starts to feel like a burden.

"I'm going to take a quick shower," Cassia says, leaning down to dig through her duffel bag.

"Okay." I should probably shower too, but a cold beer and sitting down feels like more of a priority right now. "You remember the way to the bathrooms?"

"Uh-huh. And I made it there all by myself this morning."

There's a challenge to her words, but also a hint of teasing I'm relieved to hear. I know I was overprotective last night. Just like I know letting her walk off alone in the dark wasn't an option.

Since it's still light out, I don't insist on going with her this time. I trust she'd tell me if that's what she wanted.

I nod and then head for the campfire, only pausing to grab a beer out of the cooler.

I take a seat next to Finn and crack the cold can open.

"How did it go?" He doesn't bother with any small talk. Or keeping his voice down.

I smile before I sip. "Great."

Finn's exhale is overdone and dramatic. "Thank fuck."

I roll my eyes, but I'm still smiling. "How was fishing?"

"Good. Caught a couple of trout."

"Same spot?"

"Uh-huh. It was super crowded, so I didn't have high hopes. Did better than I was expecting to."

I nod, then drink more beer.

"How far did you guys go?" Finn asks.

"Hazard's Beach."

He whistles, long and low. "Damn. That's…what? Seven miles?"

"Eleven, according to my phone."

Another whistle. An owl hoots in the distance, the low sound echoing through the trees.

"So you literally wore her down?"

I snort. "Sure."

My stomach grumbles, wanting more sustenance than beer. I get up to grab a hot dog, lathering it with plenty of ketchup.

Grace appears beside me, reaching for the mustard. "Fishing sucked," she informs me.

"No one made you come."

"Jordan said it was just our group."

"What do you have against Brooks?" I ask.

She huffs. "You know that's not who I'm talking about."

"No, I don't, actually. Because Cassia is part of my group. She's my girlfriend. She's been my girlfriend for years. And she'll be my girlfriend, up until the day I ask her to marry me. So whatever fantasyland you're living in? Whatever lies you're telling McKenzie or anyone else? We're. Never. Going. To. Happen."

I leave her standing there and return to my seat in one of the Adirondack chairs.

I eat and listen to the various conversations, not paying close attention to anything until Cassia reappears with wet hair. She grabs some food and then takes the seat closest to me.

I'm distracted by Finn shoving some of the fish he caught and cooked in my face. I take a tentative bite while he watches with rapt attention.

"Well?" he demands.

I chew carefully. "It's not bad," I decide.

That's all the encouragement Finn needs to launch into a detailed recap of the fishing trip.

I let him talk. I feel bad for barely communicating this summer and for missing fishing today. This is usually our big weekend together, and it's looked nothing like it typically does.

The s'mores fixings come out once everyone is finished with dinner.

I glance over as the marshmallows get passed around, registering the raised bumps on Cassia's arms in the orange glow cast by the campfire.

I scootch forward in the chair, tugging my sweatshirt off and then tossing the ball of fabric so it drops into her lap.

"I'm fine," Cassia says.

My response is just to sink back in my chair, barely registering the slight bite to the air. I think Cassia might roll her eyes, but it's hard to tell in the dim light. She only hesitates for a second before she's pulling the sweatshirt on. Then shocks the hell out of me by abandoning her spot to sit on my lap and lying back so her head is tucked beneath my chin.

My arms twine around her automatically, hugging her to my body. The warmth is nice. But it's nothing in comparison to the feel of her pressed against me.

It's bliss and agony.

My body is reacting to the close proximity, and there's no way she can't feel it. I shift so my mouth is right next to her ear.

"Sorry," I whisper. "It's been a while."

"I know *exactly* how long it's been." She pauses. "I'm not a cheater, either."

My hold on her tightens.

I didn't think Cassia asked for a break because she wanted to hook up with other guys, or that she would. But it's been a nagging doubt in the back of my head all summer. My first glimpse of her in two months was laughing with another guy.

Knowing nothing happened lifts a weight I didn't know I was carrying.

Finn suggests playing 21—again. For someone terrible at math, he sure does love it.

I tilt my head back to stare up at the stars, my cheek pressed against Cassia's hair. It feels right, holding her like this. It feels like a lot less time has passed than the months it's actually been since we shared this easy connection.

Commotion echoes around us, but I'm oblivious to the activity, focusing on the woods instead.

I've always appreciated how nature simplifies things. How it strips away distractions and boils down to what really matters. Always preferred being outside to staying indoors. Sitting here feels similar to the old basketball court. It's a snippet of peace amidst chaos.

I alternate between tracing patterns in the stars above and watching flames burn the pile of sticks down to nothing. It's late and I'm exhausted. But there's no inclination to move.

In groups of two or three, everyone else heads to bed. Finn is the last to leave, nodding at the bucket beside the stone circle. I nod back before he heads toward his tent.

"We can clear a group, huh?"

My head jerks at the sound of Cassia's voice. She's not asleep, like I assumed.

"I thought you were asleep."

"Nope. I am comfortable, though." She shifts so I can see a little more of her face. "Were you going to wake me up or carry me to bed?"

"Probably just wait for you to wake up. I'm comfortable too."

She huffs a laugh and then slides off my lap, moving forward and raising her arms above her head to stretch. Cool air rushes between our bodies, the loss of her touch physically painful. The temperature has dropped significantly since I gave her my sweatshirt.

"Cassia?"

"Yeah?"

I clear my throat, chickening out. "We should get to bed."

"I'm not tired."

She stands, my sweatshirt hanging to her mid-thigh.

My brain is still processing what *that* comment means when she pulls my sweatshirt off—taking her t-shirt with it. The pile of fabric lands in a heap on my lap. Goosebumps rise on her skin, the moonlight barely enough illumination to see the raised texture. The dark blue material of her bikini looks black in the limited light, contrasted against her pale skin.

"Thanks for letting me borrow that."

My tongue feels too big for my mouth. Words are a jumble in my head.

She's gorgeous.

She's always been gorgeous, and I've never been able to find the right words to convey that to her. To explain that any insecurities she has about Grace or any other girl mean nothing, because all I see is her.

"You can keep it," I manage to choke out.

Cassia smirks. "You're telling me to put clothes on? That's a first."

I want to flirt back. But I can't forget we're standing on shaky ground. That we just started walking forward and that sprinting might end in falling. "You're still wearing your suit?"

She raises one eyebrow, probably wondering why I'm bothering to ask. I'm thinking the same thing. I'm also stalling, trying to figure out how to best handle this.

"I showered in it."

I stand. "Cassia…"

"Holden…" She mimics my tone, still smirking.

I shake my head, leaning down to grab the water bucket and tossing it over the smoldering embers. They die with a low hiss, tendrils of smoke wafting upward from the damp ashes.

"That isn't why I invited you."

"I know. This little adventure was about hiking fifty miles and listening to Finn describe killing fish."

My lips curve up involuntarily. This is my favorite version of Cassia—this sarcastic, unreserved one who says exactly what she's thinking.

"It was about spending time together. Figuring out what wasn't working, so I could fix it."

"I just needed to know you were willing to work at it, that you were willing to meet me half-way. That you'd chase me a little."

"I'll chase you anywhere."

"You'd better."

Her hand moves farther south, and I grab it before I lose complete control. "Cassia."

She sucks in her bottom lip, holding my gaze as she stares at me. "You don't want to?"

"I've been hard since you sat in my lap two hours ago. I fucked my hand all summer, pretending it was you. *Of course* I want to. What I don't want is for you to regret this. Sex has never been an issue between us. Last night, you basically said it was all our relationship had turned into."

I'm immensely relieved when I see her smile.

She steps into my chest, the warmth of her bare skin against mine a heady sensation that pulls a groan out of my mouth.

"I appreciate that. I really do. And I think the space this summer was good for me, as much as it sucked at the time. I could think through how I was feeling without you as a distraction. It's not up to you to *fix* us. I should have told you how I was feeling sooner instead of dumping it all on you at the start of the summer. I'm trying to be better about telling you how I feel, when I'm feeling it, instead of shoving it down and waiting for it to go away. So this is me telling you…this is what I want. I want to have sex. *Please*."

I scan her face, looking for any trace of hesitation and finding none.

My thin willpower wears down to nothing.

The smile spreads across my face easily.

Lust and relief mix in a heady combination. The last of the invisible weight I've carried around for the past couple of months lifts, dread dissipating like it never existed.

I step closer to her, closing the gap between us.

"Since you asked so nicely, flower."

CHAPTER NINE

CASSIA

Familiar nerves fizzle in my stomach as Holden hovers over me, a slow smirk spreading across his handsome face. He leans over and turns the knob on the electric lantern between our sleeping bags. More yellow light spills across the nylon fabric, chasing away some of the shadows.

"I want to see you," he murmurs, before his lips land on the center of my chest.

My heartrate accelerates to a rapid, uneven rhythm, the gentle pressure of his mouth against my skin spiraling through me in a cacophony of sensation. He's holding all his body weight above me, so I can smell him and sense him, but can't *feel* him anywhere except that one spot.

I gasp when his teeth graze the top of my breast, then tug the polyester triangle of my bikini top to the side. Cool night air is replaced by wet heat.

My back arches, silently—but not subtly—begging for more. Holden's chuckle is low and throaty as his tongue traces circles around my sensitive flesh. Desire pools low in my stomach as my center starts to throb.

Stiff nylon rubs against my back as I run a hand through my hair and then lift my arms over my head. Holden's exhale is ragged as he lowers some of his weight, his erection rubbing exactly where I need him. All he's wearing is his swim trunks, the thin fabric straining against his sizable erection. My knee hooks around his hip, trying to pull him even closer.

"*Fuck*," he growls.

My closest friend at Richmond, Nova, was stunned when I told her Holden is the only guy I've ever been with. Laughed and said she's bored after one time with a guy.

Maybe it's because my oldest and closest friend is his sister, but I've never discussed intimate details about me and Holden with anyone. But if I had shared, I would have told Nova I don't just *not get bored.*

That there's *always* this thrill of anticipation and a heady rush of excitement, even when it hasn't been this long since we were together. That the novelty never wears off.

And it's exhilarating, hearing the desperate note to his voice as I grind against him. Knowing that after *years* of sleeping together, he's still this affected by me.

Holden rises onto his knees, grabbing the waistband of my leggings and tugging them down. There's an urgency to his movements, but he also takes his time. His thumbs run lines down the inside of my thighs, pausing to circle around my knees before yanking fabric the rest of the way past my calves.

I'm left in bikini bottoms and a top that's displaying my breasts instead of covering them. But I'm barely aware of my nudity, more focused on the clench of his abs and the bulge in his swim trunks, the shadows hiding and the pockets of light a tease.

"You're so fucking beautiful."

I smile, biting my bottom lip. My knees spread naturally,

letting him look his fill. Appreciating the way his hungry gaze roams across my bare skin.

They're not just spoken words. I can feel them brushing over my body.

His hand lands on my leg again, moving upward instead of down. I moan when his fingers brush the elastic edge of my swimsuit. Trace lightly over the thin fabric until my breaths are pants. And then whimper, when one deft finger slips beneath the material.

"Please," I beg.

Holden's dangerous grin hits my system like a shot of adrenaline. The possessive way he's watching his finger disappear inside my body drives my desire higher, knowing he's getting off on this as much as I am.

"What do you want?"

He's teasing me because of what I said earlier.

He's also really asking.

"I already told you." My tone is petulant.

He nods and bites his bottom lip, then pulls his hand away.

I rise up on my elbows. "What are you doing?"

"Waiting for specific directions."

I roll my eyes. "Are you being serious right now?"

"Did you think about this over the summer?"

"Of course."

"Did you touch yourself, pretending it was me?"

"Yes."

"Tell me what I did, and I'll do it."

My body reacts to the request. Holden notices my thighs clench. His blue eyes darken, but he doesn't move any closer.

"Is this about what I said last night?"

"A little."

"Holden, I was drunk and I—"

"You were right. I showed up at your door looking for one thing. You've never been a warm hole for me to fuck. It means something to me, every time." He leans closer but still doesn't touch me. "Use me to get off. Whatever you want, tell me."

My breath catches, arousal thundering through my body. I've always been happy to let Holden take control in our physical relationship. He was the one who knew what he was doing. I was attracted to him taking control in bed.

But the thought of *using* Holden—telling him what to do—is unexpectedly arousing. Like experiencing casual sex but being with someone I love and trust.

I nod and stand, my head brushing the side of the tent. My hands fall to my bikini bottoms first, untying the strings on my right hip. Holden doesn't visibly react as the fabric sags, but I hear his breathing quicken in the charged silence. I untie the other side even more slowly, enjoying the way anticipation thickens the air and tightens my stomach.

"I can see how wet you are."

His low voice is an erotic murmur than echoes in my head.

The knot behind my neck is harder to loosen. I finally manage it, then tug at the one on my back until my top falls away too.

I look at Holden, deliberating. Then drop to my knees and crawl closer to him.

My name is a tortured swear falling out of his mouth.

I grin, confidence coursing through me. I needed this, as much as I crave his verbal assurances.

"You're overdressed."

He smirks as I repeat his words from earlier. But it quickly disappears when I yank the elastic waistband of his swim trunks. His cock jerks free from the confines. I grip the hot skin, my thumb tracing the raised vein.

Holden hisses, his abs clenching.

I lean down, swirling my tongue around the flared tip and tasting the salty tang of his pre-cum. His hand slides into my hair, tugging gently. I suck him as deep as I can, my hand moving in tandem with my mouth.

"I'm going to come, Cas."

I pull away, smirking at the disappointment he quickly tries to hide. Then shift until I'm sitting on his lap. We both groan at the friction, the slickness of my arousal coating his cock as I rub against his erection. His hands hold my hips.

Holden doesn't guide my movements the way he normally might. He lets me move at my own pace, the tendons of his neck raised and his jaw a tense line.

I'm *so* close. My body is vibrating with need, heat pooling in my lower stomach as I clench around nothing. Pleasure glows brighter and closer. My heart races and my breathing is desperate huffs.

"Remember the first time you rode me like this? Couldn't see your boobs or feel your pussy, and it was still the hottest thing I'd ever experienced. Do you feel how hard I am for you? How much I'm dying to fill—"

That's it.

I'm done.

Teasing him is torturing me.

I lift my hips and fist him, then sink down. My teeth bite into the inside of my cheek, the burst of pain necessary to keep from coming immediately.

The delicious stretch is everything I've been missing, an ache only he could soothe.

"So fucking good," Holden growls.

"Your turn," I tell him. "I want it hard and fast."

"Yeah, I can do that."

He pulls out and repositions us so I'm splayed on my back,

then thrusts into me so deeply I swear I can feel him in the back of my throat. Skin slaps as he sets a frantic pace, just as worked up as I am.

My hands explore the topography of his back, powerful lines of muscles shifting and tensing as he moves above me. I lift my hips, opening up and taking him as deeply as I can. My nails dig into his back as I writhe beneath him.

I'll probably be sore *everywhere* tomorrow, and it will be completely worth it. He's fucking me like I'm his, possessing my body the same way he owns my heart.

The pressure that's been building forever finally explodes, my entire body awash in tingling pleasure.

I'm so lost in the haze I barely register the thickening of his cock as he finds his own release. Warmth seeps inside of me as he continues rocking into me, prolonging the tremors as euphoria slowly fades.

He kisses me.

It's not the skilled exploration from earlier. That was a special reconnection. A tentative re-creation of what we've done a million times before.

This is a possession. Our mouths imitating the motion of our hips.

Filthy and messy and desperate.

I love it.

When he pulls away, I'm a sweaty, satisfied heap.

"Cassia?"

I muster enough energy to roll my head toward him. "Yeah?"

"I love you."

He holds my gaze, letting those three words sink in. Sweet sentiment mixes with the remnants of lust and desire.

Holden leans over and grabs a sock out of his duffel bag, promising "It's clean" before he carefully wipes between my legs.

He tosses the white fabric and turns the light off before he lies back down, pulling me onto his chest.

I turn my face so it's pressed against his neck, my heartbeat steadily slowing.

"I love you, Holden Adams," I whisper.

CHAPTER TEN

CASSIA

Eileen smiles broadly as soon as I step inside the door. I pause, the bell chiming cheerfully as the door swings closed.

"Good morning?" It comes out a question, because Eileen is not a morning person and I've never seen her smile before nine a.m.

"Morning. How was your weekend?"

The smile spreads automatically.

We went to Finn's fishing spot yesterday morning, so the rest of the guys could fish again and Holden could go once. I sat with the group of girls I've never felt like I belonged with, forcing those thoughts from my head. It helped that they were all friendly, with the exception of Grace, who barely said a word to me. She obviously noticed the lack of distance between me and Holden.

We got back to Pembrooke late afternoon, then Holden came over for dinner.

Eileen is still waiting for an answer. She takes Mondays off while I'm working, so I didn't see her yesterday.

"It was really good," I say.

She nods like she already knew my answer. "You picked a good one," she tells me.

"A good…shelter to work at?"

Eileen snorts a laugh as she flips through the pile of papers on the desk. "That too. There's someone for you in the back."

I glance around the lobby.

Everything looks normal. Outdated magazines on the coffee table. Five folding chairs set up against the far wall for anyone waiting. Photo wall of pets who got happy endings.

Nothing out of the ordinary.

"Oh-kay." I wait, but Eileen says nothing else.

So I head down the hallway to the kennels, twisting my hair back into a bun as I walk. I'm running a little later than usual, still operating on a sleep deficit from this past weekend.

Holden is standing in the center of the room with a small group of guys clustered around him. I don't recognize any of them and they all look younger.

"Um, hi," I say, glancing around the room to try to figure out what's going on. I texted with him last night and he made no mention of coming to the shelter today.

Holden smiles. "Hey." He looks at the group of guys. "Head out back and wait for me. I'll be right there."

With a few grins and a couple of smirks, they all head out the side door that leads to the back lot—mostly an enclosed yard we exercise the dogs in, plus a small parking lot meant for volunteers and employees.

"What are you doing here?" I ask.

"You told me to show up more, not less, remember?"

I nod. "I remember."

"And that the shelter needs money."

I glance toward the door that leads to the front lobby to make sure there's no sign of Eileen.

I don't want her overhearing us. She's made multiple comments this summer about how she wishes that she could pay me more or hire extra help so I wasn't working six days a week. I don't want to pile on to that guilt.

"Yeah…"

"Well, I have some sway over the basketball team. And Coach Benson was always trying to set up community events when I played. I went to talk to him yesterday, figuring he'd be all over it, and I was right. They're planning a car wash here in a couple of weeks. I wanted to introduce the guys to Eileen and take a look around the place for set-up. We can plan to come back to Pembrooke for it, if you want. Or…not."

He stares at me, and I realize I haven't reacted at all.

I'm…stunned.

I feel silly.

All summer, I tied myself up into knots. Planning what I'd do at Richmond when I saw Holden on campus. Dreading seeing a photo of him with another girl.

My tendency is always to prepare for the worst, and I'm not totally sure why. My life has never weathered any calamity significant enough to justify that pessimistic mindset.

I think it's just my personality. I like to be prepared.

So, it's an adjustment to realize how far I blew everything out of proportion. That not only will I not have to avoid Holden on campus or stomach seeing him with someone else, he's showing me that he listened to what I said *and* he's actually doing something about it.

A crease of confusion—maybe concern—appears between Holden's eyes as I continue staring at him, motionless and silent.

"You didn't have to do that," I finally manage.

"I wanted to."

"Cassia, did you have a chance to—" Eileen stops talking

when she spots me and Holden. "Oh. I'm sorry. I saw the group out front and I didn't realize you were still back here, Holden."

"Of course they can't follow simple instructions," Holden mutters. "I'll text you, Cas."

He takes a step in my direction, then glances at Eileen and heads toward the hallway instead.

I sort of want to punch myself in the face. Talk about not appreciating a gesture.

"Holden!"

He turns as I half-jog toward him.

"Thank you," I tell him. "This means a lot."

He smiles, a full, beautiful one that sets off a flock of butterflies in my stomach.

"You're welcome, flower."

I glance at Eileen. She's migrated to the far corner of the room, sorting through the pile of leashes that get tangled no matter how many hooks we hang up. Purposefully giving us some privacy.

I rise up on my tiptoes to kiss him. It's soft and sweet, reminding me of our first one back in middle school. Right now, he's the boy who begged his dad to adopt a puppy because he knew my parents wouldn't let me have a pet of my own. Who named her after a flower.

The guy I thought I wanted. When he changed in high school —hardened, darkened—I thought we would never share a sweet moment again.

But I wouldn't change a thing about him.

Holden smiles as he tucks a piece of hair behind my ear; another perfect one. He kisses my temple, then steps away. "I'll see you later."

I nod and smile, watching until he disappears into the lobby.

Distantly, I hear him call, "Does this look like the back of the building to you guys?"

I laugh under my breath, then turn back to the first cage that needs to be cleaned.

"You picked a good one," Eileen repeats, passing by with a handful of leashes. She's smiling, which is a relief to see. Lately, she's seemed extra weighted.

This shelter is a lot to manage, and she doesn't have any help aside from me and occasionally Jackie.

I know Holden arranged this for me, but it will have a big impact elsewhere too.

"Yeah. I did," I agree.

———

I survey the huge pile of clothes on my bed, wondering how I managed to fit all this into two suitcases last year. My room looks like a tornado blew through recently.

"Cassia!" My mom's voice calls from downstairs.

I got home from work a half hour ago. Showered and put on a clean version of what I wore all day—athletic shorts and a t-shirt —then started on what I should have done a while ago: packing.

I've put it off longer than I should have, apprehensive about returning to campus because of where things stood with Holden. Just not in the mood to deal with any of it.

Sunday was supposed to be my packing day, but Holden was here for dinner, and I was too tired from the camping trip to do much of anything after he left. Yesterday was spent at the animal shelter, just like today. Last night I made the piles I'm currently staring at. Now I'm rapidly running out of time to actually pack.

I leave for Richmond on Thursday.

"Be right there," I shout back.

I grab an empty water glass off my dresser and then head down the hallway, dodging the piles of Legos scattered across the runner.

I pause at the top of the stairs, stunned.

"Sydney?"

My best friend turns from her conversation with my mom in the entryway, a wide smile breaking across her face.

But even from here I can see the strain. The tightness around her eyes and the tenseness in her posture. I know her well enough to tell that something is wrong.

I rush down the rest of the staircase, worry temporarily overshadowed by excitement as we hug tightly. "You're here!"

"Yep!" Sydney's tone is as excited as mine, but there's the same flicker of *something* else in her expression.

I haven't seen her in person since I visited her in July. But we talked last Thursday, and she didn't sound off then.

"You visiting this weekend reminded me how much I miss this place. So I decided to come back for a few days."

Shit, I think

There's a teasing twinkle in Sydney's eyes now. I totally forgot that I used her as my excuse.

"Here, I'll take that." My mom reaches for the empty glass I'm holding, oblivious.

She's got six kids to worry about, five of which give her a lot more trouble than I do. I feel a little guilty for taking advantage of that blind trust.

"Sydney, can I get you anything to eat or drink?"

"I'm all set, thanks," she says.

My mom nods. "Dinner will be ready soon. You're welcome to stay, Sydney," she says, then heads for the kitchen.

"I can't believe you're here," I tell her.

Sydney smiles, but the edge is back.

"Come on, let's head up to my room."

"Holden isn't here, is he?" she asks.

"Uh, no. He's playing at the court with the guys."

I wait, but Sydney says nothing else as we head upstairs.

My unease grows, realizing she doesn't want Holden to know whatever is wrong. That's always been the biggest challenge of dating my best friend's brother. Lines get blurry.

Maggie walks out of her room right as we pass by.

"Hey, Maggie," Sydney greets.

"Hi," Maggie replies. "Tell Mom I'll be back later," she says.

"Tell her yourself," I respond, then push my bedroom door open.

"Should I also let her know you lied about where you were this weekend? Sydney might be willing to cover for you, but I'm not."

I glance at her. "How do you know about that?"

Maggie rolls her eyes. "Like I wouldn't hear you went off on a sleepover with your boyfriend. Cora has a crush on a bunch of those guys. She follows them all on social media. It didn't look that fun. So, tell Mom for me."

Sydney laughs under her breath as Maggie continues down the hall. "I guess she didn't leave the dramatics in high school."

"Nope," I say. She's had more fits than Sally this summer.

"Wow." Sydney surveys the mess that's my room.

"I know. Packing got put off for too long. I have no clue how it'll all fit in my car."

"When are you leaving?"

"Thursday. Classes start Monday, and the apartments opened to everyone yesterday."

"Oh. I thought you had another week." Her tone is distant as she glances around the disaster that's my room, focusing on nothing.

I take a seat at the edge of my bed. "What's going on, Syd?"

She exhales. "I have no clue how to say this. And I hate that I'm burdening you with it, because you—"

"Sydney," I interrupt. "Just tell me."

"I think I'm pregnant."

I blink at her, those four words registering yet also sounding totally foreign.

"*Say* something." Sydney pushes a stack of shirts aside and sits down beside me, her fingers twisting anxiously in her lap.

"I… You had *sex*?" As far as I knew, she was still a virgin.

Sydney exhales. "Unfortunately, yes."

"*Unfortunately?* What the hell happened?"

She makes a face. "Well, the sex itself sucked. And now I might be pregnant. So overall a pretty crappy experience. Zero out of ten, I'd say."

I want to pelt her with more questions about the *losing her virginity* bomb, but it's overshadowed by the second revelation. "Might be? Did you take a test?"

"No. I realized I was late on Friday, freaked out all weekend, then booked a train ticket back home yesterday. Catherine picked me up from the train station. I had her drop me off here."

"Did you tell her?"

"No, of course not. She's nice, but it's not like she's my mom. She's not still in Pembrooke for me or Holden."

"You need to take a test, Syd."

She looks away. "I know. I just need to panic some more first."

"You might be panicking for no reason."

"Well, I'd rather panic about a maybe than be terrified over a yes." Sydney lies back against my comforter on top of my winter jacket.

"Okay." I push some jeans aside and lie down beside her.

"You can't tell Holden."

I exhale. "Sydney…"

"I mean it. I don't want him to know. Hopefully never, but definitely not yet."

"Okay. I won't say anything." I pause. "Can I ask… Who got such a dismal review in bed? A hunky actor in the program with you?"

Sydney doesn't crack a smile at my attempt at humor.

"You haven't mentioned a guy this summer…"

There's a *long* pause before she finally answers. "It was Harrison."

"Harrison," I repeat. "As in Harrison…*Baker*?"

"Yes." Sydney won't look at me. She's intently focused on the ceiling.

It's the third bomb she's dropped on me in a span of five minutes. I'm not sure which is the most shocking of the three—that she lost her virginity, that she might be pregnant, or that she had sex with Harrison.

"Holy shit."

"You can't tell Holden," she reiterates.

That's much easier to agree to. I'm not sure exactly how he'd react, but I know it wouldn't go over well.

"I thought Harrison was dating someone at school."

"They broke up at the beginning of the summer." She glances at me. "You know, right around when he came back here for the summer."

I roll my eyes. "You think that had something to do with me?"

"He's always had a thing for you. That's how this whole thing started. He was in New York for a night so he could get a direct flight to LA, and he replied to the photo I posted of us from your visit that past weekend."

I blow out a long breath. "How did that end with you sleeping with him?"

"We met up at a bar. Things…happened from there."

"Wow."

"I'm sorry I didn't tell you when it happened."

I glance over at Sydney. "Why didn't you?"

She grabs the rabbit that's sat on my bed since I was little and starts playing with its floppy ears.

"I was…embarrassed, I guess. It was bad. *So* bad. Awkward and uncomfortable. I had no idea what I was doing, but I was trying to act like I knew exactly what I was doing, and I think that freaked him out. Just thinking about it makes me want to crawl under the covers and never come out."

She presses Chester to her face dramatically, and despite the seriousness of the situation, I want to laugh.

"You're definitely not the only person to have that experience, Syd. Lots of people have terrible first times."

"*You* didn't, right?" The question comes out muffled beneath the rabbit.

"Uh…"

Sydney tosses Chester away and grimaces. "No details, please. Just, you know…generally."

"I was super nervous and parts of it were weird. But I was comfortable around him, and that helped a lot. I felt safe. I don't know, it was kind of like jumping, but knowing there was a safety net."

"All that *and* you managed not to get knocked up." Sydney's smile is bittersweet. "Lucky you."

"You don't know you're knocked up. Which is why you should take a test."

"But what if I *am*?" Her voice holds all the naked terror I'd be experiencing in the same situation.

"Harrison is a good guy, Syd. It isn't just your problem. You have support. And options."

Sydney sighs. "I haven't talked to him since that night. I wouldn't even know how to… We used protection," she tells the ceiling. "And he put it on, so I didn't mess that part up. He can't blame me."

"Nothing is a hundred percent reliable."

"Except for abstinence." She snorts. "Wish I'd stuck with that."

"You don't know anything for certain."

"Enough about me. What did *we* do last weekend?"

"Thank you for covering for me."

She smiles. "What are best friends for? Although I think Holden is a bad influence. You were with him, right?"

"Yeah. Maggie was right. We went camping."

Sydney's nose wrinkles. "How was that?"

"Better than I was expecting." I know she's asking about the whole sleeping and eating in the woods part, but it applies to the entire trip.

"Dinner!" my mom calls.

"Come on." I pat Sydney's leg. "Let's eat and then I'll drive you to the condo. We can watch a movie or something to take your mind off everything."

She groans but follows me into the hallway.

And the whole walk downstairs, all I can think about is how completely shocking it is my best friend might be a mom.

CHAPTER ELEVEN

HOLDEN

The ball sinks through the hoop with a satisfying swish. Finn swears—loudly.

I grin, retrieving the ball and then spinning it around on one finger. "What's the score again?"

Mark groans. "I need a water break."

We all watch as he hobbles toward the grass that surrounds the cracked pavement. Jordan drew a foul earlier.

Most of my time spent in Pembrooke, it feels like nothing has changed. Especially here on this court, it's easy to pretend that we're just kids playing a game.

I dribble a few times, then palm the ball. We've been out here for about twenty minutes. When I texted Cassia earlier, she said she had to pack tonight, but maybe she'd be up for an ice cream break. We could go to the place with the waffles that she likes so much.

"Fuck."

We all glance at Mark. He's sitting in the grass, a strange, panicked expression on his face as he looks down at his leg.

"Did you cut yourself?" Finn asks, then looks away. He's

squeamish. I got a bloody nose during a game our sophomore year and I was worried he was going to pass out.

"I got stung by a bee."

"Don't be so dramatic, Kelly," Finn says. "Just stand up and—"

"I'm allergic."

"*How* allergic?" Jordan asks.

"I dunno. I had a reaction when I was a little kid, so I've carried an EpiPen around ever since."

Finn glances at me worriedly.

"Do you have it with you?" I ask.

"It's in my gym bag."

I jog over to the bleachers, grabbing Mark's bag and my own. I drop Mark's down beside him, then fish my keys out of my pocket.

"I'll drive you to the hospital."

"Great. I'll be in the truck." Finn heads toward the bleachers as Mark pulls out a cylindrical object from his bag.

Once Mark has injected himself, I help him up. He looks fine, his face flushed from exertion. Nothing looks swollen or concerning. But my steps are quick as we head for my truck. Jordan and Finn are already in the back. Mark gets in on the passenger side and I climb into the driver's seat.

The nearest hospital is a town over. The drive takes about twenty minutes, the three of us casting worried looks at Mark until he threatens us to stop.

He still looks normal when I park in the hospital's huge lot.

"You guys don't have to stay," he says. "This will probably take a while."

"We're not going to just abandon you here," I say. "And hurry up. If you're about to collapse, I'd rather you do it inside than in the parking lot."

"Dick." But Mark's smiling as he says it.

We walk inside the automatic doors without incident. I was joking in the parking lot, but it's still a relief to be inside the building. If Mark went into anaphylactic shock, I would have no clue what to do.

Jordan, Finn, and I take seats in the waiting area while Mark goes up to the window to check in.

I pull out my phone and text Cassia.

HOLDEN: *How's packing going?*

"This *will* probably take a while," Finn mutters beside me.

"We both know you have nothing better to do."

Finn rolls his eyes and slouches back in the hard chair. My butt is already going numb. You'd think they'd invest in some more comfortable ones, considering how long most people have to sit here for.

"I'm gonna run to the restroom," I say, standing and stretching. "Be right back."

"We'll be here," Finn says.

I nod, then head to the right, down a hallway. It's empty aside from one unoccupied gurney pushed against the wall. The other side is all glass windows overlooking a courtyard splashed with orange by the sinking sun.

I reach the end of the hallway, turn left, and freeze.

"Lana?"

She turns slowly, blue eyes the same shade as mine, widening with shock.

My mother has never looked happy to see me.

A sobering truth.

My first thought.

She left when I was five. My memories of her are hazy and abstract, not happy. When she showed up, about a week after my dad died, it was to tell me she moved a whole two towns over, and she'd heard about the accident. Then she came to the high school with some half-assed explanation for why abandoning her two kids was in our best interest. I haven't seen or heard from her since, and I didn't expect to.

And now she's standing three feet away, looking like the ghost she is in my memory. Looking *unhappy* to see me.

"Hello, Holden."

I study her more closely. "Are you…okay?"

It's a stupid question to ask.

Her skin is sallow and pale, and she's lost weight she couldn't afford to in the first place. When I saw her four years ago, she was skinny. Now, she looks skeletal.

"I'm fine." A forced smile stretches the skin across her pale face.

"Then why are you here?" I challenge her because it's the only way I know how to interact with my mother. My instinct is to doubt and distrust her.

I'm not even sure the brief, rare encounters we've had since she abandoned our family can be categorized as a relationship. But we're *related*. And I care, even knowing I shouldn't. Knowing it'll only hurt more when she inevitably disappears and disappoints again.

She looks away, avoiding my gaze. Unease suffuses through me, spreading like wildfire.

A middle-aged man approaches, the strides of his heavy work boots echoing down the linoleum hallway. I expect him to pass us. Instead, he pauses. Ignores me and focuses on my mom as he tucks a folded white paper into his pocket. "We're all set, Lana."

My mom nods. "Thanks. Let's go."

"Who the fuck are you?" The question is out before I can think it through. Just one of my many impulsive decisions.

He focuses on me for the first time, raising one unimpressed brow as he scrubs a palm against his thick beard. "Who the fuck are *you*?"

I look at my mom. The common denominator.

When she told me she was living in Ridgemont, I didn't ask for any details. Where she was working. If she lived alone.

Is she married to this guy? Do they have kids? Do I have half-siblings?

Questions burning in my mouth like I swallowed acid. Questions I'm not sure I can stomach the answers to.

"Why are you here?" she asks me.

Sounding *angry* about it. Like being in the same building as her son is a fucking inconvenience.

My jaw works angrily. "I'm here with a friend."

"Go look after your friend, Holden."

She continues walking, and that's *it*. That's the end of the third conversation with my mom that I remember.

I'm expecting her "friend" to follow. But he doesn't. He remains standing a few feet away, sizing me up.

He kinda looks like my dad, which pisses me off. Broad shoulders. Trimmed beard. Brown hair.

"What?" I snap.

He shakes his head. "You coulda been nicer to your momma."

"So you do know who I am."

"Yeah." He scratches his beard again. "She told me she had a kid."

"*Kids*. She tell you she walked out on us too?"

"She explained the situation."

I snort. "Explained the situation—there's nothing to *explain*. She left."

"Life's a bitch, kid. Learn that lesson."

My fingers curl into fists as I resist the urge to punch his superior expression. Glance over one shoulder to confirm my mom is gone.

She's always been good at walking away.

The one way in which she's predictable.

"She's sick?" The question comes out as more of a statement, since I'm sure I already know the answer.

He hesitates for a minute, then nods. "Liver cancer. They caught it late. She needs a transplant soon. Odds of that happening aren't good. The focus now is pain management instead of treatment."

All I can think is *Fuck*.

In nearly every way, I lost my mom a long time ago.

But in one important way, I never did.

For the past few years especially, since she ambushed me, I've known where she lived, not just that she was alive.

She was never gone in that final, permanent sense.

The way my dad is.

I'm barely aware of the man walking past me and continuing down the hallway. The man who I'm ninety percent certain I don't like and whose name I don't even know. The man who's bringing my mom to the hospital because she has a disease that will most likely kill her.

I back up until my spine connects with plaster, sucking in a deep breath of antiseptic-scented air. Shaken in a way I can't fully comprehend. I just got sideswiped by a situation I never saw coming.

I can read between the lines just fine.

My mom is dying.

She walked away from me and Sydney without looking back. Aside from seeking me out after my dad died, she's never made any attempt to cross the distance she created.

Never apologized.

Never suggested she regrets her decision.

Families fracture in all sorts of ways.

She didn't have to ensure the break was permanent. She chose to leave. To remain gone, as we grew up and after our dad died.

Three nurses pass me before I move. Two shoot me concerned looks. One sends me a flirty smile.

I find the restroom and return to the waiting room in a daze.

Finn glances at me as I sink back down into the chair next to him. "You okay?" he asks.

"Yeah. I'm good."

My tendency is never to talk. I bury things down until there's no space left. Even then, I don't talk. I punch or I yell or I drink until the ugliness is expelled.

I lean my head back against the wall and stare at the mint green one across from me, resenting whatever coincidence landed me in the same place at the same time as my mother. Mark's allergy. Her illness. My need to pee.

My mom is dying.

And I wish I didn't know.

———

Music is blaring from the condo when I reach the entrance, audible even through the closed door. I exhale before fishing my keys out of my pocket. Catherine must be home.

I haven't seen her since I got back from camp.

I'm grateful to her for stepping up after our dad died. For taking in Sydney and Lily. I wouldn't have gone to college otherwise.

But it's an awkward dynamic. She's a full decade younger than he was, meaning she's closer to my age. Not much of an authority figure. The only reasons she stuck around after Sydney graduated high school had nothing to do with us.

And I'm in a crappy mood already. Predictably, it took a while at the hospital for Mark to get the all-clear. Then I had to drive everyone back to the court to get their cars.

I unlock the door and step inside the condo. The front hallway leads right into the kitchen. All the lights are on, but the room is empty. I follow the music to the right and toward the living room, pausing in the doorway.

There's no sign of Catherine.

My little sister and my girlfriend are the ones dancing and jumping around and singing at the top of their lungs.

Sydney looks the same as she did when I saw her in May. She came back to Pembrooke for a week before returning to New York for a summer theater program at her school. She's smiling widely, her long hair pulled up in a ponytail that bounces around as she tosses her head around.

Cassia's eyes are closed, her arms raised over her head as she sways in place.

The song blaring sounds familiar, but I don't know any of the words. They're hard to hear. Cassia and Sydney are singing loudly enough to drown out the original artist's voice.

Cassia spins around to face Sydney. Then they're moving again. This portion must be choreographed because they're in perfect sync as they shimmy and twirl their way across the fluffy rug that covers the floor.

The song ends.

"Killed it!" Sydney exclaims. "Once more with…" She spots me and her voice trails.

Cassia glances over, stilling when she sees me.

"We didn't hear you come in," Sydney says.

"Shocking," I drawl. "It's so quiet in here."

Sydney rolls her eyes. "I'm going to grab some water."

"Nice to see you too, sis," I call after her as she heads toward the kitchen.

Cassia attempts to fix her hair as she walks toward me. Half of it is falling down again by the time she reaches me.

"How was the court?" she asks.

"Eventful. Mark sat on a bee, and it stung him."

"Poor bee."

I roll my eyes. "Poor Mark. He's allergic."

Her eyes widen. "Is he okay?"

"Yeah. He had an EpiPen. We took him to the hospital, just in case. He's fine."

I haven't decided what to do about my mom. If I'll do anything. If I'll say anything.

I really don't want the responsibility of telling Sydney. And I don't want to burden Cassia with the secret.

But she knows me too well. Her head tilts, studying me closely. "Are you okay?"

I let my gym bag slip off my shoulder and step forward so I'm just inches away from her. Rest my hands on her waist and then slip them under the hem of the oversize t-shirt she's wearing to pull her against me.

"Better now," I say into her hair.

I mean the words.

Talking to her, touching her, it soothes the ache that's always there when I think about my parents and got amplified today.

Cassia Nolan is the only person who's ever *chosen* to love me.

And if I have my mom to thank for anything, I guess it's the lesson that love is never guaranteed. That just because someone is supposed to care doesn't mean they will.

Her nose wrinkles as she tilts her head back. "How do you still smell like cinnamon even when you're sweaty?"

I grin as I play with the end of her ponytail. "I'm not that sweaty. We'd only been playing for about twenty minutes when the bee attacked Mark."

"Were you winning?"

"Of course."

"I was wondering why you were texting mid-game," she says.

I raise one eyebrow. "You didn't answer."

"I know. I'm sorry. Sydney came over, and I got distracted."

My hands move an inch higher, fingers brushing across the sides of her rib cage.

"Holden…" Any chastisement in her voice is drowned out by the lust.

"What? Your shirt is soft."

"It's your shirt," she whispers. "I stole it out of your gym bag…that night."

I know which night she's referring to. It's an ugly, unpleasant memory, but her words erase a little bit of the sting.

"Why?"

Her fingers twist the fabric of my shirt, her gaze focused on my chest instead of meeting my eyes. "You weren't supposed to agree." She mutters the words, so softly I can hardly hear them.

My brow furrows. "You told me—"

"I know what I said. I was trying to—I don't know. I wanted you to fight. And when you didn't…I got scared. So I stole your shirt." She makes a face. "It felt stupid when I did and it sounds even stupider now that I'm admitting it."

My grip on her tightens. "It's not stupid. I-I didn't know you wanted me to fight, flower. I was fucking terrified of losing you. I *am* fucking terrified of losing you. So I was trying to do exactly what you asked. Trying to do whatever it took to keep that from happening."

"I know," she says softly. "I know I sent some mixed signals."

"You can take as many of my clothes as you want, Cas."

She smiles, her eyes fluttering closed when my hands creep even higher up her back. "Don't tempt me. Not only are your shirts super comfortable, but I kinda like the way you look without them."

"Oh, yeah?"

"Mm-hmm." I feel her lips curve upward against mine.

Our kiss starts off slow and soft. Sweet. Then turns into heat and intensity.

A throat clears behind us. I pull away reluctantly, dropping my hands, then glancing over one shoulder.

Sydney smirks at us between sips of water. For the most part, my sister has been supremely cool about me dating her best friend, so I try not to make it more awkward for her.

"You guys done?"

I steal one last kiss, squeezing Cassia's hip before I step away. "For now. Text me back, Cas."

I grin at her, then head down the hallway, only pausing to grab my bag before continuing toward my bedroom. Or the place where I rarely sleep, rather. I haven't spent more than one night straight here since January. Gone at school or camp or staying at Finn's. It feels like living in a hotel.

I toss my bag on the bed, unzipping it and starting to sort through the empty water bottles and extra socks I need to clear out. Cassia isn't the only one who's put off packing. Most of my belongings are dirty or jumbled or both.

There's a soft knock on the doorframe. I glance up to see Sydney standing there.

"Hey. Just wanted to say Welcome Home."

I smile. "Yeah, you too. Theater program was good?"

Sydney glances away, so quick I barely catch it. But then she's nodding and smiling. "Yeah. It was great."

"You sticking around for long?"

"I have a week before classes start. Not sure yet. You're leaving Thursday, like Cassia?"

I nod. "Unless you want me to stay…"

"I'm twenty, Holden. I don't need a babysitter."

"Fine. It was just an offer." I toss a sweatshirt into my open suitcase, a half-hearted attempt at packing. I'll take everything in here with me, so it's just a matter of getting it all from Point A to Point B. Pembrooke to Richmond College.

"I just meant, there's no reason for you to stay. But thanks."

I nod.

"Uh, Cassia and I are going out for ice cream. Do you want me to bring you back anything? Or you could come…"

I hear the reluctance in the second offer, even as she makes it. Our group dynamic shifted at the start of high school. Changed again during Cassia and I's senior year.

I know Sydney is happy for me. For Cassia. She pushed me to fight for her during one of my many fuck-ups. But I also recognize that me dating her best friend must suck sometimes. If she and Finn got together, it would be very weird for me.

So I shake my head. "Nah, I'm good. Thanks. You guys have fun."

Sydney nods, relief flashing across her face. "Okay. See you later."

"See you."

A few minutes later, I hear the front door shut.

Leaving me with a lot of laundry and troubled thoughts.

CHAPTER TWELVE

CASSIA

After dropping Sydney off at her condo, I stop at the pharmacy. I'm not sure if she'll be grateful. She didn't mention the possible pregnancy once during our trip to get ice cream. And maybe this is a step she should take herself whenever she's ready. But I also know *not* knowing must be driving a part of her crazy. It's driving *me* crazy.

Guilt swirls in my stomach as my steps shuffle along the gray carpet past packages of pads. Not only am I going against what Sydney wants right now, but I'm keeping this huge secret from Holden. He'd want to know Sydney is struggling. The sooner Sydney knows for sure, the sooner I'll know how big of a secret it is.

When I make it to the end of the aisle, there are way more options for pregnancy tests than I was expecting. If our situations were reversed, Holden is who I would tell first. But Sydney is the person I would bring along on this trip. Maybe we'd be giggling nervously about how many different options there are. Wondering *why* there are countless choices. Aren't they all the same?

Or maybe that's just wishful thinking. Maybe I'd be paralyzed by the possibilities the same way Sydney is.

Denial isn't always a terrible place to be.

After staring at the boxes for a few seconds longer, I randomly grab one off the shelf.

My palms dampen with sweat as I rush down the aisle.

Pembrooke is a small town.

The realization I'm rushing piles on another hefty dose of guilt. Because I know I'm not the one who's potentially pregnant, but I feel ashamed by the box I'm carrying anyway.

Irresponsible and insecure.

"Cassia?"

I glance to the left, hastily angling the box I'm holding behind my back.

Mrs. Golden, my American History teacher in high school, is standing at the end of the aisle beside the display of laundry detergent on sale.

"Hi, Mrs. Golden. How are you?"

My manners kick in automatically despite the nerves pinballing around my stomach.

"I'm doing fine, Cassia. How have you been?"

Maybe it's my guilty conscience, but I swear she glances at my hidden hand.

"Good. I've had a nice summer."

"You'll be a senior at Richmond, right?"

I nod, surprised and touched she knows that. She's had a lot of other students besides me. "Right."

"That's where Holden Adams ended up as well, correct?"

It's never really occurred to me before that teachers must hear some of the gossip that circulates through the student body. Partly because I spent most of high school doing nothing that was gossip-worthy.

"Yeah, he did."

"Do you see each other much?"

I nod. "We're still together."

Mrs. Golden smiles. "I had a good feeling about you two. Only thing he aced all semester was the paper you helped him with."

"Holden wrote that himself," I say, some ancient—or never-ending—urge to defend him sparking to life.

"Oh, I know." Mrs. Golden smiles. "It takes a special motivation to get a reliably C-student to turn in A material."

Her smile fades as she glances down the aisle behind me. This time, she definitely looks at my hand. Silent questions swim in the air between us.

"It's for a friend," I blurt. Then wince, because it's an unnecessary explanation. An answer to a question she didn't ask.

I don't owe her anything.

It sounds like a lie. Like an excuse.

And also…a betrayal of Sydney and the assurances I told her earlier.

I'm not perfect. I know I'm not. But I've never been able to shake the urge to strive for it. To be responsible and successful and reliable.

"None of my business." Mrs. Golden grabs an orange bottle of laundry detergent and adds it to her cart. "But if you ever need anything, please reach out. Okay? I know it's hard to believe, but I was your age once."

"Thanks, Mrs. Golden."

She smiles, and I can't tell if she believes me or not. "Nice to see you, Cassia."

"You too," I say as she continues walking.

Then I rush toward the front of the store, relieved to find the self-checkout is open. I quickly pay for the test and then shove it into my bag before leaving.

I was planning to pick up a few toiletries for school while I was here, but my mind is a muddled mess right now. The list of items I thought of earlier seem irrelevant. I haven't fully recovered from the shock of Sydney's revelations earlier.

When I get home, my dad's car is still missing from the driveway. No one is downstairs, so I head up to my room.

My mom's crouching down in the hallway, cleaning up the Lego mess. "Did you have fun with Sydney?" she asks, glancing up.

I nod. "Where is everyone?"

She rocks back on her heels. "Maggie is out with friends. Regan is at a sleepover. Charlie and Chris are at soccer practice. Sally is showering and then we're going to watch a princess movie before I have to pick the twins up. You're welcome to watch with us."

"Dad isn't home?"

"No."

"Is…everything okay?"

My mom exhales, then stands. She glances down the hall at the closed bathroom door. If I strain to hear, I can catch the rush of running water.

"I wanted to tell you this a while ago, Cassia. And…I also *never* wanted to tell you this."

Panic expands in my chest, heavy and suffocating as I stare at her. "What?"

"Honey, your dad and I are getting a divorce."

I stare at her, uncomprehending.

"What?" I repeat.

"It's just…not working any longer. Sometimes couples grow apart and there's no solution."

It sounds like a prepared line, and I realize that's exactly what it is.

She's been *preparing* for this. Planning. Deciding.

And I've been living at home all summer with no clue that it was coming. Oblivious and not looking past the busyness to realize what was crumbling. What my mom just described is a typical schedule for my siblings.

Chaos can mask misery, I guess. It worked to hide my own heartbreak.

I'm listening as she continues talking in a quiet tone so Sally doesn't overhear, tossing out phrases like *difficult decision* and *we both love you kids so much.*

Not a single word is registering or reassuring.

I'm watching an integral part of my world tumble down around me, powerless to do anything except watch it take place.

"Did Dad cheat?" I ask. "Is that what all the work trips this summer have been about?"

"No, he didn't cheat," she answers. "We separated in the spring. Your father's job *has* been especially hectic." My mom hesitates. "And…he's also looking into some other living arrangements."

"Living arrangements where?"

"Nearby. I believe he toured a unit in the building where Holden's aunt lives."

"Does anyone know that you're separated?"

"I told your grandmother. I'm guessing your father confided in some work colleagues as well."

I'm suspicious of the way she says *work colleagues.*

"You don't know there's someone else, or you know there's not?"

Her silence answers for her.

The lump in my throat won't disappear, no matter how many

times I swallow. That's worse than *we're having problems* or *things might not work out. Different residences* and *separated since spring* sounds very permanent. So does a silence that suggests my father might have already moved on.

"I don't know what to say," I admit.

"You don't have to say anything, sweetheart. I've been debating on what to say, when to tell you. I wanted to tell you in person, and you don't usually come back from campus before Thanksgiving..." She sighs. "There will probably be some changes by then."

Changes...like my family looking totally different from how it's been for the past twenty-one years.

"You mean Dad will have moved out?"

"Most likely."

My nod is slow. "I'm...I need to go."

"Go?" Alarm threads through her voice. "It's getting late. Where are you going, Cassia?"

I head for the stairs. "I just need some air."

"Honey, I'm sorry you're so upset."

"How am I supposed to feel?" I snap. "Happy?"

My mom is silent.

I exhale. "I'm sorry. This is why, I just need to... I need a minute."

"Okay. Make sure you take your phone."

I nod, reaching into the bag on my shoulder for my keys. I pull out the box blocking them without thinking, intent on getting out of here as quickly as possible.

My mistake doesn't occur to me until I hear my mom's sharp inhale. When I look over, her eyes are focused on the pink pregnancy test.

"Oh, Cassia..."

"It's not mine."

"Honey…"

"I promise. It's for a friend."

I don't feel the same guilt I experienced earlier. Me having a baby would affect my mom in a way it wouldn't Mrs. Golden. I don't want her stressing about the possibility, especially now that I know everything else she's dealing with.

But my denial has a different outcome. I watch the pieces click together in my mom's mind—Sydney's surprise visit earlier, our long talk locked away in my room—and come to the correct conclusion.

"Oh."

"She doesn't want anyone to know. Doesn't know for sure. Please don't say anything."

"I won't. But please make sure she knows I'm here if she needs anything. Going through a pregnancy at any age is difficult, but without her parents…"

I nod, fisting my keys and shoving the box back in my bag. "I'll tell her."

"I love you, Cassia."

I walk over and hug her, inhaling the familiar scent of her perfume. "I love you too, Mom."

Tears sting at my eyes as I step back.

My movements are hasty as I hurry downstairs. Wanting to get away before I break down. Before this house shrinks even smaller than it already feels.

Backing out of the driveway and driving down the street feels strange. I haven't left the house this late all summer. I've had to work early most mornings, so I was responsible and went to bed before midnight. Sydney and Holden were both gone, so my options for people to hang out with were limited.

The court is empty when I park. Unsurprising. It's late on a Tuesday night, and people have already started to leave town and return to campus. I'm not even sure if younger grades know this place exists, let alone hang out here. Holden and his friends kind of claimed it as their own.

I climb out of the car, inhaling deeply. The night air is thick and humid, sticking to my skin and hair. Clogging my lungs.

I'm craving the cool, refreshing air from the mountains. Wishing I could rewind to being in that tent with Holden, before I knew about my parents. Before I was carrying around Sydney's secret.

Both are weighing me down, situations I can't do anything about but am burdened by.

I pull my phone out of my pocket and send a quick text.

CASSIA: *I'm at the court.*

The metal bleachers are damp and cool when I set my phone and keys down on the lowest risers.

A weathered basketball is half-rolled beneath the bleachers. I retrieve it and dribble over to the free throw line. Take a shot. Miss. Continue shooting, my percentage abysmal, but the repetition calming some of the chaos in my head.

"Isn't it like an hour past your bedtime?"

I spin, my breathing fast and my hair falling in my eyes.

Holden is walking toward me, a smirk covering his gorgeous face. A little of the tightness eases watching him approach.

I tuck the basketball I'm holding under one arm, pushing my hair out of my face with my free hand. The elastic isn't doing much.

"Wanna play?" I ask.

Confidence turns to confusion as Holden searches my face. "What's going on, Cassia?"

I pass him the ball—hard. Anyone else would miss it. Holden snags it out of mid-air easily. "I don't want to talk about it."

His nod is slow as he continues to scan my face. This is out of character for me, and we both know it.

But he doesn't voice his concern.

Doesn't push me to talk.

And I love him for it.

"Okay." He dribbles to the mid-court line. "Make it, take it?"

I nod, stripping my t-shirt off and tossing the ball of fabric toward the bleachers. I've already worked up a sweat.

Holden's eyebrows shoot half-way up his forehead as I crouch a few feet away, my gaze falling to the ball he's holding.

I love school.

I'm a people pleaser. Making my parents and teachers proud has always driven me. So has the goal of getting into vet school.

But I miss playing basketball. Regret giving it up as easily as I did.

I hate and love how it's *Holden* to me.

At times, it's been an unpleasant reminder. It's also another love we share, aside from our feelings for each other.

He's better than me. Always has been and the gap in our respective skill levels has only widened over time. I quit in eighth grade. Holden is one of the top college players in the country.

He feints left, but I'm ready. I mirror his movements, knocking my shoulder against his chest as I reach for the ball.

I spin and dribble. "Don't let me win!"

"You're the one who took your shirt off to distract me."

I roll my eyes. "I'm wearing a sports bra. It's not like I'm naked."

"Fine."

My mouth goes dry as he yanks his shirt off one-handed, tossing it toward mine.

And I sorta see his point. His shorts sit low on his hips. His broad shoulders, ripped stomach, the carved V, the line of dark hair disappearing into the waistband? All *very* distracting.

"I'm still going to win," I inform him, exhibiting a confidence I don't feel.

Holden smirks. "I thought you didn't want me to let you win?"

"I didn't say anything about you *letting* me."

He shakes his head but is enough of a gentleman not to rattle off his stats. We both know I don't have a chance of winning against him. But I like that he's pretending I do. And competition is a necessary distraction from his body.

"Okay. Your ball."

Fingers trail across my bare stomach as he moves into position with his back to the basket.

"That's a foul," I inform him.

Holden's laugh is low and throaty. "You can't play and ref, Cas."

"Why not?"

"It's a conflict of interest."

"Don't you trust me?" I bat my eyelashes.

"With my life? Absolutely. To play ref without cheating?" He grins. "Nope."

"Rude."

"Take the shot, Nolan."

"Oh, shit. Guess you mean business, Adams."

Holden smiles and shakes his head.

I move left but spin right and shoot. If I dribble, I'm sure he'll steal the ball in about two seconds.

Miraculously, it goes in.

I throw my arms up to celebrate.

Holden goes after the ball, dribbling back over to me with a serious expression that I find as attractive as his impressive physique. He's even more competitive than I am. Losing to anyone—even me—always pisses him off.

"Still my ball," I remind him, just to rub it in a little.

"Not for long."

I grin, his confidence bolstering my own.

This time I gamble, dribbling right into him. It works for a couple of seconds. But as soon as I try to get past him, Holden's hand sneaks out, snagging the ball easily. He spins and shoots, the *swish* as his perfect arc falls beautiful and irritating.

"Fuck," I grumble, pulling the elastic out of my hair and scraping it together into another ponytail. As if that'll help.

Holden grins, spinning the ball on one finger.

I push him toward the center court line. "Stop gloating and start playing."

"*That* was a foul. You're not going to call yourself?"

"You told me I couldn't be ref," I remind him.

Holden rolls his eyes but dribbles back to the line.

He shoots from there this time, not even taking one step forward. I turn to watch it sink in, sighing when it does.

"What's the score, ref?"

I groan. "We're not calling fouls."

Holden would never hurt me. Physically. He's inflicted plenty of emotional scars, some on this very court.

And he's right, I'm not above blurring the lines a little bit.

He smirks, then goes to retrieve the ball.

I rush him as soon as he's back into position, deliberately colliding our bodies together.

Holden holds the ball above his head, out of my reach.

"Whatcha doing, flower?"

I want to kiss him.

His skin is hard and hot against mine. His smirk is teasing me. Daring me.

"Playing basketball."

"Not baseball? Because this feels like second base."

I make a desperate grab for the ball.

He chuckles as he spins around me, wrapping an arm around my waist to hold me away while he shoots one-handed.

It goes in. He hasn't missed a single shot yet.

And I'm running out of swear words.

Holden's hand is still wrapped around me, spread across my stomach and searing my skin.

I step back into him. Grind my ass against his crotch.

"This is cheating," he says. "Illegal interference."

His breathing is fast beside my ear and I take a lot of pleasure out of that. Either I challenged him to exerting himself some or he's affected by my proximity.

"Cassia." There's a warning in his voice as I continue to circle my hips.

I eye the basketball where it landed beneath the hoop, then lean back so he's supporting all of my weight.

Fuck it.

"We'll call it a tie."

His hand slides down to my hip, thumb tracing the line of my shorts. I still, absorbing the thrill of his touch. "Sure. It's not like I was ahead or anything."

"Don't be a sore winner."

"I thought we tied?"

I start moving my hips again, a soft gasp leaving my mouth when I'm rewarded by his reaction.

"Cassia." His other hand lands on my hip, caging me in place. "Are you okay?"

"Move your hands lower, and I'll be amazing."

"I'm serious."

"So am I."

His chin brushes the top of my head as he looks around the empty court. "What do you want me to do? Fuck you on the ground?"

"I have my car."

There's a pause before he replies. "Car sex, huh? I don't know if I should be flattered or concerned that you're so desperate for my dick."

"You get drunk and fight people when you're upset about something. I want you to fuck me."

"I don't do that anymore."

"*Please*, Holden."

I don't want to talk about my parents. I can't talk about Sydney. Instead of thinking or worrying or feeling sad, I want an escape. And nothing—no one—has ever distracted me the way Holden Adams does.

"Okay." He releases all of me except for my hand and leads me over to the bleachers, snagging our two shirts and my phone and keys before we continue to my car.

He tosses everything he's holding into the front seat and then opens the door behind it and nods to the backseat. "Get in."

I crawl in, expecting him to follow. But he only leans in, his hand landing on my thigh and pulling me back toward him. I reach for his shorts and he shakes his head. "This is about you."

Like I'm going to argue with that.

He tugs my shorts and underwear down. Tosses them into the front seat, leaving me wearing just a sports bra and socks. Not exactly a sexy outfit, but the heat in Holden's gaze makes me feel like it is.

We've fooled around in Holden's truck a few times before, but never in my car. I'm not sure I'll be able to drive this sedan again without picturing this scene playing out in the back seat.

His fingers find the sensitive spot between my legs, his touch light and teasing.

I shift closer, trying to force more contact.

"You're so wet," he tells me, watching his fingers tease me.

"You took your shirt off."

Holden chuckles. "Thought that wasn't distracting."

"I lied," I breathe.

"Yeah, I kinda figured that out when you started rubbing all over me."

A low buzzing begins by my ear. I swat toward the sound. "Mosquitoes found us."

"I don't know how. It's not like we're next to a light and it's dark out."

"You're such a smartass—*oh*." He slides one finger inside of me, making my back arch.

Holden grins. "You were saying?"

I moan as he adds a second finger, too distracted and desperate to think of anything smart to say in response. "Keep doing that."

The buzzing begins again, closer this time. I wave both hands, trying to smack it away. I don't even care if they're inside the car. I just don't want to *know* they're in the car or listen to the incessant drone.

"You look like a crazy person," he tells me.

"I hate mosquitoes and I'm basically naked. I don't want them to eat me alive."

"Are you having second thoughts?"

"No." I'm turned on and throbbing. Stopping sounds like a horrible idea. "Can't you get in the car?"

Holden eyes the backseat. The *small* backseat. "How the hell is that supposed to work?"

I scootch back as far as I can. "Just get in. We'll figure it out."

He still looks dubious, but he listens to me, climbing inside and shutting the door behind him. I can't hear the mosquito anymore, so hopefully it already flew out.

I crawl into his lap, my head rubbing against the sedan's roof. His thighs are spread to take advantage of as much space as possible, his knees still smushed against the back of the driver's seat. The mesh of his basketball shorts brushes against the wetness between my legs, both of us groaning when I settle on top of his erection.

"Can you come this way?" he asks.

"Yeah," I tell him. "But I want your tongue."

His eyebrows rise, surprised. "We would have been better off doing this on the court," he tells me.

I roll my eyes. "Lie down."

Holden listens, his eyes darkening to navy when he realizes my intention. His head and torso span two seats, his legs folded up in the rest of the remaining space.

Carefully, I move over his chest, wedging one knee between his body and the leather seat and the other half-hanging off the edge. It's not roomy or ideal, but the maneuvering ends with my center directly above his mouth.

"I knew dating a smart girl would pay off," Holden says. "This is genius."

I laugh, not dropping my hips yet.

I want to savor this moment for a few seconds longer. It must be close to or after midnight by now. Later than I usually stay up, as Holden pointed out. Seven a.m. is going to come really early tomorrow morning.

But I'm exactly where I want to be right now.

And that's when the car's lights go off.

So much for being smart. It didn't occur to me they'd turn off once the door was shut.

"Dammit," I say. "I—"

I stop talking when his tongue swipes against my slit. My knees buckle against the seat, so I'm literally sitting on his face.

Holden doesn't seem to mind. His hands slide up and grip my thighs, angling me exactly where he wants me. Exactly where I need him. Forcing me to accept the pleasure that's rapidly building to a devastating peak.

I wanted to watch.

But there's something sinful and exciting about him touching me in the darkness. The court's lights a distant glow that barely reaches the car. My eyes have adjusted enough I can make out his silhouette, but that's about it. The lack of sight heightens my other senses.

His tongue swirls and his lips suck until I'm falling apart, pleasure pummeling through me in relentless waves.

"Fuck." My breathing is ragged and uneven as I collapse against the seat. My muscles are useless right now, numb with pleasure. "You're so good at that."

His hands run up and down my thighs, rubbing the sensitized skin. My whole body is still humming with awareness.

"I've had a lot of practice."

I tense. It's not a decision, just a reaction.

He feels it, because he huffs. "With *you*, Cassia. If you want to get jealous, here's a fun fact: you're the only girl I've ever gone down on. Okay?"

I exhale. "I'm sorry. It's not that I don't trust you, and I know I need to get over it. I just…wish it had only been me. Thinking about you doing this with someone else makes me want to punch something. And maybe it would be different if it had all been before I knew you." *But it wasn't.* "I'll stop mentioning it. I promise."

"Cassia." Holden sits up, his hand finding mine in the dark.

"I'm sorry. I am. I'd have happily punched Douchenerd after seeing him just talking to you. That day in the library, when you helped me with my history paper? I was furious with Harrison for sitting at the same table with you. If I knew that one of them had touched you…" He exhales. "I was in a bad place in high school. Those other girls? They were a distraction, like fighting or drinking. And I hope you never find this out for yourself, but having sex with someone you don't love feels different. It wasn't that I wasn't attracted to you back then. Or that I didn't care about you. It's that I was scared and selfish. Trying to protect you from myself."

I smile. "Who's Douchenerd?"

He chuckles. "Uh, Brooks."

"That's mean. He's a nice guy, not a douche."

"His name is *Brooks*."

"I like that you're jealous," I whisper, squeezing his hand.

"Great. I'll punch guys around you more often."

"I'd rather you did other things with your hands."

"You just came."

"Yeah, but you didn't." I slide my hands down his chest until I reach the elastic band of his shorts, the stretchy material expanding easily as I tug it down. His boxers yank away just as effortlessly. I find his cock by feel, my fingers brushing against the hard length.

I want to take him in my mouth. But that's logistically impossible in the current situation. I settle for rubbing him against my clit until I can barely think straight, then lining the tip up with my opening and sinking down.

I come after only a few strokes, desperately chasing the euphoria of release. Craving the closeness of being so connected to him. This feels right, while so much feels wrong.

It's too cramped in the backseat to make cuddling comfortable. We both get dressed as best we can. Holden climbs out first, and I'm right behind him.

"Good game, flower."

I smile in response to his teasing, but it fades quickly. Holden's does too, watching me closely. A shadow of dread appears in his expression, same as I glimpsed earlier. Or maybe I'm just projecting my own churning emotions onto him.

I spin my keys around one finger, glancing at the bleachers.

This place that has seen so much of our history. The beautiful and the ugly. The sultry and the sad.

My mouth doesn't open. I'm dreading speaking the words.

They sound so…final.

Real and permanent.

Divorce is an ending.

Having parents who aren't together isn't something I ever wanted to have in common with Holden. I liked the idea of him having my whole happy family to fill the gap of his fractured one.

Holden's gaze grows increasingly concerned.

"You're freaking me the fuck out, Cassia." He takes a step closer, the comforting scent of cinnamon invading my senses. "Whatever it is, it'll be okay. We can figure—"

"My parents are getting divorced." The hot burn of tears stings my eyes, making me feel like a child.

Holden's inhale is sharp and sudden. "When did you find out?"

"Tonight. My mom didn't want me to go back to school without telling me. My dad hasn't really been around all summer. They said it was because of work. His firm is opening a new office in New Jersey."

"I'm so sorry, Cas."

I blink rapidly. "I didn't see it coming. Twenty-four years of marriage. Six kids." My fingers dig into my palm, the pain a welcome distraction. "I thought they'd...last." I exhale, then switch to fiddling with a stray thread on the hem of my t-shirt. "And my siblings... I grew up with two parents. Maggie is in college now too. But Regan, Charlie, Chris? They all live at home. Sally is only eight! More than half her life, she'll have to deal with shared custody and all the confusion that goes along with that."

"Cassia..."

"And I feel guilty telling you. My parents are both alive, and *here*, even if they're not together. I know I'm lucky to have that. It's just—"

"Hey." He steps closer, grabbing my chin and tilting my face up. Forcing me to meet his gaze. "Never apologize for something you're upset about. Never, and especially not to me. Okay?"

I nod. "My mom felt terrible and none of my siblings know, so I just came straight here. And I don't want to go home and know. Don't want to leave for school and also can't wait to." A long sigh leaves my body. "I'm just...a mess, I guess."

Holden's hand wraps around my waist, tugging me into the warmth of his body. "You don't have to explain. I don't have anywhere else I need to be. And even if I did, I'd still be right here."

I tilt my head back so I can see his face better. "Thank you," I whisper.

There's another secret weighing me down, one I'm not allowed to share with him. Hopefully Sydney isn't pregnant and he'll never know. But God, if she is, it'll affect him. They're the only immediate family each other has.

Like he's reading my mind, he asks, "Did you tell Sydney?"

"No. She's got enough going on." My guilty conscience speaks without thinking.

"She does, huh?"

I gnaw on my bottom lip, debating what to say.

"And she asked you not to say anything to me?"

"I don't tell you everything Nova says to me."

"That's different, Cas. She's not my sister."

I blow out a long breath. "I know. But I…there are boundaries. There are plenty of things I keep between us that I don't tell Sydney."

"If she's upset about something, she should trust me enough to tell me herself." He sighs. "I'm a shitty brother."

"No, you're not."

"You're not exactly unbiased."

"I'm not a liar either," I reply.

One corner of Holden's mouth curves up. "Not a good one, at least."

"What's that supposed to mean?"

"You have tells."

"Tells? What do you mean?"

"Whenever you lie, your eye twitches."

"Bullshit."

He grins. "I'm right. If you'd played the game that night, I would have known the lie."

"If you knew the lie, it would have been because you know me."

"Mmhmm," he hums.

"Or because I lied about something stupid, like my favorite ice cream flavor."

Holden rolls his eyes. "I wasn't in the mood for games."

Slowly, the light moment fades.

His hold on me tightens. I make no attempt to pull away.

"They're not us, Cas."

I pull in a deep breath.

"I know more than your tells, flower. But your parents aren't us. They made it really far. Just not all the way to the finish line. We will."

"We don't even know where we'll each be living next year. After graduation, we could—"

"We've done long-distance before. If we have to, we'll do it again."

"By long-distance, you mean us not talking for the past eight weeks?"

He half-smiles. "Okay, it was a rough trial run."

I snort. "As long as you realize there's room for improvement."

"There's definitely room for improvement. But that doesn't mean we're doomed. It means we're worth working on."

I nod. "I know we are."

"Thanks for texting me back."

I manage a smile. "Anytime."

He kisses me and then heads for his truck. I stare at the court for a few seconds longer, then climb into my car.

CHAPTER THIRTEEN

HOLDEN

I shut my laptop and scrub at my face with one hand. My mind is spinning from the amount of medical jargon I just tried to absorb, my stomach tied into uncomfortable knots.

I haven't mentioned my mom's illness to anyone. I considered telling Cassia, but that was before I found out about her parents' divorce. She's got enough going on right now.

The easy option would be to do nothing. To continue with my life exactly as it is. It finally feels settled after the upheaval of the summer.

My senior year.

The beginning of the end of college.

Since arriving back on campus yesterday, it's felt like I never left. I transferred the terrible packing job I managed—Sydney and Catherine had a good laugh watching me load the car in the condo's parking lot—and am officially moved into the off-campus house I'm sharing with two teammates.

I should be thrilled to have Cassia nearby and a bedroom in a house where none of my few family members live. The car sex was hot, but it's never happening again. I have bruises and mosquito bites in places I never thought I would. After being separated all summer, it feels like we have a lot to make up for.

And I should be excited about getting back on the court with my teammates. Games that actually count toward our season's stats won't start for a while. But practice is picking up right away and we have a few scrimmages scattered throughout the fall. I won't lose any momentum from the intense training camp I just attended.

Everything should be good. Great, even. Classes haven't even started for me to stress about. I have three days to chill on campus and do absolutely nothing.

I can't stop thinking about my mom, though.

The surprised, scared look on her face.

The way her skin matched the grayish hue of the linoleum floor.

The random guy with her.

I should be relieved, I suppose, that she has someone. But it's a glimpse into her present I didn't get the last time when she showed up alone.

How long have they been together? What did he offer her that my dad didn't? Does he treat her well? Make her happy?

I'm the furthest thing from a medical expert—I got a C in Biology—but everything about my mom's appearance indicated she's sick. Really sick. That she doesn't have long left and any chance to get those answers is disappearing fast. That any chance to talk to her at all is fading.

A knock on my bedroom door is a welcome interruption.

I drop my hand from my face and call out, "Yeah?"

"Hey, man." Henry opens the door and peers inside, his usual friendly smile fixed on his face. "How's it going?"

"Good." I'm not sure if it's a lie or not. "You?"

"Great. Good to be back."

"I thought you weren't coming back to campus until tomorrow?"

"What can I say? I pictured you guys having a blast without me and got FOMO."

I snort. "We've just been unpacking. Nothing that exciting."

"Yeah. Solid progress." Henry eyes the stack I haven't touched. I haven't even unpacked my sheets yet. I just tossed a blanket on the mattress to sleep last night.

"Well, I'll leave you to it. Pizza later?"

"Yeah, sounds good."

He grins, nods, then heads toward the door.

"Wilson."

Henry spins back around. "Yeah?"

I exhale. "What do you know about liver cancer?"

A wrinkle forms on his forehead. "Uh, it sucks?"

I stand, pushing my desk chair away. "I'm serious, man. Like treatment, outcomes. Stuff like that."

"I'm *pre*-med, Adams. They teach us about cell structure and the periodic table. I'm not an oncologist."

I deflate. "Okay. Nevermind."

"Anything you want to talk about?"

"No. Forget it."

He shoots me one last concerned, curious look, then leaves.

I drum my fingers against the desk, then unlock my phone and pull up the number for Walker-Moore Memorial Hospital. I'm on hold for a few minutes before a tired-sounding woman answers and then transfers me to the Oncology department. A man answers, then transfers me a second time, to the doctor who is supposedly treating my mother.

I spend every second of the fifteen-minute process second-guessing making this call.

There's a click, then a man's voice says, "Dr. Meyers speaking."

I clear my throat. "Hi. My name is Holden Adams. I was told you're treating my mother. Lana Harris?"

Her last name is a guess. She and my dad never got married, but I have no idea if she is now.

"Yes, she's a patient of mine."

"How long does she have?"

I hold my breath, waiting for his answer.

Dr. Meyers sighs. "I'm afraid I can't share any patient information. That's all kept confidential."

"I'm her son."

The words burn like acid coming out, a truth I'd adamantly deny under any other circumstance.

"Regardless of your relation, she needs to agree to any information being shared. The hospital has a legal obligation. If you'd like, I can contact your mother and request her permission?"

Part of me wants to let this doctor reach out to her. See how she reacts to me giving a shit about her health. But the rest of me knows she won't agree, and I'll get nowhere.

"I heard she needs a transplant. I've been doing some research online, and I…is it true you can donate a liver and live through it?"

Silence. I can hear the hesitation in it as the doctor deliberates whether or not to respond. I wonder how well he knows my mom. How long he's been treating her. If he had any idea she has kids.

"Yes, that's true," he finally says. "The liver is an incredible organ. With a living donor, we take about half to transplant. There are risks involved, like with any surgery, but the donor's liver will regenerate to its normal size. After a recovery period, they're able to live a normal life. And save a life."

"And is it true that family members are often matches?"

A longer silence this time.

Dr. Meyers has obviously figured out where I'm headed with this. Maybe he knew as soon as he answered the call.

"We don't know if someone is a match until we've done testing. But certain factors, like blood type, are hereditary. It's true that a family member has a better chance of being a match than a stranger off the street."

I stare down at the floor, tracing the grain pattern in the wood with my eyes. Uncertainty gnaws away in my gut. I was hoping he'd tell me I was wrong. That her rude companion was wrong, and there's no need for a transplant. That they already have one lined up for my mom. That there's no chance I could be of any help.

He isn't saying any of those things.

"How do I get tested?" I ask.

"Holden, that's a big decision. You should talk with your mother and—"

"We don't *talk*," I snap. "She left when I was five. I have no relationship with her. But…I don't want her to die. So if I could keep that from happening, I want to at least know."

"It's not a simple process, Holden. We would run blood tests, take a chest X-ray, do an electrocardiogram, and also do an ultrasound of your abdomen. And if all those tests suggested that you could be a viable donor, we would have to do a CT scan to make sure that your liver is big enough to donate a piece."

"I want to know if I can donate," I tell him.

"In those circumstances, the transplant recipient's insurance typically covers the costs of the donor, beginning with evaluation. It hasn't come up as a possibility in your mother's case, so I need to check and see if—"

"The money isn't an issue. I can pay for the testing if I need to."

Thanks to my dad, I'm set financially. Thanks to the days, months, and years he spent driving thousands of miles to provide for us. I wonder how he'd feel about me spending it to help the woman who abandoned us.

The doctor sighs, caving to my determination. "All right. I'll transfer you back to the front desk. They'll get you set up with an appointment. I understand the situation with your mother is… complicated but I would *strongly* advise speaking with her before going through with the testing."

"Okay." I won't, and the doctor's sigh suggests he realizes that.

I have to wait on hold for another ten minutes before I reach the front desk.

"We had a cancellation this afternoon, if you're available at three thirty," the woman tells me. "Otherwise, our next appointment is in two weeks."

I eye the clock. If I speed, I can probably make it. And I would really rather get this over with.

"Okay. I'll be there."

———

I'm sitting on the bleachers, staring into space, when Cassia calls me. I stare at her smiling face on the screen, debating on whether to answer. When I left Richmond, I didn't consider what I would say to her about this trip. I told Henry I was going to the gym and Robby wasn't home.

I could drive back to campus now instead of spending the night here. It's after dinner. I left the hospital and stopped for a pizza before coming here.

The drive back to campus would be dark and long, but I'd make it before midnight.

Motivating myself to move is more the problem. Now that I've gotten tested, it's a waiting game to get the results. Dr. Meyers expected it to take two weeks because Walker-Moore's lab is backed up and they're sending it somewhere else. I'm eager to know the answer and also want to put it off as long as possible. If I am a match, it'll be a harder decision than choosing to get tested in the first place.

And this is always the place where I've come to think. I'd rather worry here than in my bedroom off-campus.

My phone's screen goes dark, then lights up again.

I answer this time, concerned something is wrong.

Relieved when her tone is cheerful. "Hey! Nova and I are getting ice cream. Do you want me to bring you anything? Or come? I haven't seen you since you got here."

Guilt twists in my gut. "I'm okay, thanks. I just ate a whole pizza."

"Is everything okay?" The cheerfulness has faded, replaced by concern.

"Yeah. Everything is fine." I pick at the Band-Aid stuck to my arm. The crease of my elbow stings in the spot where they took two vials of blood earlier. "I'm just...not on campus. I'm back home."

"Home as in—you're in Pembrooke?" All I can hear in her voice is surprise.

"Yeah, I realized I forgot a few things. And Catherine wanted help with a couple of projects around the condo."

The lie is out before I've thought it through—before I've thought at all.

I want to tell her about my mom, but I also don't want to discuss it. And I won't know the results of the testing for a little while. If I'm not a match, if I can't do anything, I'm not sure there's anything worth telling Cassia. It'll be something I bury, along with all the other problems in my family I couldn't fix.

"I feel bad that I wasn't around to help this summer, after everything she's done for me and Sydney." More bullshit spills out of my mouth. "I'm just spending one night, then I'll be back tomorrow."

"Okay. Say hi to Syd from me."

"Yeah, I will."

Sydney is one of the reasons I came here after leaving the hospital. I'm not ready to face her yet.

She's the other person I can't decide on whether to say anything about my mom to or not. Part of me thinks she deserves to know.

The rest of me wants to protect her. I couldn't shelter her from our mom leaving or our dad dying, but I could shield her from this. Pretend I never saw our mom in that hallway. Chances are she'll never find out about this on her own. In Sydney's mind, our mom has been dead for a long time.

But if I'm not a match…Sydney might be.

I'm torn about whether she deserves to make the same decision I did.

She's an adult, technically. But she's also my *little* sister.

"Holden?"

I straighten from my slouch. "Yeah. Still here. Sorry. What did you say?"

"Come by tomorrow, okay? I miss you."

I smile, rubbing a hand against the back of my neck. "I will. I love you."

"Love you too."

She hangs up and I sink back against the bleachers.

Stare at the hoop.

Dr. Meyers was very thorough. Before I started the testing, he ran through the recovery process if I am a match and do decide to donate. I'm looking at eight to ten weeks after surgery until I'd be cleared to play basketball.

Between the delay for test results and actually scheduling surgery, that period wouldn't start until early October at the absolute earliest.

I wouldn't be able to play basketball this season.

My senior year.

My last chance to chase a professional career.

Gone, just like that.

That scares me more than the risks of bleeding, infection, or liver failure that Dr. Meyers also ran through.

As pathetic as it sounds, I don't know who I am without basketball.

I've always played.

Basketball has been there for me in my darkest moments. The only thing I love anywhere near as much as I love Cassia, and many special moments with her are mixed in with the sport.

We played together as kids.

Now she comes to my college games, wearing my jersey.

Losing my shot at playing professionally? I don't know what that would do to me. Part of me *needs* to know if I could make it. If I have what it takes.

And it would be a bitter irony, losing basketball—which makes me happy—because of a woman who gave me life but then offered nothing but misery.

My phone buzzes again. I pull it out of my pocket, glance at the screen, and answer.

"Hey, Finn."

"Hey! How's Richmond?"

"Fine, I assume. I'm in Pembrooke."

I continue staring out at the basketball court that's been my happy place for as long as I remember. I don't have a spot like this on campus. The basketball gym in the sports center is state-of-the-art. Everything is new and shiny and clean.

This court fits me better.

Cracked asphalt. Faded lines. Ragged strings hanging from the hoop.

"You are?" Finn's voice pulls me out of my thoughts.

"Uh-huh."

"Come to Arlington!"

"What?"

"It's Friday night and classes haven't started yet. There are about a hundred different parties happening on campus tonight. Come here! It's the least you owe me after ditching all summer."

"I was at camp."

"Whatever. I'm serious. Come here! Harrison is here." Finn says that like it's some sort of enticement, which isn't the case.

But even considering Baker's company, I'm tempted. *Very* tempted.

Partying with Finn sounds way better than moping here or having to face Sydney at the condo.

I'll find out if I'm a match before potentially involving her, I decide. If I am a match and go through with the transplant surgery, I'll have to tell her. And if I'm not a match, then Sydney can choose if she gets tested or not.

"I'm leaving now."

Finn is still celebrating when I hang up.

CHAPTER FOURTEEN

HOLDEN

The drive to Arlington University takes just over an hour. I've been here a handful of times, the last visit more than a year ago. Between basketball and Cassia, there's not much motivation to leave Richmond when I'm there.

Finn is waiting for me outside the frat house he's lived in since freshman year.

I park my truck on the street and climb out, stretching. Rip the Band-Aid off the crease of my elbow and toss it in the footwell before slamming the door shut. There's a tiny red dot visible over the vein. I stare at it for a few seconds, half-expecting a trickle of blood. Nothing happens.

Finn grins as I approach. "Gonna be a great night."

"Fuck yeah," I respond.

It's been a while since I experienced the reckless energy humming through me right now. Worrying about my mom isn't just unpleasant, it's probably a waste of time. Definitely more time than she's spent concerned about me.

I knew you were better off without me.

That's what she told me when I confronted her about abandoning me and Sydney. And our dad. I'm not sure if he ever got over it. He buried himself in working. Half the time, he felt as absent as she did. With one crucial difference—he was working *for* us. She was just selfish.

Just like I am.

But unlike in high school, I know there's someone I would sacrifice for. There's a difference between me and my mom, something I know separates us.

Harrison and a few other guys are waiting down the block beneath one of the massive trees that line the street. The closest house to it is clearly our destination, loud music audible even from here.

I greet the guys—Finn's friends who I've met on past visits—and tap knuckles with Harrison.

"I'm sorry about the camping trip," he tells me quietly, as we head up the brick walkway toward the party. "You were right. It was none of my business."

I glance at him. "Because I told you we'd work it out, and we did? Would you be saying this if Cassia and I weren't back in a good place?"

Harrison shrugs. "I don't know. But you are, so…"

I shake my head. Snort, because at least he's predictable in his meddling.

"You didn't make any sense together, Holden. I noticed Cassia in high school, okay? She was sweet and smart. You were throwing punches every Friday night. I thought you were going to destroy her. I didn't get it then and I'm not sure I get it now. But there's not a fucking chance Cassia doesn't know what she got into by now, so…" He shrugs. "You were right; your relationship."

"If anyone's destroying anyone, it would be her obliterating me." I say the words quietly, not wanting the rest of the group to overhear.

But I mean them.

Cassia has always had the power to shatter me.

Harrison's expression is all surprise as he glances over.

"Make fewer assumptions, Baker," I say. "I never got why girls—including my sister—had a thing for you in high school. But it probably had something to do with the 'good guy' thing, you acting like a saint who could throw a spiral."

Harrison looks away.

"I don't blame you for being interested in her. What pisses me off—then, now—is you not respecting our relationship. I *love* her. Unless she tells me to fuck off, I'm sticking around. There isn't her side and my side, it's just *us*. You think you want what's best for her? That's nothing compared to how much I care. Accept that, respect our relationship, and we won't have any issues."

"Okay," he says.

"Great."

We reach the front door.

The party inside looks similar to Richmond's parties. With important distinctions.

Cassia isn't here.

My teammates aren't here.

Unless any guys on Arlington's basketball team show up and decide to start shit, I'm just one more person in a crowded room.

I push all my responsibilities, all my obligations, all my worries far away. Follow Finn into the kitchen, shrugging off the girls who approach me as we push through the living room.

The air is hot and heavy, weighted by the scent of smoke and alcohol and sweat. It smells like loose inhibitions and bad decisions.

Finn knows exactly where he's going. He heads straight

toward the cabinet to the left of the sink, pulling out an unopened bottle of amber liquid. Whiskey. My favorite.

I take the shot he hands me and down it, the burn of alcohol sliding down my throat a relief. I don't cough or reach for a chaser. I hold out my cup for a refill.

"Hell yeah, Adams!"

Finn fills it with twice as much this time.

I glance at Harrison, who trailed in here behind us. He looks away, grabbing a can of beer out of the fridge for himself.

I down more whiskey, the warm burn turning into numbness. The buzz is hitting me faster than usual, probably because of the pint of blood they took from me earlier. I shouldn't be drinking at all, let alone this much.

Stupid and reckless are two synonyms for my name, though.

So I keep taking sips, the bitter five-year-old in me feeling satisfied I'm destroying the organ I might be donating.

Somehow, that feels fitting.

If I offer something to my mom, it *should* be damaged.

The same way she mangled me and Sydney by wrecking our family.

The same way she injured my dad. If she'd stuck around, maybe he'd be alive right now.

The same way she's messing with me, by forcing me to help her or live with the guilt of knowing I could have done something and didn't.

I don't just want to be different from her. I want to be better.

My glass gets drained and is filled again.

And I keep drinking.

Until I'm not thinking about my mom anymore.

Until I'm not thinking about anything.

CHAPTER FIFTEEN

HOLDEN

A pounding headache is the first thing I'm aware of. I roll over in bed, my eyes blinking open blearily as a jackhammer continues working on my skull.

For the first time, I'm not looking at a dark head of hair in bed beside me.

There are blonde strands spread across the pillow next to me.

Everything in me freezes, realization and dread trickling through me like a cold stream of water.

Fuck.

I emphasize each letter in my head, ratcheting the pounding in my head up to an intolerable degree.

The pain isn't enough.

The word *fuck* isn't enough.

I can't think and can barely breathe. It feels like a lead weight is resting on my chest, pushing down, down, down until there's nothing left to demolish.

I squint around the room, trying to figure out where I am and look for clues about what might have happened.

There are pink curtains covering the windows and there's a bunch of makeup on the table beside the bed.

I'm wearing boxers, which is a small relief. But the rest of my clothes are scattered on the rug, mingled with a lacy red bra and a black dress.

Panic heaves in my gut, making me feel like I'm going to puke. I sit up, scrubbing a hand across my face.

Fuck.

Fuck.

Fuck.

I can't believe this is happening. Maybe this is a nightmare, and I'm about to wake up for real.

"Morning, Holden."

My gaze snaps to the left, at the blonde who's stretching and smiling sleepily at me. She's pretty. Confident of it too, based on the way she's flaunting her body.

Once upon a time, she was exactly the kind of girl I'd take upstairs at a party. Eager and hot.

She's also completely naked. And she knows my name.

My heart takes an abrupt nosedive.

"Did we—" I clear my throat. I'm an atheist, but I send up a small prayer anyway. "Did we hook up last night?"

She raises one eyebrow. Then shakes her head. "No."

The rush of relief is so strong I slump back against the white sheets, my eyes closing and my breath leaving me in a long exhale.

Cassia has forgiven me for a lot of shit.

I don't think she would have forgiven a *yes*.

I don't think I could have asked her to.

"Thank God," I breathe.

"But I'm up for it." A warm hand brushes my abs, dangerously close to my dick, and I realize lying back down was a big mistake. I'm in bed with a naked chick who is not my girlfriend, for fuck's sake.

I jump out of the bed like someone just electrocuted me and grab my shorts. "I have a girlfriend."

"So? That didn't matter last night."

I glance at her, my heart back in my throat. "You said nothing happened."

She rolls her eyes. "Nothing did. I came up to *my* bedroom, and you were passed out and half-naked. I couldn't move you, so I just went to sleep. Plus, you were hot." Her gaze roves my shirtless state appreciatively. "You obviously came up here looking for something."

I snort. "Yeah. A *bed*."

I lean down to grab my shirt. When I stand again, the blonde is still lying in the same spot, making no attempt to hide her body. The sheets are *right there* to cover up with, and she's flashing her tits.

"Well, *you're welcome*," she snarks. "I could have called Campus Security, told them there was a random guy in my bed."

I exhale. "I'm sorry. I was wasted, and it will *definitely* never happen again."

"Is it serious?" she asks. "With your girlfriend?"

Her eyes are a contrast to her bored tone. Alert and aware, skimming over my body with interest.

I quickly yank my shirt on and start hunting around for my sneakers.

"Yes," I reply firmly. "It's very serious."

"Too bad." She clicks her tongue and stands, still naked as she strolls over to the adjoining bathroom and shuts the door.

I put on my shoes as fast as I possibly can.

Open the bedroom door and slip into the hallway, well aware it looks like I'm doing a walk of shame. Trash—empty red cups and crumpled beer cans and a condom wrapper—litters the hallway as I walk through the silent house.

Every creak makes me flinch.

I get downstairs without seeing anyone.

But there's a familiar face standing in the living room, straightening up the mess.

The house is even more of a disaster down here.

"Wasn't expecting to see you here," I say.

Brooks raises one eyebrow as he glances over. My memory of last night is hazy enough, I can't even recall if he was at the party. He must have been, I guess, if he's helping clean up.

There's a black trash bag at his feet, half-filled with garbage he's collected. "I go here, remember?"

I rub the back of my neck. "And you live here?"

"In the *sorority* house?" He raises one eyebrow, then shakes his head. "No, I live down the block. Just came over to help clean up."

"Big of you."

He studies me. "Finn wasn't sure where you ended up last night."

"Yeah, I crashed. Crazy night."

"Crashed here?" he asks, glancing at the stairs I just descended.

"I should get going."

I pass Brooks, headed in the direction I think the front door is.

"She deserves better than you."

My steps slow until I glance back at him. "You don't know anything. About her. About me. And it's none of your fucking business."

God, I'm sick of saying that.

Maybe I don't deserve Cassia. But I *want* her. *Need* her. *Love* her.

"I know she deserves better than a guy who spends the night at a sorority house."

Brooks has balls, I'll give him that. Most guys would be shrinking under the glare I'm aiming his way. He's wearing the same superior expression Harrison used to always aim my way.

I know I fuck up more than my fair share and that this is a particularly terrible example.

But Brooks doesn't know me. He doesn't know anything about my mom or why I ended up here. He doesn't know Cassia, and he sure didn't write down his feelings for her in a ragged notebook for years or comfort her when Lily died.

Instead of saying any of that, I head for the front door, slamming it shut behind me.

Wishing this was how I left—that I'd left—last night.

CHAPTER SIXTEEN

CASSIA

I'm sorting through the textbooks I picked up from the campus bookstore this morning when I hear the doorbell ring. I'm probably the definition of a nerd, because preparing for the first day of classes tomorrow has me excited instead of apprehensive. For so long, vet school has felt far away. A finish line that never drew any closer, no matter how fast I walked.

It finally feels like I'm making some progress. Like I'm close.

I add my Genetics textbook to the stack on my desk, stand, stretch, and then leave my bedroom to answer the door.

My roommate, Nova, is on Richmond's soccer team and so has already been back on campus for a couple of weeks. With the exception of my room, our apartment is well-settled. The open layout of the living room and kitchen is homey and organized.

I open the door, expecting it to be Nova forgetting her key.

It's not.

I stare at Sydney, stunned. She's come to see me—and Holden —on campus before, but those were always announced visits.

"Hi," I greet, when she doesn't speak first.

"Hi," Sydney replies. She glances away, toward the apartment next door. Her arms are wrapped around her waist and her face is pale despite the heat.

Dread expands in my chest, my mind spinning with the only logical conclusion of why she's shown up here without so much as a text. "Come in."

She follows me into the kitchen.

"Want anything to eat? Or drink?" I ask, playing hostess.

"I took the test," Sydney tells me.

I dropped the one I bought off at the condo on Thursday morning before leaving Pembrooke. And I hadn't heard from her since. Part of me thought—hoped—that meant it was negative.

Sydney opens up the tote bag she's carrying. It's canvas, the side decorated with the logo of a famous New York theater. She pulls out a plastic baggie and tosses it on the counter.

"And then I went out and bought three more because I was hoping that one was wrong."

"They were *all* positive?"

"Yep." She draws out the word.

Sydney leaves both of her bags on the counter and wanders deeper into the apartment, passing the kitchen island and heading toward the living room.

The far wall is all windows, overlooking the woods behind campus that are in the shadow of the Green Mountains.

"Wow. This place is really nice," she says, glancing over the couch and coffee table.

I pick up the plastic bag on the counter.

Sure enough, the four tests are all positive.

My best friend is pregnant. With Harrison Baker's baby.

Even the thought sounds absurd.

And a crazy reminder of how quickly and completely life can change.

I exhale, setting the baggie back down and walking toward

Sydney. She's collapsed on the couch, head tilted back, feet up on the coffee table and eyes focused on the distant peaks.

"Do you have any alcohol?" she asks. "I could *really* use a drink."

I huff a laugh. "Sydney."

Even if she wasn't pregnant, I wouldn't think she was serious. She's never been much of a drinker. Something to be said for having the choice, I guess.

Holden and I have never had a scare like this. I've never been late. This isn't a situation I've ever come close to experiencing first-hand, but I easily can imagine how terrifying it would be. Any escape would sound pretty good to me too.

"I'm supposed to leave for London in ten days. What the fuck do I do, Cassia?"

"Wait, what? I thought you decided against that program."

"Well, I applied anyway. Because I didn't think I'd get in. But then I did. And *that* was supposed to be the end of summer surprise. Not…this."

I take a seat next to her, tucking my feet underneath my legs. "You need to go see a doctor so you can find out for sure."

"I took four tests. They couldn't have *all* been wrong."

"You never know. And you should hear what your options are. Tell Harrison. And then…" I exhale. "You'll have some decisions to make."

Sydney chews on her bottom lip. "Yeah. You're right."

"You drove all the way here by yourself?"

"I couldn't keep sitting in that condo alone. Catherine's gone on a work trip, so I had a car."

"Catherine's gone on a work trip?"

"Yeah." Sydney sighs, oblivious to the trickle of unease running through me. "And she's barely home, even when she is in town. For the best, I guess. It's not like I've felt like talking. But there's not much to do except freak out when I'm alone."

I hum an agreement, my mind still spinning too fast to form more of a response.

He lied to me about helping Catherine.

Why?

"Does Holden know you're here?" I ask.

Sydney huffs, eyes focused on the mountains. "No. I haven't talked to him since he left on Thursday."

I swallow, trying to ignore the unease as I realize…he didn't go back to Pembrooke *at all*.

I push the questions away for now. Sydney has plenty to deal with at the moment. She doesn't need my drama.

"Want to spend the night?" I ask.

"Don't classes start tomorrow? I don't want to get in the way."

"You're not in the way." I stand. "Just let me change. We can go get some lunch and buy cookie dough for later."

Sydney gives me a watery smile. "You're sure Nova won't mind?"

"I'm sure. Soccer is in full swing for her already, so her schedule is super hectic. She's only been back here to sleep."

I head into my bedroom to grab a shirt.

The air conditioning is on, but it's not doing much. I'm just wearing a sports bra and shorts. I was half-considering going to the gym later, but I need no convincing to abandon that plan.

"So I ran into Grace Harper yesterday," Sydney says when I walk back into the common area.

"My condolences," I say before tugging the t-shirt down over my head.

When the fabric clears my face, Sydney is smiling. Then she

tilts her head. "She asked if you and Holden were *actually* back together…which kinda implies you broke up?"

There's no accusation in her expression but definitely some confusion. Wondering why Grace knows more about my relationship with her brother than she does.

"It wasn't a big deal," I say.

I walk toward the kitchen table—where I'm ninety-nine percent certain I left my car keys earlier—grateful I can hide my face.

I don't want to lie to Sydney.

But I don't want to get into this either—not when she's got all this other stuff going on.

Not when Holden and I are back on stable ground. I *thought* we were back on stable ground, at least.

Not when I just found out he lied to me yesterday.

That feels like tremors.

"Why didn't you tell me?" she asks.

"It was a rough patch. We got through it."

"Holden did something?"

"Syd…"

"Okay, all right. Not my business. If you want to talk about it, I'm here."

"Thank you."

"I told Grace to shove it, by the way."

I grin. "No, you didn't."

"Well, I didn't hold the door for her, even though she was right behind me."

"How rude."

"I tried."

"I know." The world would be a way better place if everyone had the same low tolerance for cruelty as Sydney does.

We head outside into the heat. And I try to shove all thoughts of Holden far away.

CHAPTER SEVENTEEN

HOLDEN

Henry does a double take when I walk into the kitchen. "I thought you were asleep upstairs."

I head straight for the fridge, grabbing a sports drink and draining most of it in one go. Now I just need a couple of painkillers to combat the pounding headache.

"Way to bail last night."

"Sorry," I say, taking another long pull.

Henry studies my wrinkled clothes. "You never came home?" he asks.

I shake my head and gulp more liquid.

"Hangover?"

"Yeah. It feels like a construction crew is working on my skull. I drank way too much last night." I toss the empty bottle into the recycling. "Woke up in some random girl's bed."

Henry gapes at me, spoonful of cereal suspended halfway to his mouth. "You cheated on Cassia? You fucking asshole."

I shake my head. "No. I didn't cheat. There was a bed and a girl, but I didn't have sex with her. Didn't touch her. I got wasted at a party, went upstairs, passed out, and then next thing I know there's a naked chick I'd never seen before in the bed."

Henry's spoon falls into his bowl with a crash.

His eyes are wide and horrified, and I realize he's the worst possible person I could have confided in about this. His moral compass is straighter than the rest of my friends'.

Finn would have shrugged it off.

At least, I think he would have. I didn't talk to him this morning. Just texted him, letting him know I was leaving. Then got in my truck and drove straight here, leaving my bad decisions behind.

"She was *naked*?"

I wish I'd left that detail out.

"Yes. But *nothing happened*." I heavily emphasize those last two words.

"How do you know?"

"Did you miss the part about how I was wasted? I wasn't in any shape to have sex with some random girl."

"*Ri-ght*. Because drunk people never make dumb decisions. Or hook up at parties." Henry raises both eyebrows, fixing me with an incredulous look.

"I've never been *that* shit-faced before. I doubt I even could have gotten hard."

Whiskey dick must be a saying for a reason, right?

"Did you talk to this chick? Flirt with her?"

I shake my head. "Nah, I don't remember her at all. I went with a bunch of guys. Last I remember, we were drinking. Hanging out. Then I woke up in her bed. She told me nothing happened."

"And you believe her?"

"I..." *want to*. "Why would she lie? I've never met her before. I don't even know her name. She said I was passed out in her bed when she came upstairs, so she just left me. And…I wouldn't do that to Cassia. I don't think I physically *could*."

I know too many guys who have girlfriends and still fool around on the side. Who get some stupid high from the forbidden attention. Who say they love a girl but that they're bored of only being with one person.

It's not a line to help her feel secure when I tell Cassia I only want her. The calculating, mean-girl vibes were a turn-off, but the blonde was what most guys would consider a bombshell. She was in bed, *everything* on display, and I couldn't have been less interested.

Cassia has always been the girl I compare other ones to.

I've never compared anyone to her and not found them lacking.

Henry's attention has returned to his cereal. Either he's bored by my drama or just hungry.

"Do I tell Cassia?" I ask him.

The question I debated the whole drive here.

Other girls are a sensitive subject with her. I've always been able to tell her it was before we were together.

This time, I can't.

"I don't know, Adams. If she got drunk at a party without you and woke up in bed next to a naked dude, would you expect Cassia to mention it to you?"

Henry's heavy sarcasm is *not* appreciated.

I'm seeing scarlet at the thought.

I know if the roles were reversed, I'd lose my shit. I wouldn't be mad at *her*, per se, if she promised me nothing had happened with the guy, but I'd be furious. Even if he hadn't touched her, he would have seen her in basically nothing. Slept in bed beside her. Gotten special moments that should only be mine.

Yeah, I'd lose my shit.

If this hypothetical happened, I would get my knuckles bloody and then drink a bottle of whiskey.

And I'm a fucking hypocrite, hoping she'll be understanding. For considering keeping it from her.

Fury mixes with self-loathing, making me feel like a shaken bottle of something carbonated. Close to exploding.

Cassia's world was just upended by her parents' pending divorce. That's why I haven't told her about my mom, and that had nothing to do with *us*.

This is the last thing I want to burden her with—another mistake of mine she has to suffer because of.

"If nothing happened, why do I need to tell her?" I ask.

"If nothing happened, why did you tell me?"

Yeah, Henry was definitely the wrong person to confide in about this.

"Tell who what?" Robby strolls into the kitchen, tugging a sweatshirt on. He almost collides with the wall, changing course at the last second to grab a banana from the bunch by the fridge.

"Holden woke up in bed with a naked chick." Henry spills, unhelpfully.

Robby's mouth falls open, giving me a disgusting view of half-chewed fruit. He swallows quickly. "Wait. You and Cassia broke up? When? What did I miss?"

"We did not break up."

"You cheated?" Robby raises both eyebrows, then opens the fridge. "You're a fucking idiot, Adams. She's smoking hot and she's loyal. I hit on her every time I see her, and she's never flirted back. Not once. That *never* happens."

"I did not cheat," I grit out.

My headache is growing worse by the minute. I thought stating the situation out loud would help. That by spelling out what happened, it would be easier to see everything rationally.

Instead, more panic is splintering my chest as Henry and Robby exchange a loaded look.

Expressions that tell me I *have* to tell her, no matter how terrible the innocent situation might sound. No matter how much I don't want to.

"I'm going to the gym," I say, heading for the stairs.

Before I talk to her, I need to think through exactly what I'm going to say. Pummel a punching bag until I'm less anxious and angry than I feel right now.

———

I pull in a deep breath and then knock on her door.

A few seconds later, it opens.

"Sydney?"

Dread shifts to surprise.

My sister takes a step back from the door. "You're not Nova."

"You're not in Pembrooke." I step inside the apartment, closing the door behind me and following Sydney into the kitchen. "Is everything okay…?"

Speaking becomes challenging as my eyes snag on the plastic sticks in a clear baggie that's sitting on the counter.

My vision tunnels to those pregnancy tests.

The *positive* pregnancy tests.

It feels like a load of bricks was just dropped in my stomach. Like I'm sinking down, and everything is moving in slow motion around me.

"What did she…"

I tear my gaze away from the counter to look at Cassia. She's the one and only thing that could distract me right now.

Her voice trails the same way mine just did as soon as our

gazes connect. She's frozen, her hands tangled in a knot of hair above her head, eyes darting between me and the countertop.

Betrayal and anger heat my blood. Rapid math and my sister's random appearance leading to one logical conclusion.

Cassia's face has paled, her expression guilty as she takes a hesitant step closer to me. "Holden—"

"They're mine."

I'd forgotten Sydney was even here.

"What?" Thanks to shock and being extremely hungover, my voice is the same consistency as gravel.

"I'm pregnant," Sydney says.

My off-kilter world spins around again.

"What?" I repeat, turning to stare at my sister. My reliable, responsible sister, who's never had a boyfriend. Who's always been the angel to counteract my devil. Healing instead of destructive. Communicative instead of silent.

"I'm pregnant." Her voice is a little louder, slightly more confident. "I've been worried for a while, and I found out for sure last night. I didn't want to tell you until I knew…until I processed it a little bit more."

"You're pregnant."

Sydney nods.

I glance at Cassia. Recall her comment at the court about Sydney having a lot going on. "You knew?"

"Don't blame Cassia," my sister says. "I asked her not to say anything."

I exhale, trying to find my bearings.

This is all…too much.

I came here to tell Cassia about last night.

I'm carrying around my mom's secret. Waiting to find out if I have a huge decision to make concerning basketball.

My head was already spinning with guilt and uncertainty.

And now…this.

"Are you keeping it?" I don't know if that's the right thing to say right now, but it's the next question that comes out.

"I don't know."

"Who's the guy?" I ask.

Sydney grimaces.

She's never discussed boys with me. I assume she tells Cassia everything. Graham Warner, back in high school, is the only guy I've seen her act flirty around.

Cassia looks down at the floor. Her cheek twitches, like she's chewing the inside.

Red flags fly up.

"*Sydney.* Who's the guy?"

"Harrison," she mumbles, so low I barely hear her.

It takes a second to sink in.

There's no way she means… "*Harrison?* Harrison Baker? Are you fucking kidding me?" I pinch the bridge of my nose. "Please tell me you're kidding to make the theater tech who *actually* knocked you up sound better."

"Is it that shocking one of your friends found me attractive? God, Holden!" Sydney huffs, then looks away.

"It's shocking he *touched* you, knowing I'd kill him."

She rolls her eyes. "I'm an adult. I can make my own decisions. And you're not my father. I can have sex with whoever I want."

I sort of wish I was still drunk for this conversation. "You weren't even in Pembrooke this summer. When—how did this happen?"

"What does it matter?"

"I'm just trying to figure out what the hell happened, Sydney."

"Do you want to know what position we had sex in too?" she snaps.

"I found out five fucking seconds ago, okay?" I retort.

"Syd," Cassia says softly. "It's a lot to take in."

My sister sighs. "He was in New York to catch a flight the next day. It just…happened."

Jesus Christ. Baker had a one-night stand with my little sister. And then he came back to Pembrooke and had the fucking nerve to lecture me about *my* mistakes.

I swallow in an attempt to forcibly tamp down my anger. "I'm…glad you told me."

Sydney snorts. "Yeah, you seem it."

"I mean, this isn't something I want you to deal with alone. Have you told Harrison?"

I know the answer before she shakes her head.

What little of last night I remember, he was drinking beer and making out with a redhead. He didn't look like a guy who just had his life upended.

If my sister wasn't part of the collateral damage, I'd take some selfish satisfaction in this turn of events. All of Harrison's morally superior lectures and judgmental looks, and then he knocks up my little sister.

"I didn't mean to tell you, at least not until I decided what I'm doing. I came to see Cassia, but I should have assumed you'd show up." Sydney glances at Cassia and rolls her eyes. "He's so needy."

Cassia smiles, but it's her fake one.

There's no genuine amusement in this room.

And I realize…Sydney came from Pembrooke.

Where I was supposed to be.

Which means…Cassia knows I lied yesterday. Knows I didn't spend the night in Pembrooke.

"I have to pee. I'll let you guys make out, or whatever."

Sydney disappears down the hallway, the bathroom door banging shut a few seconds later.

Cassia doesn't step toward me.

She sure as hell doesn't kiss me.

"Where were you?"

I shove my hands into my pockets. "Finn called me, wanting to hang out. So I ended up spending the night at Arlington."

All true.

I haven't lied to her again.

Yet.

This is the obvious opening to come clean. To tell her *exactly* where I spent the night.

But my little sister—my *pregnant* little sister—is just down the hallway.

Cassia didn't even tell Sydney we all but broke up this summer. I'm certain she doesn't want to air out our dirty laundry now. And me sleeping in another girl's bed isn't exactly the sort of thing I can mention to her and then say we'll discuss it more later.

So, that's all I tell her.

"How's Finn doing?" Cassia asks.

"He's…Finn."

"Did you see Harrison?"

"Yep." My molars grind, recalling our conversation before the party. There must be some sick irony in him apologizing just before I found out he slept with Sydney. "I'm gonna kill him."

"It's not his fault."

I raise one eyebrow. "It's *absolutely* his fault."

Cassia glances over one shoulder to make sure Sydney isn't back yet. "You really think this is what he was after? Come on, Holden, you know him."

"Turns out, I really don't."

"He's a good guy. It could be worse."

"Yeah. A *good guy* who's spent years telling me I'm too much of a fuck-up for you, but then turns around and knocks up my sister."

"Everyone makes mistakes."

I silently pray she's still this forgiving when I tell the rest of what happened last night.

"Sydney's spending the night here?" I ask.

"Yeah. I bought cookie dough. The plan is to stuff our faces in our pajamas."

I smile. "She's lucky to have a best friend like you."

Cassia closes the distance between us, running her hand up my arm. "I'm lucky to have *you*. You're my best friend too. And you're not a fuck-up."

It's hard to smile while what feels like a rusty blade saws my chest open, but I manage it. I want to rewind time so I can punch myself in the face last night.

I tilt my head down and kiss her. Once, tentative and soft. But as soon as I feel her respond, self-restraint dissipates.

"I'm glad you came over."

"I wanted to see you." I kiss her jaw. "I missed you." My lips move down to her neck, and a breathy moan leaves hers.

"I was *kidding*. You guys didn't actually need to make out." Sydney's voice douses the moment immediately.

I press one final kiss to Cassia's forehead and then step away.

Walk over to my sister. Beneath the bravado, I can see the strain in her expression. No matter what she decides, this will affect her.

"I'm sorry I freaked out."

"Actually, you reacted better than I thought you would," she says.

Any other day, I might have. I still feel like shit and I'm carrying around a lot of guilt about last night. I showed up here dreading telling Cassia and now I have to *keep* dreading telling her. Sydney's news—while shocking and concerning—has a lot to compete with.

"If there's anything you need, let me know, okay? If there are doctor visits or other stuff—" God, I have no clue what equipment babies require. "Just let me know. There's money Dad left that—"

"That money wasn't meant for…*this*."

"It was meant for *you*," I tell her. "However you need—or want—to spend it."

Sydney's smile wavers. "God, Dad would be so disappointed in me. I'm a cliché. History repeating itself."

"He would *not* be disappointed in you," I say.

Cassia walks down the hall and then slips into her bedroom, subtly giving us a moment of privacy.

"He loved you, Syd. *So* much. He'd love your kid the same way."

She exhales, chewing on her bottom lip. "I don't know if I can do this, Holden. I've never even thought about if I want kids. I'm supposed to go to London this semester. I got a scholarship for that program."

"You didn't tell me."

"Yeah, well…" She looks away. "It was supposed to be a 'Surprise, I'm going to London!' thing. Not a 'Surprise, I'm pregnant!' conversation."

"I can't make any decisions for you, Syd. But I'll support whatever you decide. And I'll kick Baker's ass if he doesn't do the same."

Her smile dies as quickly as it appeared. "What if I *am* history repeating itself, Holden? What if I'm *just like* Mom?"

"You're not."

"You don't know that."

"Yeah, I do. You're nothing like her now, Sydney. If you decide to be a mom, you'll still be nothing like her."

I want to tell her *selfishness isn't genetic*, but I'm not sure it's true. I used to use it as an inherited excuse. But now I know it has limits. Cassia ranks above any of my own interests. It's part of why I was so shocked when she told me she didn't think she was a priority to me. All the lies I've told…they were to protect her, not me.

"Yeah. I hope not," she says.

I didn't show up here planning to discuss my mom with Sydney.

And all it's done is remind me I'm keeping secrets—from both her and Cassia.

"I *know* not."

Sydney nods but I'm not sure she believes me. Maybe it's something she needs to realize on her own, the same way I did. Sydney has always seemed unscathed from our mother's abandonment. I was the one who acted out and resented. She simply acted like our mother never existed, and I'm now wondering how much of a performance that was.

"Thanks, Holden."

I hug Sydney and then force a smile. "I mean it. If you need anything, let me know. Okay?"

She nods. "I will. Thanks."

"I'll be around in the morning. Say bye before you leave."

"I will."

I glance toward Cassia's room, debating my next move.

Leaving without saying goodbye to her feels strange. But so does talking to her when I know secrets are piled between us. When I know I haven't been the only one withholding.

I'm not mad, exactly. I get why she didn't tell me, and I get it was a terrible position to be in. I even understand why Sydney didn't want to tell me.

But it stings, knowing Cassia knew and chose to keep this from me. It feels like a small betrayal. If she'd told me and asked me to keep it to myself, I would have. I thought we had the type of relationship where she would have trusted me on that.

It's absolutely my guilty conscience talking. The realization that I came here to get something off my chest and am leaving with more piled on is stifling.

"I begged her not to say anything."

"Yeah, you said."

"I mean it, Holden. Don't you dare get angry at her about this."

"I won't. I mean, I'm not." I glance toward the front door, then back to her room again.

"Then go *talk* to her. I'll cover my ears and close my eyes if you want. Just remember…" Sydney points to her stomach. "Consequences can happen."

"Jesus," I mumble as I walk past her.

Almost as bad as the pregnancy news is that Sydney seems to have lost her filter. She used to get all shy when anything remotely scandalous—drugs, drinking, sex—came up.

This brash version of my sister is unnerving, uncomfortable, and makes me a little sad.

She grew up fast, we both did. But this feels more like bitterness or cynicism than taking on responsibility.

Our mom resented the hell out of us for existing.

I don't think Sydney would ever abandon a child the same way our mom left us. She's too loving, too loyal. But I hate there might be some resentment beneath. That this baby is going to affect her whole future, the same way that we changed our mom's.

Cassia is sitting cross-legged on her bed when I enter her room. She's organizing her textbooks, which makes me grin.

"Nerd."

She glances up, then climbs off the mattress. "Slacker."

Both our smiles fade fast.

"I'm heading out. But, uh, we should talk soon. Once Syd leaves."

Cassia nods. "Yeah."

"Okay. Have fun with your girls' night." I muster another smile, this one forced. "Don't do anything I wouldn't do."

She smirks. "That rules out nothing."

"Yeah, well, you've always made better decisions than me."

Cassia steps closer, gnawing on her bottom lip. "I'm sorry I didn't tell you…"

"It's okay. I get it."

She studies my expression. "You're mad, though."

It's convenient and inconvenient, having someone know you so well. I'm surprised she can't read *I'm keeping secrets from you too* stamped across my forehead.

"I'm…shocked."

She nods, wrapping her arms around her waist. "Yeah. Me too."

I exhale, then glance around her messy room. It's still more settled than mine. "I'd better go unpack. I don't even have sheets on my bed yet."

"That's disgusting, Holden," Cassia tells me. "I'm not staying over unless you do."

"Cool. All the incentive I need." I step forward and kiss her. Her hands fist the front of my t-shirt, holding me in place. I wish I could stay here forever. Just keep kissing her and not have to think about all the messy shit I need to sort out.

But the longer I stay in here, the more safe sex comments Sydney will probably make when I leave.

Reluctantly, I pull back far enough to see her. Tuck a piece of hair behind her ear. "I love you, flower."

She smiles. "I love you too."

I kiss her one last time, then head for the door.

I didn't think it was possible to feel worse than I did when I arrived.

Turns out, it is.

CHAPTER EIGHTEEN

CASSIA

I'm changing into my pajamas when my mom calls. I hobble over to the door with one leg in the cotton shorts and one leg out, carefully closing my bedroom door. Sydney is in the kitchen, making cookies out of the dough we bought at the store earlier.

Placing them on the sheet and putting them in the oven, basically. We used to make homemade ones when we were younger, and they always turned out terrible.

She's probably out there wondering why I shut my door.

But I haven't told Sydney my parents are getting divorced.

Haven't told anyone, except Holden.

According to my mother, the list of people who know are me, my grandmother, and whoever the ambiguous work colleagues my dad talks to about his personal life are.

"Hi, Mom," I answer, leaning down to pull the other side of my shorts up.

"Hi, sweetheart. I just wanted to call and check in. How's everything going?"

"Uh, good. It's nice to be back."

"The apartment is nice?"

"Yeah, it's great."

Only half-unpacked, but nice. It's my mess in Pembrooke, just transplanted to a new location.

Proof running escapes nothing, maybe.

There's a prolonged pause as we both deliberate what else to say.

"How are you?" I ask.

"Oh, I'm fine." Her answer is quick. *Too* quick.

"Mom…"

"Don't worry about me, honey. Everything here is fine. Busy, like usual."

"Did you tell Maggie about the divorce before she left for college?" I ask.

"Cassia, it's nothing you need to concern yourself with."

I exhale, the huff saturated with annoyance I feel guilty aiming at my mom.

Nothing I need to concern myself with, which affects my entire family. Which affects me.

She's trying to protect me, I know.

To shield me from the ugliness of what I always viewed as a perfect relationship. An ideal marriage. A happy ending.

"Classes start tomorrow, right?" Her cheerfulness is deliberate. Forced.

I can hear the twins arguing in the background.

My mom is trying to hold everything together. I'm not going to be the one who tugs at the stray thread.

"Right. I got all my textbooks earlier. My Genetics one is about a billion pages. A little intimidating."

My mom laughs. "You can handle it, honey. You always do well."

That's me.

Reliable. Dependable. Studious.

Part of me wonders what she would have said if I hadn't corrected her about the pregnancy test. If my future had just been affected the same way Sydney's was. Would she have been supportive? Disappointed?

"I know. God forbid I get a B."

A beat of silence. "Cassia, that's not what I meant. I'm always proud of you, no matter what grades you get in school."

I exhale. "I know. I'm sorry. Just…long day."

I'm taking everything out on my mom, which isn't fair. She's only one half of the equation and the only one available to direct my feelings toward.

I thought my dad working constantly was a sign of his devotion to our family. Turns out I couldn't have been more wrong.

He might be providing financially, but that's it. He didn't attend one of Regan's swim meets this summer. Wasn't there to pick the twins up from soccer camp once. The sedan malfunctioned in July, and he said he'd look at it on one of the rare evenings he was home for dinner. It had to be towed to a mechanic.

"I've had a few of those myself," my mom says. "I should go serve up dinner. I'll talk to you soon. Okay, honey?"

"Yeah, sounds good."

"Bye, Cassia. I love you."

"I love you too," I say, then hang up and toss my phone onto the bed.

Finish getting dressed and find Sydney standing at the kitchen island scrolling on her phone.

The timer for the cookies buzzes a couple of minutes later. We transfer them to a plate without bothering to let them cool, the chocolate smearing across the china in a gooey brown mess.

We settle on the couch with the cookies, plus seltzers and

popcorn. The air conditioning is finally working. The living room vent is right next to me, raising goosebumps on my skin.

"What do you want to watch?" I ask, turning on the television and starting to scroll through the options. Thanks to my lack of a social life this summer, I've already seen all the recent releases.

"I'm jealous of you," Sydney says suddenly.

I glance over at her. She's playing with the hem of her shirt, a glum look on her face. "What? Why?"

"Because you got the guy." She makes a face. "Don't get me wrong, it's weird that he's my brother. But if I pretend that he's not, that he's just *a* guy who looks at you the way Holden does… We both know I heard all the same rumors you did in high school, about the fights and the drinking and other girls. You always acted like you didn't care."

Her expression turns wry, both of us knowing I cared a whole lot, even if we never discussed it at the time.

"I just mean, you have a person. Someone has your back and cares no matter what. If you got pregnant accidentally, you'd know he was *in*," she continues. "That sounds pretty freaking nice right now."

"Harrison will—"

"It's *different*, Cassia. I know Harrison will step up. But it'll be different. You have someone who would see it as more than an accidental obligation. Holden would be excited. Supportive. Protective."

I open my mouth, ready to refute. Recall Holden's stunned expression earlier. That didn't look like excitement to me. I have no clue how he'd react, honestly.

Sydney shakes her head, stopping me. "You don't have to say anything. Maybe I'm a terrible best friend for saying anything. I'm not trying to make you feel guilty or feel more sorry for me than you already do. I'm hormonal and scared." She snorts. "Who would have thought, out of the two of us, that Holden would end up in a long-term relationship and I'd get knocked up from a one-night stand?"

"We've had plenty of problems, most of which you've witnessed. No relationship is perfect, but ours definitely isn't."

"You got through it all, though. That means something too."

Your parents aren't us. They made it really far. Just not all the way to the finish line. We will.

I heard the confidence—the certainty—in his voice. I believe him. And I appreciate it more, absorbing what Sydney is saying. My feelings for Holden terrify me. They also symbolize the safest I've ever felt.

"I want you to be happy, Cassia. Same with Holden. You guys give me hope of finding that person. All I'm trying to say is…I know I don't have what you two have with Harrison. It wasn't just the sex that was uncomfortable and awkward. None of it felt right or easy. And…" Her hand falls to her stomach, rubbing tiny circles. "That's *sad*, more than scary. I was the kid born to two parents who didn't love each other. I never wanted that for my own baby."

I study her profile, deliberating how to respond. Not sure what I can say to make her feel better. "All you can do is make your own choices, Syd."

She exhales, nodding.

"You and Holden grew up without a mom, and you both turned out pretty great." I second-guess it as soon as I say it. Her mom is a topic Sydney and I don't discuss. "You don't need a perfect family. You'll meet another guy, who it *does* feel right and easy with. Harrison will be there, even if it's not the exact way you wish it was between you. And you have me. Holden. If you think this kid will lack love…it won't."

She sniffles and nods. "Thank you." Grabs a cookie. "Can we

watch a comedy? So far, this has been the most depressing girls' night we've ever had."

I huff a laugh. Hand her the remote.

"We can watch whatever you want."

Sink back against the cushions.

Wonder what Sydney would say, if I told her that I know of a couple who had *six kids* together, then decided to separate. Who went through all the steps you're supposed to and still ended up walking on different paths at some point.

That what you're aiming for—what you're jealous of—is rarely as ideal as it looks.

That nothing is as solid as it seems.

It's reassuring and discouraging.

There's nothing to fall short of.

But if that's the case, what's the point of even trying?

CHAPTER NINETEEN

HOLDEN

I spin, dodging the reach of an invisible opponent. The smack of rubber against varnished wood echoes around the cavernous space before I shoot, the orange ball arcing through the air to swish through the net.

My sneakers squeak against varnished wood as I pivot to grab another ball off the rack. I go in for a layup next, my fingers brushing the metal rim as I watch the ball fall through.

"I figured I'd find you here."

I turn, watching Sydney walk across the empty court.

I'm alone in here, just a bunch of basketballs littering the ground that I'm putting off picking up.

Sydney has come up to Richmond for a few of my games over the past three years, but this is the first time she's been in the gym when it's like this—hallowed and silent.

It's quieter than a church. Huge and empty. And while it's not the same as being at the court back in Pembrooke, it's the closest thing to it. It's so huge in here, all my problems look small.

I could really use that perspective right now.

"You weren't answering your phone," she says, stopping a few feet away and shoving her hands into the pockets of her shorts.

I glance toward the bleachers, where my bag sits. "Sorry. I lost track of time."

Sydney nods, chewing on her bottom lip.

"Did you guys have fun last night?"

"Yeah, it was great. Aside from the obvious. Felt like the old days when she'd sleep over on Friday nights."

I smile, nostalgic for those nights too. I was always eager to get home and find out if Cassia would be in the kitchen. Should have figured out back then I was a total goner for the girl. That the feelings I thought were an adolescent crush wouldn't go anywhere, no matter how hard I tried to ignore them. And God, did I try.

It's always been her for me.

"Good." I pause, trying to figure out what else to say.

"This isn't your problem, Holden," Sydney says. "It's mine."

I nod, although I'm silently disagreeing. We both know that isn't true.

We're the only reliable family each other has. It would be different if our dad was still alive. If our mom had stuck around. If she and Harrison were in a relationship.

But if Sydney decides to have this baby, she'll need me.

And I'm not just stressing about that.

Her pregnancy added a new, complicated layer to the decision of whether or not I tell her about our mom's illness.

I rest the basketball I'm holding on my hip. "When are you going to tell him?"

She looks up at the row of shiny banners hanging from the ceiling. "I don't know."

I shake my head. "Fucking Baker."

Shock and guilt dulled a lot of my anger yesterday.

It's back this morning in full force. I'm trying to tamp it down because I know it won't help the situation and won't change anything. But it's still there, festering. Even if he hadn't gotten her *pregnant*, I can't believe he touched her.

He should have taken her out on a date first, at the fucking least.

Mentioned his interest to me.

That he didn't do either of those things tells me she didn't mean anything to him, and that makes me furious.

And he *did* knock her up. I can't direct any of my anger about the situation toward Sydney without making her feel worse than she already does. But Baker? As far as I'm concerned, he fucked up my sister's whole life. Put her in this impossible position.

"Harrison didn't do anything wrong, Holden," Sydney tells me.

I lift an incredulous brow. "You've gotta be kidding me."

"I'm positive he didn't mean to knock me up."

"So he's incapable of putting on a condom?"

Sydney's cheeks flush dark pink. "I can't believe we're having this conversation."

That makes two of us.

"Not that it's *any* of your business, but we used one."

"*You're* my business, Sydney. This...it affects you, so it affects me. You should have told me sooner."

"I was..." She exhales. "I was scared. I needed some time to process the possibility before I knew for sure. Cassia was the one who risked public embarrassment and bought the test for me."

I run my palm across the ball, recalling the terrible seconds yesterday when I thought the test was hers.

"Grace Harper is running her mouth around town about you, by the way. She cornered me at the coffee shop, asking questions that made me think stuff happened this summer that neither of you told me about. If it's none of my business, it's definitely none of hers. And if you fuck up things with Cassia, I'll never forgive you."

I swallow. I guess Grace has a short memory. Our conversation on the camping trip clearly didn't stick. Fortunately for Grace, I have bigger problems right now.

"I'd never forgive myself," I tell her.

Sydney smiles, hearing the honesty in my voice. "Good." She glances around. "Don't you have class?"

"One, this afternoon."

"Cassia left at seven this morning to go to the library before her first lab."

I grin. "I'm sure she did."

"Don't flunk out, okay? This is your last year."

"I won't flunk out," I promise.

"I'd better get going."

"Okay. Text me when you're back at the condo."

Sydney rolls her eyes, but nods.

I drop the basketball and hold my arms open. She steps into them, releasing a ragged exhale as I squeeze her tight.

"Love you, little sis."

"Yeah. I love you too."

———

I'm in the pasta line when the third stranger tells me he can't wait for this season. It's weird. Having strangers weigh in on my performance. Knowing the exact expectations in place.

I've always played basketball for myself, not the name on the front of the jersey.

Cheers and applause don't really register on the court. I'm focused on one goal: winning. Distractions don't help.

But it's hitting me a little differently this year. I want to play well so I have a chance to chase my own dreams. But I'm also conscious that this is possibly my last season. That this year could be as good as it gets for me.

And then there's a terrifying whisper in the back of my head, reminding me there's a chance I won't play this season at all. That I already peaked, and it's all downhill from here.

By the time I'm through the line and have my food, Cassia is already sitting at a table. I texted her after leaving the gym and showering to see if she was free for lunch.

So far, I haven't done anything to reassure her this year will be different from last year. She said we barely saw each other all spring, and she wasn't wrong. We haven't even had sex since we've been back on campus.

There are extenuating circumstances this time. Sydney's pregnancy. The Nolans' divorce. My mom's health. The blonde.

But Cassia only knows some of those secrets, so I add *another break* to the long list of things I'm currently stressed about.

She looks up from the textbook she's flipping through when I take the seat across from her.

"No way you're behind," I tease. "It's literally the *first* day of classes."

Cassia rolls her eyes and closes the book with a thud. It's as thick as all her science textbooks, well over a thousand pages.

"Just trying to figure out how many hours of reading I have tonight."

I mock-shudder at *hours*. I'm a business major, same as most athletes here to play sports, which requires plenty of reading but nowhere near the same workload Cassia carries. "How were your classes?" I ask.

She nods, taking a bite of her sandwich. Chews and swallows. "Good. Intense."

I nod too. For so long, senior year seemed a ways away. Now, all of a sudden, it's here. And it's different from high school. There was some uncertainty about where I'd end up then, but nothing in comparison to all the choices stretching ahead in front of me now.

"Sydney stopped by the gym earlier."

Cassia is focused on opening her salad. "Yeah, she said she was going to. How'd she seem?"

"Okay, I think. Better than…it's a lot to take in. If she keeps the baby, I'll be an uncle. Harrison will be a dad." I shake my head. "I'm still processing, I guess." I pause. "She said you bought the test for her."

"Yep. I ran into Mrs. Golden at the pharmacy. And then accidentally showed it to my mom."

My eyes widen.

Cassia's expression is wry. "I told them it wasn't for me. But…*you* thought it was mine."

I swallow, knowing she'll read the truth on my face. "For a second, yesterday, yeah."

"And you freaked out."

"Only because of the math."

Twin lines form between her eyes. "The math?"

"We were apart all summer, Cassia. If you just found out you were pregnant, it wouldn't be mine."

"You thought I'd do that?" Confusion has turned into hurt. A little anger.

"*No.* I wasn't thinking straight, Cas. I wasn't expecting… I walked into your apartment and there was a positive pregnancy test right in front of me, all of a sudden. I just…it caught me off guard."

Understanding flashes across her face. "You're the only guy I've ever been with," she whispers.

I knew that already.

But it doesn't temper the rush of relief and primal possessiveness from hearing her say it. It's the biggest turn-on, knowing it's a gift she's given to me alone. Which makes me the biggest hypocrite in the world, considering I've been with other people and can't say the same thing back.

I lean forward. "If we'd been together this summer, I wouldn't have freaked out for a second."

Cassia raises one eyebrow. "No?"

"No. I would have been thrilled."

She snorts, then stabs her salad with a fork. "You're just saying that because you freaked out and I brought it up."

"Nah. I'm not."

"We're twenty-one, Holden. I'm planning on four years of vet school. You want to play basketball professionally. And you would be *thrilled* about tackling parenthood?"

"I'm not saying the timing would be ideal. It would be hard. Challenging and stressful. But having a kid with you? I wouldn't freak out about that. I would wish for that."

A tiny smile appears on her face. "I can't picture you with a baby. I didn't even think you liked kids."

"I would like *our* kid."

She rolls her eyes. "Pretty sure it would scream and cry like anyone else's."

"Yeah, probably." I grin, then turn serious. "I mean it. If it happened…I want you to know I'd be more than okay with it. I hate that Sydney is going through this. That I can't fix it for her. But if it had to happen, I wish it was with a guy who meant something to her. I know Baker is a decent dude. I know he won't pressure her to end the pregnancy or ghost her and leave her to handle things herself. He'll step up. But..." I exhale. "It'll be about obligation and taking responsibility, not love. I mean, she hasn't even told him."

"It's a lot to dump on someone. I know you feel like she—I—kept it from you, but she didn't tell me right away. She'd been stressing about it on her own."

I hesitate, not sure if I should voice the question. Then decide to go for it. "Who's the first person you would tell? Honestly."

She plays with the lettuce. "You," she finally answers.

"You don't have to say that just because—"

"No, I mean it. And you're right. It would be different for us. I'd be nervous to tell you, knowing what impact it would have on our lives. But that's also why I would talk to you first."

I suck in a deep breath. I want that transparency and honesty from her.

And it's not fair to expect it if I'm not returning it. I have to tell her about Friday night.

"Hey, Adams. Hardly surprised to see you here, considering the fridge is empty."

"It's Henry's week to get groceries," I tell Robby.

"Uh-huh, sure. Hey, Cassia."

"Hi, Robby," she greets.

"Mind if I join you guys?" he asks.

"Of course not." Cassia slides her massive book over, making space.

"This yours?" He taps the shiny cover.

"Uh-huh." She takes a bite of salad.

"I figured. I don't think Adams even got his books yet."

Cassia looks to me, eyebrows raised.

"I *ordered* them," I tell her. "I just haven't picked them up."

"Hey, Reynolds! Johnson!" Robby calls. "Over here!"

A couple more of my teammates head this way.

I glance at Cassia, realizing that's the end of our private conversation. And I still haven't told her about Friday night.

Part of me is disappointed.

Most of me is relieved.

CHAPTER TWENTY

CASSIA

I'm the first one in my Genetics class. There were only fifty spots available during registration, but this lecture hall could easily fit a hundred students. It's a giant, cavernous space.

I choose a seat a few rows back and pull out my laptop and my textbook. Open up a fresh notebook and write the date at the top of the page.

There's still no sign of anyone else.

I'm ten minutes early.

Holden's teammates are all nice, but they're a rowdy group. I left lunch as soon as I was finished eating, stopping for a coffee and then coming straight here.

I look around the lecture hall, then quickly discover there's nothing interesting to see. Cream walls, gray carpet, whiteboard at the front of the room.

So I pull out my phone. I text my mom first, asking how she is. Text Maggie second, asking how her freshman year is going. Odds are I won't hear back from her for a while. The last message I sent is still unanswered. Finally, I text Sydney, asking if she's back in Pembrooke yet. I doubt she is, and it's an unnecessary question. But I don't want her to feel like she's alone. I didn't ask when Catherine will be back or if Sydney is planning to tell her about the pregnancy. But she's probably returning to an empty condo.

No one responds right away, so I switch to scrolling through social media. Predictably, Maggie has posted on there. I look through a few photos of her smiling and laughing, unsurprised she's already made more friends in a few days than I have in three years of college. We've always been so different that it's hard to contemplate that we're siblings. Maybe it's an anomaly we'll study in this class.

A few other students have started to trickle into the lecture hall, but none of them are people I recognize.

There's no sign of the professor yet.

I open my school email, clicking through the new messages about various campus events.

"...so hot, right?" A female voice says.

"I know," another girl responds. "Even better in person. How is that possible?"

"He has huge hands. And feet."

"That's what you were looking at? I was focused on his face."

I'm still looking at my phone screen but am shamelessly eavesdropping on the girls' conversation because it's more entertaining than reading about the library's hours or which school the football team is playing in the season opener.

"Well, you know what they say..." A giggle. "I wonder if we'll cover that theory in class."

"I don't care about the theory. I just want to see his dick in person."

"Good luck, girl."

My eyes are still on my phone, but I'm very tempted to look toward the voices behind me. The most scandalous thing I'd overheard in a lecture up until now was about petty drama with a roommate.

Maybe I've been sitting in the wrong spots.

Embarrassingly, I've often ended up seated in the front row. Most of my classes allow laptops, and it's distracting seeing people in front of you shop for clothes or play games instead of taking notes on the lecture.

"God, can you imagine walking up to *Holden Adams* and asking if you can see his dick? You know, for science?"

Both girls start laughing.

I freeze, realizing exactly who this conversation has been about.

Having no idea how to feel about it. Flattered? Annoyed?

Right now, I'm just uncomfortable.

I know Holden attracts female attention, obviously. And he *always* has. Back in elementary school, long before he'd kissed me or ignored me, he was the guy all the girls made paper Valentine's Day hearts for. I used to tease him about it when we'd play basketball in his driveway, saying if everyone knew he lost to a girl, they wouldn't still have crushes on him. Back before I identified the uncomfortable prick in my chest as jealousy.

Knowing is different from experiencing.

Before I can decide how to react—*if* I should react—Christine slides into the seat beside me. She's also pre-vet, so we've had nearly identical schedules since freshman year.

"Hey!" Her smile is bright and cheery as she settles into the chair.

"Hi!" I push away the awkwardness I'm experiencing and focus on Christine, watching as she unpacks her laptop and textbook from her backpack. "How was your summer?"

"It was great." She sits up, tucking a piece of hair behind one ear. "How about yours?"

I tap my pen against my notebook. "Uh, yeah. It was okay. I worked at the shelter a lot."

Christine is from Utah, so she's never visited me in Pembrooke. But I've told her plenty about the animal shelter.

My last day there this summer was especially difficult since I had to say goodbye to Milo. I'm hoping he'll still be there when Holden and I go back for the car wash. And also wish Milo finds a forever home sooner than then.

Christine and I continue catching up until the professor arrives. She just met with her academic advisor about vet school applications, which I'm supposed to do next week.

The course syllabi start circulating the room, and everyone settles down.

I stretch down and reach into the side pocket of my backpack for my water bottle, quickly glancing at the two girls sitting in the row behind me as I do. They're both beautiful, with flawless makeup and styled hair.

I spent about five minutes on my appearance this morning. I left early to go to the library before my first lab. My hair is pulled back in a messy ponytail, I'm wearing no makeup, and my t-shirt is a boring white cotton one.

Quickly, I turn back toward the whiteboard, not wanting the girls to catch me staring.

I'm not worried about me and Holden. I no longer feel like I'm clutching onto our relationship with both hands, the way I felt last spring. Doesn't mean I want the unwelcome reminder he has lots of options. That girls mob him after games and approach him at parties. I've seen some of the messages he gets sent on social media, despite the fact he's posted photos of the two of us, and it's pretty obvious he has a girlfriend.

It's hard to just *ignore* all that.

But I force myself to, flipping through the syllabus when it reaches me and starting to take notes as soon as the professor begins speaking.

I've worked so hard, for so long.

This is the last semester vet schools will see on my application. My final chance to make sure I have as many options as possible. I'm on the fourth lap of four, approaching the finish line. This isn't the time to slow down.

I direct all my attention to that goal.

Although part of me does wish I had turned around and told those two girls that *my boyfriend* does, in fact, have a huge dick.

Just to see the looks on their faces.

CHAPTER TWENTY-ONE

HOLDEN

Cassia's hand tightens around mine as we step into the crowded, hot house. Tomorrow is our first official practice of the season. It's just a weight session, one more of a thousand I've participated in. How I spent most of my summer. But it's also one of the first *lasts* of my college basketball career.

We always have a party the night before. It's a team tradition.

"I'm going to get a drink," Cassia tells me.

I nod, letting go of her hand. "I'm going to try to find Finn."

He always comes up to Richmond for this. I think he has more fun than the team does. He opted not to play in college, and I wonder if this is his way of admitting he misses it. It's hard to experience the camaraderie of sport anywhere else. The shared mindset, winning or losing together, it creates a different, stronger bond.

I wander deeper into the living room, bumping fists with a few teammates when I see them. Robby tosses me a can of beer.

I crack the can open, scanning the room for Finn. There's no sign of him. But I spot someone I wasn't expecting to see here. Deliberate for a few seconds, then walk over to him.

"No parties at Arlington this weekend?" I ask Brooks.

He studies me for a few seconds, then shrugs. He looks uncomfortable and out of place, standing alone in the corner. No drink and no girl. "Finn made the trip here sound like an open invitation," he tells me.

I look away, taking a swig of beer. I can't decide how I feel about Brooks. He reminds me of Harrison. He's friendly and chill, for the most part. But also gives me a judgmental vibe. And he was, or is, into Cassia. He lost to her that night at the court, and still spent the whole time grinning. Didn't exactly ignore her on the camping trip either.

"You rushed off fast the other weekend."

Unease ripples through me, recalling our interaction that morning. Finn never questioned where I spent the night, probably assuming I passed out on a couch somewhere. Brooks has a much better idea where I was.

I decide I'd be just fine with never seeing Brooks again.

"Had stuff to get back for," I say.

Brooks says nothing else.

My eyes focus on a figure headed this way. The crowd shifts slowly. I follow the admiring looks to her face once it becomes fully visible.

Fuck.

Brooks follows my gaze. "Bailey asked around about you." He pauses. "She came downstairs that morning, right after you did."

"Nothing happened. I got wasted and crashed in the first empty bedroom I found. It happened to be hers. I told her I had a girlfriend and got the hell out of there as fast as I could when I woke up. The end." The words are a panicked rush. I never expected to see the blonde again. Never even considered the possibility. I mean, what are the damn odds?

Brooks nods slowly. "Bailey doesn't give much credence to anyone's relationship status. Or her own."

"You're speaking from experience," I surmise.

He releases a long exhale. "Yeah. The one girl?" He nods toward the blonde. She's paused to talk to some guy. "Her."

"She cheated on you?"

"Yeah." Brooks shakes his head, then takes a long pull from the can he's holding. "With my best friend."

"That's brutal, man. I'm sorry."

"Me too. You can't buy loyalty. Shouldn't take it for granted either."

He aims a pointed look my way, and my molars grind together. There are lots of guys—at this school and on this planet—who would be better for Cassia. Who are richer and smarter and less likely to make stupid, drunken mistakes that result in waking up next to a naked stranger.

But none of them know her the way I do.

None of them love her the way I do.

Oftentimes, history gets a negative connotation. We avoid repeating it. Learn from it. Sometimes, we celebrate it.

But we rarely revel in it. Appreciate it. But so much of my past with Cassia—the first time we met, playing basketball in my driveway, the first time we kissed—is history. And there's a weight and importance to that.

Something unique we share with each other and no one else.

Cassia appears beside me, holding a red cup.

Finn is right behind her, grinning widely. "Hey, Adams! Been looking for you."

Panic spirals through me as I nod at him. Nowhere near meeting Finn's enthusiasm.

I'm focused on her.

"Cassia, I need to talk to you."

She's not paying me any attention. Ignoring the urgency in my voice that's lost in the commotion around us.

"Hey, Brooks," she greets, smiling at him. "Finn just mentioned you were here."

The blonde—Bailey—is looking this way.

Walking this way.

I can't believe this is happening.

It's one of those terrible moments where everything is happening in slow motion, but you can do nothing to stop it.

I'm still planning to tell Cassia about the drunken mistake that was last weekend. But I *haven't*. I've put it off and allowed interruptions because I never foresaw this situation. I knew it would look bad—the longer I didn't tell her.

The test results are supposed to come back next week, and I was waiting to lump it all into one sucky conversation.

To explain the entire situation at once.

Why I was in Pembrooke.

Why I was so upset that night.

What my choice is. Either I'm not a match and my mother will most likely die, or I am a match and I'll have an impossible decision to make.

Knowing the blonde's name.

Having her here—in the same house as my girlfriend—means my time has whittled down to nothing.

I waited to tell Cassia so I could share the full story, and now I don't even have that. I just waited to tell her, and that makes a bad situation look even worse.

Brooks glances over at me. He's the only one who has any clue what's about to take place. His expression is caught somewhere between distaste and pity, like a judge handing down a guilty verdict.

"So this is where you guys all went off to. Stick around so a girl can get her bearings next time, huh?" The sound of her voice grates my ears, like nails screeching on a chalkboard.

"What happened to Kayla?" Finn asks.

I guess he knows her too.

Bailey shrugs, then tosses her hair over one shoulder. She's wearing a tight, short dress meant to draw attention. The nearest group of guys are all laser-focused on her ass.

Her eyes settle on me. "Nice to see you, Holden."

I want to walk away, but I force myself to stay still and simply nod. I feel Cassia's eyes on me.

"I didn't know you guys knew each other," Finn says, glancing between me and Bailey. He's drunk or oblivious or both.

"We don't, really. He just spent a Friday night in my bed." Bailey smirks, then takes a sip from the cup she's holding.

Cassia stiffens beside me.

I want to punch something.

Finn scoffs. "What the hell are you talking about? Holden wouldn't—" Then he catches a glimpse of my face, which must convey that I *would*, that I *did*, and he finally shuts up.

"Excuse me," Cassia says. Then walks off.

I don't bother with a pleasantry.

I bail on the group and chase her down.

She's already in the hallway by the time I catch up.

"Cassia!" I call. "Cassia, stop!"

She does. Whirls on me with an expression that chills my blood.

"What the *fuck*, Holden?"

She's speaking at a normal volume, but I flinch like she's shouting.

"I…"

She's looking at me, waiting for an explanation, and I feel about two inches tall. Wish, more than anything, that I could tell her I have no clue what that girl was talking about and that I've never seen her before in my life.

Wish I wasn't having to ask her forgiveness *again*.

"Nothing happened," I blurt.

That seems like the most important detail to convey. It sounds bad, and it probably looked even worse—at least Bailey didn't mention she was naked—but it's true.

"I can't believe this." Cassia scoffs, shakes her head, and then turns away.

I grab her arm as a reflex, holding her in place.

"I swear. I can explain—"

She steps away. "Unless you want this to be the last time you touch me, *let go of me*. And unless you want this to be our last conversation, *stop talking*."

"I just want to make sure that you know—"

She steps closer, so I can hear the anger in her voice perfectly over the loud music playing. "What I know is that you weren't in Pembrooke last weekend. You lied about that. *Nothing happened*? How do I know you're not lying about that too?"

"Because I *wouldn't*, Cassia! You know me, better than anyone. After everything we've been through, you really think I cheated on you?"

"I don't know what to think, Holden! She said you were in her bed. And you didn't deny it."

I swallow, because I can't. Not then, not now. "But I didn't touch her. I—"

"You were drunk, right?"

I hear the implication loud and clear. She has every right to be pissed at me. But some anger sneaks into my voice too.

"Yeah, I was wasted. But there's not enough alcohol in the world to make me fuck someone else."

She shakes her head. "You've told me so many lies I don't know what the truth is anymore."

Cassia yanks her arm away and stalks down the hallway into the kitchen. I don't chase her this time. I lean back against the wall, sucking in deep breaths. The window next to me is open, but I feel like all the oxygen around me is burning away.

"Holden? What the hell is going on?" Finn appears next to me, his usual grin replaced by concern.

My jaw tightens like a taut rope. I force it to relax so I can say, "I fucked up. Again."

I want to drink until I feel numb.

I want to punch something until all I can feel is the pain.

But I don't move. Don't do either of those things, because I'm trying to grow the fuck up.

And if I lose her, I'm not sure there's enough alcohol or agony in the world for me to ever feel okay.

––––––––

I last about five minutes before I go looking for Cassia. Even if she can't talk to me—won't look at me—I need to be near her. I search the backyard and the living room before ending up in the kitchen.

It's most crowded in here since it's where the drinks are located. I find a spot by the fridge and scan around, looking for a dark head of hair.

"Can you pass me the vodka?" someone asks.

I glance over, register it's Bailey beside me, then reach over and push the glass bottle on the counter even farther away.

"Guess not." She rolls her eyes.

"What the fuck is wrong with you?" I snap. "I told you I have a girlfriend!"

Bailey shrugs. "She deserved to know."

"Know *what*? You said nothing happened."

She taps her chin with a pink fingernail. "Did I say that? I don't know. I was pretty drunk too."

I shake my head. "Even if I was the kind of asshole who cheated on his girlfriend, I know nothing happened. You're not my type."

She smirks. "What? You're not into blondes?"

"I'm not into girls who stir up drama because they're bored and lonely."

"Please. I can get any guy I want."

"Looks like you're all alone to me, Bailey."

Her smile turns pleased. "You asked around for my name, huh?"

"No. The guy you *cheated on* mentioned it to me. You screwed up your own relationship, so now you're trying to fuck around with other people's? Get a life."

Bailey's smile fades slowly as she attempts to keep her composure. She looks away, hopefully regretting approaching me. "Whatever."

"Not *whatever*. You want to party here? Fine. But stay the fuck away from me."

"Sure." She smirks. "You weren't that great in bed anyway."

I force my expression to remain neutral, because I'm certain a reaction is exactly what she wants.

She says nothing else as I walk away. Maybe some of what I said sunk in. Probably not. I have other priorities right now.

There's no sign of Cassia in the kitchen, so I head into the hallway. I pull out my phone and try calling her. It goes to voicemail.

Then I spot her roommate by the front door and beeline for her.

"Nova! Have you seen Cassia?"

"Ten minutes ago, maybe? I think she went upstairs."

Heart racing, I head for the stairs. Basically sprint up them, knocking into several people.

The first door is locked. Same with the second. I continue down the hallway, deciding to try them all before I make more of a scene.

Maybe she's in the bathroom. Maybe Nova was wrong, and she's not even up here.

She's already mad at me.

Breaking down doors won't help.

But I've heard the horror stories about what happens to girls at wild parties. And I would never forgive myself if that happened to Cassia.

The fourth door opens, but the room isn't empty.

Cassia glances over from her seat at the end of the bed, then away.

"I don't want to talk to you."

"I know." I exhale, relief coursing through me. Close the door. Lock it behind me.

She doesn't react as I walk over and take a seat on the opposite side of the bed, leaving plenty of distance between us.

I stare at the posters on the walls.

Whoever lives in here, they've got shitty taste in art.

The silence lasts for a few minutes before she speaks.

"Don't you have something else to do?" Her voice is all snark.

"Nope." I pop the P.

"It's not even midnight. *Plenty* of time to get wasted and crawl into a hot blonde's bed."

I know she's mad.

I know I fucked up.

But I'm glad she's facing away from me so she can't see my smile. God, I love her.

"It shouldn't have happened, and I should have told you that it did. But—"

"I said *I don't want to talk*, okay? Respect that or leave."

"Okay," I say, quietly.

I don't know how much time passes before Cassia lies down on the bed.

I don't know how much time passes after she does.

My phone keeps buzzing in my pocket, but I don't pull it out.

I just sit on the side of the bed, my elbows resting on my knees in the same pose as the rare times I sit on the bench.

Staring at the signage for a band I've never heard of that features skulls and roses, waiting until she's ready to talk.

CHAPTER TWENTY-TWO

CASSIA

He hasn't left.

I keep waiting for him to leave, but he hasn't.

The silence is both peaceful and tense.

I can hear the muffled beat of the loud music downstairs. Occasionally, someone will shout in the hallway or bang against a door. There's a steady pounding in the room next to this one that makes me think another couple is making very different use of the bed in there.

I don't even know whose bed I'm lying on right now. One of his teammates'?

I don't know what to think. How to feel.

I just got blindsided.

And I didn't think Holden would blindside me. That he *could*.

I thought we were honest with each other, almost painfully so. He knows all my insecurities and fears. I'm stripped bare and vulnerable, feeling stupid for not asking more questions about his visit to Arlington last weekend. Wanting to know exactly what happened and also feeling like I'll fracture into tiny pieces talking about it.

My feelings for Holden have always balanced on the fine line between love and hate.

That line has never looked thinner.

I love him. I love him so, *so* much.

But right now, I also hate him to a painful degree. It actually *hurts*, like there's a splinter shoved into my chest.

Do I think he cheated on me?

No.

But the smug expression from a blonde in a low-cut dress and the guilty, panicked expression on Holden's face had me considering the possibility.

He admitted he was drunk. *Wasted* was the word he used. And I've always known Holden has the tendency to self-destruct. To make stupid choices without thinking or caring about consequences.

The blonde's superior smile is burned into my brain.

She wants him.

Girls have *always* wanted him, and I'm sick of always second-guessing myself. It's the girls in my Genetics class all over again. You can only rise above so many times before the low road looks a lot more appealing.

It feels like I'm sixteen again, staring at Grace Harper draped all over him in the hallway outside my homeroom.

My parents have been married for more than two decades and have six kids. They couldn't manage to make it work forever.

Instead of the success story I always thought they were, they're proof that sometimes love isn't enough. That's an open wound that's burning right now.

I can't tell my best friend because Holden is her brother. I don't want Sydney knowing and getting angry on my behalf when she needs his support with everything she's got going on right now. I can't talk to my mom, who's dealing with plenty already.

She doesn't need to worry about my relationship on top of her own. Nova is never home to talk to, and it feels too personal to confide in anyone else.

I feel betrayed, and not just by Holden. I always felt like love was something I had a solid example for, some model to follow.

Now it feels like I'm groping through a dark room, just hoping I'll make it across without crashing.

I roll my head to glance at him.

Holden's back is stiff with tension, his posture rigid as he leans forward on his elbows.

He hasn't said a word since I told him to be quiet or leave. And he's stayed. He didn't listen when I told him to stay away earlier. He fought like I wanted him to when I brought up a break.

I know I'll forgive this.

Maybe it makes me pathetic or at the very least a hopeless romantic, but I know he's *it* for me. Know I'll never love another person the way I love him.

I'm not sure there's anything he could do that I *wouldn't* forgive, which is terrifying.

But it's also the truth.

If the alternative was never talking to him again? Never touching him again? I couldn't live that way, voluntarily walk away, having experienced being with him and knowing what it was like.

He's the person with the power to hurt me most in the world.

Even hearing about my parents' divorce didn't invoke this level of devastation. They'll always be in my life individually. No matter what happens between them, they'll always be my mother and father.

If Holden and I end, there's no guarantee he'll be anything in my life. Nothing more than my best friend's brother, at least.

And I can't imagine anything more crippling than that—having all of him and then going back to anything less.

Anger is harder to hold onto when I accept that inevitability.

I'm still upset and hurt though.

I sit up, reaching down and picking up the plastic cup I poured before coming up here to brood. Take a sip and gag because I wasn't exactly measuring. It tastes like straight tequila.

Maybe it is. I can't remember if I put anything else in here.

When I glance over at Holden again, he's already looking at me.

I clear my throat and stand, rounding the side of the bed until I'm standing right in front of him. His forearms flex but he doesn't reach for me. His head tilts back to meet my gaze.

We stay like that. Me standing and him sitting.

So many emotions expanding in the air between us they feel like a third presence.

I'm not really sure what to say. How to vocalize the conclusion I just came to. Everything we've already overcome and everything we will still face seems like smaller obstacles after my little epiphany.

Inevitability is scary and reassuring.

His blue eyes scan my face, filled with worry and silent questions.

I keep waiting for him to speak first. Of the two of us, he's the one who owes explanations.

I take another sip of tequila, making a face when the smoky liquor burns my throat.

Then I remember why he's not saying a word.

I step into him, his knees parting to let me in closer. Drag my fingers through his messy hair, the red cup teetering dangerously close to spilling in my loose grip.

"Stop doing things I'll have to forgive," I whisper. "Because I'll hate you a little more, every time."

He swallows, his Adam's apple bobbing. Nods.

"Remember that party in high school? The one Harrison invited me to? If I'd been in bed with him upstairs, even if nothing else happened, how would you have felt?"

"I would have punched him instead of that cabinet."

My eyes fall to his right hand. His fist is clenched, the white scars on his knuckles evidence of the many times Holden has chosen violence.

"Look at me, Cassia."

I raise my gaze slowly, reluctantly, worried poking a sore spot from our past was the last thing this conversation needed. "You have every right to be pissed at me. If you don't want to talk to me or look at me, I'll respect that. But I need you to know I love you and I'm in love with you and that won't ever change."

A huge lump appears in my throat. "It could," I whisper. "Lots of people fall out of love."

"We're not lots of people, flower. We're not your parents. We're us."

I nod, running my hand through his hair again. He leans into my touch, some of the stiffness disappearing. Sip more tequila.

"I had no idea she'd be here."

That, I believe. I saw the surprise on his face. "I don't want to talk about it yet."

"Okay."

We revert to silence until my cup is empty.

I set it down on the side table and step away.

All of Holden's attention is on me, his eyes tracking every movement like I'm an opponent on the basketball court. It feels good. Right.

I hold his gaze as I pull up the hem of my dress. It's daring—for me—short with an open back.

I felt pretty in it until I saw the blonde stroll over in her skintight outfit. But those are my insecurities. Nothing to do with her.

And I feel more than pretty as I tug the fabric up my thighs. I feel sexy and confident. Loved.

There's a full-length mirror attached to the wall next to the dresser. I can see half of my reflection, the flash of lace as my underwear comes into view. The length of my leg.

I lean back against the wall, holding my dress up with one hand and rubbing my clit through the lace with the other. The last time I touched myself in front of him, Holden went absolutely feral.

And I need that right now.

Nothing sweet or soft or tender.

He stands, and my heart stutters.

"I hate that poster so much." He nods toward the frame on the wall next to me. "Been staring at it for what feels like forever."

I laugh, and it feels good.

He reaches me. "This view is *way* better."

"That's not much of a compliment." My voice breaks halfway through *compliment*. Because touching myself in front of him—having him watch me—is almost as arousing as having him touching me.

"Yeah, you're right," he says. "How about this? You're the most loyal person I've ever met. How you stand by your friends? Your family? Anyone you care about is so lucky. And you're so smart, Cassia. Anywhere you apply is going to accept you, because there isn't a vet school in the country that wouldn't be better off for having you as a student. And you're gorgeous. The most beautiful girl I've ever seen. No matter what you're wearing, when I get to see you wearing nothing at all…I have to remind myself that you're real."

"You're not bad at loving," I whisper.

Holden smiles, then his gaze falls to my hand. It's no longer moving. My focus is all on him instead of chasing pleasure.

"You sure?"

"Yeah."

He steps closer, his hand landing on my thigh and sliding up until he's the one holding my dress.

I press my face into the hollow of his throat, inhaling the scent of cinnamon. The smell of home.

Deliberately, I graze his dick before lifting my hand and tangling it in his hair. My lips press to the side of his neck, and I suck the skin—hard. It's a punishment and a prize.

It's also a marking.

A reminder for all the girls downstairs.

He's *mine*.

Holden's cock thickens against me, in response to the hickey or the way I'm grinding against him, or maybe both.

He pulls back, just far enough to unbuckle his belt and tug down his boxers. Our bodies press together and our mouths collide in a desperate, messy kiss.

Holden devours me like I'm oxygen.

Like I'm something vital to him.

My hand finds the thick length bobbing between us, and he groans as I stroke, breaking our kiss. "Fuck." He hisses when I squeeze tighter than usual, but there's pleasure laced in the pain. "I love you so much."

I roll my eyes. "You love hand jobs."

He chuckles, but then something grows still and serious between us. "Only from you."

I hold his gaze. He reaches for my underwear, pulling the lace taut so it rubs exactly where I want his cock.

"Only you," he says.

I swallow, the words rubbing and soothing a wound that hasn't fully healed.

"For now."

"For*ever*." There's a sharp note to his tone that wasn't there before. His hips push into mine, erasing all the space between our bodies.

"Prove it," I whisper.

He smirks as I writhe against him, trying to get his dick inside of me.

"There's an old condom in my wallet," he tells me. "If you want me to wear one."

I blink at him, not missing the way he emphasizes *old* and *you*. We haven't used condoms since before starting college. At first, I think it has to do with Sydney and his reaction to seeing the pregnancy test. And then I realize exactly what he's doing.

He's forcing me to admit I believe him.

To not hide from what happened downstairs.

If I think there's a chance he cheated, I'm jeopardizing my health by letting him come inside of me.

I shake my head and shift my hips, savoring every inch that stretches me open.

There's something indescribably intimate about being completely connected with someone you trust and love that runs much deeper than physical pleasure.

Because I *do* trust Holden.

I'm demonstrating how much I trust him right now.

"It's only you, flower. It's only ever been you and it only ever will be you."

He hooks one of my knees on his hip, hitting a deeper spot inside of me that makes stars spark behind my eyelids.

"I'm insanely attracted to you. I'm addicted. To your tits and this tight pussy and this mouth."

His thumb runs across my bottom lip.

"And if you're ever doubting that, I want you to remember this moment."

The speed of his thrusts picks up, pounding into me in an unrelenting rhythm. We're making way more noise than the couple next door.

"I want you to remember how deep I am inside of you. How hard I am for you. I'm buried inside of you, and I already want to fuck you all over again. You're *mine*, Cassia, just like I'm yours."

That last declaration is what sends me over the edge.

I come with a loud cry, my inner muscles spasming around him as everything shatters in pleasure. So lost in the swell of ecstasy that I'm barely aware of the warmth seeping inside of me when he finishes, a physical declaration of what he just told me.

Him marking me in the same way I marked him.

CHAPTER TWENTY-THREE

CASSIA

Brooks is the first person I see when I step inside the campus coffee shop. His eyes light up as soon as he spots me, heading straight this way.

"Hey."

"Hi." My greeting is more hesitant than his, so I force a smile to make up for it. "Are you transferring here or something?" I tease.

"Uh, no." Brooks chuckles, but it comes out sounding a little forced. "I never sleep well in a new place. Especially if that *new place* is a flat sectional at a frat house."

"Yeah, I'm the same way," I admit. "Technically, we call it the basketball house, not a frat house."

"I thought the party last night was at the basketball house."

"The JV house. Holden's place is called Varsity."

"That's a thing in college? I thought that was just high school."

"It depends on the university. Basketball is big here, so they do."

"Bishop and James are on JV? They're massive."

I smile and shake my head. "No. They're seniors on varsity too. But Holden was the only freshman to make it onto varsity, so the nickname is more for him."

"Ah. He must be pretty good, then."

I nod. "He is." I glance ahead, wishing the line would move faster. "Are you guys headed back to campus today?" I ask.

"Yeah. Whenever Finn drags his hungover ass out of bed. That'll probably be a few hours from now, based on experience. Which you probably know."

I shrug a shoulder. "Sort of."

"What do you mean? Didn't you go to high school with him?"

"Yeah, I did. We weren't exactly part of the same social scene, though."

His nod is slow. "Listen, I'm sorry about Bailey."

I tense at the sound of her name. "Not your fault," I say.

"I should have seen it coming. I saw Holden leaving her house that morning. Then she decides to come up here this weekend, when she's never joined Finn before? All sus. I figured it was because I came. She sometimes goes on these crusades for us to get back together and I—"

"Wait." I glance at him. "Bailey is your ex? The one girl—the girl who cheated on you?"

"Yeah. Holden didn't tell you?"

I'm not sure if he means it that way or not, but I catch the subtle dig. The implication that Holden feeds me scraps and I take whatever he offers. That I get sections of stories and am okay with it.

So there's a slight edge to my voice as I tell him, "We had more important things to discuss."

"Everything is okay between you guys, then?"

Brooks knows I have a boyfriend. I know he knows I have a boyfriend. Clear lines have been drawn between us and any possibilities. But it also feels like he knows too much, and so it seems smart to continue redrawing them.

Rather than nod, I turn so I'm fully facing him. "Brooks, you seem like a really nice guy. And I'm sorry about what happened with Bailey. But we don't really know each other. *My* relationship with *my* boyfriend is none of your business. And things will *always* be okay between me and Holden. I'm sorry if I ever gave you the impression otherwise."

Brooks is already shaking his head, looking so apologetic I *almost* wish I'd just nodded. Almost.

"I'm sorry, Cassia. You're right, it's none of my business."

I hate confrontation, and I avoid it. I'm proud of myself for saying exactly what I was thinking for once, even if it's landed me in this awkward situation.

"All good," I say.

We reach the register, which is a relief.

I gesture for Brooks to order first. "I'm still deciding."

He goes ahead and orders an iced coffee—black.

My usual order.

After a forced minute of deliberation, I opt for the same.

"Can't go wrong," he comments, his smile tentative.

I smile back and nod.

I already knew Brooks and I were similar. Some common coincidences—like our science majors. And then little ones—like our limited sexual experience and avoiding alcohol. I'm not sure the second one applies to me lately. It used to, though. Sydney is the only other person I have those two things in common with, and she's my best friend. And she would have ordered the pink, frothy drink being promoted on the chalkboard.

I think if I still believed in ideals, he'd look a lot like mine.

My phone buzzes, and I pull it out to see a message from Holden.

HOLDEN: *Finished with practice. Are you free?*

I gnaw on my bottom lip for a few seconds, debating my answer.

CASSIA: *I'm at Daily Grind. Grabbing a coffee and then was going to study in the library...*

HOLDEN: *I'm almost to the student center. Be right there.*

CASSIA: *Okay.*

CASSIA: *Ran into Brooks here.*

The dots take a few seconds to appear.

HOLDEN: *Okay.*

There's not much to read into that response, so I pocket my phone and pull out my credit card to pay. Brooks tries to add my coffee onto his order but doesn't push when I insist on paying for myself.

"How is TAing going?" I ask.

Brooks groans. "I jumped at the chance to leave campus for the weekend. I think that conveys the gist of it."

I smile. "It'll get better."

"Or worse."

My grin grows. "Is this the first time you've visited Richmond?"

"I toured it, back in high school. Since then, no. I know Finn comes up a few times a semester, and it's always been an open invitation in the house. But Bailey was on campus...so I never had much incentive to leave."

I nod, grabbing a straw out of the metal canister stuffed with them.

The two girls standing on the opposite side of the island that stores all the coffee shop necessities—sugar packets and wooden stirrers and extra lids, plus canisters of milk—start whispering.

After three years on this campus, my first instinct is to look for Holden. And I'm right. He's running a hand through his damp hair as he joins the line in front of the register.

Brooks glances around, noticing the same phenomenon I've witnessed many times before.

Holden draws attention. Because of his looks. Because of his athleticism. Because he has *it*, whatever that elusive, intangible quality is that's more powerful than charisma.

"I figured that's who you were texting."

Clearly, my stealthy typing skills need work.

"We had plans to study…" I lie, because I still feel awkward about what I said earlier.

No guy has been brave enough to flirt with me since rumors started circling about me and Holden our senior year of high school. I'm automatically considered off-limits, because of some invisible code that Brooks's ex Bailey could learn a thing or two from.

If my life was very different—if me and Holden had never met but Brooks and I had—I could picture us as a couple. Because we would match, line up like two pieces from the same puzzle. I think we would have the same steady, reliable relationship that I used to think was the ideal.

I love Holden because of our differences, not despite them.

And I'm no longer certain *similar* has a solid outcome.

My parents were similar. Steady. Reliable. Until they weren't.

It's given me a new appreciation for the rollercoaster relationship I'm a part of. Maybe it means we face our issues head on, instead of letting little problems fester until they become big issues.

Brooks and I focus on the neutral topic of school until Holden joins us.

"Hey, Holden."

Holden nods. "Brooks."

"Finn is still sleeping, so I thought I'd explore campus a little." Brooks glances at me. "Do you think anyone here will care if I poke around the science center?"

I shake my head. "It's the brick building just past the library. The lounge areas and lecture halls are always open. It's just the professors' offices that get locked over the weekend."

"Great. Thanks. Nice to see you guys."

"You too," I say.

Brooks smiles, then heads toward the door.

I finish adding milk to my coffee, avoiding Holden's gaze. He always gets lattes because otherwise he complains his coffee is too strong or too weak when he dilutes it himself.

Once I've snapped the lid back on the cup, I glance up. Holden's expression is apprehensive, which I'm relieved by. I'd rather that than he pretend nothing was wrong.

We left the party shortly after having sex upstairs. Spent the night at my apartment. And then he left early this morning for his weight session.

"How was the gym?" I ask.

He rolls his shoulder, then winces. "A little rough."

"Did the whole team make it?"

"Owens was ten minutes late, but yeah."

I've never understood the questionable wisdom of the basketball team partying the night before the first practice.

According to Holden, it's a boost to morale. Play hard, party hard. The team that gets drunk together wins together. Drink as a team, dominate as a team. Some mentality like that.

All I can say is it makes me grateful study groups don't follow the same twisted logic. Then again, passing an exam isn't exactly a team sport. In the end, we're all looking out for ourselves.

"Coach had a whole last season speech."

"That must have been strange for the juniors and sophomores on the team."

His smile is brief. "It's *his* last season. Coach is retiring at the end of this year."

"Oh."

Holden nods. "Yeah."

I know he was already carrying around a lot of weight about this season. Responsibility. Hope. Dread. I'm guessing the pressure of a beloved coach's final season isn't helping.

The two girls are still standing on the other side of the table. Despite the early hour, they're sporting full faces of makeup and high, bouncy ponytails. And they're both staring at Holden.

He tilts his head toward the door, ignoring the attention. Maybe it's white noise to him at this point. "Library?"

I nod. "Yeah."

One week in, and I have a long list of assignments to tackle.

"Do you have any work to get done?" I ask, as we start across the covered walkway that leads to the library.

"Probably."

Holden's lazy attitude about academics drives me crazy, which he knows.

I roll my eyes and he smirks. Then grabs my hand and pulls me to the left. If there wasn't a cover on my coffee, I'd be drenched.

"Let's sit here for a sec." He pulls me toward an open picnic table on the campus green.

Nerves pinball around in my stomach. He wants privacy, which means he wants to talk.

I haven't decided what I want to know.

Ask.

Argue about.

And I'm out of time to decide.

CHAPTER TWENTY-FOUR

HOLDEN

I glance over at Cassia. Her face is tilted back as she straddles the bench's seat, soaking up the sunshine.

"What a beautiful day," she says before taking a sip of coffee.

A robin lands on the tree branch above us, chirping cheerfully. Neither the nice weather or the merry sound do much to calm the anxiety squeezing my stomach.

After last night, I think we'll be okay. I don't think this will be the mistake that damages us past repair. But I can't get the words she whispered—*Stop doing things I'll have to forgive. Because I'll hate you a little more, every time* —out of my head.

They echoed ominously in my head throughout my entire weight session. I can barely feel my shoulders right now, the muscles are so sore.

"Crazy that you want to spend it in the library," I tell her. "We could go for a hike or something."

"Maybe next weekend," she says.

"Next weekend is the car wash," I remind her. "We were going to go back to Pembrooke for it, remember?"

"Yeah, I remember. I just… I'm not sure if I want to go back." She fiddles with the straw of her coffee, avoiding my gaze.

"You can't avoid going home forever," I say softly.

There are many times I've dreaded returning to Pembrooke. Since my dad died, it feels like there's less there for me. The house I grew up in, gone. Lily, gone. I see my high school friends elsewhere. Sydney is usually in the city living her life. Cassia is here with me.

All I really care about there is that old court.

But I know for Cassia, Pembrooke has always been special. She has the big, memory-filled house and the happy family and the shelter that sparked her dream of becoming a veterinarian.

I hate that's changed for her.

That it's less of a home now.

She exhales. "Yeah, I know."

I do too, realizing I need to get into everything I've been avoiding telling her. It's not an excuse, but my mom's illness is important context for explaining how the situation with Bailey happened.

"I might have to start going back to Pembrooke a lot," I tell her.

Cassia looks at me, a wrinkle appearing on her forehead. "What do you mean?"

"Remember that day I came home when you and Sydney were twerking in the living room?"

"We were not *twerking*."

I grin, then sip some coffee. "Whatever. I told you how Mark got stung by a bee at the court and then we went to the emergency room because he's allergic."

Cassia nods. "Yeah, I remember."

"What I didn't tell you was that I ran into my mom when I was at the hospital."

She inhales sharply as soon as she hears the m-word.

"And that I found out that she's sick, dying. She has liver cancer and needs a transplant."

Cassia bites her bottom lip, her eyes filling with sympathy.

"I didn't know what to do. How to process it. Who to tell." I sigh. "I did some research. Online mostly. Then I called the hospital and talked to her doctor."

"You got tested to see if you could donate."

I nod, not surprised she knows all the information I spent hours researching about living donors. Flattered she thinks highly enough of me to jump to that conclusion.

"Yeah. I'm still waiting to get the results. After getting tested, I was in a bad place. If I'm not a match, my mom will probably die. If I am, I'll miss most of my senior season before I'm cleared to play. Finn called, talking about some party. I drank way too much and then when I woke up—"

She interrupts me. "It's okay, Holden."

I shake my head. "No, it's not. No matter what else was going on, it's no excuse for me being that stupid. I got drunk because I was trying to forget. Because I don't want to help her and if I do, it seemed like I should damage my liver as much as possible first."

Cassia snorts, pressing her lips together to keep the smile at bay. "That's terrible logic." Her expression turns sympathetic. "I get it, though. Why you felt that way."

"I got wasted, and at some point I went upstairs to find a place to pass out. When I woke up, she was there. Nothing that happened had anything to do with her. I'm not interested in her or attracted to her. I never flirted with her or touched her or wanted to. Going to that party was a mistake. So was drinking as much as I did. But that's all I'm asking for forgiveness for. I picked a shitty spot, but all I did was sleep. I swear. And I was going to tell you.

It wasn't supposed to be a secret. I went over to your apartment the next day to tell you, and then Sydney was there. Sydney was *pregnant*."

Cassia sucks her bottom lip into her mouth, nodding. Realizing.

"I do stupid stuff sometimes, Cassia. You already knew that, and I wish you didn't. I'm trying to stop. To be smarter. But *nothing* I've ever done has been to purposefully hurt you. It was *always* my messed-up way of protecting you. Not telling you about my mom made sense when you'd just found out about your parents and were dealing with that. And then everything with Sydney… It spiraled from there, and I'm so sorry about that. But I would *never* cheat on you. That's one thing I promise you never need to worry about."

"I believe you."

I exhale, the fist finally loosening. "You do?"

"I do. But I wish you'd told me about your mom. No matter what I have going on…we're supposed to be partners. A team. I want to know that stuff, for you to share it with me. Do you wish I hadn't told you about my parents? Just kept it to myself?"

"Of course not."

"That's the same way I feel. We don't have to talk about it. But just *tell* me."

"I will. I promise."

She nods. "Okay." Then sighs. "The longer I sit here, the later I'm going to have to stay in the library tonight."

"Let's go then." I round the side of the picnic table, offering her my hand to stand from the bench.

We start walking in the direction of the library. First holding hands, swinging them between us like we're little kids. We did this as younger versions of ourselves, before I tried to talk myself out of falling for her.

I tug her into my side, securely tucked under my arm.

I press a kiss to her hair, then whisper, "Don't hate me, okay?"

Cassia tilts her head back so I can see her expression. I'm not expecting the amusement. I was walking on eggshells even bringing up what she said last night.

"You know," she tells me. "No matter how hard I try to, it just never seems to stick."

I smirk. "I've never seen you fail at anything. So maybe you're not trying that hard."

"Yeah, that's possible." She glances at me. "It helps that you're hot."

"I had no idea you were so superficial, flower."

"Well, it's mine to appreciate, right?" She flutters her eyelashes and I really want to kiss her.

My chest is squeezing again, but this time it's not with fear. It's happiness. Gratefulness. I'm so, so grateful for this girl.

"Yeah. It's yours."

She smiles. "I can see it, you know."

"See what?"

"The finish line. *Us* at the finish line."

I smile. "Good."

CHAPTER TWENTY-FIVE

CASSIA

My phone buzzes in my pocket as I rush across campus toward the science center, my backpack banging against my spine in uncomfortable smacks.

Another buzz. I make sure there's nothing right in front of me I'm about to run into and then glance down at the screen.

It's Sydney.

I slow my steps to read her messages.

SYDNEY: *I turned down London. Staying in New York this semester.*

SYDNEY: *I told Harrison.*

I stop walking entirely, barely registering the "Hey!" as someone bumps into me.

"Sorry," I say, not looking up from my phone.

CASSIA: *And???*

Her responses to my texts lately have been sporadic and vague. We haven't talked on the phone since she visited.

I was considering asking Holden if we could go to New York to see her after stopping in Pembrooke for the car wash this weekend.

SYDNEY: *He proposed.*

"He *what*?" I screech when Sydney answers the phone.

As soon as I saw her text, I called her.

"I had to ask Finn Thomas for Harrison's number, which was an awkward beginning. And then I called him, which was way worse. We made small talk for a few minutes, and then I blurted it out. There was a *long* pause, and then he asked if we should get married."

"What did you say?"

"No thanks."

I don't quite manage to stifle my laugh. "How…uh, polite."

Sydney's exhale is half-amused, half-hysterical. "I don't know what the hell he was thinking."

"It's a lot to process."

"I know! And I'm already freaking out about it. We can't *both* be freaking out about it."

"You have a head start on freaking out. You've had a little time to process everything. He just found out. Give him a minute."

"Well, I lied and told him I had a class and we could talk tomorrow. Then hung up."

"It could have gone worse?"

"Yeah, I guess so. I didn't exactly have an ideal outcome. There's no easy answer here."

"I know," I say sympathetically.

I reach the steps that lead up to the Chemistry building's entrance but don't climb them yet. A slight breeze pulls a few strands of hair out of my messy bun. I run my fingers along the wrought-iron railing, watching other students stream in and out.

There's muffled commotion in the background on her end.

"Can we talk later?"

"Yeah, of course. Bye, Syd."

I hang up and rush up the stairs. I have exactly two minutes before the start of Genetics.

"Cassia!"

I glance over one shoulder as I pull the door open, smiling at Christine as she hurries up the stairs. Her cheeks are red, half of her hair falling out of the braid it's pulled back in.

"Hey!"

"The printer in the library was jammed." She huffs. "I just ran across campus like a crazy person."

I laugh, then pull out my phone. "We still have one…"

"Cassia? You coming?" I glance up, finding Christine staring at me expectantly. Her face creases in response to whatever expression I'm wearing.

I didn't even realize I'd stopped walking.

REGAN: *Did you know Mom and Dad are getting divorced?*

I stare at the message from my little sister, my throat tightening.

I'm looking ahead but seeing nothing.

For the first time—ever—I don't want to go to class. I'm not excited about learning something new or anxious about the prospect of missing a lecture.

I'm numb.

I feel empty.

"Um, no. I'm, uh, actually not feeling great. So I'm just gonna…go."

I stuff my phone into the back pocket of my shorts.

Worry flashes across Christine's face as she takes a step toward me. "Do you want me to walk back with you?"

"No, no. I'll be fine. I'll call Holden. Can I just get today's notes from you in class tomorrow?"

Christine nods. "Yeah, of course."

"Great. Thanks."

I turn and retrace my steps to the heavy wooden door, almost colliding with a girl rushing down the hall with a stack of three books.

The pathway outside the brick building is empty. I wander in the direction of the student center, finally deciding to do exactly what I told Christine I would do.

Holden answers on the second ring. "Hey."

"Hi. Are you home?"

"Yup. What's up?"

"Can I come over?"

There's a pause before he asks, "Your class get canceled?"

"Nope."

I wait, but he doesn't ask any more questions. "Okay. See you soon."

I hang up and head for my car.

The drive to the "Varsity" house only takes five minutes. I was planning to go get groceries after my Genetics class, which is why I was lazy and drove to campus this morning.

I leave the windows down for the short trip. The heat wave that greeted my return to campus has broken, leaving the air crisp and cool with the first hints of my favorite season.

I park in the driveway that's already crowded with three cars and walk up the brick front path. Debate on knocking and then just decide to try the door handle. It opens, so I crack the door open and call out, "Hello?"

"Come on in, baby!"

I follow the sound of a male voice that does not belong to Holden into the kitchen.

Holden's roommate Robby is leaning against the kitchen counter, shirtless, eating a bowl of cereal.

"Hey, gorgeous," he says. "Here to get arrested for breaking and entering?"

I roll my eyes. "The door was unlocked, so it's not considered a felony."

"Hot *and* smart. How the hell did you end up with Adams again?"

"Stop talking, Sanderson." Holden walks into the kitchen, zipping up his *Richmond Basketball* windbreaker.

"I was just welcoming Cassia to our humble abode. It's nice, right?"

I eye the pile of dirty dishes next to the sink. There's an open box of cereal on the counter and a small pile of granola wrappers next to it.

"Yeah," I say. "Did you guys hire an interior decorator or did the mess come with the place?"

Robby grins. "For real, you're my dream girl."

"For real, *shut up*," Holden says. Then glances to me. "You ready to go?"

"Go where?"

I figured we'd just hang out in his room. Talk. Watch TV. Fool around, if he's put sheets on his bed.

"You'll see."

Holden grins at me, a carefree one that lightens a little of the weight on my chest. Lately, it's felt like all of our conversations have been heavy. Like there are storm clouds following us around. Right now, his eyes are clear and bright. Blue skies.

"See ya, Sanderson."

"Bye," Robby calls after us through a mouthful of cereal.

"Seriously, where are we going?" I ask Holden once we're outside.

"I have a plan," he tells me, confident.

I stare at him as we walk toward his truck. "A *plan*? I told you I was coming over, what? Ten minutes ago?"

"You're skipping class, flower. That's rarer than a national holiday. I've had an idea in mind since freshman year, just in case."

"I can't tell if you're being serious right now or not."

Another grin, as he unlocks his truck. "You trust me, right?"

"You know I do," I grumble.

"Then get in. Let's celebrate."

I climb into the passenger side. "Celebrate *what*?"

"Just celebrate."

"I haven't felt like celebrating much lately," I say.

He reaches over and squeezes my thigh before backing out of the driveway. "That's exactly why we should."

———

I try to guess our destination based on the turns Holden takes, but we're quickly past the immediate town and driving on back roads I don't recognize. The radio playing quietly in the background and the distant hum of road noise are the only sounds.

Holden doesn't ask why I'm skipping class for the first time ever.

Doesn't bring up going back to Pembrooke this weekend, which I still haven't given him a final answer on and am even more conflicted about after getting Regan's text.

Doesn't wonder if I've heard from Sydney or my mom.

Everything gets left behind us, only a comfortable silence filling the truck's cab.

We drive for almost an hour before Holden turns off the highway. There's no chance I'm not missing my afternoon class too, and I can't bring myself to care. I don't email my professor with a made-up excuse or text anyone asking them to take notes. I pretend there's nothing I had to do today and nothing I need to worry about.

I'm not expecting to see the water appear ahead. But it's suddenly there in a shimmering blue spread, the surface a few shades darker than the sky.

Holden parks in the lot beside the dock and glances over at me. Grins, at what I'm guessing is a startled expression.

I glance at the sign that reads *Lake Champlain Ferry*.

"We're going out on a boat?"

"Yep. Come on."

Holden's excitement is obvious and genuine as we approach the boat. There are only a few people in line to board ahead of us, tourist season probably at its tail end. He shows the attendant something on his phone screen and then we're ushered onto the metal walkway that connects the dock to the boat. It creaks ominously as I head toward the deck, water sloshing the shore beneath the silver rungs.

Once on board, I turn toward the left, figuring the front will offer the best view. Holden is right behind me.

We stand at the railing, looking out at the water and the greenery lining the lake's shore. Here and there is a splash of autumn color, a few patches of leaves losing chlorophyll early.

There's commotion on the dock as the crew prepares to depart. I rest my elbows on the railing, looking out at the water. If I had to describe a place that brings me peace, I'd say the animal shelter. When I'm there, I feel like my actions matter, like I'm making a difference. The scratch of excited paws against linoleum, the smell of the cleaning supplies used to sanitize everything, the feel of soft fur, it all soothes me.

I know Holden finds that feeling at the old court.

But this is pretty nice too.

I feel more myself than I have in a while, which is ironic considering skipping is a very uncharacteristic thing for me to do.

It probably has something to do with Holden.

He speaks first, once we're far enough from the dock I can't make out anything distinct on the shoreline. "So…remember that conversation we had about telling each other things?"

"Yeah, I do." My eyes remain on the water. The surface is sparkling in the sunshine, the view only interrupted by the strands of hair blowing across my face in the breeze. "It's stupid."

"I doubt that."

I say nothing.

"We don't have to talk about it, Cassia. Just tell me."

My eyes find his. "You were actually listening, huh?"

"It happens occasionally."

I scoff, but I'm smiling. "Regan texted me, asking if I knew about the divorce. I saw it right before class, and that's why I skipped. Going didn't feel…important. I feel guilty for being gone. And I'm…angry at my parents, which isn't fair. I get ending a marriage isn't something you plan on. But when I talked to my mom, she didn't want to talk about it. I have no clue when my dad is going to move out, when they're going to tell my siblings. I haven't talked to my dad at all. It's all so uncertain."

"They're probably trying to figure things out for themselves."

"Yeah, I know. But they're upending our lives. The least they could do is figure out how to tell us."

"You didn't tell anyone about us over the summer," he says.

"I was pretty sure we'd figure it out."

"Pretty sure, huh?"

"You…weren't?" I ask.

"I… No, I wasn't."

I might regret asking, now that it feels like we're finally past it all, but I do anyway. "Why not?"

He drops my gaze, looks out at the water instead. "Because part of me has been waiting for you to change your mind about us ever since I handed you that notebook and you showed up at my game." His gaze returns to my face. "You like safe bets, Cas. I'm not one."

"You've never been a *bet* for me, Holden. Our odds were never great. I thought you regretted kissing me for years, so I never thought there was even a chance we'd be here. You've always been the one part of my life that I have no control over."

"Will you still love me if I follow you wherever you go to vet school and do who knows what?"

"Yes."

He smiles.

"When are you supposed to get the test results?" I ask softly.

The only reason he'd follow me was if he didn't have his own dreams to chase anymore.

"Any day now."

"If you donate…if you can't play this season, is there still a chance you'd get drafted?"

Holden looks out at the water. "I don't know. It's a unique situation and I haven't said anything to Coach Jackson yet." He glances at me, his expression wry. "Pro basketball likes safe bets too."

"And fans like an underdog."

He snorts. "Right. That's worth the risk of infection or liver failure."

I still. "What's the risk of infection or liver failure?"

I've been preoccupied by the mental toll donating might take on him. The impact of losing basketball. It's just now occurring to me—and I feel stupid that it didn't before—that he's risking a lot more than his pro career. He's risking his health. His *life*.

Whatever expression I'm wearing strains the corners of Holden's eyes. "I was just kidding, Cassia. Forget it."

"What are the chances of that happening, Holden?"

"It was a stupid joke."

I hold his gaze, not wavering.

He exhales. "It's a major surgery. Yeah, there are risks, and the doctor ran through them with me. But I don't even know if I'm doing it. And if I did, everything would be fine. It's probably more likely I get hit by a car tomorrow."

"That's not fucking funny," I snap.

His humor fades. "What do you want me to do, Cassia? Let her die?"

Yes, I want to say. If it's a choice between him and her, that's an easy one. But that's too terrible to say. And it's not my impossible choice to make—it's his.

"Like you said, you might not even do the surgery. We'll worry about it then."

And I will. Worry about it.

Holden exhales. "This is why I didn't want to tell you about it. Not until I had the test results, at least."

"Well, I know."

He steps back from the rail, motioning me closer. I step in front of him, so I'm caged between warm muscle and hard metal. His chin rests on the top of my head.

"It'll all be okay, flower."

"I know," I say. *Lie.*

Lately, it feels like I'm sure of a lot less than I used to be.

And nothing I'm worried about feels that far away anymore.

CHAPTER TWENTY-SIX

HOLDEN

All of my teammates at the table order another round. I shake my head when the waitress looks my way, pulling my phone out to check the time and then drumming my fingers on the surface of the table.

"Your girlfriend is really hot." Sebastian's tone is admiring. I can tell how drunk he is based on a) the slur in his voice and b) what he's saying.

"I know." Mine is cutting.

If I punched him once, he'd probably be unconscious on the floor.

And he's not wrong about Cassia. Just currently oblivious to the fact that I'm wildly possessive when it concerns her, and my tolerance is getting tested to its max.

In the past two hours we've been at this bar, I've witnessed a lot more guys than that check out Cassia.

Right now she's in the center of the throng, dancing and singing with her roommate Nova and a few other girls on the soccer team. After driving back from the ferry and getting dinner, we came to Dirty Mike's, one of the most popular bars off-campus. It's packed despite being a Tuesday night.

"Who's up for darts?" Ezra, a junior on the team, stumbles over to us.

Great, the whole team is wasted.

"Can you even throw straight right now?" I ask.

He grins. "Only one way to find out."

Ezra probably can. His accuracy is similar to a sniper's.

I roll my eyes, then spot Cassia pushing toward the edge of the formerly open space now serving as a makeshift dancefloor.

"Stay away from sharp objects," I advise, then head straight for her.

Cassia stiffens when I grab her arm. Then smiles when she registers who it is, wide and sloppy. She steps into me, flinging her arms over my shoulders and shoving her hands into my hair. She's draped over me like a blanket, letting me support most of her body weight.

"You okay?" I whisper into her hair. Actually, considering the noise level in here, it's probably more of a shout.

"*So* good," she tells me. Her face turns into my neck, her lips warm and wet.

"Yeah, remember that in the morning," I say, steering her toward the bar. "Let's get you some water."

If I had no idea why she was so upset, I'd be more worried. But even knowing, I'm uneasy.

This isn't her, skipping class and suggesting we come here after dinner. She faces things head-on, like showing up at the campsite. She doesn't duck and avoid the way I try to.

And I guess I now know how she's felt every time I've spiraled into self-destruction. It's *awful*, watching someone you love struggle and being powerless to fix it.

She squints at me as I hand her the cup of ice water the bartender helpfully provided. "Why do you look so…serious?"

"Probably because I switched to water a while ago, but you stuck with tequila."

"Ugh." She drinks most of the cup and then leans into me, resting her forehead on my chest. "Can we go outside for a minute?"

"Uh-huh." I steer her toward the door, nodding to the bouncer as we step out into air that's much cooler and quieter.

There's a bench about halfway down the block that I guide her toward.

"I'm a mess." Cassia sighs as soon as she takes a seat.

"No, you're not." I sit beside her.

"I am." She drops her head in her hands. "I'm acting like a little kid throwing a tantrum."

"Little kids throwing tantrums don't get drunk in college bars."

She huffs a laugh. "I'm twenty-one, Holden. I'm an adult. I'm all grown up. Who cares if my parents are getting divorced?"

"*You* care, and you should."

She sniffles, running a hand through her long hair. "I feel dumb for assuming they'd stay together forever."

"You're the smartest person I know. That's not dumb; it's sweet."

Cassia wipes a cheek. "You know, if someone had asked me a month ago who would still be together now—us or my parents…" She shakes her head, staring at the ground for a minute longer before glancing over at me. "If I hadn't grabbed that bottle, would we still be sitting here together?"

"Honestly?"

Cassia nods.

"I don't know. I'm selfish and self-centered—"

She interrupts. "No. You're not."

"Come on, Cassia. Yeah, I am."

"You spent today cheering me up and discussing what might happen if you donate an organ to save your mom's life. *No one* would call that selfish or self-centered."

"I guess you've been a good influence."

"You didn't answer my question," she says.

"Yeah, I did. *I don't know*, Cassia. If you've been a good influence on me, I've been a bad one on you. The only person who's ever depended on me at all was Sydney. And she always had it together, so she never actually relied upon me. If I fucked up, I didn't feel like I was letting her down. With you…I want to be reliable. I wasn't sure if I could be that guy for you, so I avoided you. Ignored you. Told myself that you didn't care. And if you'd never grabbed that bottle…never climbed into my lap… there's a chance I could have convinced myself of that. But you did grab that bottle, and I'm so grateful. I wouldn't change any of our past, flower, even the messy parts."

I lean closer to her.

"And if we're placing odds on couples who will last? I'd pick us every time. Because now that I have you, I can't imagine ever letting you go."

She stares at me for so long I'm not sure if she registered a word I just said. At least she hasn't fallen asleep. Or puked.

"Can we go back to your place?" she asks.

"Yeah, of course," I reply.

Another surprise.

We usually sleep at hers. She has one roommate, instead of two. And Cassia's apartment is nicer than mine. Cleaner. Her floors don't have dirty clothes flung across them. But I don't question her decision. I'm just relieved we're leaving and I can stop glaring at every guy who looks in her direction.

We head toward the street corner where I parked my truck. I sneak glances at Cassia as we walk, trying to gauge exactly how drunk she is.

Nova and some other girls who Cassia is friends with showed up about an hour after we arrived, so I lost track of how much she continued drinking after she went off with them.

My phone buzzes with a message in the team group chat, wondering where I went. I reply, letting the guys know I left, shoving my phone back into my pocket before the inevitable messages about me being whipped come in.

We're one of the smaller teams on campus, tighter knit than most. And I'm currently the only one with a girlfriend. Henry dated a sophomore named Amanda for a few months last year, but they broke up mid-season. Several guys on the team are in a constant state of shock that I choose to be in a relationship when they've seen first-hand the attention I get from girls.

Cassia connects her phone to the speakers as soon as we're in the cab, flipping between songs as I drive. Her mood seems to be shifting just as quickly. I glance over at the first light, and she's frowning. At the next stop sign, her lips are tipped up.

When I park in the empty driveway, she speaks.

"Nice place." She glances over at me, still smirking. "Have you lived here long?"

I raise one eyebrow, trying to assess her angle.

She raises one right back at me. "What, your sister got all the acting skills in the family?"

I shake my head, then decide *what the hell?* I turn toward her as much as the truck's seat will allow. "How do you know my sister is into theater stuff?"

Cassia beams when she realizes I'm playing along.

I roll my eyes.

"Lucky guess," she replies.

"Want a tour of the house?" I ask, popping my door open.

"Sure. Although I'm really just interested in, you know, your bedroom."

I chuckle under my breath and shake my head as I lock the truck, then follow her up the brick path that leads to the front door. The porch light is on, but the house is dark. Robby was supposed to show up at Dirty Mike's but never did. No clue where Henry is.

I watch Cassia carefully as she climbs the steps. She doesn't stumble or trip, walking confidently up to the front door and waiting for me to unlock it.

I guide her into the kitchen first, pulling a glass out of the cabinet and filling it with water before handing it to her. Pretty sure she'll wake up with a hangover regardless, but I tried.

"Drink this, Cassia." She takes the glass, then asks. "How do you know my name?"

I roll my eyes. "Seriously?"

Her smirk remains, waiting expectantly.

I take the glass back, then hold it out to her. "Drink this, Random Girl From The Bar."

She drains it, then sets it on the counter, holding eye contact the entire time. "What's your name?"

I huff a laugh as she steps closer, deliberately trailing her fingers down the center of my chest.

"You're drunk and upset," I remind her.

"Yup." Cassia confirms.

But instead of backing away, she takes another step closer.

Our bodies brush together as her hand slips into my hair, fingers tangling in and tugging on the short strands.

"Only you could get me wet right now." She whispers the words like they're a secret no one else is supposed to know. To anyone else, they'd sound hot. They'd be an ego stroke.

But I hear the hidden meaning.

The first time we hooked up, I was the drunk and upset one.

As soon as she was in my lap, I couldn't focus on anything else. So I told her that—*Only you could get me hard right now*—in an unplanned admission.

An acknowledgment, to her and to myself, that the past few years of denial had done nothing to curb my attraction toward her. That with other girls, it was just physical. Not mental and definitely not emotional. Maybe I didn't even realize that was missing or was supposed to be there until her touch lit my body up like a supernova.

"What's your name?" she repeats.

I huff a laugh that turns into a groan when she unzips my jeans and palms my cock through my boxers.

At first, I thought this was ridiculous. That's turning to intrigue.

"If you make me come, I want to know what to scream."

Holy shit.

Blood is rapidly rushing south as I harden beneath her touch. It's hard to think straight, much less focus on what she's saying. But I register enough key words to have a pretty good idea. She's seducing me, and I'm the farthest thing from unwilling.

"*When* I make you come," I correct.

"Lots of guys talk a big game but don't follow through."

I know she's talking hypothetically. Know she's acting out a part from stories she's heard or movies she's seen or books she's read. Know this act is another distraction from an entire evening that's been an escape from reality for her.

This is a game. A fantasy. Whatever.

But my dick rises to the challenge like it's never been inside this girl before.

"Then you've been fucking the wrong guys."

Cassia smirks. "Prove it. I already know you can talk a good game, Adams."

"I thought you didn't know my name." I push her toward the stairs, smiling when she laughs.

Her long hair is loose, strands tangled from my hands.

"*Everyone* knows who the star shooting guard is," she says as we head upstairs. Her fingers trail the banister the way I wish they were still touching me.

"Everyone, huh?" I ask once we're in my bedroom. I close the door, then lock it. I have no idea when Henry and Robby will be home or if they'll be alone.

"Yeah." She steps closer, tugging at my shirt. "Take this off."

I shrug off my t-shirt, letting the cotton fabric drop on the floor. Cassia sighs appreciatively, running her warm hands down the center of my chest and then carefully tracing my abs.

Her hazel eyes heat. "Fuck, you're hot."

She's seen me naked as many times as I've seen her. It's still an ego boost to see her looking at me like that, the desire so obvious it's written across her face.

I can feel attraction humming in the charged air between us.

Her fingers move lower, brushing skin so lightly it's barely a graze. She follows the trail of hair down until she reaches my cock, easily displacing my shorts and boxers.

I groan when she grips me, her fist a devastating combination of pain and pleasure. My cock jerks in her hold, the tip flushing an angry purple-red color.

"Wow. Your dick is even bigger than the girls in my Genetics class were saying."

"That's…oddly specific. Was this a class discussion?"

Cassia snorts. "No. They were just talking before class."

I stare at her, trying to figure out if this is real or if we're acting. "Wait, that really happened? Don't they know that we're…"

"That we met tonight?" She shakes her head. Then her thumb swipes the tip of my dick, and it's a struggle to stay focused.

"That's fucking rude, Cassia."

"They don't care I'm your girlfriend. Or more likely, they don't even know that I am. It's a big campus."

"That's bullshit. Don't make—*fuck*."

She's on her knees, the tip of her tongue tracing the throbbing vein on the underside. I can't focus on anything except the wet heat of her mouth.

We can pretend to be strangers all she wants. I'm responding this way to *her*, to the way she's learned exactly what drives me insane.

I'm dangerously close to coming when she pulls away and stands.

"I don't swallow," she tells me before pulling off her shirt.

I smirk at the lie. "Smart. Nothing in it for you."

She steps out of her jeans, then her bra joins the growing pile of clothes on the floor. "Exactly."

Cassia sprawls out on my bed wearing nothing except lacy underwear. She wasn't lying about being wet. The sight of the soaked fabric clinging to the outline of her pussy is pornographic. I could get off just staring at it.

Even hotter is the way she spreads her thighs as wide as they'll open. Wanting me to look. Practically begging for my attention.

Her hands trail up her stomach until they reach her bare breasts, pushing her tits together.

I get naked as quickly as physically possible, stroking my erection as I approach the bed. Cassia's attention is focused on my dick like she's never seen it before.

"Will it fit?" She bites her bottom lip, her expression purposefully suggestive as I hover over her.

I hook her knee over my hip, lining our bodies up perfectly. "We'll make it fit, baby."

"I was so freaked out it wouldn't, our first time," Cassia whispers. "I stood in that hotel shower for like twenty minutes, worried I was going to humiliate myself because I had no clue what to do."

"I wish you'd told me," I say, rubbing tiny circles on her thigh with my thumb.

It's fucking with my head a little, jumping between familiarity and the façade that we're strangers.

She breaks eye contact. "I knew you were experienced and confident and I didn't want to be the shy, good girl."

"I wasn't confident that night," I tell her. "I was fucking terrified."

"Then you used to be a better actor."

I scoff. "You broke character first."

Cassia smiles, then lifts her hips. We both groan when my cock slips into the wetness gathered between them. One rock of my hips, and I'd be inside her.

"Do you have a condom?"

It takes my lust-addled brain a few seconds to figure out why she's asking. "No."

"I've never let a guy fuck me bare." Her fingernails dig into my back. "I guess you'll be the first."

"I like the sound of that." I thrust forward slowly, savoring the stretch as her tight heat spreads around me.

"Wait," she says suddenly.

I freeze halfway inside her. "What's wrong?"

"Roll over."

I hesitate for a second, trying to figure out what's going on.

Then pull out and shift away, sprawling on the comforter next to her. "I'm not a damn dog."

Cassia giggles, and the sound makes me smile.

All the amusement fades when she straddles me.

"I want you to watch."

She leans forward, her long hair dragging across my chest. So close, I think she's going to kiss me. But she pulls away at the last minute, rising up on her knees and gripping my dick. I hiss at the contact, so hard it's painful.

If she needs—wants—this distraction, I'll give it to her.

I'll give this girl anything she wants.

CHAPTER TWENTY-SEVEN

CASSIA

When my eyes blink open, it feels like heavy bags of sand are sitting on them. Dry and gritty.

Sunshine is sneaking in around the corners of the shades, straight lines illuminating sections of the hardwood floor.

My head is pounding, and my throat feels raw.

I fling an arm across my eyes in an attempt to block out the light. Parts of yesterday are hazy and translucent, like my memory is a faded photo. But my recollection of other moments—specifically late last night—is completely clear. I lift my arm so I can raise the covers and confirm—yep—I'm naked.

There's no sign of Holden.

I sit up in bed and grab my phone, scowling when I see the time. I only got a few hours of sleep, but it feels like even less.

There are a few new messages, including a couple from Christine asking if I'm okay. I reply to her first, letting her know I'm feeling better, and I'll see her in class. She replies right away, liking the message.

I groan and toss my phone onto the comforter without looking through any more texts. I'm so, so tempted to skip class again today. To hide a little longer.

But that's silly and selfish. I'm not even having to deal with any of the repercussions of my parents' divorce first-hand.

I wonder how Regan found out. Wonder if Maggie knows.

I need to talk to my mom. But I also don't want to, for the first time ever.

While I'm on campus, it's easy to pretend like nothing has changed back in Pembrooke. Like the conversation I had with my mom never happened and we're still the big, happy family I thought we were.

Does my dad know she told me?

Too many questions I'm not sure I want answers to.

Answers won't change the outcome.

I hunt around Holden's room until I locate my clothes. His room isn't as messy as I've seen it, but it's not exactly neat either. At least his bed has sheets on it.

My shirt smells like tequila, and the smoky scent makes my stomach turn as I pull it on.

Once I'm dressed, I cross the hall into the bathroom. I clean up as best I can with limited tools, splashing some cool water on my face and using a finger to rub some toothpaste around my mouth. I'm not sure which toothbrush is Holden's.

The hum of voices is audible as I walk downstairs. Holden has lived in this house since sophomore year, but I've only woken up here a handful of times.

Nova and I have chosen to live together ever since we were randomly assigned as roommates freshman year. Since our place is quieter—and cleaner—we usually end up sleeping there. Plus, Holden doesn't seem to mind "roughing it" the next morning, whereas I could really go for a clean shirt and some facewash right about now.

Henry and Robby are both sitting at the island when I enter the kitchen. Holden is standing at the stove, cooking eggs.

Henry spots me first and grins. "Morning."

"We didn't think you'd be up for a while," Robby says. "According to the team group chat, you had a wild night."

I have a vague recollection of basketball players being at the bar last night. And considering my definition of a wild night is probably different from theirs, I'm sort of glad I don't have a clearer memory of that part of the evening.

Henry leans forward, grabbing the pot of coffee and pouring some into a water glass. He slides it my way. "We're out of mugs," he says.

I huff a laugh. "Thanks, Henry."

The coffee does help wake me up a little more. The hot drink also washes away the coating of alcohol that still feels like it's clinging to my throat. The minty aftertaste of toothpaste isn't a pleasant combination with the coffee's nutty flavor, so I sip some more.

Henry stands and stretches. "You can have my seat. I've got to run to the library to print something before our weight session." He yawns. "Sorry if I woke you guys up coming back last night."

"Nah, *you* didn't wake anyone up," Robby says.

The heavy emphasis on you has me blushing.

I know I was loud last night. The house was empty when Holden and I got back. Once we were in his bedroom, I didn't consider that might not remain the case.

Me of last night did not care.

Me of this morning is more than a little embarrassed.

Henry glances between me and Holden, then smirks. "Good for you, Adams."

"I thought you were leaving, Wilson?" Holden says.

"Yeah, yeah. I am. Good to see you, Cassia."

"You too," I say, drinking more of my coffee.

"I should get going too." Robby finishes the smoothie sitting in front of him. He glances at me and grins. "You guys might have changed my opinion on long-term relationships being boring."

"Sanderson," Holden snaps.

Robby chuckles. "Bye, guys."

As soon as Robby is out of the kitchen, I drop my face in my hands. "Fuck," I groan.

"Here." I glance up to see Holden setting a plate of steaming eggs down in front of me. "This will help with your headache."

"Thanks." I pick up the fork and stab a piece. "Do you have anything for the humiliation of knowing Robby heard us last night?"

Holden smirks. "If it helps, there's a long list of stuff I can tell you Sanderson has done that's way more embarrassing than having sex."

"Still, I was loud."

His grin widens. "I didn't mind."

"Of course you didn't."

Holden helps himself to his own plate of eggs.

"What time is your practice thingy?"

"My *weight session* is at eight."

"Do you have a morning class?" he asks.

I nod. "Yeah. Genetics. Plus a meeting with my class advisor before."

"Fall semester just started."

"I know. But different vet schools have different requirements. I have to make certain I've completed all the necessary classes for anywhere I'm applying. Next semester is my last chance, if I haven't."

Holden nods, then continues eating.

Our plan for the future has always been some version of wait and see. Wait and see where I get into vet school. Wait and see if he gets drafted, which now has the added complication of his status this season.

Look at all of our options and then decide.

It's really the only option. Once my applications have been submitted and his final season is over, our roles in shaping our futures will be over and everything will be beyond our control. Which is freeing and terrifying, all at once.

Once we're both finished eating, Holden leans closer.

I wait for him to say something serious. About next year or about my mini-meltdown yesterday. Some assurance everything will be okay or a plea to revert to my responsible self.

Instead, he grins. "Last night was fun. Can I get your number?"

I start laughing, then push him to the side so I can reach my glass of coffee again. I can feel the warmth in my cheeks.

Last night was out of character for me on several levels.

Most of the time, being steadfast and mature suits me. It's gotten me to this place where I've accomplished a lot and have a promising future.

But as long as I can remember, Holden has been the person who draws out the reckless streak I didn't even know existed. Being sensible can also be exhausting.

I like knowing I can still surprise him.

Love knowing I can let go and he'll be there to catch me.

"Thank you," I say.

"You don't ever have to thank me for that. It was my pleasure. Literally."

I roll my eyes. "Can you be serious for two seconds?"

Holden smirks. "I am. You don't ever have to thank me,

flower. For anything. I've got you. Always." He opens his arms, his smile turning more tender than teasing. "Come here."

I glance down at my wrinkled shirt. "I need to shower. I smell like tequila."

"Like I give a shit." He tugs me closer before I can protest more.

Unlike me, he smells good. Like cinnamon and laundry detergent and woodsy cologne.

"It'll be okay," he murmurs.

"I know," I reply.

My answer is a little more confident than it was yesterday.

———

My advisor's office is on the fifth and highest floor of the main science center. It's a seven-minute trek if you take the stairs or a fifteen-minute wait for the elevator.

I opt for the stairs, hoping if I start sweating it won't smell like tequila. At least I know I smell fine at the moment. I took a quick but thorough shower as soon as I got back to my apartment, changed into a clean outfit, and then rushed onto campus.

I did stop for an iced coffee. Condensation drips down my fingers as I grip the cold plastic cup, forcing my lungs to take deep breaths as I climb the stairs.

My calves are burning by the time I reach the door with a large number five written on it. The walk down to Professor Miller's office is familiar. She's the youngest member of the science faculty and favors a hands-on approach. We've met multiple times a semester since I started at Richmond College.

Our meeting today takes longer than usual. Professor Miller runs through all the requirements for every vet school I'm planning to apply to, and we discuss my personal essay at length.

By the time our meeting ends, I'm running late for Genetics. I rush down the hallway, only pausing to toss my empty coffee cup before I head down the stairs. At least my class is in the same building.

When I reach it, the door to the lecture hall is still wide open. I relax slightly, since Professor Cassidy always closes it behind her.

I hurry inside, then skid to a stop.

"What are you doing here?"

Holden is standing at the bottom of the stairs that lead up to the stadium-style seating, holding a coffee cup.

He holds it out to me. "Thought you might need this."

My bloodstream is probably more coffee than cells at this point. Better than tequila, I guess.

I take the cup, smiling at the thoughtful gesture. My cheeks warm from more than exertion as I register all the eyes on us. Professor Cassidy might not be here yet, but most of my classmates are.

And they're *all* looking this way.

Not to stereotype, but the sciences aren't a super popular major at Richmond among athletes. In three plus years of classes, there have only been one or two in mine. I had one class with Holden's roommate slash teammate Henry, who's pre-med, freshman year, but our schedules haven't overlapped since.

Sports are a big deal at Richmond. And Holden's not just an athlete. He's the poster boy for the basketball team—literally. His face is plastered all over campus. You'd have to actively avoid any mention of the basketball team—and possibly be blind—to not know who he is.

I might have to move to the back row, just so no one can look at me.

"Thank you," I say

He steps closer, scanning my expression more closely. "Are you okay?" he asks quietly.

Clearly, I really freaked him out yesterday.

Guess he knows how I felt, seeing him come home bloody and intoxicated most Friday nights. We weren't dating. I wasn't supposed to care. But I did.

"I'm better," I tell him. "I'm planning to call my mom tonight. Let her know I'll be back this weekend and get some answers about what Regan knows and…" I exhale. "Just get answers."

"Miss Nolan, I hope my lecture isn't interrupting your conversation."

I glance at the desk to see the professor has arrived.

"Sorry, Professor Cassidy."

Holden steps even closer and kisses me.

"Tell them it's huge," he whispers, confirming it wasn't a coincidence *this* is the class he showed up for.

My face must look like a tomato. I avoid attention; Holden attracts it.

I shove him, but I'm smiling as I start up the stairs toward where Christine is sitting.

"Sorry, Professor," Holden says, at normal volume. "I just had to talk to my *girlfriend* real quick."

I don't miss the way he emphasizes girlfriend. I don't think anyone else in the class does either.

But it's worth experiencing all the eyes on me, seeing the wide ones of the two girls who were talking about him just before I slip into my seat.

CHAPTER TWENTY-EIGHT

HOLDEN

My phone buzzes with a call from an unknown number right as I reach the main doors of the sports center. My steps slow and my stomach twists as I accept the call.

Wondering if it's the one I've been waiting for.

"Hello?"

"Holden, it's Dr. Meyers. Is this an okay time for you to talk?"

"Yeah, now's good."

My heartbeat quickens to a dizzying pace as I walk over to the stone wall that's part of the decorative entrance to the sports center. Lean against it, barely registering the scrape of the stones against the thin barrier of my basketball shorts.

"I'm sorry, but our testing indicates you are not a viable match to…"

Blood rushes in my ears, the rest of his words nothing but a nonsensical blur.

I'm expecting the relief. I was just handed the *get out of jail free* card. There's nothing I can do for her. I can play my senior season. No choice can be made.

What I'm not expecting?

The disappointment.

Part of me wanted to do it. To save her life.

So I wasn't an orphan.

So I didn't have to bury another parent.

So I could prove to myself—to her—that I'm different. That she was right that day in the parking lot, and we were better off without her.

"Holden?" Dr. Meyers says.

"Uh, yeah. I'm still here."

"It was a beautiful gesture."

My molars grind. Beautiful and *pointless*.

"What will happen to my mom now?" I ask.

"We'll continue to search for another donor."

"What are the chances of that happening?"

There's a pause that gives me a pretty good idea of the odds. "I couldn't put a precise number on it," he finally answers. "But I can tell you we'll do everything in our power to help your mother."

I nod, then remember he can't see me. "Okay. Thank you."

"You're a good man, Holden."

"Not really the thought that counts here. She's dying anyway."

"I understand the situation between you two is complicated. But I think you should tell your mother you got tested. I think it would mean a lot to her."

"Yeah, I'll think about it."

He sighs, realizing the same thing as me—I won't.

"I've gotta get to practice. Thanks for calling."

"Of course. I wish I had different news for you."

"Bye, Doc."

"Bye, Holden."

I hang up and blow out a long breath before I head inside for practice.

Everything is autopilot. I don't remember walking inside the sports center or the locker room. If I talk to anyone, I'm not sure what I said.

I rely on grunted responses and muscle memory to get through practice. After dreading the call for so long, it's unsettling to have gotten the answer.

Coach Jackson pulls me aside at the end of practice. "What's going on with you, Adams?" he asks.

I run a hand through my hair. Look away. "Just having an off day."

"You were unstoppable all summer. We've got our first scrimmage against Lincoln in two weeks. Off days aren't on the agenda."

"I know. It was just today."

He studies me for a minute, then nods. "All right. Get a good night's sleep. I'll see you tomorrow."

I nod and leave the weight room.

Instead of heading to the left, toward the locker room, I go right.

The punching bag is located in the weight room the football team usually uses. I share a couple of classes with the starting quarterback, so I know the team is at an away game.

The room is empty, which is exactly what I was hoping for.

I head straight for the bag suspended from the ceiling.

It's been a while since I was in a physical fight. And I miss the adrenaline. The rush of facing an unpredictable opponent.

Basketball's a more civilized version. No one is throwing punches, just shoving elbows. And no matter how hard I hit the bag; it never retaliates.

I lose track of time as my fists fly.

My muscles are exhausted from lifting weights for the past hour, but I continue throwing punches relentlessly, trying to expel the chaotic energy swirling inside of me.

I don't stop until one of my knuckles splits. I swear, ripping off a piece of paper towel from the roll meant to be used to clean equipment.

By the time I reach the locker room, I'm sweaty and exhausted. All my teammates are long gone. I shower and change into sweatpants, then head for the exit.

Cassia is standing in the lobby, wearing one of my high school sweatshirts. It hangs to her mid-thigh, her hands lost somewhere in the front pocket.

Despite my dark mood, my lips turn up into a smile at the sight.

"What are you doing here?" I ask. "Because I know you're not here to exercise."

She rolls her eyes. "At least I know you didn't stand me up on purpose."

My eyes close briefly as I wince. We had dinner plans tonight. I was supposed to meet her after my practice. "Fuck. I'm so sorry."

"It's okay."

"No, it's not." I scrub a palm across my face.

"Jesus, Holden."

I drop my hand, realizing she's focused on my knuckles.

"It looks worse than it is."

I'm not sure if it does, actually. I thought the shower would clean it up. But blood is oozing out of the wound again. I definitely should have searched for a Band-Aid, at the very least. The paper towel didn't do much.

Cassia steps closer, searching my expression. "Did something happen?"

I exhale. People are walking in and out around us, but I'm totally focused on her.

"I got the results. I'm not a match." I spit the words out.

Sympathy bleeds across her face.

"And I'm relieved, which makes me feel like shit. But I'm also angry. Disappointed. Not only because she'll probably die, but because I wanted her to owe me. To *not want us* but to *need me*." I shake my head. "It's stupid. I'm just—"

"It's *not* stupid."

She hugs me. Here in the lobby of the sports center. Random people are walking past and the fluorescent lights hum overhead. And I hug her back, bending my neck so my chin rests on her shoulder. Exhale deeply, ignoring the throb of my hand and the ache in my heart and focusing on the only person I've ever allowed myself to accept comfort from.

"I could get tested," she whispers.

I pull back so I can see her. So she can see my expression, especially the certainty there. "No. Absolutely not."

"It's not as likely I'd be a match since I'm not family, but—"

"I said *no*, Cassia."

"Why not? You were going to—"

"Those are risks I was willing to take myself. Not anything I would let you chance."

"She's your mom."

"I don't care."

"I could at least get tested and then—"

I start walking, needing the fresh air outside.

She follows me. "You can't just walk away, Holden. At least let's talk—"

I whirl on her. "There's nothing to discuss."

Her chin sets stubbornly. "I disagree."

"*I don't care.* It's my mom. My situation to figure out. I have to be able to tell you things and trust that you'll respect my decisions!"

"How is me offering to get tested not respecting your decision? You chose to get tested. I could do the same. What if I'm a match? What if I could save her and I didn't? Could you live with that?"

"Yes," I tell her bluntly. "Because I love you, not her. I'm not willing to risk you to help her, and if that makes me a terrible person, I don't really care."

Cassia inhales deeply, then glances away. "Fine. The offer stands, so *think* about it instead of just reacting. But you're right; it's your mom. I would never do it behind your back, but please consider it, okay? I would do it for *you*, not her."

It feels like some cosmic error that I got this lucky. That I found someone who's willing to make that kind of sacrifice.

And maybe I appreciate it extra, since I've experienced versions of love neither permanent nor guaranteed.

My throat is too thick to speak, so I pull her into my arms again. Trying to wordlessly convey what the offer means to me. And hopefully she hears it, because she relaxes into me, her body language totally opposite from the tense anger of a minute ago.

"I don't have to think about it. But I love you for offering."

She's silent. Disagreeing, probably, but respecting my decision.

"Do I tell Sydney?"

Cassia exhales. "I haven't texted Regan back about the divorce. We're not supposed to be the adults. My parents are the ones who are supposed to tell her."

"My mom isn't going to tell Sydney. She wouldn't have told me."

"Would you want Sydney to tell you, if she had found out?" she asks.

"No. I wish I'd never found out. If that had happened…I just wouldn't have wanted Sydney to shoulder it all by herself. I can handle it."

She chews on her bottom lip. "She could find out one day. Go looking for answers. Do you want her to find out you had some?"

"She's *pregnant*, Cassia. She can't get tested. Can't donate. What's the point?"

"She could say goodbye," Cassia says softly.

I sigh.

Realizing…I have to tell her.

CHAPTER TWENTY-NINE

CASSIA

I cross my arms, eyes scanning the grooved exterior of the office building that houses the law firm my dad has worked at for as long as I can remember.

I've always known his job was stressful and important. Time with him growing up always felt finite. In high school, I'd wake up extra early some mornings just so that I could see him before he left for work. Part of that was driven by guilt—basketball was a passion we shared until I dropped it at the start of high school. My father agreed with my excuse—I should focus all my attention on academics so I could get into a good college and then vet school—but I never admitted the real reason to him. And I could tell he was disappointed by my decision, even if he never said so.

Maybe I was so wrapped up in my own drama then, the same way I was all summer, that I missed noticing all the cracks appear. That I ignored all the warning signs.

Another person passes by, giving me a curious glance before entering the building.

I've been standing out here for ten minutes, just staring. It probably looks like I'm casing the place for a planned robbery.

I'm not sure if I should do this.

When I called my mom to let her know I was coming back to Pembrooke for the weekend, she was excited. Once I'm on campus, I usually only come back on school breaks. I didn't ask her about the divorce and she didn't bring the subject up. I'm not sure what to make of that.

What I do know is that I haven't spoken to my dad in weeks.

Despite his busy schedule and missing some moments, I never felt like he was absent. I always felt like I had the whole family that I'm mourning the loss of. And I'm not sure when that shift happened.

It's probably why I asked Holden for a break this summer. Because I've spent years—my entire life—not as a priority. I know my parents love me, just like they love their five other kids.

But I've never been the main focus. I was the easy kid who got good grades and wasn't out late enough to need a curfew. My behavior was taken for granted, the same way it started to feel like Holden took me for granted. Like he could show up whenever it worked for him, and I'd be accommodating.

I needed to know I was still a priority to him and felt like I needed to shock that into happening by having him confront the possibility of losing me. I'm not sure if that was the right way to handle things. I feel silly for doubting him as thoroughly as I did, looking from the place where we are now. But I'm also unsure we'd be in this place if I hadn't asked for a break.

And now I feel like I need to give my dad a similar ultimatum. To let him know I'm upset my parents are getting a divorce, but that what scares me the most is it feels like I'm losing my father. He should have been there to tell me about the divorce too. To reassure me—and my mom—that it was a change they'd handle together. That it would be okay.

Instead, I haven't heard a word from him.

It feels like an in-person conversation, not a phone call.

But I'm nervous too. I might be twenty-one and a legal adult, but he's my dad. My hero, for a long time. Maybe he still is. And he's supposed to be the parent. The one insisting on the tough conversations, not me.

I sigh and push away from the door of the sedan, straightening.

Holden and I left for Pembrooke around lunchtime. I drove my car since it was raining and we each had a couple of bags that wouldn't fit as easily in the small back of his truck. Dropped him off at the condo and, instead of driving to my house, I came here to sit and stare at the place where my dad spends most of his time.

I remember coming here to visit him at work when I was little, getting a lollipop from the secretary at the front desk. Picking out a pen from the huge closet that stored all the office supplies.

That was a long, long time ago.

I glance at my dad's car, parked in a prominent spot in the first row. Then sigh and start walking forward, passing the huge metal sculpture with water tricking down the sides right in front of the main entrance. Step inside the revolving door and push at the gold bar until the pane of glass starts to move.

The lobby inside is nicer than I remember. The last time I was here, I was probably five, maybe six. It makes sense that they've redecorated since.

My sneakers tread silently on the polished marble floor, passing leather couches and potted plants. Glossy magazines are spread on coffee tables, the covers shiny and noticeable under the modern-looking lights.

The receptionist behind the desk that looks like a giant cement block is a young woman I doubt is that much older than me. It's strange—maybe since I've always known I planned on another four years of school after graduating college—that this will be most of the people in my classes next year. Working a nine-to-five with a salary and benefits and a retirement fund.

She eyes me skeptically when I give her my dad's name and tell her I'm here to see him.

"One minute," she tells me, then picks up the phone. I assume she's calling my dad.

But another woman appears instead, silently gesturing for me to follow her. I thank the receptionist, offering her a smile she doesn't reciprocate before turning back to her computer.

The hallway is nondescript, cream carpeting running the length. The walls are white too, occasionally decorated by abstract art. Each dark brown door has a shiny gold nameplate next to it. Most of the doors are shut. We pass a kitchen, then an open space that houses a maze of cubicles, then end up at the end of the hall in one corner of the building.

There's a middle-aged woman standing in the hallway just outside it, flipping through papers. She's about my dad's age. My mom's age.

She glances up as we approach, her smile friendly and polite. "Hello."

The greeting seems to be aimed at me, since my guide doesn't respond.

"Hi," I say.

"This is Cassia *Nolan*." The woman I'm with heavily emphasizes my last name.

I get the strong impression these are the *work colleagues* my mom was referring to. At the very least, my family has been a topic of conversation between these women.

"Oh. It's so nice to meet you, Cassia. I'm Elena. I work with your father." Her smile grows. "You look just like him."

I'm not a fan of Elena's familiar tone. The way she's talking about my father feeds all the suspicions swirling in my gut.

"That's funny," I say. "Most people tell me I look just like my *mom*."

Elena's smile quickly disappears.

"Cassia?"

I glance toward the doorway where my dad has appeared.

"Hi, Dad. Can we talk?"

I don't wait for an invitation. I walk away from the two women I'm standing with without so much as a glance, walking past my dad and into his corner office.

"I—um, sure." His tone is unsure behind me.

There's the low hum of a few words being exchanged, then his door closes.

I approach the huge bookcase that spans most of one wall, my fingers trailing across the embossed spines of the law books. His diplomas hang on the wall next to the bookcase.

I take a seat in one of the two chairs opposite the desk, glancing at the framed photo next to his computer. It's from two summers ago, when we rented a beach house on Nantucket. Me and my siblings are all piled on the porch swing, sandy and sunburned. Sally is in my lap, the twins perched on the two arms pretending to be pirates.

It's the only photo in here. I'm not sure if that's always been the case or not.

"You were rude to Elena," he says.

It's about the worst possible thing he could say. My anger grows, burning hotter and brighter.

"Just being honest." I cross my arms. "Maybe you should try it sometime."

The stern expression he aimed at my siblings a lot more than he ever aimed at me appears. "I didn't raise you to be rude, Cassia."

"Are you going to stick around to *raise* the rest of your kids after the divorce?"

My dad sighs. "Your mother spoke to you." He shakes his head. "We were going to tell you kids together."

"Don't blame Mom for this."

"For sharing something with you that we agreed to tell you together? Who should I blame for that, Cassia?"

"You weren't home to tell anyone anything. You're *never* home."

My dad points to a high stack of papers piled on his desk. "See that? That's what I have to get through before I leave for the day. Tomorrow there will be a new stack twice that size."

"You have an important job, Dad. I get it. Don't patronize me like I'm a little kid."

"Then stop acting like one."

"Being the president is also an important job. I bet she eats dinner with her family more than twice a month."

A vein in my father's temple pulses. "Do you know how much the twins' soccer camp cost? Regan's dance lessons? Maggie wants to study abroad in Italy next year. You'll be in vet school."

"I can take out loans or—"

"Cassia." He stands and rounds the corner of his messy desk, taking the chair next to mine. "Honey, it's important to me I'm able to provide for my family. I'm up for a huge promotion, and things should settle down a little bit soon. I love you kids more than anything else in the world. You're my proudest accomplishment. Not all this." He gestures around the big office. "Your mom and me...maybe I've used work as an excuse too many times. But when we spend time together, we fight or we sit in silence. That's not how I want to spend the rest of my life, and I know your mom doesn't either. People change. Relationships change. That's just part of life."

"That doesn't mean you stop trying. It means you try *harder*, Dad."

"That's always a nice idea. The reality is different. We've been together for a long time, your mom and me. We're not happy together any longer. All we have in common now are you kids. And I *will* be around to raise your siblings—and you, because you'll be my baby girl even when you're forty. I promise you that. This was a big decision, and it had been a long time coming. One I intended to be there to tell you."

I nod, chewing furiously on my bottom lip.

"Does Elena have anything to do with this?"

My dad exhales, tugging at his tie to loosen the knot. "With the divorce? No. She's a good friend and a trusted colleague. Is there a possibility we'll have a different relationship in the future? I don't know. Maybe. But my priority right now is you kids and work. That's it. And I didn't have an affair, if that's what you're really asking."

"Mom isn't a priority anymore?"

He sighs again, looking increasingly uncomfortable. "Of course she is. We're getting divorced, though, Cassia. That means our feelings for each other have changed. Not our love for you kids."

"How do you know they won't change back?" I ask.

I hear the little kid my dad accused me of acting like in the tentative question. The innocent hope that things will always be okay.

"I think we're way past that point, sweetheart."

I blow out a long breath. "Will you be home for dinner?"

His eyes dart toward the stack of papers, and I know the answer. *No.*

"I should have asked…why aren't you at school?"

"There's a car wash at the animal shelter. It's a fundraiser for the new kennels. I told Eileen I'd come back and help out. Holden and I drove down after we finished class for the day."

"And how is Holden?"

Briefly, all I can see is bloody knuckles. I think part of me is still holding my breath after seeing the devastation on his face from finding out he wasn't a match. Waiting for him to lash out again.

"He's good. Busy with basketball, even though the season hasn't even started. He's taking the train to visit Sydney tomorrow."

"He treats you well?"

I nod, my throat thick. I missed this with my dad, even if it's a little awkward that the topic is my love life. It feels like those mornings before school when we'd talk about basketball and he'd ask about my grades.

"The best."

My dad nods. "Good."

"Well, I—" I clear my throat and stand, glancing at the stack of papers. "I'll let you get back to work. Thanks for…talking."

Halfway to the door, I hear him call my name.

I glance back. "Yeah."

"I'll be home for dinner, honey."

I bite the inside of my cheek, battling the bizarre urge to cry. It's not an *everything will be okay* or *your mom and I are getting back together*, but it's something. And even if it doesn't change the outcome, I'll get to eat dinner with my entire family—minus Maggie—for the first time in a while.

"Okay. See you at home, Dad."

"See you at home."

I leave, carefully closing his door behind me.

CHAPTER THIRTY

HOLDEN

A horn blares to my left, scaring up an entire flock of pigeons. I hold my arm up to block my face, concerned a bird is going to fly right into me. Sidestep a pile of trash bags.

If by some miracle I get drafted and end up playing in a major city, it'll be a big adjustment. I liked growing up in a small town. And Richmond might be large, but the closest town has fewer than ten thousand residents.

Sydney attends a tiny, artsy school. The campus is literally just a couple of city blocks, nothing like Richmond's sprawling size.

I was worried about Sydney's future when she decided this was her dream school. Supposedly, they have one of the best theater programs in the country. But nothing in the shiny pamphlets Syd drooled over said anything about their graduates' employment prospects or median salary.

Maybe that concern was rich, coming from me. About one percent of Division I basketball players make it to pros. I'm not exactly angling for a set future. And I don't have many marketable skills. If I wasn't playing basketball, I was rarely studying. I'll graduate with a degree, but none of the accolades Cassia earned. The money my dad left me is mostly untouched. Richmond offered me a full athletic scholarship.

But I'm not about to have a kid.

Any worries I had about Sydney's future in theater are amplified now that she's pregnant. Now that she's decided to keep the baby.

I didn't raise any concerns when she decided on school here because Sydney has always been reasonable and mature. I trusted her to figure out what would work for her. And it was money our dad had left for her. Sydney's to use as she wanted.

I'm stressed about my future. Cassia's. And now I have Sydney's to worry about as well. She was supposed to be happy in New York next year. Not having a baby to take care of.

The first building I walk into is the Admissions one. I wave at the woman at the front desk apologetically and then head back out onto the street.

Sydney might not even be on campus, since it's a Saturday. But every time I've talked to her on the weekends, she's been here. She doesn't seem to spend much time at the shoebox she calls an apartment. Not that I blame her. My freshman year dorm room was bigger.

The next building I enter is the student center. I pass a bookstore and a coffee shop before I spot my sister.

She's laughing with two other girls on a sectional couch.

Laughter that comes to an abrupt stop when I approach.

"Well, *hello there*," one of the girls says, looking me up and down. It's an interest I've gotten used to over the years. As much as you can get used to it, I guess. Sometimes it's entertaining. Annoying at others.

This is the former, since Sydney has always been irritated when her friends showed any interest in me. I think the only reason she was okay with Cassia is that she saw us grow up together. Before my high school idiocy, Cassia and I were closer friends than she and Sydney were.

Or maybe she saw the same thing I realized—Cassia was always going to be *it* for me.

"He's taken, Ruby," Sydney says, rolling her eyes. "This is my brother, Holden. Holden, this is Ruby—" She points to the brunette. "And Bella." Sydney nods to the friend with overalls and a bob.

"*Very* nice to meet you, Holden." Ruby smirks, then stands. "We'll let you two catch up."

Bella waves at me and follows Ruby toward the coffee shop.

"What are you doing here?" Sydney asks, eyebrows raised. "Is everything okay?"

I take the open seat next to her, glancing around the space a little more. There's a wide array of artwork hanging on the walls, a clash of color and styles that's visually shocking. All student work, I assume.

"Everything is okay," I answer. "I just wanted to come...check in."

"What, you were in the neighborhood?"

Aside from moving Sydney in and out of the series of small, shitty apartments she's lived in, I've never visited her during the school year. We've always had separate interests that translated into separate lives. I play sports; she makes art. I like small towns; she lives in a big city. I draw attention; she avoids it. We're as different as Cassia and her sister, Maggie.

"No, I wasn't."

I didn't tell her I was coming because I didn't want her to ask why. Didn't want to get into anything I came to tell her over the phone.

"Okay..."

"Can I buy you some brunch?" I ask. "Your choice."

"I didn't think you knew what brunch was." She hikes her oversized bag up on one shoulder. "Is Cassia with you?"

"No. She's in Pembrooke to see her family."

"If you'd told me, I could have taken the train to see you guys. You didn't need to come here."

"It's not that far."

Sydney raises one eyebrow but doesn't argue. "There's a great bagel place down the block. Wanna go there?"

"Sure. Sounds good."

"Okay."

We exit the building and head down the street. The endless swirl of commotion around us that makes it challenging to keep up a conversation. Sydney is unbothered, so I guess you get used to it.

Horns blare. Workers shout. Construction equipment clangs.

I half-yell over the noise to ask Sydney a few basic questions about school as we walk. Over the years, I've heard her share enough to have some sense of which questions to ask about the production she's working on.

The bagel place is busy. It takes about fifteen minutes for us to order and pick up our food, then find an open booth to sit in.

I dig in right away. I ate breakfast early to make the train to come here, and I'm starving.

"Your friends seem nice," I say. I'd never met anyone she goes to school with before.

"Well, they're *big* fans of you."

I smirk, then turn serious. "Do your friends know? About…" I gesture toward her stomach.

Her expression shutters closed. "No."

"Why not?"

"Because when people find out you got knocked up in

college, they think you're slutty or stupid or both. I love Ruby and Bella, but they're terrible secret-keepers. Once they know, everyone will. Plus, I'm single."

My brow furrows. "What does your relationship status have to do with it?"

"Well, I'm not sure if you know this, but you have to have sex with a guy in order to end up pregnant. Since there's no boyfriend in the picture…everyone's going to wonder who the dad is. And I don't feel like dealing with that."

"Sarcasm not appreciated, Syd," I tell her. "And not to burst your little denial bubble, but you can't keep it a secret forever. Your friends will know you kept it a secret from them. And you could use the support. People to talk to. Cassia said she hasn't talked to you all week. And Harrison…are you guys talking?"

She huffs, balling up her napkin and tossing it on the table. "Is that what this little visit is? An *intervention*?"

"No. It's just me, worried about you."

She looks away, at the busy street outside. "I feel…ashamed. Like I fucked up and I should have known better."

"Sydney…" I exhale. "That's not how you should be thinking about this."

"Why not? I had sex—bad sex—once, and now the rest of my life has been upended? What kind of messed-up punishment is that?"

Details about how my little sister got pregnant is not what I was angling for on this trip. I run a hand through my hair, trying to scrub any thought of her and Harrison from my brain.

"It's not a punishment, Syd. It just…happened. Shit happens in life. And now you have to deal with it."

"Shit happens?" She snorts. "Wow. Wise wisdom, big brother. Like I didn't hear the stories about all the girls in high school. All the stories *Cassia* had to hear too."

I flinch.

"I'm glad you finally got your act together. But what if you'd gotten Grace Harper pregnant, huh? It could have happened, Holden. Because *Shit happens*, right? You think you and Cassia would still be together if it had?"

I exhale. I know Sydney is upset and scared and angry.

But this resentment from her is new.

She's made it clear when she was disappointed in me, and that's usually involved Cassia in some way. Those lectures lacked the stinging bitterness poisoning her words now.

"I don't know," I answer honestly.

I *do* know what Sydney is implying.

This should be happening to me, not her. I'm the sibling who's slept around. Who's made reckless decisions. Who hasn't cared about consequences.

She's wondering what the point of being cautious is if you're just dealt a random hand.

And I have no good answers for her. All I can do is support her through it the best I can.

Plus drop the bomb I came here to deliver.

After some awkward silence, our conversation transitions to easier topics. Sydney tells me about an art exhibit she went to last weekend and asks me about basketball. She knows better than to bother questioning me about my classes. This is her first week back, and preparations are already in full swing for the fall play.

About an hour has passed before she glances at her phone. "I didn't know you were coming, so I made plans this afternoon…"

"No worries. But, uh, before I go, I have to tell you something."

Sydney scans my face, her expression vacillating between curiosity and worry before finally landing on uncertain. "Okay…"

"It's about our mom."

She sucks in a sharp breath, her face a mask of pure shock. "The woman who *abandoned* us, you mean?"

I nod, not sure if that phrasing bodes well or poorly for this revelation. If the anger threading through her words means she won't care or reveals that she still cares too much, the same way I do.

Of the two of us, Sydney is the one I would characterize as sympathetic and understanding. I'm the apathetic asshole. I care about three things: Cassia, basketball, and my sister. Pretty sure Sydney's list is much longer.

If *I'm* struggling this much with this…I'm terrified how it'll affect her. But I'm resolved. This is the whole fucking reason I came all the way here—to tell her this in person.

Sydney's eyebrows creep higher and higher the longer I'm silent.

"What is it?" she finally asks.

"I don't know how to tell you this. Wasn't sure if I *should*. I found out by accident and I've been debating on whether to burden you with it. Especially after…" I clear my throat.

"Just tell me."

"She has cancer, Syd. It's bad; she's dying. I was at the hospital with Mark at the end of the summer and ran into her getting treatment."

"What kind of cancer?" Her voice has dropped to a near-whisper, sounding like a child's.

"Liver. She needs a transplant. I got tested, but I'm not a match. She's on a list."

"You got *tested*?" Her tone is incredulous. "You would have, what? Given her your liver?"

"Part of it, yeah. Mine would regrow."

"Still, that's a major surgery, right?"

"It's surgery, yeah." I deliberate, then add, "If I'd been a match and gone through with it, I probably would have missed most of the season."

Sydney looks shocked. "You would have given up *basketball*? For *her*?"

"I was…considering it. She's, you know, our mom."

"She's a *stranger*, Holden. I can't believe you even recognized her at the hospital. She must look totally different."

There are unspoken questions in her words. She wants to know more but isn't sure about asking.

"She looks sick," I say. "And I…" I exhale, debating and then deciding to come completely clean. Might as well get it all out there. I'm in this far. "It wasn't the first time I'd seen her since she left. She showed up when we were in high school, right after Dad died. Once at the house when you weren't home. Then again, at the high school after one of my practices. I wasn't sure if I should tell you. There was so much other stuff going on. We were both grieving…"

Sydney blinks at me. "You saw her? Talked to her? *Years* ago?"

"Yes."

"Did she ask about me?"

This. This is exactly why I never said a word. Because I hear the tentative hope in her voice, the foolishness that I had too. That she'd shown up to express regrets, to make amends. To rebuild bridges that had been reburned.

But she didn't offer any of those things. Didn't even give me the satisfaction of telling her that we wanted nothing to do with her. That she had to live with her mistakes.

And my mom isn't here to crush the hope in Sydney's voice, so I have to.

"No."

Sydney looks away, hiding her disappointment. "What did she want? Money?"

"No. It was…she said we were better off without her. That Dad was a better parent because she left." I shake my head. "No regrets. No apologies. There wasn't really anything to tell, but I probably should have said something to you. I never thought I'd see her again."

"But you'd still do that for her? Donate?"

"I was considering it. There was no harm in getting tested. Now I don't have to feel guilty about it."

"What if I'm a match?" she asks.

"You're *pregnant*, Sydney."

Her laugh is bitter. "I know. How ironic is that? We ruined her life, according to her. I messed up mine. And I could maybe save her life, except I can't because I repeated her mistakes."

"Don't think that way. It is what it is."

Sydney plays with her napkin. "I want to see her," she announces suddenly.

"What?"

"Mom. I want to see her. Do you know where she lives?"

I stare at her, stunned. I had no clue where this conversation might go, but this is the last thing I expected. "Um, sort of."

She nods. "Set it up. I'll come back to Pembrooke next weekend. You don't have to show up, but I'd like you to be there too."

"Of course I'll go with you. But, Syd… I'm not sure if this is a good idea. Honestly, I'm not sure *she*'ll show up. She's never… she still wants nothing to do with us. Her…the guy she was with is the one who told me about the cancer. She just walked away."

The determination remains on Sydney's face, no sign of second-guessing. I have no clue what that means. If it's a healthy or terrible reaction.

"There's only one way to find out." Sydney glances at her

phone. "I've really got to go. I'll see you next weekend. Thanks for the bagel."

Then she slides out of the booth and leaves me sitting here.

My phone vibrates with a text from Cassia.

CASSIA: *How did it go?*

I have no clue how to answer her.

CHAPTER THIRTY-ONE

CASSIA

"Wow. This is…wow."

I hide a smile behind my water bottle as Jackie stares at the group of shirtless guys washing cars.

Pembrooke High's basketball team turned out in full force. JV and Varsity are in complete attendance.

I'm not surprised Holden's influence surpassed our graduation. I *am* surprised by how many of Pembrooke's residents have shown up to support the fundraiser—including my own family.

My mom came by with the twins and Sally about an hour ago. Seeing my siblings excited and smiling was a highlight of the morning. It's hard sometimes, having such a huge age gap with some of my siblings.

Sydney bemoaned being so close in age to Holden plenty of times, wishing for some more separation. And in some ways, it's fun, getting to relive my childhood through the eyes of my younger brothers and sisters.

But right now it's hard, knowing they'll have a different childhood than I did.

My dad showed up for dinner last night as promised. I don't

think any of my siblings—except Regan—noticed the way my parents avoided each others' gazes the entire meal. How my dad loaded the dishwasher and kicked a soccer ball around with the twins before heading into his home office and closing the door. It was still shut when I went to sleep, long after my mom had retired. My guess is my dad slept on the couch in his office.

Regan found out about the divorce by snooping through some papers on her desk, according to my mom. Which means there *are* papers, something I didn't know.

And Maggie knows about the divorce too. My mom told her before she left for college, same as me. I'm not surprised I haven't heard from Maggie about it. We've never had the sort of relationship where she comes to me for advice or assurance. She's more of a realist than I am in some ways, and much less of a hopeless romantic. Maybe she saw the signals I missed that our parent's relationship had changed for the worse. If Holden Adams had ignored her in high school, Maggie would have dated the rest of the basketball team right in front of him. That's just never been me.

Holden shows up at the animal shelter around two. I haven't seen him since I dropped him off at the condo yesterday before heading to my dad's law firm.

He headed into the city early this morning to see Sydney. To check in with her. And to tell her about their mom, I'm guessing, although he didn't explicitly tell me what he'd decided to do about that. We've both avoided the subject since I offered to get tested.

And he never responded to my text asking how the visit went, which I'm assuming means not well. I haven't heard anything from Sydney.

But there's no stress on his face as he approaches me, smiling at the long line of cars still waiting to be washed.

"How's it going?" he asks.

"*So* good. Ten dogs have already been adopted, and there's two hours left. Plus—" I glance at Jackie, who's now off standing with a few of her friends, including Harrison's sister. "There's been a lot of interest in volunteering somewhere that holds events like this."

"Huh." He smirks. "Wonder why." Then glances at the wire pens that have been set up so people can meet and play with the dogs available for adoption. "Has Milo been adopted?"

I shake my head. "I'm sad…and relieved."

His smile is bittersweet. "I know."

"You never replied to my text. How did it go with Sydney?"

"Sorry, I was distracted. And then I got off at the wrong subway stop, almost missed my train." Holden exhales. "Sydney wants to see her. Wants me to set up a meeting to talk to her next weekend."

"Really?" Sydney avoids the subject of her mom as much as possible. I didn't consider she would want to see her. Based on Holden's expression, he didn't either. As far as I know, he had no plans to ever reach out to his mom. To leave her to her fate, as sad as that sounds.

"Yeah."

"Do you have a way to contact her?"

"We didn't swap phone numbers. But I know where she lives. If I get creative, I'm sure I can find something." Holden leans down to pat the lab in the nearest cage. "He looks like Lily."

"I thought that too."

His smile is bittersweet. "I miss her."

"Me too." She died last year.

Catherine found Lily cold and unresponsive in her bed one morning and brought her to the vet to be cremated.

Neither of us were here, and I'll always wish I'd been able to say goodbye to her. For so long, Lily was a reminder who Holden was to me. He might have ignored me in the halls and went out with other girls, but Lily was a reminder he'd begged his dad for a dog and named her after a flower. For me.

Holden gives the lab one final pat and then straightens. "Finn called on the train home. He's hosting a party tonight."

I roll my eyes. "Of course he is."

"I told him we probably wouldn't make it."

"Why not?"

"I thought you'd want to spend more time with your family."

"They're going to a barbeque tonight, so I can't anyway. I was going to come over to the condo."

Holden studies me. "So…you want to go?"

I shrug. "Sure."

His jaw works a couple of times, deliberating something. "She might be there."

"I can handle it." If anything, I might savor the opportunity to rub our relationship in her face a little. For what she did to Brooks, if nothing else.

———

Arlington University has more of a town feel to it than Richmond's campus does. We arrive just before six.

Instead of heading straight to Finn's frat house, Holden parks my sedan downtown. We wander past storefronts of bookstores and clothing shops for about fifteen minutes before he guides me into an Italian restaurant with real candles and cloth napkins.

It's one of the nicest places I've ever been to.

"Are you sure you want to eat here?" I whisper once a waiter shows us to our table.

He's usually more of a paper napkins and pizza kind of guy.

Holden grins. "Uh-huh."

I showered after the car wash earlier, but only to put on jeans and a t-shirt. I'm dressed for a college party—my version of it, at least. The woman at the table next to ours is wearing a silk dress and heels.

We're underdressed, but I can't really bring myself to care. The last time we had dinner together, Holden's hand was bleeding, and we'd just had a big argument.

This is already an improvement.

We talk about nothing important throughout dinner, and it's incredible.

The past weeks have been filled with heavy conversations, following months without a single word exchanged. It's a relief, to make predictions about the next season of a show we've watched together. To celebrate what a success the car wash was— it raised several thousand dollars. To simply appreciate each other's company.

To joke and laugh and tease and flirt, like this is our first date and we haven't known each other most of our lives.

The food is delicious. Holden gets Bolognese and I order ravioli. We split a Caesar salad and sip fancy wine.

It all feels very adult. Like a glimpse into what the rest of our lives will look like.

By the time we leave the restaurant, I'm so full that it's almost uncomfortable. There's a slight chill in the evening air as we walk back toward the parked car.

I squint at the tall silhouette in the distance. "What's that?"

Holden follows my gaze. "It's the water tower."

"You've been there before?"

I haven't been to Arlington's campus since one visit freshman year. Holden has visited here much more frequently. And recently.

"Nah. Finn has mentioned it. The guys go hang out there sometimes."

"Can we go?" I'm not dreading the party, but I'd rather spend time with him alone instead of sharing his attention. Dragging this portion of the evening out as long as possible is my preference.

Holden raises one eyebrow in surprise but agrees. "Yeah, sure."

It takes about ten minutes for us to follow the path. It leads from the small downtown section and through a wooded area. There's no gravel or map, the grass worn away by forbidden steps.

I gaze up at the tall, distinctive shape, silhouetted against the darkening sky.

"Let's climb it," I decide impulsively.

Both of Holden's brows rise this time. "You serious?"

I roll my eyes at his incredulity. I can be fun. Spontaneous. "Yeah. The view from up there is probably amazing."

"Not when you're falling to your death."

My laugh is short and surprised. "This coming from the guy who used to *fight for money* in high school?"

"That was different."

"It sounds just as reckless to me."

"You weren't involved. That's why it was different."

I still, absorbing the intensity behind his words. Processing the protectiveness.

"You can be kinda romantic sometimes, you know that?"

Holden grins as he shrugs out of his coat. "I have my moments. Here, hold this."

He hands me his basketball jacket, then starts walking toward the ladder.

"Wait, what are you doing?" I call after him.

"Climbing it!"

"You just said it was too dangerous."

"You just said that you want to climb it. So I'm going to check it out."

I bite my bottom lip, watching him step onto the first rung. Second-guessing my own sense of adventure.

"It's fine. I wasn't serious. Let's just go."

He grins over one shoulder. It's a dangerous, destructive one. The same one he used to flash on the Friday nights he'd come home late, drunk on adrenaline and who knows what else. I never thought there would be a day when I was the one who incited that in him.

"Yeah, you were," he tells me.

"Holden, I'm serious. If you think it's not safe for me to climb, do you really think I want—"

He starts climbing, a loud rattle echoing through the night air as more space stretches between him and the ground.

"*Holden*!"

His chuckle is the only response.

It only takes him a couple of minutes to reach the top.

My heart races for every single second of them.

"You were right," he calls down. "The view's great from up here."

I exhale. He still has to make it down, but that seems much more likely now that he made it up there unscathed.

"You coming?"

I eye the rusty ladder. Yeah, this was my idea. And it now seems like a bad one.

"Get your ass up here, Nolan!"

I trust Holden completely. If he says it's safe, I believe him.

I slip his coat on. The smell of cinnamon surrounds me as I walk toward the ladder and take a deep breath. Glance up, at what looks like a very long climb.

There's nothing wrong with being cautious. But I've felt a little more reckless lately.

Maybe it's being a senior, knowing next year my life will drastically change.

Maybe it's the way my family is fracturing and I can't do anything about it.

Whatever the reason, I'm not sure that it's a bad thing. Comfort zones can be as constricting as they are reassuring.

It takes me longer to climb than it took Holden, but I make it.

And the view from the top *is* amazing. It reminds me a little of our hike on the camping trip, seeing so much land stretching around. Dark forest stretches in one direction, the twinkling lights of the town and the university in the other.

I offer Holden his coat back but he tells me to keep it, his eyes darkening to navy the way they often do whenever he sees me wearing something of his.

We stand and stare at the view for a while before Holden's phone begins buzzing.

"Finn is wondering where we are," he tells me. "You ready to go?"

"Yeah," I agree.

Holden heads down and I'm right behind him. I'm not sure he could *actually* catch me if I lost my grip or a rung suddenly crumbled, but that's what I tell myself the whole trip down.

We retrace the dirt path that led from downtown here, the path hard to see now that the sun is almost gone.

I can see the lights of the town through the trees. That's what I'm focused on, when three guys suddenly appear on the path in front of us. There's an opening to the left that leads to a clearing —almost a park, but not really—that they must have come from.

They're high, by the smell of it, and a couple are also holding beer bottles.

Holden immediately tenses, so I do too.

"Wassup?" one asks, grinning at us.

They don't seem unfriendly, but I'm still uneasy. I shift a little closer to Holden, my grip on his jacket tightening.

"Hey, you're the Richmond basketball player, right?" Another guy, this one in front—the guy closest to us—waves the open beer bottle he's holding in Holden's direction.

Some splashes out of the rim, foam fizzing as it hits exposed soil.

"I play." That's all Holden says.

"And you're a real hotshot, huh?"

"Depends on who you ask."

"I'm asking you."

Holden smirks, the expression a strange contrast to the tense line of his shoulders. "No one's that lucky. Talent and skill show up somewhere along the way."

"If I put some money on you, would that be a safe investment?"

I already figured, based on the way they're wandering around in the woods, stoned and drunk, that these guys probably aren't upstanding citizens or model students. But a fresh thrill of unease runs through me, trying to figure out exactly what their angle is here. Their interest in Holden is especially concerning.

"I'm one player out of five, man. Whether we win depends on a lot of factors, including the other team."

Beer Bottle nods slowly at Holden's answer, but there's nothing stilted in the way his eyes dart toward me. I'm beginning to think it's all an act—the beer bottle and the easy drawl.

The most dangerous predators hide in plain sight.

If I were alone, I'd be petrified motionless. But I trust Holden —more than anyone else in the world. If anyone is going to get me out of a volatile situation, it's him.

You weren't involved. That's why it's different.

That's what he told me earlier.

I'm not sure that applies in a situation like this. This isn't a rusty ladder. Would he fight these guys? Would he win? The rumor in high school was he never lost a match.

"Next week, against Lincoln. What are the odds?"

"I don't know," Holden responds. "Ask a bookie."

"Again, I'm asking you."

"Any Richmond player—including me—would tell you we'll win. If you ask guys at Lincoln, they'd say the opposite."

The guy who clearly is the ringleader shakes his head. "Not helpful."

"That's all I have for you."

"Come on, give me something."

I glance at Holden, panicked. His expression is blank, purposefully so. Completely clean of emotion.

It feels like a rubber band is constricting around my chest. Blood pounds, sending adrenaline rushing through my system.

"Don't you want to impress your date? If you give me any good intel, I'll even make sure you get a cut of the profits."

The front guy—the ringleader—takes another step forward.

"What the fuck are you going to do, Nelson?" Holden snaps. Any ease is gone from his voice and posture. He looks like a coiled predator about to strike. He looks *dangerous*. And a lot more intimidating than the three guys facing us.

I've never seen him fight. Never wanted to. But the adrenaline in my bloodstream is a thrill I wasn't expecting. Random facts I remember from my animal behavior class last year run through my head.

Holden is very much giving off alpha vibes.

The guy hesitates, like he's realizing the same.

"Walk away," Holden advises. "If you want to know what bet to make next week, go check my stats."

Nelson hesitates, then nods. "Let's go, guys."

I exhale a sigh of relief as they retreat, headed back in the same direction they came from.

Holden's hand lands on my lower back on top of his jacket, which I'm still wearing. He guides me along the rest of the dirt path and onto the sidewalk, both of our steps faster than they were on the way to the water tower.

"Are you okay?" he asks me quietly.

I nod. "Yeah."

"Are you sure?"

"Yeah…just…" I exhale a laugh. "Uh, wow. That was crazy. Who was that?"

"Jimmy Nelson."

I shake my head. "Never heard of him."

Holden smiles. "Good."

"Who is he?"

"He considers himself an entrepreneur. Drugs and—"

"Gambling?"

"Apparently, yeah. Finn crossed paths with him a few times."

"Finn does drugs?"

"He experimented some. And I've heard about Nelson from a few other guys. He has a reputation for bottom-feeding. Trying to talk guys into point-shaving. Shit like that."

"What if he bothers you again?"

He shrugs as we reach the car, appearing unbothered by the prospect. "What if he does?"

"He seems…I don't know. Shady. Slimy."

Holden smirks. "I wasn't going to start anything just now. But I can take care of myself, flower. They were lucky you were there. If they bother me again, they'll regret it."

CHAPTER THIRTY-TWO

HOLDEN

Finn is standing out on the front porch when we walk up the path toward the front door of his frat house.

"Hey, you guys made it!" He grins like he didn't just call me five times and text me ten, asking how soon we were showing up.

"Just happened to be in the neighborhood," I say.

The front door opens again, and Harrison steps out.

I had no idea he'd be here, and I'm not sure how to feel about it.

Cassia heads inside with Finn after casting me a worried, warning glance. I linger on the porch and Harrison stays out here too.

Finn doesn't seem to notice how Harrison remains outside with me, happy to show Cassia around, which makes me think Harrison hasn't mentioned to him why this might turn physical.

Whatever. Harrison's news to share.

This is the first time I've seen Baker since finding out he slept with my sister. Remnants of adrenaline buzz in my veins. Maybe I should have punched Nelson the second he stepped toward me. It would have been a hell of a lot more effective than talking him out of starting shit, and it might be easier to keep from using my fists now.

Harrison exhales, facing me as soon as the door shuts. "Go for it, Adams. I know you've been dying to deck me for years."

I don't move. Don't correct him, because he's right.

But I'm not going to punch him, no matter how satisfying it would be to. It won't change anything that happened. Won't help Sydney. "My fucking *sister*, Baker?"

Harrison flinches. "I know."

"No, you don't. She was supposed to go to London this semester. Did she tell you that? She was supposed to have this whole life, which you *fucked up* when you *fucked her*."

"I made a mistake. You've made mistakes before."

"This isn't about *my* mistakes, which you've always been happy to point out. This is about *your* mistake."

"I'm taking responsibility, Adams. Whatever Sydney wants, I'm willing to do."

"What she *wants* is not having to deal with this."

"If she decided to end the pregnancy, I would have supported that decision."

I snort. "Yeah, I'm sure you would have. Easy for you to say, when you don't have to make the choice *or* live with the conse-quences."

Harrison exhales. "What do you want me to say, Holden? Do I wish it had never happened? Yeah. But it did, and I'm trying to make the best of it. My life is going to change too. Not as much as Sydney's, I get that. Nothing I can do about that either. All I can do is be there for her, and that's exactly what I've been doing. She hasn't exactly been open to a lot of support."

I picture Sydney in the bagel shop, defiant about not telling her friends about the pregnancy. On this, I believe Harrison. I'm sure she's embarrassed. Scared. Before they hooked up, I'm not sure if they'd ever exchanged a single word. Not the most solid of foundations.

"Keep trying."

"I will," he tells me. "I get she's your sister. But that's my kid. I take it seriously."

I sigh, suddenly exhausted. "I know. I'm a little on edge." It's the closest to an apology I'll come. "We just ran into Jimmy Nelson."

Harrison's eyebrows rise. He's heard the same stories I have. "Where?"

"In town. We stopped for dinner. Then Cassia wanted to climb the water tower."

"Everything okay?"

"Yeah. I handled it."

"Good."

I punch his shoulder. "Come on. I could use a drink."

The party is in full swing when I step inside into the living room. I spot Cassia standing by the couch, talking with Finn and Brooks.

I catch her eye and point toward the kitchen, indicating I'm going to grab a drink. She already has a cup in hand.

Cassia nods.

Harrison follows me into the cavernous kitchen. It's fancy, all shiny appliances and marble countertops. I've never gotten involved with any of the Greek life at Richmond, but the college definitely doesn't take any of it as seriously as Finn's frat does. It's one of the nicest houses I've ever been inside.

I mix whiskey with some cola, then head back toward the living room.

"Holden Adams."

I turn at the sound of my name, facing Travis Dennis. He's a senior as well, a center on Arlington's basketball team.

We've had plenty of altercations on the court. This is the first time I've run into him off it. And it couldn't be a worse time, because I'm still amped up on adrenaline after talking to Jimmy Nelson.

"You're a long way from home," he tells me, sneering.

"I was invited. What's your excuse for showing up?"

"This is my campus, Adams."

I scoff at that. Basketball isn't even that big here. Football reigns supreme. If Liam Stevens made that claim, I might believe it. Travis just sounds desperate.

"Technically, we're not *on campus*, Dennis."

He makes a show of looking behind me. "Doesn't look like your boys are here watching your back."

"Because this is a party, not a back alley brawl." I glance deliberately at the two guys flanking Travis. I think they're both on Arlington's team, but I can't remember either of their names. "Read the room before you bring your back-up."

"And look a little harder." Finn appears beside me, Harrison stepping up right behind him.

I'd rather Finn didn't get involved and I don't need Harrison's support, but I do enjoy the spasm of unease that crosses Travis's face.

Evidently, he doesn't like even numbers.

"Seriously, Thomas?" Travis says. The betrayed look he aims Finn's way is ridiculously exaggerated. "Richmond plays dirty."

"We *win*," I reply. Knowing it won't deescalate the situation but also unable to resist the jab.

We're undefeated against Arlington.

I regret baiting him when Cassia walks into the kitchen with Brooks.

"Your first scrimmage is against Lincoln, right?" Travis asks me.

I nod, my attention torn between him and Cassia and trying to hide it. Finn spots her too, tensing beside me.

Travis is also looking Cassia's way now. But it has nothing to do with me. He didn't catch my reaction. He's just checking her out.

"Hey, gorgeous. Can I get you a drink?"

Cassia glances his way. Holds her cup up. "I'm all set."

Her tone is polite, but firm.

"Let me get you a drink."

I have no idea what Travis is angling at. If he's trying to bow out of the conflict while preserving his pride. If he's trying to show off his subpar seduction skills.

I'd rather not escalate the situation, especially after the scene with Nelson earlier. No matter what Cassia said, I'm sure it rattled her.

But when Travis takes a step toward her, my control snaps.

"She's not interested."

"Let her talk for herself, Adams."

"Actually, he's right," Cassia says. "I'm not interested."

Travis's eyes dart between us, and I see the moment it clicks. "I thought you looked familiar. You could do a lot better than Adams, gorgeous."

I walk forward, ensuring I'm a barrier between Cassia and the dick who's incapable of shutting his mouth.

He's in good shape, but I've got a few inches and a lot of muscle on Travis. He likes to talk trash on the court, but he's never been able to follow through on it there. My gut is he won't now either, but I'm not willing to risk Cassia ending up in the crossfire.

"Keep talking, Dennis. I dare you."

"You won't do shit." Travis's voice is confident, but I catch his quick glance around the room.

We're attracting a lot of attention. And maybe this is "his campus," but I'm friendly with plenty of Finn's frat brothers. I don't think he has the home court advantage that he's acting like he does.

I shrug, purposefully indifferent. "Wanna find out?"

He doesn't.

I know he'll walk away as soon as he looks away, breaking eye contact. And he does, shaking his head like I'm not worth his time before disappearing into the next room with his buddies.

Finn exhales. "Way to keep things interesting."

I smirk. "One thing I'm always good for."

CHAPTER THIRTY-THREE

CASSIA

I'm in the library when my phone buzzes with a call from Sydney. I rush outside before the call drops, inhaling the fall air deeply.

"Celebrity sighting," she tells me, as soon as I answer the call.

"Who?"

"Scarlett Kensington."

"Really?"

Sydney and I read *Haute* magazine religiously, drooling over chic clothes we'll probably never be able to afford.

She tells me the full story—where she was, who she was with, what she was wearing—and ends it by admitting a pigeon pooped on her bag when she was walking to the subway afterward.

One minute we're laughing at the terrible luck.

Then Sydney sniffles. Once. Twice.

And I know why she really called.

"Holden told you?" she asks.

"Yeah. I'm so sorry, Syd."

"I've never had a mom, but it feels like I'm losing her all over again. How silly is that?"

"It's not silly at all. It's awful."

"How could Holden not tell me sooner?"

I inhale, staring across the campus green. It's a beautiful day out. I hate that I'm stuck in the library filling out vet school applications, but I wouldn't be getting anything accomplished if I sat outside to enjoy the weather.

"Just a guess, but I think he was trying to protect you."

Sydney sighs. "I'm sorry. I'm putting you in the middle."

"You have a right to be upset."

"But not a right to be mad at him, right?" More sniffles. "I could get tested. Just because Holden's not a match…I could be."

I don't reply right away, not sure if she's serious. When she says nothing else, I say, "Sydney, you're *pregnant*."

"I haven't decided if I'm going to keep it."

"Yes, you have."

She texted me asking if I liked the name Everett for a boy last week, before she found out about her mom.

"What if I'm the only person who can help her? The only person who could save her? She's…she's my mom."

"You don't owe her anything, Sydney."

"Holden got tested, and he hates her more than I do. I thought he did, at least. It feels like there's this big secret he's been keeping from me." More sniffles. "I'm sorry. Let's talk about something else. What's new with you?"

"Well…my parents are getting divorced."

"*What?*"

"I thought there was a chance it might not happen. But…I talked to my mom yesterday, and she signed the papers. It's going through. They've been separated since the spring."

"Wow. I-I can't believe it. They always seemed so *happy*."

"Yeah. Things change, I guess." I kick at a pebble on the pavement.

"Are you doing okay?"

"I'll be fine. I feel bad for the twins and Sally and Regan. Maggie and I are both out of the house now. They'll have the harder adjustment."

"It's still an adjustment for you."

I exhale. "I know. Not sure what Thanksgiving will look like this year."

"When did you find out?" she asks.

"A little while ago. You had enough going on and I needed some time to…process it."

"I'm so sorry, Cassia."

"It'll be all right. I want them both to be happy. If this is what they decided, there's nothing I can do. Right?"

"Yeah. Right."

We switch to catching up on other topics, which is a relief. I feel like my entire life has been overtaken by stressful, scary secrets lately. Maybe that's just a part of adulthood.

We talk for a while before Sydney has to leave for a play rehearsal.

"I hope it goes well this weekend," I tell her before we hang up.

"You and Holden tell each other everything, huh?" She sounds happy about it, not annoyed.

"We're trying out the truth thing."

She laughs. "I hope it goes well too. But honestly? I just need it to *happen*. To look at her. Now that I'm going to be a mom, it's even harder to understand how she could have made that decision."

"Maybe there's no explanation."

"Yeah." Sydney sighs. "Part of me, just—I never had any closure. Holden remembers her, but I was only four when she left. And it's not like we reminisced with our dad about the good old days. I don't even remember what she looked like. If I passed her on the street, I probably wouldn't recognize her. And she's… dying, so this is my last chance. For anything."

"I hope you get everything you need from it, Syd."

"I feel bad, making Holden do it."

I hear the question in her voice, wondering what he's told me. This is just as uncomfortable as when I was trying to share details of my first time and avoid the weirdness of us discussing her brother. Two important, distinct relationships—my closest, oldest friend and my boyfriend—with a lot of overlap.

"He doesn't do things he doesn't want to do. You know that," I say, attempting a little levity.

"Maybe that was true once," she replies. "Not anymore." Then sighs. "I've gotta get to class. I'll talk to you soon, okay?"

"Okay. Bye, Syd."

"Bye."

She hangs up. I stand and soak in a little more Vitamin D, then head back inside the library.

CHAPTER THIRTY-FOUR

HOLDEN

I drum my fingers impatiently on the scarred tabletop. Sydney glances over at me but says nothing. She's been biting her bottom lip for the past fifteen minutes.

Part of me is worried our mom won't show. It would be incredibly on brand for her.

The rest of me is scared she *will* show.

I had to look up my mother's phone number *online*. I knew what town she's living in—or I did two years ago—and pulled up a landline. Called and left a message after a generic voicemail asking her to meet me at Roxbury Diner today at one p.m.. Maybe it was the wrong number. Maybe she doesn't listen to her messages. Maybe she got it but won't show. Who the hell knows?

It's 1:05 now.

The waitress reappears, asking if we want to order anything again.

I glance at Sydney. She shakes her head.

"We're still deciding," I tell the waitress. "Thanks."

She sighs, nods, then leaves.

The bell above the door tinkles. I glance over automatically, not really expecting it to be her.

But it is.

Sydney inhales sharply next to me. I'm not sure if it's because she's recognized her or because she's reacting to her appearance.

Our mom looks worse than the last time I saw her. Paler. Skinnier. But her gaze is alert and aware as she glances around the diner, her eyes landing on me first and then sliding over to Sydney sitting beside me.

Her lips purse before she says something to the man accompanying her. It's the same guy who was with her in the hospital.

He takes a seat on one of the stools along the long countertop.

Our mom approaches us alone.

At least she didn't just turn around and leave. That would have been worse than her not showing at all, I think. For all her faults, she's never been a coward. She spent two days packing up all her belongings and left in the middle of the afternoon. She didn't desert us in the middle of the night with only her phone and wallet. It was a calculated choice, not a panicked reaction.

Sydney's knee knocks mine as it bounces below the table.

I have no assurances to offer my sister.

I'm not going to tell her it'll be fine, but I'm expecting it won't be. That this will break her heart more than it's already been shattered.

There's no welcoming smile on our mom's face as she draws closer. None of our short conversations have given me the impression she wishes our relationship was anything different than what it is.

I conveyed that to Sydney, clearly.

But I know from personal experience that's different from hearing it straight from the source. And I want to shield my little sister from that pain.

I can't, though.

She reaches our booth, pausing at the end instead of taking a seat. "Hello, Holden."

I nod in acknowledgment.

"Your voicemail didn't mention Sydney was coming."

"I'm surprised you remember my name," Sydney says. Her anger is a tangible thing in the air, humming with tension.

"Thirteen hours of labor left an impression."

"Is *that* why you left?" Sydney snaps. "Because I took too long to arrive?"

"There were several reasons I left. But no, that wasn't one of them."

It's bizarre, that's she's here. That I'm witnessing my mother and my sister *talking*. It's just been me and Sydney for a long time, it's felt like. Even when my dad was alive, he was often gone. I adjusted to that. I got used to my mom not even being a thought, much less a breathing body standing a foot away.

Sydney leans back, crossing her arms. "Care to share them?"

Our mom looks to me. "I already told Holden. I thought you called me because of the cancer."

"You have cancer?" I ask. Gasp a little dramatically.

And I think I catch a glimmer of something different on my mom's face. Amusement, maybe a trace of affection.

She blinks, and it disappears. "Vincent said he told you."

My gaze flicks to the man sitting at the counter, sipping a cup of coffee and reading the paper. Looking like he hasn't a care in the world. Acting like this is any old Sunday, and accompanying my mom to a diner to talk to the two kids she abandoned is some normal occurrence for him.

"You two married?" I ask.

"No."

My mom finally sits down. Maybe she's just tired from her

sickness. But it feels like a tiny step forward. A choice to stay, when all she's ever done is leave.

"Kids?"

Sydney straightens beside me.

"No."

Knowing that helps a little. As much as anything could. She didn't go out and replicate the life she had somewhere else. She truly didn't want it.

Sydney is saying nothing.

I'm expecting my mom to get up and leave at any second, so I ask the question that's been bugging me. I know she's dying. I know it'll happen soon. But it sucks wondering when that clock will expire. Not knowing when I won't have a mother in every sense of the word, instead of just most.

"Dr. Meyers wouldn't give me a straight prognosis when I talked to him. Did he tell you one? How long do you have?"

My mom leans forward, the first spark of true emotion I've seen from her fully appearing. "You talked to my doctor?"

"Yep." I sip some water.

"Why?"

"Just answer the question, Lana."

I refuse to call her *Mom*, even if I still refer to her that way in my head. It's a title she never earned, one she threw back at me.

She looks away, expression shuttering closed again. "I need a transplant."

"I know that. If you don't get one, how long?"

"I don't know. Months. A year at most, maybe."

Beside me, Sydney sucks in a sharp breath. It's shorter than I was expecting too.

"That's not much time."

She still won't look at me. "If you're offering some absolution because I'm sick, I don't want it. I made my choices, Holden."

"There's no forgiving what you did. I'm only here because Sydney wanted to see you."

Our mom finally looks at Sydney.

"You went to see Holden. Years ago, after Dad died. Why didn't you talk to me?" Sydney asks.

Our mother's voice is even and calm, but I can feel the emotions radiating off of her. "Because Holden was like me and you were always like your father."

Her tone is matter of fact, stating out loud what I've told myself many times before. What I spent *years* telling myself.

"Holden is *nothing* like you," Sydney hisses. "He's loyal and—"

"It's fine, Syd," I say.

I don't need her to defend me. I don't care what my mom thinks, what assumptions she's made about similarities. She doesn't know me. The only reason I'm here is for Sydney.

"Holden got tested, you know. You *abandoned* us without a second thought, and what did Holden do when he found out you were sick? He went to the hospital to get tested to see if he was a match and could donate his own liver to save your miserable life. He's *nothing* like you."

Dr. Meyers obviously didn't say anything, because there's a clear flicker of surprise on my mom's face.

"You didn't even *bother to see me*, the one time you showed up in the past decade, and I would have gotten tested too. Would've helped you too. Except I can't, because I'm pregnant!"

More surprise.

The mask she showed up wearing is slowly splintering.

The waitress appears. "Are you all ready to order yet?"

It's almost funny, her expression twisting uncomfortably as she registers the total, awkward silence around the table.

I clear my throat. "Uh, we're still deciding," I say.

"Okay."

She leaves quickly, and I'm guessing she won't be back.

"Holden, can you give us a minute?" Sydney asks quietly.

I scan her expression, reading the determination there. "Yeah, sure."

I slide out of the booth, glancing over my shoulder once before heading for the long countertop. Sydney is leaning forward, talking. I'm uneasy about leaving them to talk alone, but I'm not sure my presence was helping much anyway.

After a moment of deliberation, I take the stool one down from Vincent.

He looks up at me. Sips more coffee, still looking shockingly unbothered by the family drama he's here with. "Want me to order you a cup? It's decent joe."

I'm startled by the offer. His demeanor is a complete one-eighty from our last conversation in a hospital hallway. "No, I'm good." Reluctantly I add, "Thanks."

Paper rustles as his attention returns to his article.

I study the Formica countertop for a minute before speaking again.

"Thank you for telling me," I say. "About my mom's health. I wasn't sure if I wanted to know. But never knowing…I think that would have been worse, the more I think about it. So…thanks."

A long beat of silence follows.

"There are some decisions that are so big you can't take back," Vincent tells me. "Can never undo them once they're made. And our instinct is always survival. I guess, what I'm trying to say, is that regret is a lot to carry."

If you told me weeks ago, months ago, years ago, that I'd be sitting with a stranger in a diner and nodding along to his assessment of my mother, I'd have thought you were crazy. But I get what Vincent is saying.

I do share similarities with my mom.

Not just selfishness.

And maybe that biological connection gives me some ability to understand how convincing yourself walking away from your kids was in their best interest and then spending the rest of your life doubling down on that irreversible decision.

"I think I will take that coffee," I say.

Vincent flags down the waitress and a steaming mug appears in front of me a couple of minutes later.

I sip and continue staring at the Formica countertop, battling the urge to look behind me and check on Sydney.

The last time I was here was with Cassia. Her sister Maggie hooked me into a plan to date a freshman on the basketball team.

And it was the first time in a long time that Cassia and I talked for real. About the past—about our past. The first time I got a glimpse of how much I'd hurt her by keeping my distance in high school.

It feels like a lifetime ago.

I'm so lost in my thoughts that I jump when Sydney pokes my side. Her expression is neutral, and I don't know what that means. I'm not sure if there was ever an ideal outcome from this meeting.

Vincent is already standing, offering an arm to my mom.

"Goodbye, Holden," she says, taking his.

We stare at each other for a few heavy seconds.

And I know, somehow, that she's not just *saying* goodbye. That this *is* goodbye.

This is the last time I'll ever see her. Whether she dies in a few months or receives a transplant, she'll never be a part of my life. We'll never meet here every Sunday for brunch like a normal family.

I resent the hell out of her for that. For being too weak to carry the regret. For never being brave enough to attempt amends. For making me question if I was capable of those things.

I've had most of my life to hate her. But I still love her, just like my dad did. Just like Sydney does. And it doesn't matter that she never loved us back. Or if she did, that it was never enough. That doesn't change how I feel about her.

So I say it, one final time. The word I swore I'd never speak to her again. For me, more for her.

I swallow. "Goodbye, Mom."

She and Vincent leave. I stay sitting. Sydney stays standing.

Once they're out of sight, I glance at my sister.

"Did you get what you needed?" I ask her.

"I-I don't know." She's staring at the closed door where our mom disappeared.

"There's no happy ending here, Syd."

Even if our mom beats the odds with her illness, she'll never be *our mom*. We'll never spend holidays together. She'll never meet Sydney's kid. My kids. There will never be a time when she's in the audience at one of Sydney's plays or in the stands at one of my games.

She picked a different path.

And resenting her—judging her—will never change that choice.

———

I call Cassia after dropping Sydney off at the condo. She's spending the night in Pembrooke and taking the train back into the city first thing tomorrow. I have to get back to campus for a weight session.

"Hey." Her tone is soft when she answers on the third ring, already knowing what I'm calling her about.

"Hi."

"How…how did it go?"

I exhale, flipping on a blinker before I turn onto the highway.

"It sucked. She has a year, probably less. She looked terrible. Basically ignored Sydney, at first."

She says nothing, letting me rant.

"It sucked," I repeat. "Every time I see her, it feels like I lose her all over again. Why can't she change? Why can't it end? Why can't she *apologize*? Just once. Admit she made mistakes. I mean, she's dying. If there's ever a time to swallow your pride, that's it, right?"

"I'm so sorry, Holden. I wish I could fix it all for you. Is there anything I can do?"

"You're doing it. But you have to go, right? Don't you have your study group at seven?"

"You memorized my schedule?" She sounds surprised.

"Wasn't that the point of you sending it to me?"

Her laugh still has some shock in it. "It was for reference. I wasn't planning on testing you."

"Well, I'd get an A."

"I told them I wasn't coming this week," she tells me.

"Why?"

"Because I was hoping you'd call me after and I wanted to be able to answer."

"You didn't have to do that."

"I *wanted* to."

"We met her at Roxbury Diner, you know."

"Oh, yeah. I haven't been there forever, not since I stopped chauffeuring Regan to her dance classes."

"That was the last time I was there, with you."

"Your failed matchmaker attempt, you mean?"

I smile, even though she can't see me. "Maggie and Ben went

out a couple of times. And *we're* together, so it definitely wasn't a failure."

"Yeah, but the date was for them."

"You really think I would have showed up if you hadn't been there?"

Her silence answers for her.

"That was when I realized how bad I'd fucked up, Cas. Talking to you there, I realized my feelings for you hadn't gone anywhere. That they *weren't* going anywhere."

"Well, you always were a slow learner."

I snort. "True."

"Is Sydney doing okay?"

"I think so."

We didn't talk much on the drive home, but she seemed thoughtful, not sad. She and Catherine were going to grab dinner.

"Same as me, probably. She knew what to expect. But it's different…experiencing it."

"Can you come over later? After your weight session?"

"Yeah. I'll be there. To *talk*, right?"

She laughs. "Uh-huh. I love you."

"I love you too."

We hang up, and I focus on the dark road headed home. Headed toward her.

CHAPTER THIRTY-FIVE

CASSIA

Seven Months Later

"Is there anything to basketball aside from getting the ball through the hoop?" Nova asks me, tossing some popcorn into her mouth.

"Yes." I glance over at her. "You're an athlete. How can you not know that?"

"I play soccer. I know soccer. What does that have to do with basketball?"

I scoff, then refocus on the court.

Tonight is the last game of Richmond's regular season. Holden's final season is close to coming to an end.

And they're playing Arlington, which means Finn is here. He's sitting on Richmond's side wearing Arlington's colors, which sums up Finn pretty well.

Tonight's opponent also means the jerk in the kitchen at the

Arlington party we went to, Travis Dennis, is warming up on the opposite end of the court from Holden. The dark looks Arlington is aiming at the opposite end—toward Holden in particular—make me nervous. He hasn't lost to Arlington once in his college career. They're the underdogs, out for blood.

I know how badly Holden wants to win.

Richmond is undefeated so far this season, a feat that has garnered a lot of interest from scouts and sports commentators alike.

I snap a photo of the packed court and send it to Sydney.

She took a leave of absence for her spring semester, opting to return to Pembrooke for the rest of her pregnancy. She's living in the condo with Catherine, working at the high school as part of its theater department. She's also been working at the animal shelter with Eileen for a few hours each week. Making the best of a difficult situation.

The loudspeaker crackles to life as players leave the court, headed to their respective benches to huddle up before the game actually begins.

"What's happening now?" Nova asks.

I glance at her, not sure if she's teasing. "You know *nothing* about basketball?"

"Nothing."

I decide to quiz her. "Do you know what traveling means?"

"Like literally? Moving from one place to another?"

I huff a laugh. "Just pay attention to the scoreboard."

The announcer starts naming the starting players on each team. Unsurprisingly, Holden's name receives the loudest applause.

He's all business, talking with his coach intently before jogging onto the court.

My nails dig into my palm as I watch the jump ball.

Holden wins it easily, tipping the ball toward Henry. And then the game is off at a rapid pace, both teams rushing down toward Arlington's end.

Henry passes to Robby, who goes in for a lay-up. It misses, a collective groan echoing around the gym as Arlington takes possession.

"This is fun," Nova says. "We should come to more of these."

I snort, my eyes focused on the play. "This is the last game of their regular season. And I've asked you to come since freshman year."

Nova has always claimed she needs a break from sports after soccer season ends, which I guess is fair.

The game proceeds at a fast pace, Nova offering running commentary and me focused on the action, tracking each play carefully.

Arlington is better than I remember them being. The score at halftime is 39-33, much closer than I was hoping for.

The dance team comes out to perform. Loud pop music blares through the speakers for their ten-minute routine, then the players reappear and play resumes for the second half.

Holden makes a three-pointer to start the third quarter. But the score keeps fluctuating, the gap between the two teams never stretching more than ten points.

Richmond remains ahead, though, even as the scoreboard ticks down to the final seconds. Arlington draws a foul in a desperate bid to delay, and Robby makes both shots. Two more points get added to the board, putting Richmond ahead by seven.

Ten seconds, and the crowd starts chanting. I didn't think it could get any louder in here, but it does. I can't hear the munch of Nova finishing her popcorn or the squeak of the players' sneakers on the court.

"Five! Four! Three! Two! One!"

The remaining time ticks down to nothing, and the arena erupts. There's a decent contingent of Arlington fans who made the trip up here, but their disappointment is nothing compared to the euphoria of having clinched an undefeated season.

I'm not sure if Nova is any clearer on the rules of basketball after the game, but she's screaming along with the rest of us. Victory is an easy concept to comprehend.

Richmond's players celebrate on the court, then slap hands with Arlington's team in the typical tradition of sportsmanship before disappearing back into the locker room.

Halfway down the bleachers, Nova runs into some friends of hers I've met a few times before. We talk for a few minutes before they invite us out for pizza. Nova accepts, but I let them know I'm waiting for Holden.

The crowd filters out of the gym and into the lobby. I find a spot in a corner and pull my phone out, texting Sydney a few more photos from the game. Then busy myself on my phone, mindlessly scrolling as the lobby empties around me. Until my phone dies, giving me no distraction at all.

I huff, annoyed about forgetting to charge it, then slip my phone back in my pocket and opt to study the trophies in the case instead. Holden is usually quick to get changed and appear, but I'm guessing there's a lot of celebrating happening in the locker room right now.

"You're probably thinking you chose the right team, huh?"

I spin to see Travis Dennis standing there. His Arlington bag is slung over one shoulder and he's wearing a tracksuit over his uniform.

"It was a close game." I decide to be magnanimous.

Travis shakes his head. "Adams is a real asshole on the court. I hope he treats you better."

I watched the game he just played in. Holden didn't get called for a single foul. I know he's plenty capable of saying whatever the hell he wants sometimes, though, which is probably what Travis is referring to.

I say nothing, deciding it's better not to engage.

"What the hell are you hanging around for, Dennis?" Robby appears, his hair still wet from his shower. "Go back to Losertown."

"We were having a private conversation," Travis replies. "Nothing to concern yourself with, Sanderson."

Robby scoffs. "Like you don't know she's Adams's girl."

"What's going on?" Henry appears next, a couple of Holden's teammates right behind him.

Some of the Arlington players stop on their way to the exit, backing Travis up.

All of a sudden, I'm standing between a bunch of very pissed-off basketball players.

Richmond's side parts, and that's how I know Holden has arrived.

"Cassia? What's going on?"

"Nothing," I say. "Let's just go."

"Dennis was harassing her," Robby supplies unhelpfully.

I shoot daggers in his direction, but he's too busy glaring at Travis to notice. The same tense atmosphere as the game swirls around me, except now there are no referees. No witnesses.

Richmond just won the game. They should all be off celebrating.

"He didn't do anything," I say.

Travis grins at me. "Aw, baby. You don't have to defend me."

"Don't talk to her," Holden snarls.

"Worried she'll wise up and go for a real man?"

"Take another look at the scoreboard before you leave, Dennis. You *lost*."

Travis's smile is more of a leer. "I'm not talking about on the court. I mean keeping her satisfied in—"

I don't see it coming. I don't think Travis does either.

Holden swings, and there's a sickening smack as his fist connects with Travis's face.

Travis bends over, clutching his nose. I don't have a lot of sympathy for him—he had plenty of chances to walk away—but I'm not totally supportive of Holden's decision to punch him.

"Get the fuck out of here, Dennis." Holden takes his own advice, grabbing my hand and pulling me toward the exit. A few of his teammates slap him on the back as we pass them. One of Travis's goes over to check on him.

Cold air smacks me in the face as we step outside, chilling my lungs as I take a deep breath.

Holden says nothing as we walk toward his truck.

"That was dumb," I tell him. "And unnecessary."

"I enjoyed it."

"What if he tells his coach? Presses charges?"

"He won't."

"You sure? Because it seems like he has a vindictive streak to me."

"He also has an ego the size of Connecticut. You think he wants to spread around what just happened? He won't do anything."

"Well, congrats," I say as we reach his truck.

"Thanks."

Holden tosses his bag into the bed of his truck, then unzips it. He pulls out a blue cold pack, then climbs into the driver's side.

My breath is visible as I sigh, then get in next to him.

"Did you get hurt?"

"I'm fine. I took an elbow to the side during the second quarter," he explains. "Team doc was being extra cautious is all."

I take the cold pack from him and press it gently against his red knuckles.

"I had it handled," I say. "You didn't need to get involved."

Holden scoffs. "Yeah, I did."

"You guys won the game."

"I didn't hit him because he's a shitty basketball player. I hit him because he was talking to you."

"You can't punch every guy who talks to me, Holden."

He smirks. "Watch me."

"I'm serious. You guys should be celebrating tonight. And he wasn't doing anything."

"Yeah, he was."

I exhale, realizing this isn't an argument I'll win.

"I'm still fighting for you, flower."

When I look over at Holden, he's smirking.

"I didn't mean that literally."

"Come here."

After a second of deliberation, I crawl across the seat into his lap. I can barely fit between his body and the wheel. If my butt sets off the horn, I'll be humiliated.

But it's hard to focus on anything but Holden when his attention is totally focused on me.

"You won," I tell him.

He smiles. "I know. Wasn't sure we would."

"Undefeated." I push some hair off his forehead, and he leans into my touch, smiling.

"Yeah."

"The guys are having a party?"

"Yeah. I need to go for a little bit. But after..." Holden shifts, pulling his phone out of his pocket. He squints at the screen, then answers. "Sydney?" Instantly, his face turns serious. "Yeah, of course. Yeah. Okay. Yeah." He hangs up. "Sydney's in labor."

"What?" I pull my phone out, only to discover the screen is black. And remember that it's dead.

"We gotta go."

I nod, sliding off his lap and buckling my seatbelt.

CHAPTER THIRTY-SIX

HOLDEN

I pace the length of the hall, glance at the closed door, then start pacing again.

"Sit down," Cassia tells me. "You're stressing me out."

I take a seat in the hard chair next to her, my knee bouncing wildly. "Why is it taking so long?"

"She's pushing a person out, Holden. It's not exactly an easy, speedy process."

"Right," I mumble, sinking back in my chair.

Harrison is sitting across from us, looking more serious than I've ever seen him. He was already here when we arrived.

Sydney called him first, and I'm glad.

Another hour passes, with no news.

I slump deeper in the chair, exhausted despite the uncomfortable seating. Weeks of nonstop practice. The rush of winning. Finally getting to deck Dennis. Worry about Sydney.

I'm emotionally drained.

"Holden?"

I open my eyes to see Dr. Meyers standing in front of me.

His expression is grave as he stares at me, slumped and half-asleep.

There's a sudden, sinking sensation in my stomach, some part of me knowing what he's here to tell me before I hear the words.

He glances at Cassia, offering her a warm smile. Her expression is as concerned as mine, glancing between me and him. Probably wondering if he's one of Sydney's doctors.

I wish he was.

"Could I talk to you down the hall?" Dr. Meyers asks.

Cassia grabs my hand, squeezes it, then lets it go.

I nod and stand, my cramped, tired muscles protesting the movement. Then follow Dr. Meyers down the sterile hallway to the end.

"I heard your sister was admitted. She's still in labor?"

"Yeah." I clear my throat, my voice ragged and raw. "Uh, yeah. As far as we know."

He exhales. "There's never any easy way to say this."

"She's dead?"

Dr. Meyers nods. "It was sudden. We think it was a blood clot, a side effect of one of her medications. She was pronounced dead as soon as she arrived at the hospital." He hesitates. "I'm so sorry for your loss."

"Thanks." My voice is wooden. I prepared for this moment, I guess. As much as someone can.

"I know that this is a shock. And that you have a lot of other things going on right now. If you have any questions…if there's anything you want to talk about, you know where to find me."

I nod.

Dr. Meyers offers one last sympathetic smile, squeezes my shoulder, then heads in the opposite direction.

I stand there for a minute, the high of the game still mixing with worry about what Sydney is going through right now.

And my mom…there's a hollow, empty feeling in the center of my chest that isn't indifference.

Cassia is chewing on her bottom lip when I return to my seat. She studies me closely as I sit back down beside her, silently wondering.

"My mom's dead."

She freezes beside me. "What?"

"That was her doctor. The one who did the testing. It happened tonight."

"I'm—" Her voice catches. "I'm so sorry, Holden."

Harrison is eyeing us curiously, but I don't think he can hear what we're saying. And I'm not ready to share this with anyone else.

"I knew it was coming," I say.

And I did.

But still…I decide it *is* a loss.

I'm officially an orphan, even if it's felt that way since my dad died. Felt that a few times before he did, honestly. I know he left to help us. But still, he left a lot.

Cassia grabs my hand.

We sit in silence until a doctor clad in pink scrubs appears. Based on the way Harrison sits up, it's the news we've been waiting for.

The woman approaches Harrison first, who's sitting with his parents. They showed up about an hour after Cassia and I arrived. I don't know the Bakers well, but they seem like nice people. And I'm glad that Sydney's kid will have some grandparents.

The doctor leaves and Harrison stands.

"It's a girl," he tells us, a tentative, nervous smile on his face. "Do you guys want to come meet her?"

"You go first," I say.

Cassia nods next to me in agreement.

They might not be a traditional family, but they deserve to have this moment.

Harrison nods, then disappears into Sydney's hospital room.

I exhale and lean forward, resting my elbows on my knees. A little relief trickles into the emotional mess I'm experiencing. Cassia rubs small, soothing circles on my back.

"Do I tell her?" I ask.

Sydney and I haven't discussed our mom since we left the diner that day. I never asked what exactly they talked about when I left or if it altered Sydney's opinion of her at all. She never offered a recap of the conversation.

We both knew her death was a ticking clock. Just not when it would expire. And I'm not sure if it's ironic or fitting, that it happened tonight.

Sydney lost her mom the same night she became one.

"I think she would want to know," Cassia says.

I nod.

That's all we say until Harrison reappears. There's a look of wonder on his face and a suspicious sheen in his eyes.

"You go ahead," Cassia says softly.

I glance at her. "You sure?"

"Yeah, Uncle." She smiles.

I smile back before I stand and walk down the hall to the right room.

Sydney is sitting up in bed. Her hair is sweaty, the pieces not pulled back sticking to her temples. But she's beaming down at the bundle in her arms, looking happier than I can recall seeing her in a long time.

I walk over to the side of the bed, staring down at the tiny person she's holding. "Wow."

"Right?"

"She's perfect, Syd."

My sister smiles. "I think so. You want to hold her?"

"Uh." I clear my throat. "Sure."

Sydney carefully transfers the baby to my arms. She's lighter than I'm expecting. And warmer. I can feel the heat of her skin through the cotton blanket she's swaddled in.

"Does she have a name yet?"

"No. I thought I'd know once I looked at her. But so far, nothing."

I swallow and nod, tucking her blanket beneath my arm.

"Where's Cassia?"

"She's here. She just, um, she wanted to give us a minute." I sigh, staring down at the peaceful features of my niece. "I, um…"

"Did you guys win the game? I saw some of the texts, then got distracted." Sydney nods toward her daughter, smiling.

"Yeah, we won. But I—Syd, she's gone."

I watch those words slowly register on my sister's face.

"What? How do you know?"

"Her doctor came and told me. It happened tonight."

She exhales and looks away.

"I'm sorry, Syd."

"Why are you apologizing? Don't apologize."

"I just—it's shitty timing. Obviously."

Sydney is quiet for several minutes. I rock the baby, relieved she keeps sleeping. Giving her time to absorb the news on what's already been a crazy night.

"Do you think it's weird if I name her Lana?" she asks suddenly.

I glance up, taken aback. "The baby? Name her after Mom?"

"I've always thought it was a pretty name. And I…you were right. She was our mom. Whatever her flaws and mistakes, that was always true. Maybe she's in a better place now. Maybe she's with Dad, before everything between them got messed up. Either way, she's gone. Maybe this is a fresh start. I was going to name her Joseph, after Dad, if she'd been a boy."

"I don't think it's weird," I say. I've thought, since my dad died, that I'd probably name a son after him too. "I think she would have been touched. She just wouldn't have known how to tell you that."

Sydney sniffles. "Yeah."

The baby—Lana—blinks. "She's waking up," I say.

Sydney holds her arms out. "I'll take her. Can you go get Cassia? And Harrison if he wants to come back in?"

"Yeah, of course."

I hand my niece back, then head for the door. Sneak one glance back at Sydney staring down at her daughter.

A new beginning.

EPILOGUE
CASSIA

I roll over, burying my face in soft cotton. Inhale deeply, pulling in the scent of lavender laundry detergent and cinnamon.

For the first time in a while, I feel well-rested. My eyes don't feel gritty and dry. My head isn't swimming with exhaustion.

I crack one eye open, nothing but white fabric in front of me. Flop one arm over onto the cool material, my fingers dragging across the soft surface.

"Holden?" I croak.

There's no response.

I sit up, clearing my throat as I twist my hair up in a bun. Rubbing my eyes, I toss off the comforter and climb out of bed. My slippers are right where I left them by the dresser. I shove my feet into them and then shuffle into the attached bathroom to run through my morning routine.

The scent of freshly brewed coffee fills my nose as soon as I reach the bottom of the stairs. I pick up the two toys on the bottom stair and toss them toward the couch, then continue into the kitchen.

When I went to bed, the counters were dirty, and dishes were piled in the sink. It was a long day with Joey, and I was running on a serious sleep deficit.

Now, every surface gleams. The coffee pot is full.

I grab a mug out of the cabinet and fill it almost to the brim. Then pull the milk carton out of the fridge to top off the coffee. The first sip is heavenly, hot but also refreshing.

The muted bounce of a basketball draws me toward the back door. I step out onto the deck, fall's chill stamped in the wooden boards and stinging my bare feet.

Holden is standing in the center of the driveway, dribbling, with Joey perched on his shoulders. Our son shrieks when he shoots, grabbing his hair with tiny, strong fingers. Holden doesn't even flinch as he retrieves the ball from the row of bushes that line our driveway. It's been a year since he played basketball professionally. But of course it goes in.

I blow on my coffee and then take another sip.

Holden makes another shot. This time, Joey laughs and claps his little hands together. Then he spots me, and his claps turn into waves.

"Mama!"

Holden turns this way, holding tight to Joey's legs. He grins at me, flashing the smirk that's never lost its effectiveness.

"It's after eight," I call to him.

"I know." He swings Joey down from his shoulders so our fifteen-month-old can wobble his way toward me.

Joey took his first steps a month ago and has become increasingly mobile ever since. Based on the way he literally bounces off our furniture, our son inherited Holden's reckless tendencies.

"I thought they were coming over at eight thirty. I haven't started anything yet and there's—"

"I texted Syd last night, told her not to come until ten. You're exhausted. You deserved to sleep in a little."

Joey's little arms wrap around my legs, fisting the cotton fabric of my pajama pants in his tiny hands.

I bend down and blow a raspberry on his neck. He laughs and lets me go, walking over to the sand table set up in one corner of the deck. His favorite yellow shovel immediately gets picked up to tunnel through the sand.

I refocus on Holden, who's taking another shot. The *swish* is audible over the sound of Joey's digging as the ball drops through the net.

"Sydney was okay with that?"

"Of course. She knows how hectic your schedule is. She offered to make food and bring it over, but I told her you'd already stocked the fridge with enough to feed twelve."

I roll my eyes. "Well, you eat about as much as three adults and half of Joey's food ends up on the floor for Milo, so…"

Holden chuckles but doesn't deny it.

"Are you sure Sydney was okay with coming later? Lana usually wakes up even earlier than Joey does. Sydney will have to feed her two breakfasts."

"Then she'll feed her two breakfasts."

I nod, gnawing on my bottom lip.

I feel guilty, I guess. I found out I was pregnant with Joey during my final year of vet school, about six months after me and Holden got married. We weren't trying, but we weren't doing a whole lot to prevent a pregnancy either.

Holden was ecstatic. So were my parents and my siblings. And my soon-to-be-stepmother, Elena. She and my dad are getting married next summer. I'm not sure it'll ever not be weird for me. If I'll ever get over wishing my parents' marriage hadn't ended. But they both seem happy, and that's what I try to focus on.

Sydney was the person I was most nervous to tell about my pregnancy. She never finished college. Never dated her child's father, much less married him. Didn't have her parents to rely on for support.

I knew she'd be thrilled for me, but I was—am—hyperaware of how different our parenting journeys have been.

Harrison stepped up. He and Sydney share custody of Lana, alternating weekends and holidays. He pays child support. But they've never lived together. Sydney has never been able to sleep in on a Sunday she has Lana because someone else has already taken care of everything. I wouldn't blame her for resenting how much easier I have it.

Holden is an amazing dad and an incredible partner. He made the decision to retire from basketball when he could have continued playing so he could support me and not miss any of Joey's childhood. He's a stay-at-home-dad, and also assistant coaches the high school's basketball team. I can't imagine what these past couple of years would have been like without him, and I'm in awe of Sydney's strength.

I drain the rest of my mug. A quick glance at Joey confirms he's still happily shoveling his sand, so I set the ceramic cup on the railing and descend the deck stairs. The cold pavers that lead from the deck to the edge of the driveway wake me up more than the hot coffee did.

Holden takes a shot, watching me approach. It was the first thing he did when we bought this place, installing a hoop above the garage door. It reminds me of his driveway across from mine, and I know that was exactly his intention.

He makes the shot, of course.

But I catch the rebound, approaching him with the basketball clutched to my chest.

"Thank you," I tell him.

He grins. "For what?"

I mean to say *taking care of Joey* or *cleaning* or *letting me sleep in*. But what comes out is "This life."

His smile softens. "You never have to thank me for that, flower."

———

The doorbell rings at ten on the dot. Sydney is nothing if not punctual.

"Holden!" I call. "Get the door!"

"What?" His reply is loud but muffled. He must be upstairs.

"DOOR!" I holler.

Milo starts barking in response to my shout, the sharp sound ringing in my ears. He's been perched by my feet ever since I pulled the package of bacon out of the fridge, eagerly waiting for a piece to hit the floor. Eileen "adopted" him, only to tell me after I graduated college that she always knew he was meant to be my dog. Holden and I have had him ever since.

"What?"

"THE DOOR! Can't you hear the doorbell?"

Between Milo's barking and the sizzle of oil in the pan, I can barely make out Holden's answer. But I catch enough to gather he's changing Joey's diaper, so I turn the burner all the way down and then hustle toward the entryway. Just in time to see Sydney closing the front door.

"Hey." My best friend shoots me a bright smile before shrugging out of her fleece jacket. "I know it's probably rude to let yourself into someone else's house, but you guys did give me a key. Plus, it sounded like things were a little crazy in here."

"Just a little."

I give Sydney a hug, then bend down to kiss the top of Lana's blonde head. She's happily playing with Milo, who's lapping up the attention. My niece adores animals, which I take full credit for. She has a massive collection of stuffed animals to make up for their apartment complex not allowing pets.

"I've got bacon on the stove. Come into the kitchen." I head back that way, calling "They're here!" as I pass by the stairs.

"I heard the bell, Cassia! I was just busy! If you want to take over on wiping sh—stuff, we can switch jobs!"

Sydney laughs as she follows me down the hallway. I roll my eyes before beelining for the stove and turning the heat back up. Milo abandons Lana to sit at my feet and beg for bacon again.

"Smells good in here."

"Muffins will be finished in"—I glance at the timer—"six minutes. And the bacon will be ready before then."

"Okay if I grab some coffee?" Sydney asks.

"Of course."

"Lana is still in her *wake up three times* a night phase." Sydney shakes her head as she pours, her bob bouncing around her ears. She cut it short at the start of the summer and it's still strange seeing her with it. As long as I've known her, she's had longer hair.

"Yeah, Joey has those phases too."

"You got to sleep in this morning though, right?" Sydney winks at me.

I wonder what Holden told her. If she thinks sleeping in is code for something else, she's wrong.

"Yeah. I hope that didn't mess with any of your plans."

Sydney brushes away my worry with a wave of her hand. "Of

course not." She pauses. "Are you guys free to watch Lana on Friday night?"

I nod as I flip the bacon onto a plate. "Of course. Special occasion?"

"It might be a date."

I glance over at her, eyebrows raised. "Might be?"

"He suggested getting dinner after a school board meeting. Does that count?"

"You work together?"

"Uh-huh. He started at the middle school this year."

"What's he like?"

Sydney smiles. "He's sweet. A little shy, I think. Which is why it's hard to tell if he's just being nice or is interested. You know I'm terrible at telling anyway."

The timer goes off, so I spin around to pull out the muffins. Lana asks to go play in the sandbox and Sydney gets distracted by opening the sliding door for her.

I pull the fruit I sliced out of the fridge and set it out with the rest of the breakfast.

"Do you want it to be a date?" I ask Sydney.

She looks down into her coffee mug. "Yeah. I just don't want it to be awkward at work if it doesn't go well."

"Based on the way you described him, he's more likely to hide in a closet to avoid you if that happens."

Sydney covers her face with her hands. "Shit. I made him sound weird. He's not—"

"Is he hot?"

Sydney's hands muffle her laugh.

"Hey, sis."

We both glance at the doorway. Holden sets down Joey, who heads toward the couch. His favorite toy—a stuffed giraffe—is sitting on the nearest cushion.

"Hey," Sydney says, smiling.

Holden approaches the island, leaning a hip against the edge and snagging a strawberry from the bowl. "Should I head back upstairs so you two can gossip about guys some more?"

Sydney scoffs. "We're done."

"No, we're not. Go back upstairs, please." I flutter my eyelashes to make it extra convincing.

Holden smirks before rounding the edge of the island and coming up behind me. "Nah, nevermind. I want to hear the gossip. Go ahead, Syd."

"I haven't even gone out with him," she says. "It'll probably go nowhere."

"You never know," I tell her.

"That's true. When we first moved in across the street, I never thought you would end up with Holden. And look at you guys now."

I glance at Holden. He smirks.

Lana bangs on the glass door with one of the sandbox toys, so Sydney goes over to open the door.

Holden's hand wraps around my waist. I lean back against him, keeping an eye on the bacon to make sure it doesn't burn.

"I haven't yawned once since I woke up," I tell him. "I forgot what that was like."

His chest rumbles against my back. "It wasn't completely selfless," he tells me. "I wanted you well-rested for tonight."

I hum as his lips brush my temple, fully on board with that idea.

"Dada!" Joey calls.

Holden sighs, then drops his hand and steps away.

I turn before he can move too far away. "I love you."

Those three words are ones I make a point to tell him every

day. Because life is short and because I know I'm the only one who does.

His expression softens into my favorite smile. "I love you, flower."

Truth resonates in every syllable.

Then he goes to take care of our son.

THE END

ALSO BY C.W. FARNSWORTH

Standalones

Four Months, Three Words

Come Break My Heart Again

Winning Mr. Wrong

Back Where We Began

Like I Never Said

Fly Bye

Serve

Heartbreak for Two

Pretty Ugly Promises

Six Summers to Fall

King of Country

Rival Love

Kiss Now, Lie Later

For Now, Not Forever

The Kensingtons

Fake Empire

Real Regrets

Truth and Lies

Friday Night Lies

Tuesday Night Truths

Kluvberg

First Flight, Final Fall

All The Wrong Plays

Holt Hockey

Famous Last Words

ABOUT THE AUTHOR

C.W. Farnsworth is the author of numerous adult and young adult romance novels featuring sports, strong female leads, and happy endings.

Charlotte lives in Rhode Island and when she isn't writing spends her free time reading, at the beach, or snuggling with her Australian Shepherd.

Find her on Facebook (@cwfarnsworth), TikTok (@authorcwfarnsworth), Instagram (@authorcwfarnsworth) and check out her website www.authorcwfarnsworth.com for news about upcoming releases!